They traveled swiftly. Her stern new husband was silent, but thunder muttered, grew louder, and roared to a crescendo. Anne became aware that the carpetbag at her feet was moving.

"What's in there?" Lord Michael asked.

Before she could reply, there came another clap of thunder, a yowl from the carpetbag, and without so much as a by-your-leave, Lord Michael opened it and peered inside. To Anne's astonishment, when the kitten's furry black head popped up, he laughed and his stern expression vanished.

Juliette looked at him, wide-eyed and trembling, but another sharp crack of thunder galvanized the kitten. With a cry of terror it leapt toward Anne. Catching the lace front of her gown, it clawed its way up to the bodice edge, then tried to bury itself headfirst in the space between her breasts.

Embarrassed, Anne grabbed Juliette and said guiltily, "I had to bring her. She—" Juliette's sharp claws turned the last word into a gasp of pain.

Lord Michael reached for the kitten. "Here, let me."

"Oh, no— I-I'm sure she will not go to you. Juliette, no!" Some of the kitten's sharp claws were caught in the lace, others dug painfully into her breast, but when Anne tried to free herself, she seemed only to make matters worse.

Ignoring Anne's gasp of indignation and rigid embarrassment, he reached right into her bodice and grasped the kitten. For the second time that day she felt his warm hands on her bare skin. And when the kitten allowed him to remove it without another murmur, Anne began to revise her first impression of him. Marriage to Lord Michael might prove to be a good deal more interesting than she had expected—at least it would so long as he didn't expect her to submit to his commands as unquestioningly as Juliette did . . .

Raves for Amanda Scott's previous romances:

For *Border Bride*

"A provocative and seductive mix . . . Hours of reading fun!"
—Catherine Coulter

"Lively and entertaining . . . A must for historical romance readers!"

—Roberta Gellis

For *Dangerous Illusions*

"Amanda Scott captures the Regency with a sharp pen and her dry wit . . . Readers will be enchanted with her lively cast of characters and the unique picture of country life and strife, complete with all its subtle nuances . . . A true treat!"

—Kathe Robin

"Ms. Scott has combined intrigue, women's rights, splendid Cornwall settings, and a surprising climax—no small feat . . . so well written it would be hard to find a flaw."

—*Rendezvous*

For *Highland Fling*

"From the pen of a most gifted storyteller, *Highland Fling* is a well-crafted romance with a delightful secondary love story, sparkling dialogue, and enough humor to tickle the most discerning funny bone."

—*Romantic Times*

AMANDA SCOTT

THE BAWDY BRIDE

PINNACLE BOOKS
KENSINGTON PUBLISHING CORP.

To Georgia Bockoven
Who provided the title before there was a story.
Thanks, Birthday Sister, you're a peach!

Prologue

October 1799, Derbyshire, England

So this was Hell. The once noisy din of chatter and laughter from the next room that had gone on unceasingly despite her screams, was muted now, growing distant, as if she heard it through earmuffs in a roaring winter windstorm. But it was not winter, and Hell was no place for earmuffs.

"Her eyes are open."

The voice floated over her, far away and fading, his words nonsense. Had her eyes been open, she would have seen him.

He said, "You oughtn't to have used such a heavy whip, your lordship. She's a small wench."

"I intended that she should fully comprehend the wisdom of remaining silent, now and forevermore."

Even here and now, coming to her through airless, ever-thickening darkness, that low, purring second voice chilled and terrified her, but she would never keep silent. She had already spoken up once, and if God were in the mood to produce a miracle and snatch her to safety, she would tell the entire world what she knew about his bloody lordship. Not that God would do any such thing. He would not produce even a small miracle for such a great sinner as herself. Surely, Mary Magdalene had received not only her own share of such wonders but any share that might have come, centuries later, to a sister in sin. Unless she could manage somehow to escape on her own to tell the truth about him, the wicked man would go right on taking advantage of his lofty position to make others miserable.

Odd that with hellfire flaming through her body, threatening to consume her, she could still hear the crackling of the fire on the hearth, could still feel rough carpet beneath her cheek and the movement of the river tide below—and odder still that she felt cold. She had never known such pain, not even the many times her father had beaten her, determined to drive the devil out of her. He had warned her, so many times, that she would go to Hell. How pleased he would be now, to know he had been right.

She could not see the room anymore, though she knew its oppressive crimson elegance only too well. She could not see the fire either, for all they had said her eyes were open. Instead, in her mind's eye, like a dream, she saw a tiny golden-haired child laughing in church and being soundly switched then and there for her blasphemy, and an older child striving to memorize lines from a Bible she could not read and being beaten for forgetting. She saw a girl, free at last, going into service, wanting only to prove her worth, and the same girl learning her precise worth, learning that her father had been right all along.

A dizzy, spinning sensation threatened to overcome her, the same one she had felt when for no reason she had understood at the time, she had been turned off without a character. She knew the reason now, only too well. Like others before her, she had been doomed for failing to yield, and condemned to the *Folly*.

"She's stopped breathing, damn you!" It was the one who had so absurdly said her eyes were open.

"Mind your tongue, fool. Do you so quickly forget how to address your betters?"

Again the chill of that purring voice filtered through the heavy, dark cloud enveloping her, but how ridiculous to say she was not breathing. If that were so, she would be dead, unable to hear them at all. She could see a glimmer of light now in the tunnel of darkness ahead of her. It widened, beckoning her nearer. Surely, there was sunlight ahead, and warmth, and love.

"Beg pardon, your lordship, I'm sure, if I've offended you," the first man said, but his voice was far away and fading now. She barely sensed the irony in his words, barely heard him at all when he added, "Still and all, I tell you, the chit is dead."

"A pity, but she is no great loss, after all. There are plenty more where she . . ."

One

Dear James,

I am to be married today. I stood in front of the glass this morning and introduced myself to my reflection as Lady Michael St. Ledgers but saw only Anne Davies, as always, looking too much like a child to be a bride. That one can still look so at the ancient age of twenty seems most peculiar, but since my hair is too fair and too fine to yield easily to fashion's dictates, and my body too waif-like to stir a man's desires (or so Beth tells me, and she should know), I can do nothing to alter the matter.

I thought, once I had met Lord Michael, I would feel differently about marriage, but I do not. He is large and, I suppose, very handsome, but his demeanor is stern and his manner unyielding. I have seen him smile only once, and that was at Beth, who was flirting as usual. Tony does not seem to mind such antics, so their marriage lopes along peacefully enough, and, of course, Catherine's marriage is amiable, for she adores her grand position. I do hope my marriage will be as untroubled as theirs seem to be, James, for I mean to be a good wife. I know my duty, of course, and thanks to Grandmama's precepts and my experience here at Rendlesham, I am well trained for the position; however, since I have grown weary of constantly seeking compromise, and since I doubt that mar-

riage can require less of that increasingly tiresome occupation than the single state requires, I must admit to certain qualms . . .

Lady Anne Davies paused, nibbling the end of her pen and
absently stroking the small black cat curled in her lap as she
tried to organize those qualms into words she could set to
paper. Before she had done more than dip the nib into her
inkwell again, however, the door to her bedchamber opened
without ceremony and her maid, Maisie Bray, bustled in with
Anne's wedding dress draped carefully over one plump rosy
arm.

Looking critically at her mistress, she said, "Beg pardon,
my lady, I'm sure, but this be no time to be scribbling in that
journal of yours. His lordship—which is to say your papa, not
Lord Michael—wants to see you in his bookroom as soon as
you be dressed. It won't do to be agitating him, not today."

"I try never to agitate Papa, Maisie," Anne said calmly,
"and if I do not write now, I don't know when I shall find
the opportunity to write again." But she slipped the page obediently into the portfolio she kept for the purpose and, still
holding the small cat, arose to put the portfolio into the carpetbag she would carry with her later in the carriage. Then
she stepped to the window to take one last look out at her
beloved gardens, just now beginning to show touches of
springtime color.

The kitten purred, and Anne stroked it while she gazed at
her garden and the sloping sweep of velvet green lawn beyond.
Puffy white clouds drifted overhead, but the sun still shone
invitingly on the white pebbled walks and tidy hedged borders.
Behind her, Maisie said gently, "You'd best make haste, Miss
Anne."

With a sigh, Anne put small black Juliette down on a favored pillow on the high, pale-blue-silk-draped bed, slipped
out of her dressing gown, and stood in chemise and corset
while Maisie flung the white muslin dress over her head.

Maisie was careful not to disarrange Anne's hair, and once the gown was in place, while the maid fastened the golden ties at each shoulder, Anne gazed solemnly at her reflection in the dressing glass.

The gown was lovely, but she wished she might have had silver-embroidered borders instead of gold. She had suggested that, with her gray eyes and pale flaxen hair, silver would be more becoming to her but her mother had scorned such a notion.

"You are an earl's daughter, Anne, not a commoner," Lady Rendlesham had said tartly. "You are entitled to wear cloth of gold, just as your sister Catherine did; and indeed, had Lord Michael's family not still been in half-mourning for the late duke, I would have insisted that you display your rank properly. But for such a paltry affair as this wedding will be, gold-embroidered muslin will suffice." She sighed, adding, "Why, when Catherine was married, we had guests for three weeks beforehand, and though Beth's was not so grand as that, it was by no means an inferior occasion. 'Tis the greatest pity the duke had to die, for we might have enjoyed a truly splendid wedding."

Anne resisted the temptation to point out that had the sixth Duke of Upminster not died, the notion of marriage might not have occurred to his younger brother for some time yet to come. She said only, "There is still a Duke of Upminster, ma'am."

"A mere boy, and still in mourning at that. He will not even be present at your wedding, for goodness' sake. But others will, my girl, and you will not appear in silver trimming."

And so it was that the gown's sleeves and hemline were heavily bordered with gold. Its close-fitting, high-waisted, deep blue velvet bodice snugged her plump breasts, under which a gold, corded sash had been tied. A loose robe of gold-spotted white gauze, trimmed with a border and fringe of gold, lay waiting to be worn over the whole.

Wisps of Anne's fine hair had escaped the carefully arranged coiffure over which Maisie had labored earlier; so, commanding her to sit again, the maid tucked them into place before affixing a small blue velvet cap to Anne's head. When she had finished, Anne stood, slipped her feet into blue velvet slippers, and waited patiently while Maisie draped the gauze robe over her shoulders and pinned the matching gauze veil in place at the back of the blue velvet cap. Then she drew on her long white, delicately perfumed gloves, smiled her thanks, and turned to leave the room.

"One moment, my lady," Maisie said. "Bless me, if you haven't forgotten Lord Michael's necklace!"

The necklace, too, was gold, an exquisite chain with a pendant molded to resemble a rose and bearing a small diamond in its center. Anne liked it, and both Catherine and Beth had assured her it was a perfect wedding gift.

Having managed to fasten the necklace without disarranging her veil, Maisie moved to take one last look at the full effect, and Anne was surprised to see tears sparkling in her eyes.

"What is it, Maisie? Is something amiss?"

"No, Miss Anne, it just makes me sad to think you are all grown up and will be going away to a brand new home."

"Don't be a goose. You are going with me, after all. Indeed, were it not for that, I think I would be paralyzed with fear, for I scarcely know Lord Michael and have never met a single member of his family. That he expects me to play mother to his deceased brother's two children is especially unnerving, I think, for the poor things are bound to resent me fiercely."

"They will not," Maisie said stoutly. "For all that one's a duke before his time, they'll learn to love you like we all do."

"We will see," Anne said, smiling vaguely. "I must go now. Papa will be displeased if I tarry longer."

She left on the words, and hurried downstairs to the bookroom, grateful not to encounter any of her siblings on the way. Four of her five remaining brothers and sisters were present at Rendlesham for the wedding. Only James, the eldest and her favorite, and Stephen, the youngest, were absent, for

Stephen was away at school, and James was long dead. He had died when she was nine, but she kept him alive in her memory by writing her journal as a series of letters to him. She had never told anyone about the journal, though Maisie knew she kept one, and no one else had ever read it. Even Maisie, much as she loved Anne, did not know how very much alive James remained to her.

She found the Earl of Rendlesham pacing the floor in his bookroom, his ruddy face creased in thought, his large hands clasped behind his back, causing his waistcoat to gap over his stomach where the buttons strained. A cheerful fire crackled on the hearth, and spring sunlight streamed through the tall, leaded windows to spill across the bright blue-and-green Axminster carpet, but his lordship looked more harried than cheerful.

"There you are," he said brusquely, straightening to glare at her. "What a time you have been! Parson will be ready to begin the ceremony in a few moments."

"I beg your pardon, Papa," Anne said. "Dressing always does take longer than one thinks it will."

"Yes, yes, I suppose it does. Perhaps you had better sit down," he added, gesturing distractedly at a chair.

"Will you think me very disobedient, sir, if I do not?" she asked, smiling at him. "Maisie will be put out if I wrinkle my skirt before the ceremony."

"Do as you please," he said. "The sooner this business is done, the better I shall like it. I've any number of other things I ought to be doing."

"Problems, Papa? Is there anything I can do to help?"

"Dash it all, I don't want your help, just your obedience. I don't want to hear any nonsense about this being a hasty affair, or about being afraid to go off alone with Lord Michael."

Anne looked at him in surprise. "But I have never said I would not obey you, Papa. Indeed, I know it is my duty to marry, particularly when such an excellent connection has been made available to me. I know how fortunate I am to make such a match, and if there is haste—though I have not complained of it—it is only because Lord Michael needs a mama for his niece and nephew."

Rendlesham shoved a hand through thick, graying hair that he disdained to cover with a wig now that the price of powder had become extortionate, and said ruefully, "I suppose you haven't complained, but having listened to your mother—and to your sisters when they married—until I was well nigh distracted, I assumed your complaints would echo theirs. I ought to have known they would not. You are a good girl, Anne. Indeed, I do not know what we shall do here without you to make peace when the others choose to quarrel. But, as I told your mama, it is quite rare luck to find such a good match for a third daughter."

"Does Mama agree that Lord Michael is a good match for me?"

"Of course she does! She is convinced that whatever rakish propensities he has not already left behind him in order to manage his nephew's affairs will be put right out of his head by marriage. Furthermore, not only is he the son of a duke, but the lad's got a respectable estate of his own. Not a large one, mind you, but it ought to bring in quite a snug little income now that he seems of a mind to manage it properly. You'll be comfortable, in any event, since you will be living for some years, at least, at Upminster Priory, which is a ducal seat, after all."

"I know I will be comfortable, Papa. Indeed, thanks to my godfather's generosity, and yours, my own portion is quite respectable enough for comfort."

He did not meet her gaze. "As to that," he said, turning toward the fire, "I know you assumed you would retain a certain amount of control over your dowry, as I arranged for your sisters to do when they were married; however, as you know, your godfather left all such arrangements to me, and there has been a slight alteration in the original plan, I'm afraid."

"Indeed?"

"Yes. Michael had some pressing problems . . ." He glanced at her over his shoulder, adding with a grimace, "An expensive young man, I believe, before he was brought so rudely to his senses by his brother's untimely death. That need not concern you, of course, but I found it necessary to give in to certain demands he made with regard to the settlements."

"I see."

"I do not suppose that you see at all," he said, turning back with a sigh, "but I thought it best to tell you myself. I hope the news don't distress you."

She was shaken, albeit not by the news that her husband-to-be had a rakish reputation, or that he was expensive. In her experience, many young men shared those qualities, and despite the fact that her great-aunt Martha had married a rake, and in direct consequence, had died of a dread disease, Anne did not anticipate such an eventuality for herself. But to know that she would have no say in how her money was spent was far more alarming, for she was well aware that to have even the smallest authority would give her an independence in her marriage that she would otherwise lack. She knew better than to express her feelings to the earl, however, or indeed to anyone in her family, for they were all too concerned with their own needs to consider hers. She reassured him, as it was her habit to do, and agreed at once when he said they ought to join the others in the family chapel.

The group awaiting them was a small one, since only immediate family members and close friends had been invited to witness the marriage of Lady Anne Davies to Lord Michael St. Ledgers. Anne smiled at one familiar face after another, hoping she looked more composed than she felt as she walked at her father's side up the narrow center aisle, preceded by her eldest sister, Catherine, who was to support her through the ceremony.

The younger of her two sisters, Beth, standing between her tall, handsome husband, Tony, and Lady Rendlesham in the front row, grinned impishly over her shoulder at Anne. Beside

Tony stood Catherine's husband, Lord Crane, and next to him, two of Anne's three brothers. Harry, at twenty-three, was the eldest and had acquired some dignity, but Bernard shifted impatiently from foot to foot, wanting the ceremony to begin.

Ahead of her, standing between the one friend who had come with him to Rendlesham and the thin, elderly parson who would perform the ceremony, was her husband-to-be. Though she had exchanged only a handful of sentences with Lord Michael in the short time they had been acquainted, once the ceremony was over, she would be his wife, subject to his every command until death parted them. The thought sent a shiver up her spine, but whether it was a thrill of anticipation or one of terror, Anne herself did not know.

Dark-haired Lord Michael St. Ledgers, fashionably attired in buff knee breeches and a dark, well-fitting coat, towered over both his friend, Sir Jacob Thornton, and Parson Hale. His broad shoulders were squared, his carriage that of a military man—which indeed, he had been for a few years after leaving Oxford. He was nine-and-twenty, nine years older than Anne, and although his stern demeanor made him look older, she thought him handsome. As she approached, his gaze caught hers and held it.

She was aware that Sir Jacob also watched her. Indeed, he seemed to make a habit of watching her, and his manner was not what she was accustomed to in a gentleman, for his style was too familiar. A sandy-haired man of medium height and florid complexion, older than her bridegroom by some ten years or more, he had laughed when Lord Michael presented him, saying he thought it a great kindness in himself to have agreed to support him through the ordeal of his wedding, and was doing so only because he had pressing parliamentary business in Derby and Rendlesham took him no more than twenty miles out of his way. He had lost no time in informing everyone that he was a Member of Parliament, making it clear that he held an exalted opinion of his stature.

But even awareness of Sir Jacob's interest was not enough

just then to divert her attention from Lord Michael, whose eyes were the darkest blue she had ever seen, making them look almost black until she got near him. They were set deep beneath his dark eyebrows, and the rest of his features were sharply chiseled. He looked for a moment as if he had been carved from stone, but suddenly, as if he sensed her increasing anxiety, she detected a barely perceptible softening in his appearance.

He did not smile, but his firm, well-shaped lips relaxed, and she felt her body relax in response. She had not expected him to woo her, for theirs was not a love match like her sister Beth's to Tony, or a union arranged after months of negotiation like Catherine's to Lord Crane. Catherine, after all, as the earl's eldest daughter, her portion immense, had been the catch of the Season the year she made her entrance to society. And Beth, albeit with a smaller portion like Anne's, had not only her own vivacious demeanor to assure her of a good match but the good luck to fall in love with a man of fortune who adored her.

Anne's marriage would not be like either of theirs. As the earl's third daughter—an unenviable position in any family—she could scarcely count herself an heiress, and she had formed no attachment to anyone during the two London Seasons granted her at her grandmother's insistence. Aware that she lacked a passionate nature (and generally grateful for the fact), Anne had not expected to fall in love. Moreover, Lord Michael had made it clear that he was marrying out of a strong sense of duty, and was no more in love with her than she was with him.

Indeed, how he could have been in love with her, or she with him, was a puzzlement. They had scarcely met. Moreover, what little she knew of him included the fact that even before he was out of full mourning he had drawn up a list of possible brides as suggested by members of his family and friends—of whom only Sir Jacob had attended the ceremony—and had selected from it one who would meet his needs without demanding a long engagement. She was, in other words, no more to him than the best bride he could acquire at speed to serve as mother to his bereft niece and nephew. She was also a woman generally accounted to be docile, whose fortune could meet at least some of his most pressing financial needs. Clearly, he wanted a convenient marriage; and, since Anne had long since come to believe that any marriage was preferable to the single state, she meant to get along with him well enough so they could enjoy at least an amiable partnership.

The ceremony took less time than she had expected. When Lord Michael slipped a pretty pearl ring on her finger, the warmth of his hands startled her, briefly reminding her that the ceremony was real, not a fantasy. A moment later, Parson Hale presented the couple to the witnesses and everyone adjourned to a room opening directly onto Anne's beloved gardens for the wedding breakfast, so called despite its taking place after noon.

The next hour passed swiftly, and although the garden room was Anne's favorite, she scarcely heeded her surroundings. She ate and drank what was put before her, and replied when she was addressed, but it was as if she were inhabiting someone else's body, observing strangers. By the time she hurried upstairs to change her dress for the journey to Upminster Priory, located in the northern part of Derbyshire, she felt as if she had been participating in a dream, and someone else's dream at that.

Less than half an hour later she was ready. Pausing only to pick up the carpetbag containing her portfolio, and to slip her small black cat inside, she hurried downstairs to make her farewells. Having kissed her and given her his blessing, Rendlesham clapped her new husband on the back and said jovially, "You've got yourself a good little wife there, lad. I'll wager she never gives you a lick of trouble."

"No, sir, I'm sure she won't."

Anne experienced a sudden desire to tell them both that she would behave as she pleased now that she was a married lady, but caught the words before they leapt from her tongue, astonished at herself for even having thought them.

Then, in what seemed little less than the blink of an eye, they had said good-bye to everyone—including Sir Jacob, who was bound at once for Derby—and she found herself in a well-sprung post-chaise, next to her new husband, with her carpetbag at her feet. For the next several minutes, while the postillions negotiated first the circular sweep in front of Rendlesham House and then the oak-and-rhododendron-lined gravel drive leading to the main road, neither occupant of the chaise attempted to speak. But when it lurched onto the highroad and Anne turned to look back, her companion said, "There is nothing to see now, I'm afraid. The second carriage will not follow for some time yet."

His voice was deep and pleasant. Each time she heard it, an odd little tremor awakened somewhere deep in her midsection. Striving now to ignore it, she settled back, turning her head to look at him as she said, "I wanted to take a last look at the park, since I do not know when I will return."

"I thought you might be missing your maid. I must suppose you have never been alone with a man in a carriage before."

She had another sudden, uncharacteristic urge, this time to tell him she had been alone with all sorts of men, hundreds of times, but she suppressed it, feeling heat in her cheeks as she did. Such wicked impulses were most unlike her.

He did not appear to notice her blushes, however, or if he did, she supposed he attributed them to maidenly modesty. He did not even seem to notice that she had not replied to his comment. He was looking out the window, not looking at her at all.

She was accustomed to silence, accustomed, too, to being ignored. For many years she had mediated her siblings' battles and arguments, catered to the older one, dried the younger ones' tears, and listened to their complaints and their dreams, even though they seemed to have no time to listen to hers. From the instant she had known she was to be married, however, whenever the demands of her family members had grown tiresome, she had solaced her feelings with the hope that she would be more valued as a wife than she had been as sister or daughter. But judging by Lord Michael's present air of detachment, that would not be the case. Feeling her temper stir, she ruthlessly repressed it and said quietly, "I daresay our people will not be far behind, sir. I have not met your man, but my maid is efficient and had little left to do. How long will our journey take us?"

"About four hours. The Priory is in north Derbyshire, you know, several miles west of Chesterfield on the Sheffield Road."

"My father said we would be living there. Is that right?"

He looked at her at last. "I beg your pardon if I seem a trifle distracted. I was just reflecting on how quickly life changes from one moment to the next. No doubt your father also told you I stand guardian to my late brother's children, one of whom is the present Duke of Upminster. I believe it best for him to grow up at the Priory, particularly since I am also his primary trustee and bear the responsibility for looking after his properties during his minority. Therefore, for the present at least, we will certainly live there."

"Those poor children," Anne said. "How dreadful for them to have lost both parents in such a short period of time. Papa told me that your brother and his wife were taken within weeks of each other. Was it some sort of illness that killed them?"

"No."

When he did not elaborate, she felt it would be unwise to press him, so she tried another tack. "How old are the children, sir? What are they like?"

"Andrew is fourteen, Sylvia nine," he said, and though his manner was still brusque, she found nonetheless that his voice continued to stir that curious sensation deep within her. "As to what they are like," he added, "I cannot imagine that my opinion of them will aid you much in dealing with them. You are sure to form your own opinions once you meet them, and you will meet Andrew at once, since he is at the house. Sylvia is presently residing in Staffordshire with my sister, Lady Harlow, but she can return to the Priory whenever you like."

He looked out the window at the passing countryside again, and Anne fell silent. The day having turned blustery, the grass along the roadside was flattened by gusts. Nearby trees bent and swayed as if to unheard music, and the sun had been playing "all-hide" with errant white clouds since shortly after the ceremony. But Anne had no wish to talk about the weather, and since Lord Michael clearly did not intend either to volunteer information about his family or to encourage questions about Upminster Priory, she was at a loss. The thought of spending the next few hours in close proximity with a man who did not want to talk was daunting but not nearly so daunting as the thought of spending the rest of her life with him.

The chaise moved rapidly now, but it was well sprung, and did not sway much, for which she was grateful. She was a good traveler, but despite the increasing wind, the day was still warm and the road dusty. She knew that had the chaise been the sort to rattle her bones, she would have fallen victim to one of her annoying headaches long before they reached their destination.

She made no further effort to engage him in conversation, entertaining herself instead by watching the passing scenery, anticipating the moment when she would begin to see landscape and villages that were unfamiliar to her. The clouds grew grayer and more ominous, but the fields were green with new growth and the hedges alive with chirping birds and new color. She loved the springtime. They passed through thick woodlands of oak and silver birch, heavily populated with red deer and grouse, and traveled across lovely open moorland carpeted with bright new grass and bushy, dark green heather.

They traveled as swiftly as the condition of the roads allowed, and at Matlock, the red marls, gravel, and sandstone of south Derbyshire began to give way to limestone and gritstone, quickly noticeable because the road itself turned from reddish brown and tan to gray and pebbly white. As the lovely midland moors were replaced by steeper stone-walled hills and dales, lush, waist-high, emerging cornfields fell behind, giving way to harsher, higher grass country. The air was cooler now, and the wind-ravaged sky grew darker. Thunder muttered from glowering dark gray clouds roiling up behind the peaks to the north. At first the sound was barely discernible above hoof-beats and rattling wheels, but then the thunder groaned louder, belched, and roared to a crescendo, its echoes buffeting from rock to rock down the narrow valley through which they drove. Anne became aware that the carpetbag at her feet was moving.

The first plaintive cry, she hoped, reached only her ears. Surreptitiously, she moved her foot, gently caressing the side of the bag. The resulting silence reassured her, but that silence continued only while she moved her foot. When she stopped, there was instant complaint.

"What was that?" her companion asked.

Anne hesitated, unsure of how he would react to learning that the chaise contained a third occupant. Before she could think how to phrase the information, there came another clap of thunder, a yowl from the carpetbag, and Lord Michael leaned down and picked it up. Without so much as a by-your-leave, he opened the bag and peered inside. To her astonishment, when the kitten's furry black head popped up, he laughed, and the stern expression vanished. He said, "What have we here?"

Juliette looked at him, wide-eyed and trembling, but another sharp crack of thunder galvanized the kitten. With a cry of terror, it turned and leapt toward Anne. Catching the lace trim of her low-cut gown, it clawed its way to the bodice edge, then tried to bury itself headfirst in the space between her breasts.

Embarrassed, Anne grabbed Juliette and said guiltily, "I had to bring her, sir. She—" Juliette's sharp claws turned the last word into a gasp of pain.

Lord Michael reached for the kitten. "Here, let me."

"Oh, no— That is," she added, leaning away, "I-I'm sure she will not go to you. Juliette, no!" The kitten's sharp claws dug painfully into her breast. Others were caught in the lace, and when Anne tried to free herself, she seemed only to make matters worse.

"Let me get her," Lord Michael said firmly. "Come here, cat."

Ignoring Anne's gasp of indignation and rigid embarrassment, he reached right into her bodice and grasped the kitten. For the second time that day, she felt his warm hands on her bare skin. To her astonishment, the little cat allowed him to remove it without another murmur.

"Juliette doesn't really like strangers," she said stiffly, taking the kitten from him and settling it in her lap. "I feared they would send her out to live in the stables if I did not take her away, so I hope you are not vexed."

"Good Lord, of course I'm not. She's a little beauty." He tickled Juliette under the chin, on the spot where the only white hairs on the cat's body formed a lopsided triangle. The pointed chin went up obligingly, and Juliette began to purr. "She *will* come to me on her own, you know," he said confidently, moving his finger along one side of the furry jaw toward an ear.

Doubting him, Anne watched, fascinated, as the kitten, ignoring the thunder now, pressed its head hard against the stroking finger, purring, clearly enjoying the attention. When Lord Michael stopped, Juliette looked at him in indignation.

He wiggled the finger enticingly on his knee, then stopped. Juliette watched alertly. When he wiggled it again, the kitten put out a paw, halting it in midair when his finger again stopped wiggling. When the finger moved, the paw jabbed, and when the finger disappeared suddenly between his legs, Juliette leapt from Anne's lap to Lord Michael's knee, reaching between his legs to attack. The two played for some time before, chuckling, Lord Michael gathered the kitten up in one large hand and began to stroke it with the other. Purring, apparently perfectly at home, it tucked its front paws neatly beneath its pointed chin, and a moment later, when he lifted it to his shoulder, near Anne, the kitten blinked twice at her, then curled into a ball and settled down, purring contentedly until it went to sleep.

Watching Lord Michael with Juliette, Anne began to revise her first impression of him. He might not be a talkative man, but he was not made of stone. When he turned suddenly and smiled at her, clearly delighted by the kitten's acceptance of his friendship, she smiled back and, aware of the strange tingling again, decided that marriage to him might prove to be a good deal more interesting than she had expected.

Two

The threatening storm still had not broken when the carriage left the public road and the west front of Upminster Priory came into view. Built in the Ionic style, the enormous house stood on the east bank of the River Derwent near the bottom of a steep, rocky, thickly wooded hill. Black clouds, now laced with frequent flashes of lightning, and still grumbling and crashing with thunder, rose ominously above the Peaks to the north and roiled over the hilltop beyond the house. Slanting rays from the setting sun, now about to slip from view behind the great English Apennines bordering the valley to the west and north, lit the stone walls of the house, turning them to glittering gold.

The carriage rattled over an elegant triple-arched stone bridge, passed through a high arched gateway in the stone wall that surrounded the grounds, rolled past the low stone lodge, and continued at a smart pace through a wooded park and up a tree-lined drive, slowing only when it entered the gravel carriage sweep moments before Lord Michael's postillions drew their horses to a halt before the splendid entryway.

Engaged Ionic columns supported the pediment over the entry, approached by wide, sweeping white marble steps. The effect was stately, but Anne had eyes only for the gardens surrounding the house. The formal patterns of the low hedged borders were visible to her experienced gaze, and she could see a lake, at least one folly, and even a ragged maze. Clearly the gardens had once been splendid, but now her fingers twitched to pull the weeds she detected in the borders, to clip straggling bushes and shrubs, and to pick dead heads from rhododendrons, azaleas, and the few spring rosebushes already in bloom. She pressed her lips tightly together, wishing she had the nerve to tell the man beside her what she thought of allowing such magnificence to fall into ruin through what appeared to be simple neglect.

Lord Michael did not seem to notice the gardens. He handed Juliette back to Anne and reached impatiently to push open the carriage door and let down the steps just as the heavy white front door of the house was flung wide and two liveried, bewigged footmen hurried to meet them, supported by a much more stately personage who remained behind in the open doorway.

The two young footmen were tall and well formed, filling out their green-and-gold livery to perfection. Lord Michael nodded to them and said as he handed Anne down from the carriage himself, "Our things are all in the second coach. Be sure to send Lady Michael's maid to her as soon as it arrives."

"Yes, my lord," both footmen said together, bowing ceremoniously to their new mistress when, remembering his duty, Lord Michael presented them to her as Elbert and John.

Smiling, holding Juliette as she handed the carpetbag to the first one to reach her, Anne looked them over carefully, aware that the largest part of her duties as Lady Michael St. Ledgers would be to oversee the household and its servants. This pair looked almost like twins at first, since they were dressed exactly alike and wore powdered tie-wigs, but she quickly observed that one of them had blue eyes and the other brown, and that the first had a friendlier face while the second seemed to have more pride. Quietly, she said, "I am pleased to make your acquaintance. I am sure you will both be very helpful to me."

The friendly-looking one, John, blushed and bobbed another bow, while Elbert said rather more stiffly, "Yes, indeed, your ladyship. We look forward to serving you."

Sensing Lord Michael's increasing impatience, she looked swiftly at him, stroked the kitten beginning to tremble in her arms, and said, "I daresay it will take me some time to learn everyone's name, you know."

The impatient look softened, and he nodded, then put a hand under her elbow and urged her up the wide marble steps to the entrance and the stately person awaiting them there.

"This is Bagshaw, my dear. He looks after the house."

Anne nearly curtsied, for Bagshaw was surely one of the most imposing men she had ever met. As tall as Lord Michael and nearly as broad-shouldered, the man carried himself like a king. He did not wear livery. Instead, he wore an elegant, well-fitted black suit of clothes with snowy white linen, highly polished shoes, and his own hair neatly clipped into a fashionable style. Had she not known the sixth Duke of Upminster to be deceased, she might easily have mistaken Bagshaw for His Grace. She had met other servants who behaved with more dignity than their noble masters, but Bagshaw seemed to have turned the knack into an art form. His bow was little more than a relaxation of his stiff posture. His demeanor was stonelike, his gaze cool and polite.

"How do you do, Bagshaw?" she said gravely. "You are the house steward, no doubt."

"We have no present need for a house steward at the Priory, madam," he said with grave dignity. "I am merely the butler."

Merely did not seem to suit him in any way or fashion, but Anne nodded pleasantly, saying as she had said to the two younger men moments before, "I am sure you will be very helpful to me."

"Indeed, madam. We are all quite pleased to welcome you to the Priory. You need only make your requirements known, and they will be instantly attended to."

Lord Michael said, "Bagshaw took over everything to do with the house when my brother's steward retired, and so efficient is he that, although he keeps but a skeleton staff these days, we've seen no need to hire a new man, or even an under-butler. The house runs quite smoothly without them."

"Do you manage all the accounts then, too, Bagshaw?" Anne asked with a friendly smile. "I must confess, it was the one part of running my father's house that I most disliked, for he became enraged whenever one made the least error in arithmetic."

"Mr. Bacon, His Grace's land steward, attends to the estate's accounts, madam."

"All of them? But that must be—"

Speaking at the same time, Lord Michael said dryly, "Her ladyship does not really intend to acquaint herself with every detail this instant, Bagshaw. Pray, tell Mrs. Burdekin to be prepared to present the rest of the staff just before we dine, which"—he drew a watch from his waistcoat pocket and opened it—"I should like to do in precisely one hour. Where is His Grace?"

"His Grace went out shooting in the home wood, my lord. I should perhaps inform your lordship that the household is somewhat more reduced than before your departure. Mr. Appleby has left us."

Lord Michael grimaced, but all he said was, "Very well. I shall send a notice to the London papers in the morning. If His Grace returns to the house before we dine, inform him that I wish to speak with him in my dressing room. If he does not, he can dine when he does come in. We shan't wait dinner for him. Oh, and be sure to tell Lord Ashby that we dine in an hour."

"Yes, my lord. His lordship is in his sitting room if you should wish to make your arrival known to him."

Lord Michael glanced at Anne, and she was surprised to see indecision in his gaze. Then he said, "Her ladyship will meet him at dinner. That is soon enough."

Anne had been looking around during their exchange, and was glad to see that the house had been better cared for than the gardens. The lofty entrance hall was large and well-appointed with enormous twin fireplaces facing each other from either end, but the hall was not by any means the most imposing feature of Upminster Priory, as she discovered when Lord Michael took her through the pedimented doorway opposite the front door.

A soaring toplit oval staircase with cantilevered stairs and an intricately designed wrought-iron balustrade filled the center of the main block of the great house. Even with the darkening skies outside, light from the domed skylight overhead filled the stairwell. At the gallery landing, Lord Michael paused and said matter-of-factly, "The library, dining room, and yellow drawing room are found on the first floor. The state apartments are arranged in a circle around the stairwell on this level, and are thought to be very fine. This part of the house was used to be frequently open to the public, but I have put a stop to that practice for the present."

"I am persuaded that while the family is in mourning, sir—and with a reduced staff—you chose the wisest course."

"Yes, perhaps, though those were not my sole reasons. We pass through the state drawing room," he said, nodding to the left. "The family apartments are beyond in the southwest wing."

"I collect, sir, that this building was not the original priory but was built more recently."

"Yes, the land and its buildings were awarded to an ancestor of mine by Henry VIII at the time of the Dissolution, but the original priory was run down and of no particular beauty, so he razed it to build a more modern house, which has been much augmented over the years. My grandfather, the fourth duke, added the southwest wing less than thirty years ago. You will find the rooms there quite comfortable."

She wondered suddenly if she would share his bedchamber. Her parents occupied separate rooms, but she realized that many married persons did share a bedchamber, even in noble houses. The image was an unnerving one, as was the one that followed swiftly after it. He would soon want to claim his rights as her husband. That awareness had not escaped her altogether before now, but had, in fact, imposed itself upon her mind at much the oddest moments since the news of her impending nuptials had been broken to her. Before meeting him, she had wondered if he would be a kind man. She had even, more than once, allowed herself the luxury of hoping he might prove to be a gentle lover. Now, thinking of that moment to come, that odd but increasingly familiar little tremor stirred again.

He said, "Is something amiss?"

"No, sir," she said, turning hastily to accompany him. They passed into the state drawing room, the walls of which were lined with white tabbinet. Curtains and upholstery were blue velvet, and the furniture was constructed of dark, highly polished cherry. A faint scent of damask roses lingered in the air, and Anne noted a potpourri jar on the hearth, but despite the fact that the fire was burning, she saw that the lid had not been removed from the jar and assumed that was done only when the house was to be opened to the public.

Gesturing toward the portrait that took pride of place between two tall windows, Lord Michael said abruptly, "That is my mother, by Sir Joshua Reynolds."

Anne nodded. "She was very pretty. At least"—she looked at him in some confusion—"I know the sixth duchess died only a month or so before the duke did, but your mother—"

"—is also deceased," he said. "She died of influenza when I was a child."

"Oh, I'm so sorry."

"It was a long time ago. That jib door yonder by the fireplace leads to service stairs. The house abounds in staircases, but most of them are for the servants' use, and since those are rather steep and frequently ill lit, you will do better to use the main ones in each wing, or the central stair."

"I collect that the house is very large," Anne said.

"Large enough, certainly larger than my own house at Egremont," he said, "but I daresay there are larger houses in England. Chatsworth is larger, certainly."

Anne nodded. She had never seen Derbyshire's most celebrated stately home, but so famous was it that she imagined it must be one of the largest in the world, not just in England. "The Priory is much larger than Rendlesham, too," she said.

"You will become accustomed to it," he said.

They passed into a corridor lined with windows on both sides, and Anne saw that it connected the main block with a more modern wing. The rooms looked over the river and were backed by a continuation of the connecting corridor, which became a sort of long gallery overlooking flower gardens, lawns, and part of what appeared to be the stables, set against darkening parkland and a hillside sharply rising into black clouds pierced by jagged lightning flashes. Even inside the corridor, the air felt muggy and filled with the electrical tension of the impending storm.

"My rooms are here," Lord Michael said, indicating a pair of ornately carved doors. "My bedchamber is the first, then my dressing room. Your dressing room and bedchamber lie just beyond. Your dressing room connects with mine."

Repressing a sigh of relief that they would not share a bedchamber, Anne said quickly, "And the children's rooms, sir? Where are they located?"

"On the next floor."

"And the schoolroom?" she persisted. "I collect, since His Grace is at home now, that he does not go to school."

"Dukes of Upminster are traditionally educated at home," Lord Michael said, adding sardonically, "Only their brothers are sent away to school. That tradition may soon change, however. The Mr. Appleby Bagshaw mentioned was His Grace's latest tutor."

"Latest?"

"Latest."

"I see."

"Here you are." He opened the door to a bedchamber decorated in varying tones of gold and dark crimson.

"Good gracious," Anne exclaimed, staring in undisguised dismay at the heavy, ornate tapestries covering the walls. These were augmented by gold-and-scarlet striped curtains and bed curtains, a garish red, purple, and yellow Turkey carpet, and richly upholstered and gilded furniture, all certainly elaborate enough for royalty. She looked into the adjoining dressing room, and found it much the same. "How . . . how sumptuous!"

"Do you think so? I never liked it much, but Agnes was fond of bright colors, I suppose, since it was her bedchamber. It has certainly been redone since my mother occupied it, for I remember her surrounded by pastels and flowery fabrics. That image is so clear in my mind, in fact, that when I recall it, I can even smell her perfume. Like lilacs," he added, looking around as if he were seeing the room differently now. He collected himself at once, however, and turned back to her, saying in his customary firm way, "The bell is there by the bed if you wish to ring for someone to assist you. I believe the second coach will arrive soon, but if it does not, you need not worry about your appearance. Just tidy yourself as best you can. We rarely stand on ceremony these days." A moment later he was gone.

Anne soon realized she could see the triple-arched bridge from her windows. She could also see ever-darkening clouds from the north, moving closer, their approach announced by more frequent rolls and crashes of thunder. The sun no longer peeped over the western hills, and she knew it would not be long before its last lingering red glow would be gone. She wished the storm would break soon, then scolded herself, knowing that Maisie would not thank her for hoping the rain would come before the second carriage reached the Priory.

Wasting no time, she set Juliette on the bed and rang for a maidservant to assist with her ablutions. The kitten's plaintive mew reminded her that she was not the only one requiring assistance.

The chambermaid who responded to the bell proved to be an extremely pretty young girl, wide-eyed and nervous. She wore a simple blue frock with a white cambric apron and a mobcap from which a few light brown curls had escaped. Bobbing a curtsy, she said, "I be Frannie, m'lady. Mr. Bagshaw— That is, Mrs. Burdekin said I were to help you till your own woman arrives."

"Thank you, Frannie. Send for hot water, if you please. I see that the towels are fresh ones—"

"Oh, yes, m'lady. Oh, I beg your pardon! I oughtn't to be interrupting your ladyship, but Mrs. Burdekin wouldn't never allow musty towels to be set out. Why, she'd have a fit, she would, and if she didn't, surely Mr. Bagshaw would. Just hot water, ma'am? Nothing else?"

"On the contrary," Anne said, recognizing a tendency to chatter that would no doubt annoy Frannie's superiors more than any lack of fresh towels. She smiled in her friendly way and, picking up the kitten, said, "This is Juliette, Frannie. She is a trifle nervous of these new surroundings, but you may pet her if you like."

Frannie put out a hand only to snatch it back. "That's a black cat," she said. "They be pernicious bad luck, m'lady."

Patiently Anne said, "Juliette has white hairs on her chin, Frannie. See there." She scratched the kitten's chin, and it raised its head, beginning to purr.

"Oh, she's precious," Frannie said, succumbing. "Such a sweet face she has."

"Juliette is not accustomed to being very much out of doors," Anne explained. "She will require a box of torn paper and a private space of her own, perhaps a screened corner in my dressing room."

Frannie understood at once, and said, "There be a powder closet, ma'am, that won't be much used, unless you be wishful to have your hair powdered sometimes."

"No, that will suit Juliette excellently well."

Frannie hurried to attend to these details, and Anne put the kitten down again and, as soon as her hot water arrived, began to wash her face and hands. The outside light was nearly gone, and when Frannie, having attended to the kitten's requirements—including the provision of a bowl of tidbits to tempt Juliette's appetite—suggested that she ought to draw the curtains and light several branches of candles, Anne agreed at once.

"And light the fires here and in the next room as well, Frannie," she said. "My woman will be chilled through when she arrives, but I know she will want to begin unpacking at once. I just hope she is not so foolish as to begin doing so before she has had her dinner."

"I'll tell her, ma'am. I'm to help her in any way I can."

Thanking her, Anne noted by the clock on the mantel that it was nearly seven. Realizing that Lord Michael's allotted hour was all but gone, she said, "You may direct me to the dining room now, if you will be so kind, Frannie."

"Yes, my lady, and then shall I come back here to look after Juliette whilst you dine?"

"That will not be necessary," Anne told her. "She will be quite safe here so long as the door is kept firmly shut. She mustn't be allowed to wander about, however, until she has grown more accustomed to her new surroundings."

Frannie looked disappointed but Anne was sure that neither the housekeeper nor the stately butler would be pleased to have the maid's services usurped on behalf of a small black cat.

As they passed Lord Michael's dressing room, Anne heard the murmur of his voice and wondered if the young duke had returned. The rooms seemed to be fairly soundproof, for she could hear only enough to be certain it was Lord Michael's deep voice she heard. She could not discern his words.

Frannie, noting her glance, said, "Did you wish to speak with his lordship, ma'am?"

"Oh, no," Anne said, startled by the notion of interrupting

him, even if he were speaking only with his valet. Since it had
not occurred to her that she might interrupt him, the thought
that, as his wife, she could do so struck her forcibly. Clearly
there were things associated with the married state that would
take some getting used to.

She smiled at Frannie in what she hoped was a confident
manner and said, "Since he is apparently occupied, I daresay
there will be time for you to help me get my bearings before
I must go downstairs. I have seen the state drawing room, but
you can show me the other state apartments, Frannie."

Wax candles burned in all the rooms she entered, and fires
crackled in hooded fireplaces behind sturdy fenders in most
of them. When she and Frannie descended the spiral stairs,
the skylight overhead was dark, but candles in wall sconces
and candelabra below on side tables in the hall lighted their
way.

Bagshaw met them at the entrance to the dining room, bowing in his stately way, and saying, "You will wish to await the
gentlemen in the drawing room, madam. This way, if you
please. Frances, you may return to your duties."

Anne thanked Frannie and obediently followed the butler to
a doorway leading from the rear of the stair hall into a spacious
room with yellow-striped wallpaper and white moldings, which
was clearly much used by the family. At the moment, it smelled
of candle wax, furniture polish, and damp dog. A large retriever, curled on the hearth rug, lifted its head to look solemnly at her but took no exception to her entrance, merely
thumping its tail a time or two before lowering its head again
to its paws.

"Do you require anything further, madam?" Bagshaw asked.

Before she could assure him that she did not, another voice
spoke. "Thought we were dining at seven, Bagshaw. Where
the devil's Michael? Ought to be here to present me to his
bride, by Jove? Dashed uncivil of him to leave us to present
ourselves."

Turning her head, Anne beheld a plump, fashionably dressed

gentleman with thick, graying hair and side whiskers, who boasted some fifty years in his dish. He held a slim cane but did not seem to require its use, for he held it out with a distinct flair as he made his bow, saying, "Ashby St. Ledgers, at your service, ma'am. Pray, don't refuse to acknowledge me, for it ain't my fault my dashed, unfeeling nephew has left us to ourselves."

Anne stepped forward at once, extending her hand in a friendly way. "Of course I will not do any such uncivil thing, sir. I am very pleased to make your acquaintance. I am afraid Lord Michael has been a trifle delayed."

"Trying to lay down the law again to Andrew, most likely," Lord Ashby said, frowning slightly. "Hope the lad don't put him too much out of curl. That would not suit me just now, I can tell you, but we can't do much to prevent it, can we?" When she glanced at the lingering butler, he added, "Oh, don't mind Bagshaw. Ain't nothing about the family he don't know."

"His Grace has not yet come in from shooting, your lordship," Bagshaw said. "Lord Michael was a trifle detained by other matters, however, and begged you would forgive him."

"Certainly, certainly," Lord Ashby said, grinning at Anne and moving to pick up a wineglass containing a golden liquid. Lifting it, he said, "Care for a drop of sherry, my dear?"

"No, thank you, sir." She smiled at Bagshaw, adding, "That will be all now, thank you. We won't keep you from your duties."

"Thank you, madam."

When he had gone, she said, "Won't you sit down, Lord Ashby? I am persuaded that Lord Michael will not keep us waiting long."

Nor did he. They had been chatting in a friendly way for less than a quarter hour when he entered the room. He had changed his shirt and neckcloth, but otherwise he looked much the same as he had an hour earlier.

Lord Ashby, who had been explaining that he had not attended their wedding because it had been decided that he ought to remain with the young duke, grinned cheerfully at his nephew and said, "Thought you was trying to lay down the law to Andrew again, but Bagshaw says he ain't come in yet. Just as well, I imagine. I've been explaining to your lovely bride that it was thought best for me to stay here. Can't think it did much good though. Well, stands to reason it didn't, since that Appleby chap took a pet and left. Boy don't heed anyone, you know. Goes his own road just like his father and grandfather before him."

"He will learn to heed me." Lord Michael spoke quietly, but his tone sent a chill up Anne's spine. A rumble of thunder outside underscored the sudden tension in the room.

"Bagshaw says he's still out shooting," Lord Ashby said doubtfully, casting a frowning glance at the curtained window when the thunder muttered again.

"Yes," Michael said. "I've told them not to wait dinner for him, though, so unless you mean to carry that wine in with you, you'd best drink it down. We will go in at once."

Lord Ashby downed his wine hastily, pulled a snowy handkerchief from his coat pocket and dabbed at his lips. "Never let good wine go to waste," he said, grinning at Anne.

Lord Michael made no comment, merely stepping forward to offer his arm to his wife.

She got up at once, and as she laid her fingertips on his coat sleeve, becoming instantly aware of the hard muscle beneath, another rumble of thunder rent the air outside.

Lord Ashby, glancing again at the window, muttered, "Devilish storm's been muttering for hours. Wish it would get on with whatever it means to get on with, by Jove."

Anne said, "I was thinking the same a little earlier, sir, but I realized my tirewoman would most likely prefer to be safe and warm within doors before it breaks. She is a little nervous of thunderstorms."

"Don't like 'em much myself," he said amiably.

Approximately ten servants stood in a solemn line outside

the doors to the dining room, and Bagshaw presented them to
Anne in turn but so swiftly that she would have been hard
pressed to recall any of their names immediately afterward.
She had no more than an impression of dignity and general
nervousness as each curtsied or bowed and murmured a polite
greeting.

The interlude was swiftly over. A footman moved to stand
by the open doors to the dining room, and as they passed him,
Lord Michael said quietly, "Thunder and lightning have no
doubt delayed the second coach, for the horses will be nervous,
and their driver will have his hands full; but he is quite capable,
I promise you. They will be here soon."

She smiled gratefully, and took her seat where he indicated,
a little surprised to find herself sitting at one side of the table
rather than at the head or the foot. Then, seeing that the place
opposite Lord Michael was left empty, she realized that it was
probably where the young duke was accustomed to sit.

Lord Ashby said as he sat down across from her, "Can't
imagine what that boy's about to have stayed out so long in
this weather, by Jove. Light outside is terrible, and the thunder
will have sent any game to ground long since."

Michael glanced at Bagshaw, who stood near the serving
door, waiting to oversee the service. When the butler shook
his head, Michael said, "If he really is out with a gun, I agree
that he cannot be having much luck. He will get hungry soon,
however."

"Probably knows you're home," Lord Ashby said wisely.

Michael did not reply, and nothing further was said while
the first course was served. Anne observed the dishes and service with a critical eye, but having taken Bagshaw's measure,
was not much surprised to see that everything was just as it
should be. Whoever ruled the ducal kitchens seemed to know
his or her business as well, and the tempting aromas stirred
her to accept at least a small portion of every dish offered to
her.

Lord Ashby, signing to a footman to refill his wineglass,

said casually, "Hope you ain't meaning to be too harsh with the boy, Michael. Cuts up all our peace when he's out of curl."

"I see no reason to allow a fourteen-year-old boy to run roughshod over everyone in his path," Lord Michael said.

"He's not just any fourteen-year-old, by Jove. He's the Duke of Upminster, so if he's got a top-lofty notion of his own worth, it's not to be wondered at. We're a proud family."

"You said as much before, Uncle, but I ask you, do you really want to encourage Andrew to follow in his father's footsteps—or in those of his grandfather?"

"A proud heritage," Lord Ashby said, drinking deeply.

"Empty pride, if you ask me," Michael said. "Of what use is pride to a pauper?"

"Here now, you can't mean that. If Edmund failed to tend to business as he should have, it was only that he never cared for such stuff, and as to his gaming and that dashed inconvenient wager of his, well, that might happen to any man, but you ain't going to say my father ignored the estates, for I know better."

"I daresay Grandfather looked after things well enough, though he was scarcely a paragon," Michael said. "A more stiff-rumped old devil I hope never to encounter."

Lord Ashby chuckled reminiscently. "He was that. Lord, no one was even allowed to sit in his presence unless it was at table." Grinning at Anne, he added, "He dozed off once in his bookroom and woke to find that my sister Margaret had dared to sit down to read her book. Disinherited her on the spot."

"Goodness," Anne exclaimed, "he must have been a tyrant."

"Exactly," Michael said, "and in his own way, my brother was much the same. Thus far, Andrew has been allowed to take that same route, to believe the sun rises and sets by his wish. I have tried being firm with him but have not wanted to interfere too harshly so soon after his father's death; however, now that Appleby has gone the way of his predecessors . . ." He glanced at Lord Ashby. "What happened this time?"

Gesturing for more wine, Lord Ashby said, "Same as last time. Fellow got tired of having insults hurled at him—books too, I shouldn't wonder. Andrew ain't much interested in reading them, at all events."

"But surely," Anne began, only to fall silent when she realized she was speaking of something that did not yet concern her. She bit her lip, looking apologetically at her husband.

He said evenly, "No doubt you are surprised to hear of a tutor who allows his charge to throw things."

"Well, yes," she admitted. "I certainly was never permitted to throw anything at my governess." She gave a little shudder at the thought of what her father's reaction to such behavior would have been, from any of his children.

"A harsh woman, your governess?" Lord Ashby asked.

"Not really," Anne said, "but each week we had to tell Papa what had transpired during the week, and if Miss Turner had to punish us, he would always do so again, so my sisters and I took good care to obey her. Our brothers went away to school, to Harrow. Do His Grace's tutors *never* correct him?"

Astonished, Lord Ashby said, "By Jove, who would dare raise a hand to Upminster?"

"I see," Anne said, though she did not.

Michael said, "No other Duke of Upminster has come into his position at the age of fourteen, however, and say what you will, Uncle, even Edmund's selfishness was curtailed to some extent before my father died. If we are to prevent Andrew from becoming utterly impossible, something must be done, and soon. But we need not dwell on that at present. What other news is there?"

Lord Ashby hesitated, then said rather quickly, "Well, as a matter of fact there was something I wanted to speak to you about, but perhaps we'd do better to talk later, after you've had your dinner and a chance to relax a bit."

"How much?" Michael asked in a tone of resignation.

"Now don't fly into the boughs," Lord Ashby said hastily. "Inflammable air's dashed expensive!"

Meeting Anne's look of astonishment, Michael said, "My uncle is not content to have his head in the clouds. He must needs put his feet up there as well."

Lord Ashby chuckled self-consciously, but before Anne could request further explanation, a new voice said from the doorway, "Well, this is a fine thing! Since when is dinner in *my* house put forward without so much as a by-your-leave from *me?*"

Andrew, seventh Duke of Upminster, Marquis of Tissington, Earl of Farnham, Baron St. Ledgers and Baron Grinstead of Elstow, stood glaring at them from the doorway, his glossy dark curls damp and tumbling over his broad forehead, his gray eyes wide and as stormy as the skies outside. He was a thin boy who, though he looked to be a bit taller than Anne, had not yet enjoyed that spurt of growth common to his age. Looking at Lord Michael, ignoring both Anne and Lord Ashby, his belligerent expression challenged his uncle to reply.

With an edge to his voice, Michael said, "Try for a little conduct, Andrew, and make your leg to Lady Michael."

"It is her duty to curtsy to me," Andrew said defiantly, "and you ought to present her properly to me first."

"His Grace is quite right, my lord," Anne said calmly, getting to her feet as Elbert leapt to hold her chair. Sweeping the boy a deep curtsy, she said as she arose and held out her hand to him, "I hope you will call me Anne, Your Grace. I am sorry you were unable to attend our wedding."

Mollified and clearly surprised by her gesture, the young duke took her hand perfunctorily, released it at once, and said, "Since I am still in mourning for my father and mother, I believe it would have been inappropriate for me to attend any wedding. Is there lamb tonight, Bagshaw?" he asked, turning to the butler.

"Yes, indeed, Your Grace."

The boy moved to take his place opposite Lord Michael, and Anne sat down again, refusing to be ruffled by his rudeness and glancing at her husband to see if her action had displeased him.

He said, "Lady Michael's wineglass is empty, Elbert."

"Yes, my lord." The footman sprang to refill it.

Anne did not want more wine. Encouraged by the fact that Lord Michael sounded much as usual, she said, "I hope you mean to explain what you were saying, sir. What is inflammable air, if you please, and how can Lord Ashby put his feet in the clouds?"

Andrew looked up from the platter of sliced lamb being held for his inspection and said, "But surely you must know that Great-Uncle Ashby is the greatest aeronaut in all England!"

Three

"Are you truly an aeronaut, sir?" Anne demanded, fascinated.

Lord Michael snorted, but Lord Ashby shrugged with an air of spurious modesty and said, "I am, indeed, though the lad flatters me. Do you know much about aeronautics, young woman?"

"Practically nothing," Anne said frankly. "I once watched a balloon ascension from Hyde Park, but I know nothing about them. Isn't going up in one a very dangerous thing to do?"

"Very foolish is what it is," Michael said.

"Now, by Jove, you mustn't say that, lad. Only think what air power could mean to the military! That damned Bonaparte could scarcely afford to defend himself against ten thousand men descending from the clouds, now could he?"

"I wish I may see it," Michael said. "Your ten thousand are as likely to end up in Scotland or Norway as in France, sir. The only thing an aeronaut can control is whether he goes up or down, and he doesn't always have much choice even about that. Balloons—or aerostats, as you choose to call them—are little more than toys, in my opinion, and can serve no useful purpose until you aeronauts learn to guide them properly."

"But that is precisely why I must continue my experiments," Lord Ashby said earnestly. "It's as plain as a pikestaff that the time will come when we *can* use them to good purpose. Bound to happen, don't you know? Can't stop progress." He beamed at Anne. "Michael is one who would have scoffed at the wheel before it was perfected, but I want to ride the tide of progress as it flows into the future. Man cannot stop it any more than he can stop the course of Mother Nature. Take that storm brewing outside, for example. If I muttered and grumbled back at it each time it raised its voice, do you suppose it would pay me the slightest heed?"

"None," Andrew replied before Anne could speak. "What's more, I believe you are right about military use, too." He shot Michael a defiant glance. "There will come a day when soldiers will attack from the sky, and I just hope they will be good Englishmen and not the villainous French. I'd never deny you support for your experiments, Uncle Ashby, if only I controlled my fortune. England must control the skies as fiercely as she controls the sea."

"How dreadful," Anne said, shaken by this casual talk of more war. Then, seeing the offended look on Andrew's face, she added quickly, "Not your belief in England, sir, certainly, but the very thought of such an aerial attack on unsuspecting, innocent people. It never entered my mind, when I saw that gaily decorated balloon soar aloft from Hyde Park, that such a contrivance might one day be converted into an engine of destruction."

Lord Ashby said solemnly, "Bound to happen one day, never doubt it, and balloons won't be employed merely to take men into battle either. Two years ago a fellow actually took a horse aloft with him. Just a matter of time, I'll wager, till we put whole armies into the sky."

Michael gave a long-suffering sigh and said, "If such a day ever dawns, the most likely outcome is that the rulers of the earth will be convinced at last of the utter folly of war."

"Fine talk from a military man," Lord Ashby said with a grin.

"Ex-military, sir. I did my duty for three long years, but that does not mean I enjoyed it. I prefer to believe there must be a more peaceful way for countries to settle their differences."

"Not countries up against a devil who wants to rule the world, like Boney," Lord Ashby pointed out.

"Perhaps not," Michael said. When he did not continue, conversation lapsed, for, although Anne had given no order to do so—and had seen no one else sign to them—the servants had begun to clear away platters and dishes to make room for dessert and the wine. Once these items had been placed on the table, Bagshaw signed to the other servants to withdraw, and followed them. A heavier silence ensued, and Anne noticed that Andrew seemed suddenly to display an extraordinary interest in choosing between a slice of rhubarb tart and a cheesecake.

Lord Ashby, too, seemed absorbed in selecting his dessert. He was the first to break the silence, however, saying to Michael, "If you ain't going to have more wine yourself, lad, you might pass the decanter in this direction."

"Sorry," Michael said, pushing the decanter toward him but watching Andrew. "How was the shooting?" he asked.

Andrew looked at him from beneath furrowed brows. "Didn't see much to shoot, if you must know."

"Then don't you think you ought to have come in sooner?"

Andrew shrugged. "Didn't want to."

"And so you kept your loader tramping at your heels on no more than a mere whim."

"Why not? It is his business to tramp at my heels."

When Anne saw Lord Michael's lips press tightly together, and a muscle twitch high in his cheek, she said wistfully, "I have never actually been tempted to shoot anything, myself, but I confess, I have often thought the sport must provide gentlemen with the perfect excuse for just walking through the woods, observing the birds and trees and flowers."

Andrew shot her a quick, measuring look, but she was more interested to learn how Michael would react to her intervention. At the first hint of his anger, she had experienced an instinctive desire to defuse the situation. The impulse was second nature to her after years of intervening in such cases on behalf of her brothers and sisters. She abhorred dissension, even feared it, viewing subsequent explosions as failures on her own part to maintain a more peaceful state.

Michael was still watching Andrew. His tone was even, however, when he said, "Knowing that I was bringing my new wife home today, you ought to have been here to greet her, Andrew. I expect you to extend an extraordinary courtesy to her, for it is your duty, you know, to see that she quickly feels welcome here."

"Oh, certainly."

"And you, Uncle, I hope you will keep a protective eye on her till she finds her feet."

"Glad to oblige, dear boy. Easy on the eyes, she is—protective or otherwise—and that's a fact."

Anne blushed but said quickly, "I hope no one need look after me. I can look after myself quite well, you know."

"Can you?" Michael asked, and she thought she detected some slight amusement in his eyes. "What will you find to occupy your time here, I wonder?"

"Good gracious, sir, all manner of things. There is this huge house, for one thing, and the gardens, not to mention the children, for I do hope you mean to send for Sylvia at once. She must long to be in her own home again after so many months away."

"If you really want her, I shall send for her tomorrow, but as to the house, Bagshaw and Mrs. Burdekin have everything well in hand, so I cannot imagine what you think you need do."

"They seem competent, certainly, but I have been trained to supervise my household closely; and the gardens are quite another story altogether, I fear."

"What's wrong with them?"

"Goodness me, they are chockful of weeds, and nothing looks as if it's been pruned in a year or more. Do you stock that lake for fishing? For if you do, I'll be bound it's empty now."

"We fish the river," Michael said. "The lake is purely ornamental."

Lord Ashby said, "Could be she's right though, Michael. Quigley's getting on in years, by Jove, and his eyesight ain't what it used to be. Under-gardener's not precisely bursting with initiative either. Can't think of the lad's name just now, but you know the one I mean."

"It doesn't matter," Michael said. "Do as you like with the gardens, madam. It will at least give you something useful to do with your time until Sylvia returns."

Anne was sure she would find many things to occupy her, both inside the house and out. Gentlemen, in her experience, had little understanding of the effort required to keep a household running smoothly, but the servants would surely expect her to take the reins at once, and must be wondering whether she would drive them with a light or heavy hand. From what she had seen, the duke was fortunate in his household staff, but she had already seen a few details that could be altered without inconveniencing anyone. For example, if Lord Michael was concerned about money, surely they did not need a score of wax candles and a fire in every public room.

Knowing that such extravagance might well have been in honor of her homecoming, she resolved to make no suggestions until she had had a chance to see just how the household was run on a daily basis. For that same reason, she forbore to point out that, although she had been introduced to the servants as their new mistress, they had not once looked to her during dinner for their orders. They had even begun clearing the table without so much as looking to her for a sign that they should do so. Telling herself that such behavior was merely habitual in a household of gentlemen, and not done by intent, she decided to have a private word with Bagshaw, but only if the same thing happened again.

Conversation lapsed again until they had finished their dessert, and during that whole time Andrew scarcely took his eyes from his plate. When Lord Michael pushed back his chair and stood up, however, the boy stiffened visibly.

"I will see you in the library now, Andrew," Michael said. "I have a few things to say to you." He rang the bell, and when Bagshaw appeared, he said, "We don't want a tea tray tonight unless Lord Ashby requires one for himself." Then, looking at Anne, who had risen from the table when he had, he added, "You may go up now, madam. I will come to you when I have attended to Andrew."

Anne felt a tightening in her midsection but whether it was one of those odd tremors born of anticipation, or just annoyance at being treated as much like a child as Andrew, she was not certain. She curtsied to the boy, saying, "Good night, Your Grace. I look forward to increasing our acquaintance."

He nodded curtly and strode from the room without a word. Grimacing, Michael followed him.

"Foolish brat," Lord Ashby muttered with a sigh.

"It must be difficult for him to see me in his mother's place," Anne said as the two of them moved into the stair hall.

"Bosh, the boy scarcely ever saw her. Made a pet of young Sylvie, Agnes did, but she left Andrew to his nurses and his father when she and Edmund were here at home. Agnes preferred living in town and spent as little time as possible here. Edmund was here more, but he often came without her."

"Oh," Anne said. "I suppose it was much the same in our family, or it would have been if my mother enjoyed town life. She goes every year for precisely two months of the Season, but that is all. And although we had nurses and governesses, she was always nearby. My sisters are closer to her than I am, but we would all miss her dreadfully if she were to die. I suppose this family is different though—the mothers generally not close to their sons—and that is why Lord Michael . . . that is—" She broke off, realizing she should not be speaking of her husband in such a way.

"Showed you Marianne's portrait, did he?"

Anne nodded.

"Casual about it, ain't he? Don't let him fool you." Lord Ashby smiled in an altogether different way, a softer, gentler way. "Marianne was the merriest thing, so full of life and laughter, and she adored her children. Doted on them all in a scandalously unfashionable way, and they adored her. Think I was a bit in love with her myself. She and her special friends were quite a group. Never found anyone my own age or younger to match them. Not that they were much older, mind you. I suppose Marianne was about five years older, and she was the eldest of them all, and the merriest. The youngest, a chit called Hermione, was—is, I should say—just a year older than what I am, myself." He sighed reminiscently, adding, "My brother was never the same after Marianne died. Oh, he had his amusements, of course. Who does not? But he never could bear to think of marrying again and became as stiff-rumped as our father was, and as distant of manner. Edmund—despite being all of twelve or thirteen at the time—carried on right royally, demanding to know how she could do such a thing to him and ordering that she be brought back to life. Threw royal tantrums, too, when he found he couldn't get his own way with the Almighty, but Michael turned overnight from a merry child into a solemn one. Took it upon himself to tell Hetta. That's his younger sister—Lady Armstrong she is now. She wasn't even a year old at the time."

"He has another sister, does he not?"

"Aye, the eldest of the lot—Charlotte, Lady Harlow. Young Sylvie's been staying with her and her brood. Daresay it's done her a world of good." He glanced toward the closed library door, and tugged at a side whisker, adding, "Guess I'll toddle along to my little parlor, my dear, for you'll want to be going upstairs to your woman, and I've some sketches I want to look over."

"I am sorry you will not get your inflammable air now, sir," she said sympathetically.

"What's that you say? Oh, I'll get it, never fear. Got to. The

Royal George is fitted up with a valve, so I can't use plain hot air to fill it. Besides, I've already ordered the makings."

"But Lord Michael said—"

"Bosh, he frets and stews too much. Not my fault if the stuff's expensive to produce, is it? You just run along now. Don't want to displease him your first night." And with that, he said good-night and walked away, idly swinging his stick as if he had nothing at all to worry him.

Anne stared after him in bemusement for a long moment, but a clatter of dishes from the dining room reminded her that she had better go upstairs as Lord Michael had bidden her to do.

To her relief, she found Maisie waiting for her in her dressing room, directing the filling of a tub with hot water.

"How glad I am to see you," Anne said. "I was afraid all this thunder would fidget the horses and make you ever so late."

"Oh, aye, it was a dreadful journey," Maisie replied, "but at least it did not come on to pour yet, as we was expecting it to do any minute. Let me undo your hair, Miss—that is, my lady. Did it up all nohow, I see. Those back bits look like a broom in a fit."

Anne sat on the cushioned stool in front of the dressing table and smiled at Maisie's reflection in the mirror. "I thought you would be exhausted and grumpy by now," she said, adding in response to a plaintive mew, "Yes, Juliette, you may come up if you like."

The small cat leapt to her lap as Maisie said, "I'd have been as mad as fire at the snail's pace we set, for them horses shied at near every mutter of thunder. Coming from all directions like it's been doing, you'd think that wicked storm would have broke over our heads by now. We did get a battering of hail for a time, but Mr. Foster directed the coachman to draw into a thick grove of trees, and the worst was soon over."

"I don't think we had any hail here," Anne said, surprised, "but perhaps I just did not hear it. Surely, His Grace would have mentioned it though. He was outside apparently, shooting."

"Well, I'll tell you, Miss Anne, I'd have been fed up hours ago but for Mr. Foster. I did not quite like traveling alone with a man, but he turned out to be very pleasant indeed."

"Goodness, Maisie, don't tell me you have formed a tenderness for Lord Michael's valet!"

"No such thing! As if I would. Now, go along with you, Miss Anne, and no more of your teasing. I only said the man was a pleasant traveling companion. Behaves quite like a gentleman, he does, and no wonder, for he's traveled a good deal by the sound of it, with his lordship. He was with him when he was in the army, you see, and in London, too, of course. We'll just have that dress off you now, so you can have your bath. I've got essence of verbena or lilac to put into the water. Which shall it be?"

"Verbena," Anne said quickly, remembering that Michael associated the scent of lilacs with his mother.

Her bath was performed swiftly and soon, swathed in a warm blue dressing gown, she sat and let Maisie brush her hair again.

"Shall I plait it or leave it loose?"

"Loose, I think," Anne said. She was tempted to have it plaited, tempted too, to find numerous other small tasks to keep Maisie busy and at her side. She knew she was only attempting to delay the inevitable, and decided she was being foolish. Dismissing the woman a few minutes later, she soon found that she was listening intently for sounds of Lord Michael's approach.

The noise of the impending storm had diminished, making her wonder if it would pass them by without breaking, after all. She could still hear wind rattling the window panes, and an occasional rumble of thunder, but there had been no cracks or crashes for some time. She wandered idly around the dressing room for a short time, looked out the window at thick, impenetrable blackness, then went into her bedchamber to stir the fire there. Finally, she took her portfolio from the carpetbag and took out the page she had begun that morning, sitting down at the little writing desk against the wall opposite the windows with Juliette curled in her lap.

. . . It is hard to believe I am still in today, James. I am a married lady now, and the day is still not over. I am waiting for my husband to come to me. Upminster Priory is a magnificent seat, and could be truly splendid, I think, but the gardens are not what they might be, and it seems that all is not in perfect order with the family either. Not only my new husband but his brother, the late duke, appear to have enjoyed an extravagant nature, and consequently—

At the sound of a light rap on the door to the corridor, just before the latch clicked, Anne snatched a piece of blank paper over her writing, but her pen dripped ink over the sheet as she did so, and she stifled an exclamation of dismay, startling Juliette, who jumped to the floor.

"There is silver sand in the drawer, I believe," Lord Michael said from the threshold as he bent swiftly to foil the kitten's intended escape. "I apologize if I startled you."

"It is nothing, sir, mere scribbling." She fought to retain her serenity as she opened the drawer, but to her profound relief, he crossed the room to the powder closet with the kitten in his arms. Shaking silver sand between the two sheets of paper, hoping to minimize any damage, she hoped, too, that he would not ask to read them, which, as her husband, he had every right to do. When he came back without the kitten and bent to tend the fire, she took advantage of his preoccupation to pour the sand off into the dish provided for it, and returned her pages to the portfolio.

Capping the inkwell, she stood, turning to face him. He had straightened but was still gazing down into the fire. She saw then that he, too, was wearing a dressing gown.

He looked up at her approach, and said, "I expected to find you in bed."

"I did not know what you expected, sir, though I do recall now that you said I should go to bed. I am a trifle nervous, you see, which no doubt accounts for my having forgotten. I beg your pardon, and hope you are not vexed."

"Not at all, though I must say you don't seem nervous to me but, on the contrary, quite serene, as usual. And I don't know why you feel you must beg my pardon, though I do recall your father telling me—more than once, in fact—that you are a paragon of obedience. That must certainly be accounted a rare virtue."

"I have been told it is," Anne said. Not knowing what else to say, she waited expectantly for him to tell her what to do next.

He looked at her with some amusement. "Shall I lower myself in your eyes, I wonder, if I confess that I, too, am nervous?"

"You, sir? But I thought you . . . that is," she amended swiftly, "that all gentlemen had vast experience with such matters. Do you not know what to do?"

"Yes, Anne, I know what to do. That is to say, I know how one goes about the process of mating."

"Well, that's good, because I don't know much about it at all. You will have to tell me what to do, but if you are truly nervous or disinclined to do it tonight, there can be no great hurry, after all, and I have no objection if you should prefer to . . . to—"

"There is no good reason to put it off," he said quietly. "It is our duty, after all, to produce children. I meant only that I have never had a brand new wife before, or engaged in such activities with a lady who was not practiced in the activity."

"I . . . I see." Again, she was at a loss for words. Though she had known that gentlemen, as a rule, were far more experienced in matters of sexual conduct than ladies were, and that rakes flirted with all sorts of females, it had not occurred to her that her own husband would have engaged in sexual activities with other women. "Papa—and my sisters, too—said you were once a great rake," she said, "but since I did not know you . . ." She let the sentence trail to silence, unsure how to end it without vexing him.

"You would not have been likely to meet me in London," he said. "I did not frequent Almack's Assembly Rooms or the *ton* parties unless there was gaming involved. I am afraid that until six months ago I was as extravagant in my own way as any other St. Ledgers male, and as active in pursuit of entertainment."

"I see."

"You don't, of course, and I'm not inclined to explain. I think, for both our sakes, we had better agree to forget the past and proceed into the future. You get into bed now, and I'll put out the candles."

Anne waited until his back was turned before slipping hastily out of her dressing gown. Then, using the steps at the window side of the high bed, she sprang into it and snatched the eiderdown coverlet up to her chin. Watching him move methodically to snuff each of the many candles Maisie had left burning, she was glad she had put away her journal pages, for two branches of candles stood on the writing desk, and she was certain that he—like any other man—would have been tempted to read what his wife had written.

He left till last the candle burning on the bed-step table but snuffed it before he slipped off his dressing gown. When he climbed into bed, she realized at once that he was naked, and she was glad he had put out the light. She had never actually seen a naked man, but she had seen her younger brothers in their childhood and certainly knew that men were fashioned differently from women.

When he moved to take her in his arms, she stiffened.

He murmured, "Don't you want to take off your nightdress?"

"Must I?"

"I suppose not, but we must move it out of the way a little."

She swallowed hard, exerting every ounce of control she had over her limbs not to leap from the bed and run away. His hands on her body stirred a number of unfamiliar sensations, but her own modesty made it difficult to accept his taking such liberties with her person. When his hand moved between her legs, she jumped, quite involuntarily, and tried to pull away from him.

"Be still," he murmured. "Let me see if I can help you relax. One of his large hands moved up over her stomach, over her nightdress to her breasts, touching first one then the other, stroking her like he would have stroked a skittish colt or a kitten. His touch was sure but gentle, and the sensations he awoke within her now were such as she had never imagined. She began to relax, even to enjoy his caresses, and when his lips suddenly touched hers, coming to her unexpectedly out of the darkness, she welcomed them.

A flash of lightning instantly followed by a crack of thunder made them both jump. Lord Michael's kisses had been soft, exploratory, but now his lips hardened against hers, and to her astonishment, he thrust his tongue between her lips into her mouth.

His body stirred against hers and when a second crash of thunder came, while his tongue continued to explore her mouth, he moved a hand between her legs again, caressing the insides of her thighs briefly before his fingers sought entrance at the delicate opening where her legs met. Anne stiffened again, but he murmured against her lips, "It will be easier for you if you can relax."

"But you are hurting me," she protested.

"I know I am, and I'm sorry for the pain, but it must be done, and it will only hurt the first time, I promise you."

"How can you be certain of that?"

"I have been told by those who know."

He shifted his weight then, adjusting himself, fitting himself to her body, and despite his effort to be gentle, the pain increased from a dull ache to a much sharper one. Then he began to move, thrusting into her slowly but rhythmically, and Anne, her teeth clamped together, kept her hands at her sides, fists clenched, resisting an overwhelming urge to push him away, enduring the invasion of her body as she knew it was her duty to do.

A third crack of thunder louder than the rest roared through the room, shaking the walls, and Michael, startled, plunged into her. Anne screamed, and in a single, sharp, slicing movement, her fists shot between them, connecting forcefully with the part of his body that invaded hers. With a cry of pain nearly equal to hers, Michael reared back, and the ache within her eased at once.

Anne waited, breathless, feeling his body shift away from hers. When he did not speak at once, she said in a small voice, "I hope I did not injure you. The noise and the pain coming all at once like that was just— I didn't think. I'm dreadfully sorry."

"I'll live," he said, and there was a dry note in his voice that she had not heard before. "I have been warned that the taking of virginity can be very painful, but I was naïve enough to believe it was only the female who suffered. Or perhaps it was arrogance rather than naïveté. If so, I have been well served for it."

He was silent, and she could think of nothing to say. A moment later, she felt his weight shift as he sat up and swung his legs over the edge of the bed. She could see the shape of him by the glow of the little fire on the hearth, but not his expression.

He said quietly, "Good night, madam. I'll ring for your woman to attend you. Next time will be easier for both of us, I hope."

Lightning flashed again, and thunder shook the house as a roar of wind blasted torrents of rain against the bedchamber windows. The storm had broken at last.

* * *

The storm had diminished by the time he was able at last to summon a maid to ease the ache in his loins. Having suffered degrees of that ache from the moment he saw that good cause existed for bringing a new female to the Priory, he knew he could not expect to alleviate it in a trice, but neither had he expected to suffer like he had tonight. From the moment he laid eyes on pretty little Anne, he had wanted her, and being in the same room with her made him long to touch her, to stroke her fine flaxen hair, to—

The door opened to reveal a pretty, trembling maidservant.

He murmured, "I do not think you can have made very great haste, girl. I rang nearly fifteen minutes ago."

Paling, she bobbed a curtsy and said quickly, "I beg pardon, sir. Indeed, I thought you were—"

"Never mind what you thought. Your mental exercises do not interest me. But what do you wait for now? Get undressed at once. If you make me get up to you, I will make you very sorry."

Gasping with fear, she hastened to obey.

He wondered how long it would take to teach little Anne to fear him, and to obey. A wife would certainly create a few problems at the Priory, but perhaps that could be turned to good account. She seemed docile enough; nonetheless, it remained to be seen whether her coming would prove a windfall or a pity.

Four

Following orders, Maisie wakened Anne earlier than usual the next morning, and although portions of her body still ached from the previous night, Anne made light of the discomfort, assuring her tirewoman that she was as fit as a fiddle. She knew from past experience that Maisie could become a veritable tyrant—forgetting her place and issuing orders like a general—if she believed her beloved mistress was ill or, for that matter, if she suspected only that Anne suffered from one of her occasional, annoying headaches.

"Now, see here, my lady," Maisie said as she flung wide the curtains to reveal a brilliant, cloudless sky, "I know you must still feel a good deal of pain, so perhaps you ought to—"

"I am perfectly all right," Anne insisted. "My experience was no more than what all brides must endure, after all."

"Indeed, my lady," Maisie said stiffly, "never having been a bride myself, I never expected to find so much blood."

"It is perfectly normal, I'm sure," Anne said firmly, concealing the fact that she had been astonished to learn she was bleeding. Determined to change the subject, she said, "Have you encountered many members of the household staff yet?"

Maisie sniffed but Anne was quick to note the gleam of amusement in her eyes when she said, "I've been told, madam, that as my lady's personal servant, I am not expected to fraternize with the inferior members—which is to say not with anyone other than the housekeeper, Mrs. Burdekin, for I cannot believe she means for me to fraternize with Mr. Foster or Mr.

Bagshaw, and certainly not with the likes of Mr. Wiggins, who is His Grace's man."

"No, indeed," Anne said, twinkling as she accepted the cup of chocolate Maisie handed her. "How kind of her to explain all that to you, as I collect she must have done."

"Yes, and though it would be impertinent for me to approach Mr. Bagshaw," Maisie went on, raising her voice as she moved from the bedchamber to the dressing room to collect Anne's clothes for the day, "I am expected to relay your orders to that cheeky Elbert when necessary *and* to be certain Frannie has made up your fire in the morning and satisfactorily prepared your dressing room—which means properly dusting the hearth, as I shall shortly inform her. I doubt I shall have much to do with anyone else. Although," she added in a normal tone, appearing in the doorway, "there is a new upper housemaid who seems to be a most superior person." Scarcely pausing to draw breath, she went on, "At all events, I am expected to devote the greater part of my time to serving you, madam."

"Are you, indeed?" Anne said with a chuckle.

Assuming an air of great dignity, Maisie said, "Yes, madam. My duties have been made quite clear. Having assured myself of the chambermaid's efficiency, I am to waken you, inform you of the hour, lay out your clothing, and order hot water for you to wash. I am then, if you please, to take my breakfast with the housekeeper and other principal servants until you ring for me to attend you in your dressing room."

"Good gracious," Anne said, awed, "did Mrs. Burdekin actually have the temerity to recite all that to you?"

Maisie nodded, adding with a wry smile, "But only for my own benefit, madam, on account of Mrs. Burdekin's having no way of knowing if I was trained in such a superior establishment as this one is. And on account of the fact that I am, of course, rather young for so august a position as the one I presently hold, and will no doubt benefit from a bit of friendly guidance."

"She never said all that!"

Maisie abandoned her dignity, grinning as she returned to the dressing room and raised her voice again to say, "She did, but she also gave me some useful information in the process."

When silence followed this announcement, Anne called out, "Well, what else did she tell you?"

Maisie came back with Juliette squirming and growling in her arms, and plopped the kitten down beside Anne, where it began at once to purr. "Little puss was carrying on to be let out of yon powder closet," Maisie said, adding as she took away the empty cup, "Next Mrs. Burdekin said, when you ring for me, I'm to attend you in your dressing room to comb your hair and help you dress, after which I'm to fold and put away your night clothes, clean your combs and brushes, and adjust your toilet table. I am then to retire to my workroom—on the floor above this one, that is—to be ready when wanted. Mrs. Burdekin expects I shall employ myself there in making and altering dresses, millinery, and so forth."

"The woman must think you a ninnyhammer," Anne said frankly, getting out of bed and donning her dressing gown, before following Maisie into the next room. The kitten scampered at her heels.

"Well, I think so," Maisie said, adding as she handed a fresh towel to Anne and poured hot water into the basin, "but here's the most useful bit. At half past twelve, she said, a nuncheon is set out for the family in the dining room while the servants have their dinner. So you see, Miss Anne, it is just like Rendlesham, because dinner, she said, is usually served at six. But to get back to my duties, after the servants dine, I am to attend you again in the event that you should wish to change your dress to pay calls in the neighborhood, or to visit sick or elderly tenants. When you return, I am to help you dress for dinner, then occupy myself in useful pursuits until it is time to help you prepare for bed. Indeed," she added, primming her voice, "Mrs. Burdekin very kindly suggested that, in the meantime, I might find the opportunity to practice reading aloud, but only from books by superior authors."

Anne stared, choking on suppressed laughter as she dried her hands. "Why on earth would you want to do any such thing?"

With a perfectly straight face and a resumption of her dignity Maisie replied, "So that when you grow old and infirm, madam, I shall acquit myself well when I am called upon to entertain you by reading aloud from such works as you will most enjoy."

When Anne could stop laughing enough to speak again, she sat down at the dressing table to let Maisie attend to her hair, saying, "Oh, dear, I do hope you were not impertinent to her."

"No, madam, for despite what others may think, I do know my place. I simply agreed with her where I could do so, though I made no bones about the fact that once *my* mistress is wakened in the morning, she does not dawdle abed till all hours but gets up and gets dressed at once. I further informed Mrs. Burdekin that I shall require my breakfast either before that hour or after you had gone to the breakfast parlor. Since it appears that the *superior* servants in this house do not break their fast till eight o'clock, our schedule will not require any adjustment of theirs, except perhaps where that cheeky footman of yours is concerned."

"Goodness, did you actually say all that and look down your nose at her in that odious fashion when you spoke to her? That expression looks just like Mama's Miss Price, Maisie!"

"I have not observed Miss Price's habits all these years for nothing, madam," Maisie said complacently. "A most superior woman Miss Price is."

"I suppose she must be," Anne agreed, though she had never warmed much to Lady Rendlesham's stiff-as-a-poker abigail. "Still, I hope you will not become quite such a pattern card as Price is, and pray, do not keep calling me madam. It sounds most odd coming from you, who have always called me Miss Anne."

"Well then, I shall continue in my old ways when we are

alone, Miss Anne, but I must begin as I mean to go on here, and if I am to hold my own in this stiff-rumped household, I can see I must be as pompous as even Mr. Bagshaw is, at least in the presence of the upper servants. When you're dressed, I'll ring for Frannie to show you to the breakfast parlor. I already put a flea in that Elbert's ear, telling him he'd best change from his work dress into his livery, because you'd be downstairs by half past seven."

When Anne entered the breakfast parlor twenty minutes later, she saw that the footman had taken Maisie's advice. He was precise to a pin, although he had not yet powdered his hair. She assumed that, as was the practice in other great houses, his appearance would become more formal as the day progressed.

She discovered at once that although she was an early riser, Lord Michael had already had his breakfast and left the house, and she was just as glad, for she felt shy of him after the events of the previous night and wanted time to collect herself before they next encountered each other. Finding that she had the breakfast room to herself, she asked if anyone else might be joining her.

"His Grace be still abed," Elbert said, turning at once to the sideboard. "He generally takes his breakfast in his bed-chamber. And Lord Ashby don't take it at all. Stays up late with his papers and contrivances, he does—for he's always got some newfangled notion in his head—and then he sleeps till noon."

Accepting without comment the plate the footman had prepared for her while he talked, but requesting coffee in place of the ale he set out for her, she asked him to inform Mrs. Burdekin that she wished to speak with her after breakfast.

"Yes, madam. I am to take you to the housekeeper's room when you have finished. Mrs. Burdekin said she would hold herself in readiness to explain the household schedule to you."

Concealing her astonishment, Anne said calmly, "You may tell Mrs. Burdekin that I will receive her here when I have finished breaking my fast, Elbert, since neither His Grace nor Lord Ashby will make an appearance. And henceforth," she added, "I would prefer that you describe the various dishes prepared for breakfast, so that I can make my own selection."

Smiling and unabashed, Elbert said, "Mr. Bagshaw said I should begin by giving you a taste of each one, madam, so that you might more quickly become conversant with what dishes we generally serves for breakfast here."

"That is no doubt an excellent notion," Anne agreed, hiding a smile at his careful pronunciation of *conversant,* which was clearly the butler's word and not his own, "but I will not eat half of what you have served me. Moreover, Elbert, I do not intend to discuss the matter at length with you. Please just do as I request."

"Yes, madam, certainly." He poured her coffee and set the cup and saucer near her right hand, adding, "If that will be all for the moment, madam, I shall go and tell Mrs. Burdekin that you wish to speak with her here."

When he had gone, she breathed a sigh of relief. He had not been the least discomposed by her reproof, but she did not want to set the servants against her from the outset by continuous carping and correcting. No doubt they would rub along together well enough once the household staff came to understand her ways, but so far, the upper servants seemed to be treating her like a guest, and a rather backward guest at that. Their behavior was disconcerting, but she knew what her grandmother would recommend as a remedy.

"Be firm without being severe," the Dowager Lady Rendlesham had advised Anne on numerous occasions when she had descended upon the family. "Be kind without being familiar." The welfare and good character of any household, according to the earl's autocratic mama, depended upon the active supervision of its mistress, whose aim ought to be to manage with economy but without parsimony. Anne could almost hear her now, speaking her favorite maxims aloud.

She was rapidly coming to the conclusion that the late

Duchess of Upminster had not taken such an active role in her household, that by and large the upper servants had managed the house. That it seemed to run smoothly was evidence of their abilities, but Anne knew well that eventually, without proper supervision, problems would arise. Moreover, since by both habit and training she was accustomed to watch closely over her household, the servants might as well learn her ways quickly.

The housekeeper made her appearance while Elbert, having cleared the dishes, was removing the baize cloth from the table. Anne was gazing out a nearby window, which faced the east and the sun rising over the hill behind the house. Though leaves and branches had been blown about by the storm, making the grounds even more untidy than before, everything looked fresh and sparkling. A light mist rose from the ground as the dampness evaporated, and the day promised to be a glorious one.

She dismissed Elbert when the housekeeper arrived but did not sit down again. Nor did she invite Mrs. Burdekin to do so.

"I will not keep you long," Anne said. "I can see that the household is well in hand, and I make you my compliments."

"Thank you, your ladyship," the woman said complacently.

The housekeeper was a little taller than Anne, with light brown hair smoothed neatly into a bun at the nape of her neck. Black bombazine encased her compact figure, and around her waist she wore a golden cord, to which was attached a ring of keys that clinked musically when she moved.

"I presume that you have begun spring cleaning," Anne went on, "and so I shall want a copy of your schedule of service to the various rooms of the house. I shall also want to see the menus each day, of course, to approve them, and your linen lists."

"Traditionally, Mr. Bagshaw approves the daily menus, madam."

"No doubt he has done so in the past, Mrs. Burdekin, at

least since the late duchess's death, but I shall relieve him of that task now that I am here."

"I will speak to him," the woman said calmly. "As to spring cleaning, it's not what you would call really well in hand as yet. What with his lordship's saying the house is to remain shut to the public—and a good thing that is, in my opinion—we did not deem it necessary just at present to set everything at sixes and sevens."

"I quite understand that matters have been unsettled these past months," Anne said, "and gentlemen—at least, in my experience—frequently do not understand that certain tasks must be accomplished with stern regularity if the house is not to fall down around their ears. But you and I, Mrs. Burdekin, know what must be done, particularly in a house as large as this one. I will leave it to you to draw up a list of tasks and a schedule for attending to them. I know you are presently short-staffed, so if you need extra help for rough work, I will arrange for that, as well. I know, at Rendlesham, we always bring in extra girls from the village to help with the spring cleaning."

"Yes, madam." But Mrs. Burdekin's tone was doubtful. Anne did not press the matter, preferring first to see what the housekeeper accomplished on her own. She said, "Before you go, there is one other matter that I wish to mention. I am persuaded that we can make do with fewer wax candles, and since the worst of winter is past, we can certainly dispense with the practice of lighting fires in all the public rooms every day."

"His Grace likes a fire in every room, madam."

"His Grace? The young duke?" Anne did not trouble to hide her astonishment. Andrew had not struck her as one who would notice if the state bedchamber fire had been kindled or not.

Mrs. Burdekin flushed. "His late Grace, I should have said, madam. Duke Edmund was most particular about such things."

"Yes, well, I can see that you have continued to go on as

he liked you to do, but economy is necessary in any well-run household, as I am sure you know. We can easily dispense with quite half of those fires. Make a list, Mrs. Burdekin, and inform the servants who attend to such matters that they are to light fires in half the rooms one night, the other half the next—only in those rooms the family does not use daily, of course, but you know that without my telling you. Now then, if you will show me the kitchens, dairies, still rooms, linen presses, and so forth. I'll look round the rest of the house on my own later."

Though she looked surprised by the request, Mrs. Burdekin obliged, but Anne could not flatter herself that the interview had gone well. By exerting herself to compliment the woman whenever she found an opportunity to do so, she hoped when they parted two hours later that Mrs. Burdekin at least respected her knowledge of the effort necessary to manage a large house; however, even that respect could not be taken for granted, for Mrs. Burdekin had certainly not agreed when Anne had pointed out near the end of their cursory tour that although the huge kitchen fireplace seemed to be equipped with an astonishing array of contrivances for roasting, boiling, baking, stewing, frying, steaming, and heating—including three clockwork bottle-jacks and a smoke jack designed to turn spits by a heat-propelled vane in the chimney—it was woefully lacking in cinder guards or even a proper fender.

"There ought at least to be a bucket of water nearby," she said, "in case of accident."

"We've no need of such," Mrs. Burdekin said placidly. "Our water is piped right to the kitchen, madam, as you saw. Lord Ashby contrived it so three years ago, just as he has contrived other labor-saving devices here and elsewhere round the Priory. With water so handy, there can be no need to add to the clutter around the fireplace with another bucket. As to guards and such, I can assure you that if more were needed, we would have them."

Anne was not convinced, but she was tired and had by that

time had enough of Mrs. Burdekin's company. She had also had enough of being indoors on such a lovely day, and wanted to look over the gardens. With this object in mind, she parted with the housekeeper and had turned toward the family wing to change her shoes and fetch a cloak, when, passing one of the salons, she overheard a cry of protest, instantly hushed.

Curious, she pushed open the salon door, confounding the two persons inside. Elbert stepped hastily away from the housemaid, straightening his shoulders and assuming his footman's dignity like a familiar garment. The maid, slender but curvaceous, and very attractive even in the plain stuff frock, crisp white apron, and mobcap she wore, was not so quick to recover her composure.

Sunlight streaming through a pair of tall windows, revealed her reddened cheeks and the spark of anger and confusion in her blue-green eyes. She held a feather duster uplifted in one hand, as if she had been about to strike the young man. Now, in some consternation, she lowered the duster to her side and, bobbing a hasty curtsy, said, "Did you require assistance, your ladyship?"

It was not the first time in her life that Anne had interrupted such a scene, nor was it the first time she had had cause to deal with budding personal relationships among members of her household staff. But in general, both culprits had looked equally guilty. In this instance Elbert said coolly, "Were you looking for me, my lady?"

Anne's gaze shifted from the blushing, indignant maidservant to the footman. "What are you doing in here, Elbert?"

He showed her a rag he held in one hand, saying glibly, "The looking glass over the table yonder has got fly specks all over it. Mr. Bagshaw wanted it cleaned, and he don't trust the younger lads with anything so fragile. Since I didn't have time to attend to it before your ladyship came to breakfast, I'm doing it now."

"I see. You ought not to be doing such a messy chore in your livery, you know, and in future, if you rub the frame of the glass well with garlic or onion, you will not have so much to clean."

He grinned at her. "I'll be sure to tell Mr. Bagshaw, ma'am. No call to attend to it now though, if you've need of me. I'll just be putting this rag away, and then I'm yours to command."

"Not just now, Elbert," Anne said gently. "I have no commands for you, so you will do better to finish the task Bagshaw assigned to you. First, however, you must go and put on an apron to protect your livery, and I suggest that you take off your jacket, too, so that it does not become soiled."

He stared at her, but her gaze remained steady, and after a long moment, he bowed and moved toward the door. In the same gentle tone, Anne said, "Ask Mrs. Burdekin to provide you with some powder blue, Elbert, and a woollen cloth to polish the glass after you have cleaned it with that damp cotton rag you have. And please do not forget to rub the frame with garlic afterward."

"Yes, madam." His cheeks now as red as the housemaid's, Elbert fled.

Anne waited until the door had shut behind him to say, "What is your name, please?"

"Jane, your ladyship. Jane Hinkle." The maid's voice was low-pitched and well modulated, and Anne surmised from her careful speech and increasing air of confidence that she had been well trained and was an upper housemaid, not one of the menials. That she was still nervous was also clear. "I-I'm sorry, madam," she said when Anne did not immediately reply.

"Why are you sorry, Jane? Did you encourage his attention?"

"Oh, no, madam." Tears welled in her eyes. "I would never do such a thing, for I was raised strict. Please, ma'am, believe me."

"I do believe you," Anne said, remembering the indignant protest she had overheard. She regarded the maid thoughtfully.

"Please, madam, I hope you will not think it necessary to

complain of this incident to Mrs. Burdekin or Mr. Bagshaw. They will not be so willing to take my word, I fear."

"Why not?" Anne asked, surprised, since Jane Hinkle seemed at first appearance to be more sensible and dignified than most young maidservants, and certainly more worthy of belief than Elbert.

"I-I am rather new to Upminster, madam, and Elbert was born on the estate. They are bound to take his word over mine."

"And would he speak falsely to them?"

"H-he would say that I provoked him," Jane said. "He said as much to me, so no doubt he believes it to be the truth, but indeed, madam, I did no such thing."

"I think I will have a word with Mrs. Burdekin," Anne said.

"That won't help," Jane said with a sigh. Then, clearly recalling her place, she bit her lip and looked worriedly at Anne.

"But surely, since it is Burdekin's duty to see to the maids' welfare, she ought to be told when these things occur," Anne said.

"She is Mr. Bagshaw's cousin, madam. Indeed, save for myself and one or two other maids, all the servants here at Upminster are either sons and daughters of other servants or of tenants on the estate. And Mr. Bagshaw, ma'am, holds firm by the notion that any such encounters between maids and menservants are provoked by the maids. I value my position, madam. I do not want to lose it."

Anne nodded. "Very well, Jane, then I suggest that henceforth you make certain to have one of the under-housemaids accompany you while you attend to your duties. Two can work more quickly than one, after all, and attend to twice as many rooms as one alone."

"Yes, madam." But Jane gave her the doubtful look she was quickly growing accustomed to seeing on the servants' faces whenever she made a suggestion.

She said, "I believe you have made the acquaintance of my personal maid, Maisie Bray."

"Oh, yes, madam. She spoke most kindly to me."

"Since you are both new here, perhaps you can be friends."

"Oh, but Miss Bray is too far above me, madam. She will not wish to associate with one so inferior to herself."

"Nonsense," Anne said bracingly. "You are not a scullery maid, Jane." But when Jane only shook her head, Anne realized that in the strict hierarchy of the servants' hall, Maisie would have to make the overtures. She dropped that subject but did not leave Jane before sending for an under-housemaid to assist her, so that when Elbert returned he would not find Jane alone.

Less than a quarter hour later, having changed to footwear more suited to the outdoors, and put on a dark blue wool cloak, Anne was hurrying down the grand stair toward the entrance hall when she encountered her husband on his way up.

"Good day to you, sir," she said, controlling with difficulty the wave of shyness that threatened to overcome her, and knowing from the sudden heat in her cheeks that she was blushing deeply.

"Hello," he said, looking surprised, almost, she thought, as if he had altogether forgotten her presence in the house. He recovered rapidly, however, adding, "I trust you slept well."

"Yes, sir, very well. A-and you?" The heat in her cheeks increased when she remembered their rather sudden parting.

"Quite well, thank you." If he was embarrassed by the same memory, he did not show it. In fact, she thought she detected a twinkle in his eyes, and the sight of it did much to relieve her tension. That it also stirred tingling warmth deep inside her, she strove to ignore. He said, "Have you found something to occupy you? I suppose I ought by rights to take you out and about, or somehow see to it that our neighbors are made aware of your presence here so they can make you welcome, but indeed I cannot spare the time for that just now. My brother's affairs, as you must have guessed, are still in a tangle, and I no sooner seem to unravel one knot than another forms in its place."

"Perhaps I can be of help, sir."

"I doubt that very much. I merely wanted to make plain to you that my duties are to blame if I seem to be a neglectful husband."

"Then you must attend to them," Anne said. "In my experience, news travels quickly whether one wishes it to or not. Indeed, even if your people have not spread the word, Sir Jacob Thornton will no doubt do so when he returns from Derby. The neighbors nearby must be aware of my presence in any case, and even if they do not call at once, I shall find plenty to occupy me here in the house."

"Excellent," he said, smiling. He was two steps below her, so she was face to face with him, and she was struck once again by the way his smile altered his generally stern features, softening them and making them less formidable.

She was encouraged to say, "Perhaps you might take one moment to advise me, sir. I have encountered a small problem, and although at Rendlesham I would know precisely what to do, apparently such matters are dealt with differently here."

"What is the problem?"

"I walked in upon a footman who had cornered a housemaid and was attempting to force his attentions on her."

Lord Michael chuckled. "The minx had probably been flirting with him."

"She said she had not, and I believe her."

"Well, don't bother your head about it, my dear. Bagshaw sees to it that such matters never go too far. We do not keep immoral servants at Upminster Priory."

Anne knew she ought simply to accept his advice and let the matter drop, but a stirring of annoyance pressed her to say, "The footman was Elbert, sir. It does not suit my dignity to have my personal footman making a nuisance of himself to the housemaids."

"Then tell him so. If you are going outside," he added, evidently just becoming aware of her appearance, "Elbert will no doubt be attending you, and you can say what you like to him."

Having a sudden suspicion that she would be unwise to tell him that she had set her personal footman to rubbing garlic on looking-glass frames, she said, "I told the maid to ask an under-housemaid to assist her, so there will always be two of them together."

"That's fine then," he said, but it was clear that his thoughts had shifted to other, more important matters, and she was not surprised when he excused himself in the next breath and hurried on up the stairs.

An elderly hall porter, hastening to open the front door for her, suggested in a paternal way that she ought to have an attendant if she was going outside, but Anne dismissed his words with a kindly smile, saying, "I shan't go far, you know. I just want to look over the gardens and perhaps speak with the gardeners. I shall be perfectly all right, thank you."

She wandered happily from one garden to the next, exploring the tangled, overgrown maze and peering inside a rustic folly before making her way toward the lake and the pathway around it. She noted a number of chores to be done in both kitchen and flower gardens, and she itched to hire an army of men to weed and scythe the vast lawns, but the parkland bordering the lake path was lovely and lush, and no doubt provided excellent coverts for pheasant and grouse. She soon realized that the lake had been formed by damming a brook, and when she found the dam, she followed the brook as it tumbled merrily on through the shady woods. When the thick trees ahead parted to reveal the River Derwent, she saw at once she was no longer alone. The young duke stood atop a huge boulder where the brook met the Derwent, casting his line upriver.

She waited until his fly lit on the rippling surface of the water before she said in a tone loud enough to carry to his ears over the sounds of the water, "Catching anything?"

The boy's concentration was fixed on the fly, and at the unexpected interruption he started, turned sharply and lost his balance. One moment he stood atop the boulder. The next, his mouth agape in horrified dismay, he vanished beyond it.

With an exclamation that was half laughter, half distress, Anne snatched up her skirts and ran to the riverbank. At first she did not see him, but then he bobbed to the surface, sputtering and coughing, a short distance from the riverbank.

Seeing her, he waved his arms frantically and cried out in panic, "Help me, I can't swim!"

When he disappeared beneath the surface again, Anne realized with a sharp stab of terror that the river was carrying him away.

Five

Fortunately, Anne was on the south side of the brook, and her stout shoes made it possible for her to scramble along the riverbank in pursuit of the struggling boy. Casting her heavy cloak aside, she tried to keep one eye on him, while with the other, she searched the bank ahead for a pole or stick long enough to reach out to him.

When she realized the current was drawing him away from the shore, she shouted, "Kick your feet and keep your eyes on the bank ahead! Don't fight the river. Let it carry you as you make your way toward shore farther downriver."

"But I can't swim!"

"You're doing fine," she yelled. Clearly he had some small notion of what was required of him, but he was certainly not a skilled swimmer, and she knew he would not last long without help. Not a soul was in sight. "Kick!"

"I can't!"

"Yes, you can. Kick your feet, paddle your hands, and keep your eyes fixed on the bank ahead. You don't want a mere female to have to jump in and save you, do you?"

She was still running, slipping and stumbling over rocks, wrenching her way past bushes and shrubs, half in the water, half out. The river was running higher and faster after the previous day's storm, and she had all she could do to keep ahead of Andrew as the current carried him downstream. Her shoes were soaked. Bushes and branches seemed to reach out to scratch and bruise her arms, and each time she grabbed at a boulder, another fingernail broke, but she ignored her pains and kept her attention focused on the boy. She saw that he had collected himself and actually had made some progress toward shore, but though she took courage from the fact, she could see, too, that he was tiring rapidly.

At last she spied a dead tree limb that looked long enough and yet light enough to serve her purpose. Snatching it up, she swung it toward Andrew only to see it fall short. Recklessly, without any thought now for her own safety, she tore ahead and, holding her skirt high, leapt to a flat boulder jutting well out into the river. As the swirling water swept him toward her she saw that the branch would still fall short by a foot or more. Inching her way right into the river, she leaned forward as far as she dared.

Scrabbling wildly, Andrew grabbed the tip of the branch, and when his full weight caught it, Anne's feet went right out from under her. Slipping and sliding, holding onto the branch now with both hands, lest she lose it altogether, she was able to catch one foot in a crevice where two stones came together, but by the time she managed to drag the boy to shore, she was as wet as he was. Dragging themselves onto the flat rock together, both lay on their stomachs, trying to catch their breath.

"Why the devil didn't you run for help?" he gasped.

"You'd have drowned by the time I'd found anyone."

"I never thought you could do it alone."

"You did the most important part," she said. "Luckily, you *can* swim a bit, even though you didn't think you could."

"I've watched some of the lads," he muttered, breathing more normally, "but it's dashed harder than it looks."

"Why didn't you get one of them to teach you?"

"They were just servants' or tenants' brats," he said. "Wouldn't be suitable. Subject never came up with the few real friends I've got. They're at school, mostly, and they already knew how to swim before I was allowed to go out and about with them."

Realizing from this glib explanation that he had never admitted even to his friends that he could not swim, Anne was tempted to point out that his pride had nearly cost him his life, but what little she had seen of the young duke warned her that he would not take criticism well. So, instead, after a pause for thought, she said, "My father says a good landlord must know his tenants well. He always encouraged my brothers to be friendly with ours, for he says they will be better served by friends than by men they keep at a strict distance. No doubt things are different for dukes though, and you were quite right not to ask one of yours to teach you. I should think, however, that teaching a person to swim would foster quite a strong loyalty to him."

He did not reply, and she saw that he had laid his cheek right against the rock and closed his eyes. He was still shivering. She could feel the granite's warmth and hoped it would soon warm them; however, the breeze over her back was cool, even chilly, and she did not think it wise to stay long where they were.

"We should move," she murmured, "at least get out of the wind. I suppose we should go back to the house, but I own, I'm not looking forward to walking in these wet shoes. I shudder to think how many bruises I've collected, stumbling over all those rocks along the riverbank, and this poor frock is in tatters, I daresay, not to mention soaked through."

"My shirt will dry quickly enough," he said, "and I've got a jacket somewhere back by that boulder I was standing on. Took it off 'cause it's too tight. Couldn't cast properly."

"Well, it's a good thing you weren't wearing it when you fell into the river then," she said. "A tight jacket probably would have been the death of you."

"Wouldn't have fallen in if you hadn't startled me," he pointed out sulkily. "Ought to know better than to shout at a fellow when he's casting."

"I don't think I actually shouted."

For the first time he looked a little sheepish, saying, "Guess

I was a bit nervous. I'd been keeping low, so as not to be seen, but I knew I'd get a much better cast from that boulder." He paused, then added in a tone that he strove to keep casual, "I say, you don't mean to tell Uncle Michael about this, do you? He'll fly into even more of a rage with me than he did yesterday."

"Just because you tumbled into the river?"

"Because I was even near the river. He was devilish put out to learn of old Appleby's departure, you see, and he ordered me to continue my lessons by myself till he finds me a new tutor. Until half past twelve every day without fail, he said."

"Well, I shan't tell him unless he asks," Anne said, "and I daresay he won't unless he sees me looking half drowned, which must be how I look right now. For that matter, is it not nearly half past twelve?" she asked, feeling a stir of alarm when she recalled that Maisie had said a nuncheon would be served for the family just before the servants enjoyed their chief meal of the day.

"We've time," he said, not moving. "The sun's not directly overhead yet, so I'd guess we've at least an hour." He looked at her searchingly for a moment, then said, "I say, I nearly had you in with me at the last, didn't I? Good thing you were able to catch yourself or we'd both have been as dead as mackerel."

She said, "I am glad, certainly, that you did not pull me in with you, but I can swim, so it would not have been fatal. I am not certain, however, that in my frock and these heavy shoes I'd have been able to hold onto that branch for long, though."

"If you can swim so well, why didn't you just jump in and pull me out?" he demanded.

Despite the note of resentful bitterness in his voice, Anne answered matter-of-factly, "My eldest brother, James, who taught me to swim, commanded me most strongly never to do such a thing. He said the most likely end would be for me to drown right along with the person I was trying to rescue."

"And I suppose James knows all there is to know about everything, or so *you* think."

"James is dead," she said evenly. "He was killed in a hunting-field accident when I was nine."

He did not reply, and after some moments, she sat up and said, "We really must return to the house, I think. I've got a cloak somewhere back there on the riverbank, and we can collect your jacket, though if it is truly a tight-fitting one, you may have trouble getting it on over your wet shirt. Why did you choose such a tight one when you knew you would be fishing?"

"They are all tight."

"Gracious, I know that fashion dictates—"

"Not fashion. I've grown, that's all."

"Then you should have new ones made."

"One does not quite like to mention new clothing when Uncle Michael is constantly preaching economy," Andrew said stiffly. "The way he carries on, anyone would think I've got no fortune at all, but I know that cannot be so, for my father always had vast amounts of money to spend."

When he sat up, Anne noted that his shirt looked much the worse for wear, and that not all the damage could be ascribed to his ducking. "I will talk to Lord Michael at once," she said. "You must have proper clothing, for goodness' sake, and no doubt, Lady Sylvia will also require some new things."

Andrew stood up, and she could hear the squishing sound of water in his shoes. He said, "Uncle Michael said last night that he would send for her, so I suppose she will be home by midweek or so."

"I daresay you will be glad to see her."

"Sylvie don't bother me. She's a quiet little thing."

They soon found Anne's cloak and his jacket but not his fishing pole. She expected him to be angry over the loss, for her brothers were obsessively attached to all their sporting gear, but Andrew said only that he had other poles.

"If that is so," she said, "perhaps you might be kind enough to lend me one some morning."

"Do you fish?" He looked at her in astonishment. "I must say, you are very unlike other ladies of my acquaintance. Does Uncle Michael know you enjoy such masculine pursuits as fishing and swimming?"

"I don't know. Would it matter? I have always preferred being outdoors as much as possible, which reminds me . . . I hope you have a horse in your stables accustomed to carrying a lady."

"Certainly we do, more than one, for that matter."

"Good, because as far as I know, no arrangements have yet been made to transport mine from Rendlesham. My brother Harry said he would see to the matter, and so did Papa, but like as not, each will assume the other has done so, and nothing will be accomplished until I attend to it myself."

They soon reached the lake, where they agreed to separate, Andrew assuring Anne with a resumption of his habitual loftiness that he could easily slip into the house and up to his bedchamber without being seen. She wished she might do likewise but did not feel that she knew the huge house well enough to be certain of finding her way without getting lost if she entered by any door but the main one.

Leaving her when his path led through the home wood, Andrew turned back abruptly after taking only a few steps, to say gruffly, "Thank you. I'm sorry I said that about your brother."

She could tell the words did not spring easily to his lips but cost him an effort, as though he were unaccustomed to expressing either gratitude or apology. Smiling, she said, "I should just be grateful, I expect, that you are not still vexed with me for startling you. I hope you don't catch a chill from your wetting."

She was rewarded with a slight smile that instantly reminded her of Lord Michael, and found herself wishing that she might see each of them smile more often.

If she did not manage to avoid being seen, at least her cloak hid the worst damage, and since she had chosen not to wear a hat, she could hope the porter would blame the mischievous breezes for her untidy hair. He did not seem to notice anything amiss, and when she encountered Elbert, she quickly took a high hand by asking if he had attended to all his duties.

"Yes, my lady, but I should perhaps tell your ladyship—"

"It is not your place to tell me things, Elbert," she said firmly. "No doubt you ought, in any event, to be helping in the dining room. They are laying out a nuncheon, are they not?"

"Yes, my lady. I shall be ringing the bell in fifteen minutes, but before you go up, I think you should—"

"Thank you, Elbert," she said repressively. Knowing from experience that personal servants soon began to take an almost parental interest in their mistresses, she did not intend to let Elbert forget his place. She was no longer, after all, a daughter of the house, but its mistress, and she did not intend to allow any of the servants to order her about. "I must go," she said, "for I have been out in the gardens and am in no fit state to be seen."

Hurrying upstairs, hoping her shoes were not leaving a trail of revealing damp footprints, she was aware that she had snubbed her footman rather rudely. Such behavior was not her normal custom, but she was growing tired of being instructed by the Upminster servants. It was clear now that taking control of the household was not going to be as easy as she had hoped. When she neared her bedchamber, she realized what she had been thinking and gave herself a mental shake, wondering how she had thought she could take command of such a vast place in the space of a day.

Maisie and Juliette were both awaiting her in her dressing room, and both, in their own ways, began scolding her for her tardiness. The kitten fell silent the moment Anne picked it up and began to stroke its soft fur, but Maisie was not so easily stilled.

"Merciful heavens, Miss Anne, what have you done to your-self? Just look at them nails, and those scratches on your arms!"

Setting the kitten down on the dressing table, Anne bore with the maid's reproofs patiently while her still damp frock and shift were whisked off and replaced with fresh ones. Juliette watched the process critically, jumping to Anne's lap the moment she sat down to have her hair brushed and her nails pared.

"I don't know how you've gone and got yourself in such a mess, Miss Anne. I didn't even know it had begun raining again, but I'd certainly have thought you old enough to know to come inside before your clothing was soaked right through. Just look at yourself! You look as if you was dragged through a hedge backwards, and you've broken nigh onto every fin-gernail. I declare, the last time you looked like this was when Mr. Harry threw you into the pond at Rendlesham, but I should hope that even such a hoyden as what I know you can be would not—"

"That will do, Maisie," Anne said quietly, meeting the maid's astonished look in the mirror with a direct one of her own.

Maisie folded her lips tightly together and continued her work. She was efficient, and Anne, looking calm and serene in a high-waisted afternoon dress of pale pink muslin, was on her way downstairs soon after Elbert had rung the bell.

He and another man were alone in the hall when she ap-proached the dining room, and Anne thought the second was Lord Michael until he turned, and she recognized Bagshaw. Encountering Elbert's gaze just then, she thought he was trying yet again to convey a message to her, but she could scarcely stop and ask him what he meant by it right there in front of the butler. She understood soon enough, however, and under-stood, as well, that she might have been wiser to have let Elbert speak to her earlier.

No sooner had the footman seated her than Lord Michael

said, "I understand that you left the house unaccompanied this morning, madam. I thought I made it plain that Elbert was to go with you."

"You did, sir," Anne said, meeting his stern gaze calmly, but aware, too, that Andrew—his hair still noticeably damp—had grown very still. "Elbert had duties to attend to in the house, my lord. Not realizing, you see, that I have formed the habit of arising quite early, he had not finished his work before I came down to break my fast. And since I meant only to walk in the garden—"

"Elbert's primary duty is to serve you," Michael said in a tone that brooked no argument. "When you do not require his services, Bagshaw will assign him tasks to do, but you must not leave the house without him. Surely, you did not leave your father's house without being attended by a servant."

"I am sorry to contradict you, sir, but in fact, I did so frequently. My eldest sister never did, of course, for she was a great heiress and knew the ceremony due to her position. But I was in and out of the house all day, supervising gardeners as often as I did the household staff, so it was just too cumbersome always to be sending for a footman to accompany me. We always had one in attendance when we drove out in the carriage, of course, but surely . . ." Finding it impossible to proceed in the face of his stern, unblinking gaze, she fell silent, conscious of the interest of the others at the table, and the servants. Even her father had never taken her to task before the servants, and she found herself wondering if Lord Michael, during his time in the army, had scolded his junior officers in front of the rest of his men.

"In future," he said sternly, "you will not go outside without a proper attendant. Is that clear?"

"Yes, sir," she said quietly.

"Excellent. Do you also understand, Elbert?"

"Yes, my lord."

Anne felt warmth flooding her cheeks, but Michael's attention had already shifted elsewhere. Signing to the servants to leave the room, he said to Andrew, "I trust you were able to keep yourself properly occupied this morning."

With an air of studied indifference, the boy helped himself from a tureen of vermicelli soup. "I kept myself occupied," he muttered with a scowl. "How you expect me to teach myself anything worth knowing, I cannot imagine."

"You would not have to do so had your behavior not convinced Appleby he'd be happier elsewhere."

"He was no better than an old hen, always clucking and pecking. He did *not* treat me with proper respect."

"I've a good mind, this time, to hire a tutor who will treat you as you deserve," Michael said grimly.

Lord Ashby, intent till now upon his food, looked up and said hastily, "Now, dash it all, Michael, don't be saying what you don't mean. By Jove, the lad's the seventh Duke of Upminster. He is quite right to demand that his inferiors treat him with respect."

"Respect must be earned," Michael retorted, "and a duke who cannot read or write properly will not merit much respect from his so-called inferiors."

"I *can* read and write perfectly well," Andrew snapped, "even Latin and Greek. I just don't happen to like it much, that's all. If I had as my tutor someone other than an ancient decrepit, I might become more interested, but to be shut up for hours on end with an old chap who preaches and lectures from dusty books and notes is more than anyone should have to tolerate, let alone me."

Michael regarded him thoughtfully for a long moment. "No doubt it would do you good to go to school," he said gently.

Lord Ashby said, "No Duke of Upminster has ever gone away to school, Michael. It just ain't done."

"If," Anne said quietly, "you are looking to find a tutor for His Grace, sir, you might also seek a governess for Lady Sylvia at the same time, since I collect that she does not already have one."

"She does not," he said, "but before you begin to offer

advice as to the best course, I think you had better meet her."
Clearly thinking that matter closed, he turned his attention to
his plate.

Well aware that she had a good many things to learn about
her new family, Anne hoped Michael would take time that
afternoon to talk with her and show her more of the house
and grounds if for no other reason than to allow them to become better acquainted. But no sooner did the servants return
to clear than he stood up, said cryptically that he would be
with Alsop, and excused himself.

"Manager of one of the lead mines, Alsop is," Lord Ashby
said when Anne looked bewildered. "Michael don't usually
take a nuncheon, you know. At least, you don't know, but he
don't. Did today, I'll wager, only because it's your first day
here and he thought it the thing to do."

"That was kind of him," Anne said.

"Was it? Suppose it was. Man works too hard, if you ask
me. Don't seem natural when you recall what a dashed care-
for-naught he used to be. Edmund would laugh at him and say
he'd either outrun the constable or get himself shot by a jealous
husband, and then, by Jove, if it wasn't Ed— But there, I
shouldn't be talking like that. I tell you what it is, my dear.
Andrew's holdings are vast and seem to be complicated, and
Michael's having to learn about matters that never interested
him before. Told him I'd be glad to help out, but he'd rather
tend to things on his own. I'll say this for the man. He takes
his duties to heart. Ain't seen the like since he sold out. Always
took his military duties seriously, of course, but once away
from his unit—" He shrugged expressively.

"I'm sorry he's so busy," Anne said a little wistfully. "I'm
sure you could be helpful. I've seen your contrivances in the
kitchen, for one thing, so I know you have the sort of mind
it takes to think up solutions to problems. If he won't let you
help, I know he does not want to hear advice from someone
who has not yet been here two days, but I did hope to spend
some time with him."

"Quite natural, by Jove, under the circumstances, but he'll come about," Lord Ashby said cheerfully, getting up and poking Andrew with his stick. "At least he would if you didn't insist on making him ride rusty nine hours out of ten, you young jackanapes."

"I'll just show him one day that he can't ride *me* too hard," Andrew said grimly. "You just see if I don't."

As they left the dining room, Anne said to Elbert, "I shall return to the gardens when I have changed my shoes and fetched my cloak. Please be ready to accompany me in ten minutes time."

When she rejoined him, wearing yet another pair of the stout shoes she preferred outdoors, she said, "I want you to take me to the head gardener now, Elbert, for I am determined to discover why he has let everything fall to rack and ruin."

He stiffened as if he would actually dare to protest her decision, but he did not, and when she found Quigley, the head gardener was soon able to explain what she wanted to know.

"Ain't had no direction at all, your ladyship, since His late Grace's death. There be acres of gardens, not to mention the lake, and I've got two inexperienced yard boys to help, though one of 'em does call hisself an under-gardener what shouldn't."

Knowing she had found something at last that she could really turn her hand to, Anne spent a happy hour conferring with him, and several more letting him show her over the gardens again. When she finally returned to the house, the sun was low over the western hills. Knowing the sullen Elbert had had more than his fill of gardens, she wished she could simply dispense with his company in future, but knew she would not attempt it. She had no desire to displease her new husband if she could avoid doing so.

When they entered the house, Bagshaw greeted them in the hall, saying politely, "There you are, my lady. We have been looking for you, I'm afraid. Lady Hermione Englebourne has called. I put her in the yellow drawing room."

Anne looked at Elbert, who said, "An old friend of the family, my lady. Lady Hermione grew up here in Derbyshire but married an Irishman and went to live in foreign parts. He died two or three years ago, I believe, and she recently returned to take up residence with her brother, Viscount Cressbrook, at the Hall."

"How is it that she is Lady Hermione if her brother is only a viscount?" Anne asked.

"Oh, their papa was an earl, but Lord Cressbrook, he's a younger son," Elbert said. "He were something of a dab at politics back before his memory got so bad, and the old king gave him a title all his own. He and Sir Jacob Thornton used to get into some spirited political arguments, I can tell you, when they both was used to dine here with His Grace."

Bagshaw shot the footman a look of disapproval, but for once Anne did not care that Elbert had overstepped the bounds of propriety. She was grateful for the information.

"Please tell Lady Hermione that I will join her shortly," she said to the butler. "I've got mud on these shoes, and must change my frock in any case. Ask if she cares for refreshment in the meantime, and tell her I hope she will stay to dine."

"I have already served her ladyship some mountain sherry, madam," Bagshaw said, "and she said when she arrived that she expected to dine. Lady Hermione is a rather uncommon female."

Anne saw what the butler meant when she entered the yellow drawing room a short time later to discover that her guest had made herself perfectly at home. At once, however, Lady Hermione arose gracefully from her sofa, set aside the sporting magazine she had been glancing through, stepped around the retriever asleep at her feet, and strode forward to greet her hostess. Thirty years older and several inches taller than Anne, Lady Hermione was built on much more generous lines. Her hair, an improbable reddish orange, was styled fashionably with curls piled atop her head in an apparently artless manner that had allowed several locks to escape, tumbling over her brow and teasing the nape of her long neck. And despite her intention to dine with them, she wore riding dress, and Anne noted a riding whip lying on a nearby side table.

Extending one well-manicured, gloveless hand, her unusual visitor smiled and said, "Good afternoon, Lady Michael."

"Thank you for coming so soon to welcome me, ma'am," Anne said warmly, accepting the outstretched hand. "I understand you come from a neighboring estate. I hope I've not kept you waiting long."

"Good gracious me, what if you have?" Lady Hermione said cheerfully. "I've nothing more interesting to do, you know, and I've been in a fret to meet you, though at least one of your new family," she added with a mischievous grin, "will insist that I am merely in a pelter to look you over and decide if you are suitable, so that I can begin at once to offer you unsolicited advice."

"I hope no one from Upminster would be rag-mannered enough to say any such thing," Anne said, gesturing for her to sit down again. "I am told you lived for some years in Ireland, ma'am."

"So I did," Lady Hermione agreed.

Bagshaw said from the doorway, "Begging your pardon, Lady Michael, but Lord Michael's man has just come in with a message saying that his lordship will be delayed, and ordering that dinner be put back an hour."

"Thank you, Bagshaw. I hope you don't mind, ma'am, and still intend to grant us the pleasure of your company."

"Oh, certainly."

Bagshaw said, "Will there be anything else, madam?"

Noting her guest's glance at the decanters set out on a side table, Anne said, "Would you care for more sherry, ma'am?"

"Yes, indeed," Lady Hermione said frankly. "The mountain you served me earlier, Bagshaw. I remember when John—the fifth duke," she added for Anne's benefit, "put that down in his cellar."

"Do tell me about Ireland, ma'am. I have heard it described as a most beautiful country."

"Tolerable," Lady Hermione said, her gaze still fixed on Bagshaw, who stepped to the side table to refill her sherry glass. When he had set it on the table near her and departed, she said abruptly, "That Bagshaw of yours puts me all on end, my dear. I declare, one feels as if one were ordering King George about."

Anne bit her lower lip to keep from laughing, then said carefully, "He is marvelously stately, is he not? Just what one expects of a butler in a ducal establishment."

Lady Hermione's eyebrows flew upward. "Why, I suppose he has grown into the sort one encounters in gothical novels, at least. The trouble is, you see, that I remember him best as a boy—a youth, at all events. It has been more than twenty-five years now since I last actually lived in England, after all, and when I left, Bagshaw had not even been elevated to serve as Edmund's valet but was still some sort of a footman."

"Have you been out of England all that time?" Anne asked, still hoping her fascinating guest would tell her about Ireland.

"My goodness me, no. I have been home for long visits many times. A person must not allow herself to be buried back of beyond forever, after all, and it never seems to stop raining in Ireland. Though, to be fair, I suppose it must," she added thoughtfully. "It is just that as soon as it begins to drizzle, one forgets one has enjoyed a few hours of sunlight. Just look at that now," she added, gesturing toward the western window.

Turning to look, Anne saw that the western sky had begun to change color, turning drifting clouds to pale pink above the darkening landscape and the winding silver ribbon of river.

"Lovely," she said, getting up and moving toward the window to enjoy the view to its fullest extent.

Lady Hermione followed her, and the two stood side by side, looking out at the magical sight.

"This is what I missed most," Lady Hermione said softly. "My brother's estate also commands a view of the river and those hills beyond, and even as a child, I used to stop whatever I was doing as soon as the sky began to change. Every season is different, of course, but in the spring, the changes seem most magical to me."

"Good God, you here? Bagshaw, dash it all, you ought to warn a fellow when his house has been invaded!"

Startled to hear Lord Ashby's voice, Anne turned to see him in the doorway with the butler just behind him. Bagshaw raised his chin a fraction of an inch above its usual position but did not lower himself to respond to his lordship's undignified dismay.

Lady Hermione said placidly, "Of course, I am here, Ashby. Did you think you were seeing a specter? You cannot have thought I would delay in paying my respects to Michael's wife."

"But, good God, where's your carriage, woman? I never laid eyes on it. Came through the stable yard, too—from the south meadow, you know." To Anne's astonishment, he reddened, adding in a harsher tone, "Fetch out the whisky, Bagshaw. Dash it, I won't addle my insides with that sherry."

Lady Hermione, without moving from her position by the window, said in the same calm tone, "You did not see a carriage because I rode over, Ashby. No reason to have a carriage out only to drive over here, when I can come by the river track in half the time."

Taking the glass handed him by the butler, Lord Ashby nodded dismissal, and when Bagshaw had gone, he said, "You may have come over in half the time, but you'll be caught by darkness if you dawdle much longer, and then just see how long it will take you."

"Lady Hermione is staying to dine, sir," Anne said, adding to her guest, "I hadn't thought about your going back in the dark, ma'am, which will surely be the case now that Lord Michael has ordered dinner put back. That won't do at all."

Lord Ashby muttered, "And if I know you, woman, you didn't even see fit to bring a groom along with you."

Amanda Scott

"Well, you're mistaken, Ashby, for I did, and very virtuous I felt, too. You need not bother your head about me, Anne dear—"

"Got upon close terms already, I see," Lord Ashby said. "I expect you've already given her a load of unwanted advice, too."

"I have not," Lady Hermione said, looking daggers at him. Turning to Anne, she added with a charming smile, "I do hope you don't mean to stand on ceremony with me, my dear, for I must tell you that I am thrilled to have found a new friend so nearby. The only other woman of quality near enough to be a bosom bow is Maria Thornton, and I simply cannot abide her whining and die-away airs for longer than it takes to pay a formal twenty-minute morning call."

"Well, I shall be glad to see you whenever you choose to call, ma'am," Anne said sincerely, "and I am truly delighted that you can stay to dine with us tonight."

"Her brother might not be, however," Lord Ashby said dryly.

Lady Hermione shrugged. "That Wilfred does not attempt to interfere with me is one of the great advantages to being a widow. Moreover, his housekeeper has just returned at last from tending her sick mother, so he will be quite all right without me tonight."

"Well, by Jove, if you're staying, why don't you take a seat and let a fellow do likewise," Lord Ashby demanded. "What the deuce were the pair of you staring at out that window, anyway?"

Anne glanced outside again, then back at him. She said, "Only the sunset, sir. The colors are quite marvelous tonight, but already they are beginning to fade. It is too bad that even the best sunsets fade so quickly, but I suppose they must."

A gleam of mischief lit his eyes, and he exchanged a glance with Lady Hermione before saying, "Since Michael's gone and put dinner off, what say we treat ourselves to a second sunset?"

Lady Hermione said at once, "Oh, yes, let us do so. I saw—"

"Hush, Hermie, not another word. I want to surprise Anne. Fetch out a warm cloak, my dear, and we will show you how to enjoy two sunsets in a single day."

"But how on earth—"

"Ah, now, that would be telling," he said with a grin.

Six

For some moments after leaving the house—without so much as a word of explanation to the servants but with two of the ubiquitous dogs following at their heels—Anne felt exactly as she had felt as a child being led into mischief by an older sibling. There was the same sense of exhilaration and secrecy, the same breathless wonder and anticipation, and the same fear of discovery and retribution. She felt as if they ought to keep to the shadows, to tread softly, even to tiptoe.

Her two companions did not speak in whispers, as her siblings had done under like circumstances, but they did speak cryptically, and as old acquaintances, even erstwhile playmates.

"You saw it, did you, Hermie?"

"When I rode over."

"What did you think?"

"Not so vast as Lunardi's."

"Perhaps not, but safer and much more efficient."

"Rather gaudy, I thought. What do you call it?"

"Royal George, but hush now. You'll spoil the surprise."

But Anne, who had first been silently scolding herself for indulging in foolish fantasies, and secondly wishing she had not changed from her stout shoes into the flimsy slippers she now wore, had begun to suspect where they were taking her. That suspicion, in light of Lord Michael's strictures the evening before and her own escapade with Andrew earlier in the day, only heightened the feelings she had of mischief and wonder afoot. Even so, when they topped the low rise separating the house and parkland from the more open meadows along the river, the first view she had of the huge red, white, and blue striped balloon, its colors brilliant even in the rapidly fading light, nearly took her breath away.

"You've had it filled!"

"Aye, I told you I'd ordered the makings. We make our own inflammable gas from iron and sulfuric acid, you see, and once it's filled, it can remain so for a month if it's well tied down."
. He and Lady Hermione paused to let her drink in the sight, but only a moment passed before he said, "Got to hurry now. Won't do to let nightfall catch us on *terra firma*." He glanced at the western hills, adding with satisfaction, "Still enough light and practically no wind. Gives us an edge, you know. All these hills make for an early sunset in our little valley."

Anne suddenly remembered his promise of a second sunset and realized exactly what he had meant. "Merciful heavens," she said, "you don't really mean for us to go up in that thing, do you?"

"Certainly, I do," he replied over Lady Hermione's chuckles.

"But three of us, and in near darkness? Surely, it's far too dangerous. You'll never manage that thing alone, and I don't know the first thing about what to do. Do you, Lady Hermione?"

"Oh, yes, a bit," she said calmly.

"That *thing* is called an aerostat, and it's only difficult to manage on the ground," Lord Ashby said as he hurried them across the meadow toward the balloon. "As to darkness and danger, we'll keep it on a tether. Two of my lads stay with the *Royal George*—to guard against mischief, you know—so they can help. Here we are. In you go now, the pair of you—unless, of course, you are afraid!"

Glancing at Lady Hermione, Anne considered the suggestion only until she saw the older woman's grin. Realizing that she was grinning herself now, and just as widely, she said, "Have you truly done this before, ma'am?"

"Oh, yes. Three or four times with Ashby here, when I was

home for visits, and once, in London, with the famous Italian aeronaut, Vincent Lunardi. I took care to make out my will first, of course," she added with a chuckle.

"Well, I have not made a will," Anne said, "so I shall just have to trust to Providence to bring us safely home again."

One of Lord Ashby's assistants sprang to unlace the narrow gate to the gallery, which, to Anne, looked like nothing more than a large wicker basket connected to the huge balloon by netting draped over its top.

"Is it really safe?" she asked as she stepped inside. "If the gas is truly inflammable . . ."

"We won't set off any fireworks," Lord Ashby said cheerfully. "Scientists call the stuff hydrogen. Fellow name of Cavendish discovered it twenty years ago, and it's safe enough so long as one don't set fire to it. One fellow tried to set a balloon filled with hydrogen atop a cylindrical neck filled with hot air, thinking he could go farther that way. That notion proved unwise, but in point of fact, hydrogen is easier and safer to use than hot air. One is not so likely to burn up the container, for one thing."

Taking care not to step on any of several odd items on the floor of the basket as she moved over to make room for Lady Hermione and his lordship, and watching in fascination as the two assistants scurried about, detaching all but two of the ropes tying the craft to the ground, and the coiled tether, Anne said, "But what keeps the air in the balloon?"

"We use flexible varnish made with India rubber, over taffeta. Makes the cloth quite airtight, I assure you."

But Anne scarcely heard his words, for he had given the signal to release the last pair of ropes, and the balloon was rising. Its ascent was slow, majestic, and sure. Lord Ashby held a bag of sand over the side of the gallery, and when their ascent slowed, he poured some out of the bag to the ground below.

When they reached the end of the tether, he snorted in annoyance. "Dash it all, not high enough. Find the knife on the floor, Hermie, and the trumpet. We'll have to cut the tether."

"But if we cut loose, Ashby, we shall be late for dinner."

"I didn't ask for advice," he said, "and if we're late, it certainly won't be my fault. The tether's too short. Promised Anne a second sunset, I did, and by Jove, she shall have it!"

Taking the speaking trumpet from her, he shouted to the men below, "Slight wind from the northwest now, lads. Follow us as best you can. We won't go far, for I mean to set her down on the east moor near Wadshelf, if the wind don't change." Exchanging the speaking trumpet for the knife, he cut the tether.

As the balloon began swiftly to rise again, the men below waved, looking like dolls, the Priory like a large doll's house. The shadowy, rapidly receding landscape began to look like a crazy quilt with a shimmering silver satin ribbon running through it. Anne could still make out details—the houses and cottages in the village near the Priory, and even a large, well-lighted boat tied up at a long dock opposite and a little above the north end of the village. For a time the silent balloon followed the Derwent, but when they rose above the hilltops into sunlight, the river soon fell behind and Anne saw that Lord Ashby would keep his promise.

"Hermione," he said suddenly, his voice loud in the silence that had enveloped them, "that lacing's not fastened at the gate there. Can you secure it?"

"Certainly," she said, kneeling at once. At the sound of a loud crack, she added ruefully, "I believe I've knelt on some piece of equipment or other, Ashby."

"By Jove, if you've broken the barometer— You have! Dash it all, Hermie, why didn't you look before you knelt down? Now we shan't have the least notion of our altitude."

"Well, if you wouldn't put your stupid instruments and such all higgledy-piggledy on the floor—"

"That's hardly my fault. Where would you have me put them?"

"What house is that?" Anne asked, pointing to one she was sure must be as large as Rendlesham.

"That is the Hall, my brother's house," Lady Hermione said without looking. Her attention was still fixed on lacing the lower half of the little gate shut. As she rose carefully to her feet again, she added, "And yonder, on that rise, is Sir Jacob Thornton's home. You'll meet him soon, no doubt. He is well acquainted with my brother, and he knew Edmund quite well, too. Used to go to the Newmarket races together every year."

"I have met him," Anne said. "He stood up with Lord Michael at our wedding."

"My goodness me, did he indeed? I did not know."

"You need not sound so shocked," Lord Ashby said dryly. "You don't know everything. He offered and Michael accepted. Would have been dashed uncivil to refuse, and not everyone is as offic—"

Anne interrupted hastily. "Sir Jacob said he had important business in Derby, which was why he offered to support Lord Michael. He seemed to think it rather a good joke, in fact."

"Not surprising," Lady Hermione said. "They are not the close friends that Jake and Edmund were, nor is Michael of their cut. And, too, wasn't there something about a wager, Ashby?"

"None of your affair if there was," he said bluntly. "And as for Michael being so unlike Jake or Edmund, considering his past career, I'd say the only great difference is that he had the good sense not to saddle himself with a dashed cold fish for a wife."

"Well, I won't argue that Agnes was a bit chilly or that Maria is anything but an insipid woman. No doubt she will pay you a bride visit, Anne, but she is not, by and large, a social person, even now that most of her children are away at school. Her oldest is by way of being one of Andrew's few friends, I believe."

Lord Ashby began pointing out various villages and houses, and when Anne said the landscape looked like a child's map, he chuckled and said, "I own, I see it all now in terms of good landing places or bad ones, but I suppose it does look like a map of sorts. One certainly sees where things are in relation to towns and villages. There in the distance you can see the rooftops of Chesterfield. But look to the west. Your second sunset is beginning, by Jove."

Anne looked and her breath fairly caught in her throat, for the entire western horizon—a much more expansive horizon than before—glowed crimson and was already beginning to deepen to shades of purple. The colors blazed behind the dark undulating shapes of distant hills, as the great red half-ball of sun slipped with surprising swiftness below the dark horizon, leaving ribbons of mauve, maroon, and purple in its wake.

Anne realized the balloon was turning on its axis, and the sensation was particularly odd because there was little sense of any other motion. They were traveling with the wind, which she had discovered meant that unless she watched objects on the ground, the balloon felt as if it were standing still.

Realizing she could scarcely identify one object now from another in the darkening landscape below, she said, "Will it not be quite dangerous to land in darkness, sir?"

"Only if one cannot determine one's altitude," Lord Ashby said with an accusing look at Lady Hermione.

"Poppycock," she said. "You need not try to cast the blame on me, Ashby. You could not read the instrument in the dark, anyway. I say, *have* you ever landed in darkness before?"

"Oh, yes," he said with an air of confidence that Anne hoped was not spurious. He reached up to pull the line that opened the valve, and she heard the hiss of escaping gas. The sound was eerie, for in the absence of conversation, the silence had been nearly absolute. "We can descend quickly now," he said, "for we're over the moor. And it won't be totally dark, either, for there'll be a bit of moon to give us light once the last of the sunset is gone. At all events, we should come down near Wadshelf, just as I promised the lads. There's a large field there that's excellent for landing. I've put down there a number of times before."

Except for occasional bursts of escaping gas when he opened the valve, a companionable silence fell as the balloon drifted steadily onward and the sky around them darkened. Anne, still fascinated by the odd sensation of floating above the land, looked down and watched lights begin to appear below, scarcely noticing the falling temperature until Lady Hermione said quietly, "Is the wind not beginning to rise rather sharply, Ashby?"

"Aye," he murmured, pulling again on the line. "Believe you're right. Realized when we began twisting about on our axis that we'd encountered crosswinds. Don't tease yourself, though. I'll just let the gas out more quickly. You can see the lights of Chesterfield yonder, Anne. That small group there to the east ought to be Wadshelf. We'll overshoot it a bit, I'm afraid, but the lads ought to be able to find us easily enough."

"The first time Ashby took me aloft," Lady Hermione said, "we soared right into a cloud, and then above it."

"Goodness, I didn't know one could pass right through a cloud," Anne exclaimed. "What was it like to do so?"

"Damp," Lady Hermione said wryly. "I was soaked to the skin, but it was truly awe-inspiring to be drifting above the clouds. You must get Ashby to take you up in daylight next."

Despite their calm voices, Anne was beginning to feel nervous. What had been exhilarating moments before was rather frightening now. She could indeed see the lights of Chesterfield in the distance, and she could see the much smaller group of lights his lordship had identified as the village of Wadshelf. But she could not see much more, and she wondered how he could be certain they would not crash into a grove of trees, or even into a cliff. To divert her thoughts, she said abruptly, "Perhaps the children would like to go aloft one day. Is it safe enough for them to do so?"

"Safe enough for anyone," Lord Ashby said stoutly. "Daresay Michael wouldn't agree to it, though."

Lady Hermione said, "You know, Ashby, that might be the very thing to bring young Sylvia out of herself."

"Or frighten her totally witless," Lord Ashby said. "Not right in her head, young Sylvia ain't, if you ask me, by Jove."

"Why, what do you mean?" Anne asked, diverted from her fears at last. "Is something wrong with the child? Why has no one mentioned it to me? She is coming home very soon, you know."

"Is she, indeed?" Lord Ashby said.

At the same time, Lady Hermione said stoutly, "Nothing wrong with her at all. Her mother's death distressed her, that's all, and no one can be surprised by that. She's no doubt her old self again by now, after being with Charlotte and the children."

"But what was wrong?" Anne tried to see Lady Hermione's face, but it was too dark to read her expression. "Losing their parents one right after the other like they did must have been dreadful for both children. I assumed the duke and duchess had fallen to some disease or other, but Lord Michael said that was not the case."

A silence fell before Lord Ashby muttered, "No, that was not the case with either of them."

Lady Hermione said, "If you do not tell her, Ashby, I will, for it is nonsensical to think she will not hear the truth from someone, and quite soon. Indeed, it's astonishing to me that some well-meaning servant has not already told her."

"By Jove, Hermie, there you go again. Always interfering and offering unwanted advice. Our servants know better than to gossip about us, if you do not. Ireland didn't change you much; that's plain enough."

"No, thank the Lord, it didn't. Not that Clarence didn't try, for he did, but I was never intended to be a sweet, submissive wife, you know, not for anyone, and certainly not for a self-important Irish earl. His son's just like him, too," she added with a sigh. "But never mind that. Anne, you might as well know now as later that Edmund was killed in a duel by an understandably jealous husband. I can't tell you the whole, since they took care to hush it up—for the lady's sake, no doubt—but Edmund's behavior was not that of a properly grieving widower, I'm afraid—nor, before Agnes's death was it that of a dutiful husband."

"Now, Hermie," Lord Ashby said hastily, "you can scarcely blame the man, what with all the talk after she died. Didn't suit his dignity to hear folks speculating the way they did."

Anne felt a sudden chill that had nothing to do with the air around her. "Her reasons? Good gracious, surely she didn't—"

"She did," Lady Hermione said. "Took her own life and didn't so much as leave a note behind to explain why she did it. Poor Edmund was distraught, insisted that her death was an accident and that the lack of a note was proof that she had never intended any such thing as suicide. Thankfully, the parson agreed with him—bound to do so, of course, when the grieving husband is the Duke of Upminster—but I'm told it went against the pluck with him to do so. No one knows why Agnes did it, for she did not confide in a soul, though to my mind, young Sylvia knows more about the incident than anyone wants to believe."

"But how could she, ma'am?"

"She couldn't," Lord Ashby said flatly. "She was only a baby at the time."

"Nonsense," Lady Hermione said. "Sylvia is nine, quite old enough to be awake on most suits, and there's no knowing what Agnes might have said to her. Not a sensible woman, Agnes wasn't, for she married Edmund, didn't she—no doubt just to become a duchess."

"Can't recall that she had much to say about it," Lord Ashby said. "Marriage was arranged by my brother John and her father. Even Edmund hadn't much to say about it. Usual sort of thing, of course. One good thing about being a younger son is that no one cares much about whether one gets married, or to— By Jove, hang on, ladies," he exclaimed when the balloon lurched in a sudden sharp gust of wind. "These winds get trickier near the ground, and I can't make out much below us anymore. We passed right over Wadshelf, so I hope that open space ahead is the field I recall."

The pale crescent moon overhead cast but a dim glow on the ground, and Anne could not tell what lay below. She hoped she could trust Lord Ashby to get them down safely, but just as she had begun to breathe properly again, her thoughts shifted as of their own accord to Lord Michael. Knowing that by now he must have learned of their absence, and certain he would discover what they had done and would not be as confident of their safety as Lord Ashby was, she trembled to think what he might say.

They lurched again when Lord Ashby threw something overboard and, before Anne realized how low the balloon had drifted, its basket checked suddenly as if it had caught on something solid.

Lord Ashby said, "The hook's slowing us. We're nearly down now, ladies. Whoa, there!" The last exclamation came as the basket tilted dangerously, hit the ground hard, and bounced up again, nearly flinging Anne out. Had Lady Hermione not grabbed her and yanked her down to the floor of the basket, she was certain she would have been thrown out.

Moments later, they bounced again and yet again, then stayed down, the grappling hook apparently holding. Bruised and battered, and not a little dizzy, Anne slowly straightened.

Lady Hermione said, "I'll unlace the entrance."

"Do that, but don't get out," Lord Ashby said, "or the thing will soar upward again. Let me release more gas first. Hate to do it, because I'll have to fill it again, of course. I'd hoped we'd come down close enough to a house or village to shout for help, but there don't seem to be anyone about. Nothing for it but to collapse the balloon, dash it, and walk back to Wadshelf where the lads will be bound to find us."

Anne realized that a great deal of the air had been let out of the balloon already, for she could see its shape against the sky now, and it was no longer round but tear-shaped. At last, they managed to deflate it enough so that she and Lady Hermione could hold it in place while Lord Ashby secured the grappling line to nearby shrubbery. When at last he was certain the craft would remain grounded, they set off to look for help.

Again Anne was sorry she had not changed back into her garden shoes, for the ground was still muddy from the previous day's rain, and by the time they found the first cottage and were able to rouse the inhabitants and explain that they required assistance, she knew she looked like one of the scaff and raff. She let Lord Ashby do the talking, hoping no one would even ask who she was, and began to fidget more than ever about what her husband would have to say.

More than an hour passed before Lord Ashby's men arrived, and by then Lady Hermione had grown as impatient as Anne. "Just one moment, Ashby," she said imperiously when he began to tell the men where they would find the balloon. "I hope you do not mean to leave Anne and me here to kick our heels until Haydon and Douglas can collect your fool balloon and load it onto the wagon."

"Dash it, Hermie, I've got to go with them if they're to find the *Royal George* tonight. If you're in such a rush, we can hire a gig from one of these folks to take you and Anne home."

"Don't be absurd. Anne cannot go home in a gig, and if she did, just who do you think is to drive her? Me?"

"Well, you could do it, couldn't you?"

"So I could, but I doubt we'll reach the Priory before ten or eleven now, and if you think Michael will be pleased to see his wife come home at such an hour, in a gig and escorted only by an old woman, you must be all about in your head."

Lord Ashby sighed but agreed that she had made her point. "Very well. Let me see what sort of vehicle can be had here."

The best the village had to offer that would carry the three of them in any degree of comfort was a cart and pair, but Lord Ashby became reconciled to the plebeian vehicle the instant its owner, hearing the field described to him, expressed will-

ingness to guide Haydon and Douglas to the balloon. His lordship then took up the reins almost cheerfully. They arrived at
Upminster hours after they had been expected to dine, however, and in no grand style.

Lord Michael was waiting for them, and his set expression
warned Anne that he was extremely displeased. His tone was
even, however, when he said, "Good evening, Lady Hermione.
I am afraid you've long since missed dinner, but I'll order
something at once, for I assume that you mean to spend the
night with us."

She chuckled. "No need to hide your teeth with me, young
man. I daresay you are livid with us all, but you know how it
is with your uncle. He meant no harm, just wanted to show
off his favorite vehicle to your delightful wife. We came to no
harm, I promise you, and I believe she enjoyed her adventure
very much."

"Oh, I did," Anne exclaimed. "Please, sir, do not be too
angry with us. I have never enjoyed such a marvelous experience before! Indeed, it was most magical. Have you never
gone aloft with your uncle?"

"Never," Michael said curtly.

"Then you should. The earth looks just like a patchwork
quilt, all squares and odd shapes where the fields and villages
are, and the total silence is amazing. We did not hear so much
as a single bird. Oh, you must let him take you up one day."

His expression softened, but he did not reply. Instead, he
turned back to Lady Hermione and said, "You have not answered me, ma'am. Shall I tell the servants to prepare a room
for you?"

"No indeed," she said, "for although Wilfred does not command me, he will look for my return before dawn. My horse
is in your stable, with my groom. I'd be grateful for some
bread and cheese and perhaps a glass of wine, but I require
nothing more."

Lord Ashby spoke with annoyance, "Now, see here, Hermie—"

"Don't bluster, Ashby. I shall do very well on my own."

Lord Michael said calmly before Lord Ashby could reply, "I have no doubt you would, ma'am, but it does not suit my notions of propriety to send a female guest home on horseback after dark. You will go in a carriage with a coachman and footman in attendance. Your groom may return your horse tonight or tomorrow, as you wish. As to bread and cheese, I think you will find that Bagshaw will arrange something rather more appetizing for you than that."

"It will take twice as long by road," Lady Hermione protested.

"Nonetheless, that is how you will go."

Anne expected him to insist that they all sit down to a proper meal first, but he did not, and she soon discovered he had ordered a basket of food prepared for Lady Hermione to take with her.

Having seen her off, they returned to the house. The hall was still lighted, but the rooms on either side of it were dark.

Lord Ashby said, "Where's young Andrew? Rather expected him to make one of the welcoming party, by Jove."

"He has gone to bed," Michael said curtly.

"Don't tell me you came to cuffs with the lad again! I daresay you were short-tempered because of our little adventure, but you needn't have taken your irritation out on him."

"You may rest assured, Uncle, that any irritation I feel toward you will be expressed to you when I have sufficient time to devote to the exercise. My displeasure with Andrew arose solely from the fact that I learned he had not spent the morning with his books as he had taken pains to lead me to believe he had."

Anne gasped, but he did not so much as glance at her before adding in the same chilly tone, "He went fishing instead."

"Can't blame a fellow for that," Lord Ashby said. "Ain't his fault he prefers fishing to studying. Did myself. Daresay at his age you did too, for that matter."

"And suffered the consequences, just as Andrew did."

An arrested look leapt to Lord Ashby's eyes. "See here, you didn't do anything reckless, I hope."

"No doubt it will offend your sense of the respect due to his great rank, Uncle, but I have lost all patience with the notion that being a duke entitles him to do as he pleases. He is still a boy, and I am his guardian, and I can no longer see any reason not to treat him like any other boy. It is time and more for him to learn that his actions will result in predictable consequences."

"I suppose you sent him to bed without his dinner again," Lord Ashby said on a hopeful note.

"I did that, but I thrashed him soundly first, and I certainly do not mean to apologize for it. I won't tolerate a liar."

"He did not lie, exactly," Anne said without thinking. "You asked if he had occupied himself properly, by which I am persuaded you meant with his studies, but he replied only that he had occupied himself. I remember that quite clearly."

"That, madam, is a mere quibble, and you know it. I hope it does not also mean that you were aware that he had disobeyed me."

"Do you mean to send her to bed without supper, too?" Lord Ashby demanded. "Or perhaps you mean even to—"

"Don't try my patience too far, Uncle. I do have a number of things to say to you about tonight's business, but I'd prefer to regain control of my temper first. Come along, madam." Grasping Anne's arm none too gently, he urged her toward the stairs.

She waited until she was certain Lord Ashby would not hear her. Then, striving for a light note, she said, "I certainly hope you don't mean to send me to bed without my supper. I'm ravenous."

"Serve you right if I did," he said, "but I won't. Nor do I mean to thrash you, though I'll admit the temptation to do so occurred to me more than once during these past few hours. Do you realize it is after eleven o'clock?"

"As late as that?"

"Yes. You deserve that I should be very angry. Did it never occur to you that to let my uncle take you up in his balloon at night—or indeed, at any time—was dangerous folly?"

"I did not know at first what he meant to do," Anne said, "but once I did, I own that I thought more of the adventure than of the danger. And to be truthful, sir, I am very much afraid that, had I truly recognized the danger, I might have refused to go, which would have been too bad, for I enjoyed myself hugely, except for the very last minutes, which were admittedly rather frightening. But, oh, sir, you must let him take you aloft one day. The experience is beyond anything you could ever imagine."

"Is it?" The hard edge was gone from his voice, but she scarcely noticed, for they were passing through the state drawing room and her attention was drawn to the fire blazing on the hearth.

"There are fires in all these rooms again," she said, vexed.

"There always are," he said.

"But I gave orders today to reduce their number for economy's sake. Surely, it cannot be necessary to keep fires blazing in every large room of the house, every evening."

He said with a sigh, "It cannot cost as much as all that, and no doubt Bagshaw has excellent reasons or he would not order them lit. The house is in capable hands, my dear. I know you shouldered many responsibilities at Rendlesham, for your father was justly proud of your abilities and recited them all to me, but such constant supervision is not necessary here. Bagshaw and Mrs. Burdekin have kept things well in hand for years, and you will only set up their backs by interfering with their ways, you know. You can quite safely leave everything to them."

She wanted to ask if he would be content to leave the running of the estates to the duke's bailiff or land steward, but before she could screw up her courage to do so, he pushed open the door to her dressing room and she saw further proof of the servants' efficiency. A table had been laid for her supper before the cozy fire, with chafing dishes to keep the food warm.

Maisie awaited them, but Michael said gently, "You may go. I will bear your mistress company and see she gets safely to bed."

She glanced at Anne.

"Thank you," Anne said. "I will see you in the morning."

Lord Michael drank a glass of wine while she ate. She described their journey in the balloon, and was relieved to note that he listened without visible annoyance, even chuckling when she told him about Lady Hermione kneeling on Lord Ashby's precious barometer. When she had finished her supper, he arose and held her chair for her. His nearness stirred a tingle of anticipation, but although he escorted her to her bedchamber and assisted her with her disrobing, his demeanor remained matter-of-fact and dutiful rather than romantic. And though he undressed and climbed into bed with her, the interlude that followed was a brief one. He had been right in predicting that the second time would not be so painful, but that was about all she could say for the experience.

When he had gone to his own bedchamber, leaving her wide awake and oddly frustrated to be alone in her bed, Anne lighted her candle again and fetched her portfolio.

Dear James,

I don't yet understand the art of being married. I had expected a sort of partnership, particularly since Lord Michael clearly wanted a mother for his brother's children and—I thought—a mistress for Upminster Priory. But none of that appears to be the case. Instead, he treats me more like another child than a partner. He does not consult me even about the children, or support my authority in the house. Indeed, today he scolded me in front of both family and servants, which even Papa never did. Perhaps things will change when Sylvia arrives. I certainly hope they do.

She wrote for some time longer, describing her adventure in the balloon and Michael's reaction to their return, and then fell asleep at last, dreaming that she floated on clouds and could control their direction, and her own, as well.

His admirably discreet footman awaited him with three of the younger girls from which to choose his pleasure. One looked him boldly in the eye, one looked straight ahead, and the third, the smallest, stood trembling, her gaze flitting anxiously from him to the carpet and back. He wondered if little Anne might someday tremble in a like fashion. She had already tried her wings more than once apparently, but without support for her efforts, she would no doubt quickly learn her place.

He gestured toward the trembler, and the footman, smirking now, pushed her forward. No doubt the lad expected to enjoy the chit afterward. Perhaps he would, at that.

"Take off your clothes," he murmured.

"Oh, please, sir, spare me," she cried, falling to her knees. "I oughtn't to be here. I'm a good girl, I am."

"I will be the judge of how good you are," he murmured in the gentle, purring tone he affected at such times, a tone he knew well could turn a girl's blood to ice. Nodding at the footman, he said, "Strip her. I would know if her body is like to entertain me before we send these others away."

Seven

Lady Sylvia St. Ledgers returned shortly after noon the following Wednesday in the company of her aunt, Lady Harlow, a plump matronly dame some eight years Lord Michael's senior. Since Lady Harlow traveled with an entourage consisting of her postillions, the coachman who drove her second carriage, two footmen clinging to the back of her chaise, several outriders, and her personal dresser, their arrival caused quite a stir.

Even Andrew had run downstairs by the time Lady Harlow, entering the house with both footmen and her dresser in attendance, had finished greeting Bagshaw, Mrs. Burdekin, and several other old friends. Everyone seemed to be talking at once, and in all the bustle, Anne, emerging from the stair hall just behind Andrew, almost missed seeing the small golden-haired child walking silently in her ladyship's wake, nearly concealed by her bulk.

Lord Michael came through the front door just then, and moved to receive his sister's embrace. Encountering Anne's gaze over her shoulder, he said, "Charlotte, I must present you to my wife. Anne, I do not believe you have met my sister."

"No, indeed, I have not," Anne said, moving gracefully forward. "How do you do, ma'am. It is a great pleasure to meet you. I do hope you can stay with us for a few days."

"Well, it is kind of you to invite me," Charlotte said bluffly, "but I don't mean to do so. Harlow don't know how to go on without me, and the children begin to fret if I am absent for long. Nor would I impose myself on a newly married couple, for I am not so rag-mannered as that, say what anyone will. I shall stay only the night and be off again in the morning. But mercy me," she exclaimed, looking around distractedly, "where is Sylvia? Oh, there you are, child. What on earth are you doing clinging to my back-skirts where I cannot even see you? Come here at once and make your best curtsy to your new aunt."

Obediently the little girl stepped forward and bobbed a curtsy, watching Anne through wide and solemn gray eyes.

"I am glad to meet you at last, Sylvia," Anne said, smiling at her. "I trust your journey was a pleasant one."

A silence fell, during which Michael exchanged a glance with Lady Harlow. She shook her head.

Abruptly Andrew said, "Such journeys are generally tedious, in my experience. How did you leave my cousins, Aunt Charlotte?"

"All perfectly stout," she replied, her eyes twinkling. "How *very* kind of you to remember to inquire about them."

"Now that I am head of the family, it is my duty to remember such things," the boy replied, his dignity unabashed.

"So it is," she said. "A most promising beginning, too. No doubt your sense of duty will soon grow to match your uncle's."

"I doubt that," Andrew said with a grimace. "Uncle Michael takes his duties much too seriously."

"Well, if he does, it must be for the first time in his life," she retorted, turning with a teasing grin to her brother. "I daresay your new responsibilities have turned you from a scapegrace into a consummate pattern card by now, my dear Michael."

His grimace was nearly as expressive as Andrew's, but he said only, "I would like to talk privately with you, Charlotte."

"To be sure," she said, "but I shall want a few moments to tidy myself first. If someone has had the foresight to take a ewer and basin to my bedchamber, I can be with you again in a trice."

Bagshaw said, "That has all been seen to, my lady."

"I'm sure it has. Will you come with me, Sylvia dear?"

Without waiting for the child's reply, Michael said, "Ask one of the maidservants to look after Lady Sylvia, Bagshaw. She may dine with us later, if she likes, but she ought to go up to her own room now to rest and make herself tidy."

Anne said quickly, "Ask Frannie to look after her, Bagshaw. I think the two of them will get on famously."

"Begging your pardon, my lady," the butler said deferentially, "but Frances is still considered too young for such an important charge, and in any event her ladyship is accustomed to being served by Nurse Moffat, who has looked after her from the cradle."

"Is Moffat here at the house then?" Michael asked.

"Yes, my lord. I took the liberty of sending for her as soon as we knew when her ladyship would return."

"Excellent," Michael said, turning to the little girl. "Run up to Moffat then, Sylvie. She can order you a bite to eat if you are hungry now, and you may dine with us later if you like."

The child nodded, turned, and ran up the steps. Watching her go, Anne realized that she had not uttered one word since her arrival, and realized at the same moment that no one had seemed to expect her to do so. Seeing Lady Harlow about to go upstairs, she said quickly, "I will accompany you, ma'am, if you don't mind."

"Mercy me, no. Glad of your company." Leading the way to a charming bedchamber that she said had been her own as a girl, Lady Harlow instantly dismissed her dresser and the maidservant who was assisting that haughty dame, and said bluntly, "We shan't want either of them standing about with their ears aflap, for I know you must be bursting with questions." Untying her bonnet strings, she pulled off the bonnet to reveal a mass of bright red curls; and when Anne stared, she chuckled, casting the bonnet onto the bed and saying, "The color is real, my dear, and you needn't state the obvious. I am

the only one ever in the history of the St. Ledgers family to
have red hair. Fortunately, I inherited my mother's face, so no
one is unkind enough to declare me a complete changeling—
not to my face at all events."

"But it's beautiful," Anne exclaimed. "What a pity neither
Sylvia nor Andrew inherited that lovely color."

Lady Harlow laughed. "Not at all, for it would surely have
created the deuce of a scandal if Andrew had got it. But then,
Agnes was not at all like my mama. I doubt she ever dared
to play Edmund false, not even after she'd presented him with
his heir."

"Good gracious, ma'am, you cannot mean—"

"Of course I do. I don't blink at facts, my dear, and I
never got this hair from a St. Ledgers, or from dearest
Mama's family either, bless them. I've a strong suspicion
where I did come by it—but 'tis only suspicion, and I've
never said, nor never will. It is my belief that Mama enjoyed
a small affair after Edmund was born, to pay Papa back for
his many indiscretions, and I don't blame her in the least if
she did. Papa, you see, like Edmund after him, sowed his
seed wherever the soil was fertile, so to speak. But for Mama
to do likewise was exceedingly courageous, because the St.
Ledgers temper—as you may already have discovered for
yourself—is quite formidable. Enough about me, however. I
simply must use the pot in yonder closet and soon we must
hurry back downstairs, for Michael is no more patient than
any other St. Ledgers male. Still, I know you are dying to
ask about poor Sylvia, for I could tell by the way everyone
acted downstairs that no one had yet had the good sense to
warn you about her."

"She does not speak, does she?"

"Not a word. But be a dear and hang this cloak of mine
somewhere and excavate my comb from my reticule whilst I
attend to more pressing business. I'll return straightaway to tell
you the whole, or as much of it as I know, at all events."

She was as good as her word, and while she washed her

hands and face, and tidied her hair, she explained. "Sylvia is not backward, I promise you. In fact, she began talking earlier than most children do, and was a regular chatterbox, because Agnes doted on her and encouraged her when anyone else would have banished her to the nursery whenever she chattered too much. But both those children were badly spoilt—Andrew because dukes of Upminster traditionally have been raised to believe themselves grander than God, and Sylvie because she was such an amusing little moppet."

"Then why does she no longer speak?"

"Haven't a notion, but she hasn't said a word since her mother died." Lady Harlow paused, then added tactfully, "I don't know how much you know about Agnes's death."

"I know she is believed by many to have killed herself," Anne said. "Lady Hermione told me as much; however, she also told me that the local parson accepted the death as an accident."

"Is Hermie here in Derbyshire? That almost makes me wish I had not promised Harlow I'd turn straight about and hurry home. I quite adore Hermie. You must present my compliments to her and tell her how sorry I am to have missed a chance to visit with her."

"I will, and gladly," Anne said. "Was it an accident, ma'am?"

"Nothing of the sort," Charlotte said flatly. "Parson Dailey agreed to that only to soothe Edmund's pride and allow him to bury her in hallowed ground. I don't know what really happened, of course, for I was not here." Her tone made it clear that had she been there she would quickly have got to the bottom of things.

"Lady Hermione said the duchess left no note of explanation."

"Perfectly true. I do think Sylvia knows something, and said as much to Edmund at the time, but he disagreed, since he was the one who'd discovered Agnes's body and told both children. But if she knows nothing more than what he saw fit to tell her, I can't think why she has not spoken. She's not a melodramatic child, you see, so this unnatural silence simply don't match her character."

"How am I to deal with her, ma'am? I've no experience at all with such behavior."

"I just treated her the same as my own. She's such a gentle little thing that mine all looked after her, and as you saw when that arrogant snip Andrew jumped into the breach a bit ago, even he feels protective toward her."

"I suggested to Lord Michael that he hire a governess for her, but I can see now that it would not answer."

"The right sort of woman might do very well," Lady Harlow said. "I shall write to the headmistress of my daughters' school if you like, and put the problem to her. She might know someone suitable. You can do the same—that is, if you went to a school."

"I didn't," Anne said. "My sisters and I shared a governess—a very good woman—but she died several years ago. I'd be very grateful for your help, ma'am."

"That's settled then," Lady Harlow said, getting to her feet. "Michael will be pacing the floor by now, you know, so perhaps I ought to go down, but I hope you will write to me if you want any advice, my dear. You must realize by now that there is no need to couch your wishes in honeyed words where I am concerned. I am a plain-spoken woman and I appreciate plain speaking in others."

Anne expressed her gratitude, wishing with one portion of her mind that Lady Harlow did not live quite so far away, and being extremely grateful in another portion that she did. Leaving her ladyship to enjoy a comfortable prose with Lord Michael, she sent for Elbert to accompany her into the garden, where she passed a productive hour with Quigley, discussing the few improvements he had already set in motion.

She did not see her guest again until it was time to join the others for dinner. That meal passed uneventfully, but Anne noted that Michael, Lord Ashby, and Andrew each seemed to keep one eye on Sylvia. Even the servants seemed protective of her. The child's behavior seemed perfectly natural and unaffected, however. It was almost, Anne thought, as if Sylvia were unaware that she was in any way unusual. She was sent upstairs when the ladies left the table, and Andrew followed soon afterward. The adults spent the evening playing whist, a favorite game of Lady Harlow's, and retired at an early hour.

The following morning the family took breakfast together, and afterward the others escorted Lady Harlow to her coach, where her servants were already waiting. She hugged everyone in turn, pausing last to say to Anne, "I am glad to have met you, my dear. Never thought Michael would show such good sense in selecting his bride, but you are nothing like the females he was used to dangle after, for which I'm exceedingly grateful. But have a care," she added with a teasing look at her brother. "Though he is not so demanding or so arrogant as Edmund was, take my advice and do not let him constantly take the upper hand. All St. Ledgers men have a bullying streak in them. One simply learns not to bow before it."

"Preaching insubordination to my wife, Charlotte?" Michael said, moving to stand next to Anne, who was a bit unnerved at hearing such odd advice. "Not very judicious of you," he added. "Nor would it be particularly wise for her to follow your counsel. A good wife submits to her husband's authority."

"I must remember to inform Harlow of that," Charlotte said, smiling at him and reaching out to pat his cheek. The gesture began as a teasing one but turned uncharacteristically gentle, and Anne saw at once that Michael occupied a special place in his sister's heart. Letting her hand fall, Lady Harlow said quietly, "You have found yourself an excellent wife, Michael. Don't try to alter her too much, will you, dear?"

With that Parthian shot, she allowed herself to be helped into her carriage, and a few moments later, she and her entourage had disappeared around the first curve in the carriage drive.

Seeing Sylvia move away from the others toward the house, Anne hurried to catch up with her, saying, "Would you like to come up to my dressing room, dear? I brought a small gift for you from home, sort of a get-acquainted present, and I'd like to give it to you."

Sylvia looked soberly up at her and nodded.

Hearing Michael call out to Andrew with a stern note in his voice, Anne added in a swift undertone to Sylvia, "Do you like to ride?" When the child nodded again, she turned back and called out, "Andrew, do you remember that you promised to go riding with me today and to provide me with a proper mount from your stables?"

He looked taken aback but responded at once, "Yes, of course I do, but Uncle Michael insists I must study."

"Elbert can ride with you," Michael said, "and you should take one of the grooms, as well."

"It wouldn't be at all the same thing," Anne said, showing her disappointment. "I've scarcely had a chance to become acquainted with Andrew, and I thought Sylvia might like to accompany us."

Sylvia fixed her wide, solemn gaze on her uncle, and with a sigh, he said, "Very well then, but Andrew, before the day is out I shall expect you to finish the work I set for you."

"I won't be ready to go for at least an hour," Anne said. "Perhaps you could get some of your work done before we go."

She could see annoyance in the boy's expression, and rebellion as well, but with a glance at his uncle and another at Sylvia, he shrugged and said, "I'll just go to the stables first, shall I, and give the order to have our horses saddled in an hour's time."

Realizing that he was asserting himself in order to avoid any appearance of complete submission, Anne hoped Michael would not be so tactless as to tell him to send a servant with the order. To forestall such an occurrence, she quickly thanked Andrew for his thoughtfulness and urged Sylvia to make haste. "You will want to examine your gift before changing into your riding dress, my dear."

When they reached Anne's dressing room, they found Maisie there, and Anne introduced her to the little girl before saying, "Fetch out the red silk scarf and the book I brought for her ladyship, will you please, Maisie?"

"Yes, madam, certainly." Maisie turned away at once to the wardrobe, her back stiff, her motions indicating anger.

Anne stared at her, the child temporarily forgotten in her astonishment at this most unusual behavior. "What is it, Maisie?" she demanded. "What's wrong?"

"Nothing at all, madam. Here is the scarf. And here," she added, reaching up to the wardrobe shelf, "is the book you want." Handing both items to Anne, she began to move away again, but this time Anne stopped her with a hand on her arm.

"No, Maisie, don't go. Here, darling," she added, turning to give the gifts to Sylvia. "Try the scarf on by the looking glass yonder, and have a look at the book. It is one of my favorites." When the child had turned obediently toward the dressing table, Anne focused her attention on Maisie. "Now, tell me."

Maisie looked doubtfully at Sylvia, but Anne said, "Pay her no mind, for she will not repeat a word you say. I want to know what is troubling you, and I want to know now."

"I am to forfeit my next day out, that's all," Maisie said, her voice edged with indignation.

"By whose order?"

"Mrs. Burdekin informed me of it, but I've no doubt in the world it was Mr. Bagshaw who gave the order. I had the bad luck to encounter him when I returned to the house after my walk earlier, and it was he who asked where I had been and then demanded to know by whose leave I had gone out."

"I hope you said I had given you leave," Anne said, her own temper stirring.

"No, of course I didn't, when you had done no such thing.

I just told him I often walk in the garden when my early-morning duties are done, but he said that female servants are not permitted to leave the house without his consent or Mrs. Burdekin's."

"I'll deal with this," Anne said. She was halfway to the door when she remembered Sylvia. The child sat on the dressing stool with her back to the glass, the red scarf draped around her neck, the book lying open but unheeded in her lap. She regarded Anne with her solemn, unblinking stare. Despite the lack of expression, Anne sensed distress, and said, "I will be back directly, darling. If you do not want to go to your room just yet, why don't you curl up on the window seat with your book and Juliette until I come back. But I forgot! You have not yet made Juliette's acquaintance. Being wary of strangers, she did not come at once to greet me like she usually does." Finding the little cat curled on its favorite pillow in the bedchamber, Anne scooped it up and returned, stroking its fur and saying, "If you are quiet and don't startle her, I think she will soon come to like you, Sylvia, but though she is purring now, she might scratch if I just hand her to you, so I will put her down on the window seat for now."

Sylvia approached the kitten slowly, her gaze fixed upon it, and Juliette stared back with the same solemn expression. By the time Anne left the room, the two of them were sitting stiffly at opposite ends of the window seat, still staring at each other.

She found Mrs. Burdekin in the housekeeper's sitting room, and said without preamble, "I am told that you have taken it upon yourself to admonish my maidservant."

The housekeeper remained seated for a long moment before she clearly realized that she ought to stand. When she had done so, she said, "The Priory has strict rules for its maidservants, my lady. I am sorry if Maisie did not understand them, but we cannot make exceptions even for her. To do so would be very bad for discipline, as I am certain you will agree."

"Miss Bray is not subject to your discipline, Mrs. Burdekin, only to mine," Anne said. "Surely, *you* understand *that*."

"Why, no, your ladyship, I don't. Since she is now an Upminster servant, she must obey the rules of the house."

"Miss Bray is my servant and has been my servant since I was a child," Anne said calmly. "She answers only to me. I will say no more than that, but I hope I have made myself clear."

The housekeeper hesitated, but at last she met Anne's steady gaze and said, "It shall be as you wish, madam, of course."

"I am glad we understand one another," Anne said. "Miss Bray will take her half day or day out when it pleases her to do so."

"Yes, your ladyship, certainly."

"Good day, Mrs. Burdekin," Anne said, turning away with a sense that her grandmother's enormous dignity had suddenly descended upon her shoulders like a warm and well-fitting cloak.

As she reached the door, however, Mrs. Burdekin said, "I spoke to Mr. Bagshaw about a new fireguard for the kitchen fire, madam, and it is his decision that one is not required."

"Is it?" Anne said without turning. "Well, we shall see."

Back in her dressing room, she found Sylvia curled up on the window seat, reading, with Juliette purring contentedly in her lap. "You must have your uncle's magic touch with animals," Anne said. "Until I made the acquaintance of your family, Juliette allowed no one but myself to stroke her!"

Sylvia had watched her gravely from the moment Anne entered, but when Anne smiled, the child rewarded her with a wavering little smile in return. Sensing that it would be a mistake to comment on it, Anne turned to Maisie instead, saying, "Everything is settled. Mrs. Burdekin now understands that you answer only to me."

"It is to be hoped," Maisie said dryly, "that Lord Michael don't find himself moved to alter that understanding."

Anne had nothing to say to that. She knew as well as any

woman that her husband could quickly destroy what little authority she had managed to establish with the servants, and it occurred to her with unpleasant force that if Mrs. Burdekin or Bagshaw chose to lay the matter before him, he might well contradict the order she had given. She hoped he would not do so but realized that hitherto he had given her no cause whatsoever to believe he would support her against the upper servants, and rather more than a little reason to think he might support them against her. Indeed, she hesitated even to bring the matter of the fireguard to his attention, certain that he would tell her Bagshaw knew best.

Exchanging a look with Maisie, she suddenly recalled Sylvia's presence, and turned back to the child with a strained smile. "If we are going to ride with Andrew, darling, you had better change into your riding dress. Gentlemen do not like to be kept waiting, you know, particularly dukes."

She had hoped to elicit another smile, but Sylvia got to her feet without any discernible expression, set Juliette back on the window seat, and walked silently from the room.

When the door had been shut again, Maisie said, "At first I thought she was mute, Miss Anne, for she said not one word while you was gone. It is not my place to make personal comments, of course, even to so young a lady, but really . . ."

Anne explained about Sylvia, and as she had expected, Maisie was instantly sympathetic. "In an ordinary household, I'd have heard all about her within an hour of my arrival, but I've never known such folk as them what inhabit the servants' hall here. The only one who talks to me is Jane Hinkle, and she don't know the first thing about the family, being nearly as new as what we are ourselves. The others are as close as onions. Even that Frannie don't talk like one would expect of a youngster like her. They're a nervous lot, too, always looking about before they speak, as if they expect someone to be lurking, trying to hear what they say."

"Nonsense, they are simply well trained," Anne said. "The servants at Rendlesham would not betray family secrets to newcomers either, and like it or not, Maisie, that is precisely what we are."

"Nonetheless, Miss Anne, it ain't natural. I've never had the least trouble getting on with folks, either in my own home or in someone else's, and when we was in London, I heard a right good amount about business in dozens of homes other than our own. You know yourself that the news travels fastest from servants' hall to servants' hall. Why should Upminster be different, I ask you?"

Anne was sure Maisie had failed to take into account the facts that most servants she had known in the past had been acquainted with one another for years and that Upminster servants were more strictly trained. Like it or not, the pair of them were intruders in the ducal household, and would remain so until they were truly accepted, by servants and family alike.

Requesting her riding dress, she changed swiftly, so intent on what she was doing that she did not realize that Sylvia had returned until, turning around on her dressing stool, she found the child standing silently before her. Starting, she laughed and said, "My goodness, I never even heard you come in. I must have been lost in my own thoughts."

As the days passed, she learned that Sylvia had a knack for turning up in odd places, and in time Anne became almost accustomed to looking up and finding her in the room, or to turning around and finding Sylvia at her heels as she passed from the drawing room to the hall, or from the garden to the stable yard. She enjoyed the child's undemanding company and soon formed the habit of spending several hours each day with her. But Sylvia also had a knack for disappearing as silently as she appeared, a habit Anne found much more disconcerting, particularly when she could not find her. Eventually the child would reappear, however, none the worse for her absence, and Anne could never quite manage to scold her.

Her own time passed swiftly, for although she could not seem to induce the household servants to alter their habits, she took both children into Chesterfield to be measured for new clothing, and found occupation in the gardens when she was not receiving callers. These were frequent, and although none but Lady Hermione spent more than the requisite twenty minutes with her, there were so many that Anne began to feel rather like Miss Fanny Howe, the young lioness she had once seen at the Tower of London menagerie—or Miss Nancy, the gentle ant bear from Canada.

Lady Hermione called nearly every day, for, as she told Anne, there was little to amuse her at her brother's house.

"Shuts himself up with his books, does Wilfred, though his memory's getting so bad I don't know how he recalls what he's read. Only yesterday, he forgot he had given his cook leave to visit her daughter, then demanded to know why he was served an indifferent dinner, which put Mrs. Medbury's back up. She's his housekeeper. I don't think much of her, though to be fair, her mother has been ill, and she frets. If Wilfred would but listen to me . . ."

Anne found it easy to sympathize, and indeed, had soon found herself confiding some of her own troubles to her friend. Lady Hermione, in consequence, offered her a great deal of advice, none of which seemed practical since Anne could not imagine threatening to turn Bagshaw off, or Mrs. Burdekin, let alone telling Lord Michael to do so. Still, it had been a relief to unburden herself.

One afternoon, a fortnight after Sylvia's return, Anne went to her dressing room to change her shoes. Hearing odd noises from her bedchamber as she approached the wardrobe, she went in there instead, to find Maisie on her hands and knees, peering under the bed, muttering, "Come out, you little rascal, if you're there."

"What is it? Who's under the bed? Not Sylvia, surely."

"Nothing is there." Maisie got to her feet, frowning. "That dratted cat's disappeared into thin air, Miss Anne. She was here ten minutes ago, when I left to fetch two hats I'd trimmed for you, and when I came back, she was nowhere to be found."

Returning to the dressing room, Anne saw that a window

was ajar. "Did you open this?" she demanded, hurrying to push it wider. The distance to the ground was dismayingly far. "Surely, Juliette would not have attempted to jump from here."

"I didn't open it today," Maisie said, frowning, "but it's been opened before to air out the room, and Juliette's shown no desire to climb out. Perhaps it weren't shut properly, and she pushed it open. Could she have got onto the roof?"

"I don't know," Anne said, alarmed, "but perhaps we had better ask the servants to look for her."

With that thought in mind, she hurried downstairs, intending to find Elbert or Bagshaw; however, when she reached the hall, she found Lord Michael instead, with another gentleman, who was clearly on the point of departure.

Until the other man turned, she did not recognize him, but when he did, she did not require Michael's saying, "You remember Sir Jacob Thornton," to know him. It was not his height or stature that she recalled, or his sandy hair and red complexion, but rather the knowing look in his pale blue eyes. As she approached, he watched her too closely for comfort, just as he had before, as if he could see through her clothing.

"Of course I remember Sir Jacob," she said, nodding in a polite way but without extending a hand to him. "I trust your visit to Derby was a pleasant one, sir."

"Stap me, that were parliamentary business and I ain't just getting back, Lady Michael, if that's what you think. Been back a week, but not being one to rush my fences, didn't want to intrude straight off." He smiled broadly. "Never thought I'd meet a wench as could bring Michael round her thumb—not after all the barques of frailty I've known him entertain. Oughtn't to mention them to you, of course, ma'am, but I can see you'll keep him up to his bit. Like I said before," he told Michael with a smirk, "she's a dashed fine little beauty. I'd sure like to know where you find them."

Annoyance flitted across Michael's face, but he deftly turned the subject, and Sir Jacob took his departure moments later.

When he had gone, Michael said quietly, "Is something amiss? Where were you going in such a hurry?"

"Juliette is missing, and one of the windows was ajar. I thought she might have got up onto the roof or—"

"Nonsense," he said, taking her gently by the arm and turning her back toward the stairs. "You don't give that kitten enough credit for intelligence. Very sensible little cat, I thought. Where did you leave her?"

"In my dressing room. I haven't wanted to let her roam free in such a big house until she grew more at home here."

"She's been here nearly three weeks, Anne," he said with some amusement. "She ought to feel right at home by now."

"But the dogs! They wander in and out of the house at will."

"They won't trouble her, and I doubt she wandered far. Come along. I'll help you look."

They went up to her dressing room to be greeted by Maisie, looking amused and holding a finger to her lips. In response to Anne's raised eyebrows, she moved toward the wardrobe, whispering, "Didn't look here before because the door was shut tight, Miss Anne, but thought I'd find your garden shoes while I waited for you. Look what I found instead." Silently, she opened the well-oiled wardrobe door. On the floor amidst Anne's slippers and shoes lay Sylvia, fast asleep, curled around the purring black kitten.

No one said anything until Maisie had shut the door again and they had moved away from the wardrobe. Then, frowning, Lord Michael said, "That child should be with her nurse. What on earth is she doing in there?"

Anne said, "Please, sir, don't wake her. Moffat tells me Sylvia tosses and turns at night and rarely sleeps soundly. If she fell asleep there, it is because she needs rest and because she feels safe in my wardrobe."

"I don't believe in coddling children," he said, but Anne saw doubt in his eyes when he glanced back at the wardrobe, so she was not too surprised to hear him add gruffly, "I suppose you will do as you think best."

She was tempted to tell him that if she were allowed to do as she thought best, there would be a number of changes at the Priory. Despite her efforts, fires and wax candles still burned daily in all the public rooms, the servants still rarely looked to her for orders, even at the dining table, and whenever she suggested the smallest change, she was still told politely but firmly, "That is not how we do that at Upminster, madam."

But she could not complain that the household did not run smoothly, or that she had accomplished nothing. Quigley had ordered the kitchen gardens prepared for planting, and sown with a multitude of vegetables. Even the depleted asparagus beds had been forked over and replanted, and he had set boys to killing snails and slugs, and to watch for the first weeds in the new beds.

As the month of May progressed, Anne realized also that she was slowly but surely making friends with both children. Sylvia still did not speak, but she followed Anne like a silent shadow; and Andrew was not only more civil to her but actually took her fishing twice. He also went up with Lord Ashby once in the balloon, which adventure resulted in a stern lecture from Lord Michael on the folly of wasting money on inflammable air, but the participants apparently enjoyed themselves very much.

Toward the end of the month, to Anne's surprise, her father sent her own mare from Rendlesham at last; and when she rode or fished with Andrew, she caught glimpses of the boy he might have been had he been raised like other boys, but generally he remained aloof, and she frequently saw resentment flare in his eyes when Michael spoke sharply to him or demanded obedience to an order.

Privately, Anne thought her husband too strict and demanding where Andrew was concerned, believing it was unfair to expect the young duke suddenly to submit to authority after so many years of being allowed to do as he pleased. However, although she was slowly finding her path, she was by no means the partner she had hoped to be, or mistress of the house as she had expected to be. Nor, though she tried to be a good and submissive wife, did she see as much of her husband as she had thought she would. His many duties kept him away from the house most days, and though his connubial attentions were still dutiful rather than romantic, he did not neglect her, and was kind and even charming to her, which meant—as she confided to her journal—that she had no great cause for the odd sense of dissatisfaction that seemed to plague her.

Eight

One morning, a week later, as Anne sat at the escritoire in her dressing room, making a list of things to discuss with Quigley, she realized the time had come to convince Michael to hire more help if they were ever to begin work on the flower gardens. The men they had could barely handle the thinning and transplanting of the vegetables. It had taken two days just to move the cucumbers from their frames and plant them out under hand glasses.

She did not count her chance of success very high, knowing he would likely say it was too expensive to hire more men, and suggest that she would be better employed in beginning to repay some of the many bride visits she had received. But although she knew it was her duty to do so, and indeed had even told Lady Hermione that she meant to begin paying calls soon, she was more concerned about the garden. She felt as if she had exerted the patience of Job, moving at a snail's pace to get things done, but every time she looked at the neglected lawns and borders, she itched to set them to rights.

When Maisie entered, Anne glanced up briefly before adding one more item to her list. Realizing her woman had neither moved farther into the room nor spoken, she looked up again to see an uncharacteristic look of indecision on her face.

"What is it, Maisie?"

"Oh, Miss Anne, something dreadful's happened."

Fear for Michael or one of the children brought Anne instantly to her feet. "Tell me at once! Is someone injured?"

"No, no, but Mr. Bagshaw's gone and turned off Jane Hinkle. He says she's to leave at once, today, and without a character, Miss Anne. Please, you must do something."

"What did Jane do?" Knowing Maisie had formed a friendship with the upper housemaid, Anne hoped it was nothing too dreadful.

"She come in late last evening, Miss Anne, from her half day. Half an hour late, Mr. Bagshaw says, though she don't think it were as much as that. Said she went into the village and mistook her way coming back. Jane says Mr. Bagshaw don't like her, Miss Anne, and nor does Mrs. Burdekin, on account of Jane weren't raised here at Upminster, but she's a good girl, Miss Anne, and it ain't fair to turn her off without a character just for coming in a bit late."

"If that is all she did, she ought to have a second chance, certainly," Anne said, annoyed that Bagshaw meant to discharge an excellent servant for so small a fault.

"It's that cheeky Elbert, if you ask me," Maisie said. "He's had it in for Jane ever since that day you sent him off with a flea in his ear when he tried to take liberties with her. Mr. Bagshaw thinks the sun rises and sets with that young jackanapes, all on account of Elbert's another nephew or cousin or some such thing."

Anne was not surprised to learn that Jane had confided in Maisie about the incident in the salon. Nor did she doubt Maisie's assessment of the present situation, but she knew she would have to tread lightly if she meant to intervene between the butler and one of the servants. She could not simply make the same demands for Jane that she had for Maisie.

"Please, Miss Anne," Maisie begged, evidently believing her unconvinced. "If Jane is turned off without a character, she won't be able to get another situation in a decent house. You know as well as I do what becomes of such girls."

"I do," Anne said calmly. "I like Jane and would be very distressed if she were to end up serving tables in a tavern, or worse. I will do my best to see that she is not sent away."

"Thank you," Maisie said fervently.

Informed by Elbert that Bagshaw was not available just then, Anne ran the butler to earth herself in the lantern-lit wine cellar, where she found him with two of his minions. As she entered, he was pouring something through a wooden funnel from a bowl into a hogshead. "I want to speak with you," she said.

Straightening and accepting a linen towel from one of the men to wipe his hands, he said, " 'Yes, madam. I shall come at once."

"I have just learned that you intend to discharge Jane Hinkle without a character."

"Yes, madam." He turned back to his men, saying, "Stir it with the staff for five minutes. Then leave the bung out for a few hours so the froth can fall before you close it up. Now then, madam, I am at your service. Shall we go upstairs?"

"What sort of wine were you fining?" Anne asked curiously when he held the green baize door for her to pass through to the hall.

"An excellent claret ordered by Lord Ashby, madam. In eight or ten days it will be fit for bottling."

She said nothing more until they reached the drawing room, but when the doors were shut, she said, "I'd like you to reconsider your decision about Jane. Not only is she an excellent housemaid, whom I would be sorry to lose, but if you dismiss her without a character reference, she will be unable to find work elsewhere."

"I fear she has proven herself unsuited for work in a decent house," Bagshaw said. "Perhaps she did not tell you the whole story."

"I have not spoken with Jane," Anne said. "I would not attempt to undermine your authority in that way, which is why I came directly to you. I thought you had dismissed her because she exceeded the maids' curfew."

"That would certainly be sufficient cause, madam. Maids who defy our house rules have no place at the Priory."

"Nor should they," Anne agreed, "but I do not agree that Jane meant to defy the rules. I believe she had good reason for her tardiness, and since the infraction is a small one, after all, she might surely be forgiven just this once."

"I am afraid the fault was not so small as that, madam."

"Have I been misinformed?" Anne asked, struggling to retain her calm. "Was she more than a half hour late?"

"No, madam. The extent of tardiness alone might not condemn her but for the fact of where she passed the time, and with whom."

"Who was it?" Anne asked, wishing she had thought to ask Maisie where Jane had gone and hoping the pretty housemaid did not have a secret lover hidden away somewhere.

Bagshaw stiffened. "I am afraid I could not reconcile it with my conscience to discuss that topic with you, madam."

"Indeed?" Anne raised her eyebrows, trying to imitate her grandmother's haughtiest look when her will was crossed. At the same time, she pressed her clenched fist into a fold of her skirt so the butler would not see her increasing annoyance clearly displayed. "May I ask why you refuse to explain the matter to me?"

"The subject is not one that is suitable for a man to discuss with a lady of quality, madam," Bagshaw said with a hint of rebuke in his voice. "His lordship would be most displeased were I to engage in such a distasteful conversation with your ladyship."

"Then his lordship already knows about this," Anne said, repressing her shock at the thought that Lord Michael would agree to dismiss a house servant without so much as telling her. Seeing a flicker of wariness in the butler's eyes, she added swiftly, "He does know, does he not?"

"Since Lord Michael leaves all such matters to me or to Mrs. Burdekin, madam, I did not think it necessary to burden him with what is, after all, no more than a minor household difficulty."

"It is not minor to Jane Hinkle," Anne pointed out, "or to

me. I have been willing to allow you considerable license with regard to managing the servants because Lord Michael has faith in your competence, Bagshaw, but I must insist that you reconsider this decision about Jane."

"I regret that I can see no reason to do so, madam."

She had caught a fleeting, enigmatic look when she had spoken of allowing him license, and she realized suddenly that he did not view her as much of an adversary. Taking courage in hand, she said quietly, "Do you dare to defy me, Bagshaw?"

"No, madam, certainly not."

But she could see from the look in his eyes that he meant to do precisely that, and she could not be much surprised. If he did not look upon her as the mistress of the house, how could she blame him, when she was not certain herself that she was any such thing?

"If you wish, madam," he said, "I shall engage to bring the matter to his lordship's attention when next we speak."

"When will that be?"

"Today or, failing that, tomorrow, certainly."

"But Mai— That is, I was given to understand that you had ordered Jane to depart immediately, today."

"Yes, madam, that is correct."

"Then you must speak to Lord Michael at once, Bagshaw."

"His lordship is very busy, madam, and the young person in question is not likely to leave the area, since she has no means by which to do so. In the unlikely event that his lordship should choose to overrule my decision, she can be invited to return."

His obvious certainty that no such likelihood existed both irritated Anne and, at the same time, nearly extinguished her waning hopes, but she strove to sound both self-possessed and firm when she said, "I will speak to Lord Michael myself." She wished now that she had done so at the outset, before the butler had reminded that her position at Upminster was ambiguous at best. Giving herself a mental shake to revive waning resolution, she said, "I believe he is still in the house, is he not?"

"His lordship is in the library," Bagshaw said, adding stiffly, "If you insist, madam, I can submit the matter to his judgment at once, though he will certainly think it odd to have such a petty matter of household management forced upon his notice without proper warning. In any event, you need not accompany me. Had I realized the young person was so important to your ladyship, I would have conferred with his lordship from the outset."

His clear assumption that he could dismiss her so easily was the final straw. Anne gritted her teeth, drew a steadying breath, and said, "You may accompany *me* if you wish, but it is I who will speak to Lord Michael." Turning, she walked briskly away, determined to confront Michael before her courage failed her.

In the front hall, the porter sprang to open the library door for her, but when Lord Michael looked up in annoyance at the interruption, Anne knew that her timing could have been better. Aware of the butler's solid presence behind her, and the air of undiminished dignity radiating from him, she collected her scattered wits and said, "Forgive me for disturbing you, sir, but the matter is an urgent one."

With obvious reluctance, he rose to his feet behind the large library table. "Indeed, my dear, I believe that it must be. I am exceedingly busy, as you can see." He gestured toward what looked like a pile of accounts on the table before him, but his gaze had shifted to the butler. "What do *you* want, Bagshaw?"

Quickly, Anne said, "He means to discharge poor Jane Hinkle without a character, sir, although I have told him I do not want him to do any such thing." Striving to appear calm, she sat down in the chair nearest the library table as she spoke.

Michael remained standing, his gaze still fixed on the butler. "I assume that you have a good reason for your decision, Bagshaw."

"Indeed, I do, my lord. The girl behaved in an inexcusable fashion. She must leave at once."

"I see," Michael said, adding as he turned to Anne, "One of Bagshaw's less agreeable duties is to make such decisions, my dear. For us constantly to be second-guessing them would be most unfair."

Exerting iron control over a nearly irresistible urge to stomp her feet, even to throw something, Anne ignored the fire in her cheeks and the fury in her mind and, wishing now that she had not sat down, said with rigid calm, "He agreed to submit the matter to your judgment, and since he refuses to tell me why he dismissed Jane—and seems determined not to provide her with a character reference, which he ought in all fairness to give her under any circumstance when she has served us so well these past weeks—"

"To be truthful," Michael interjected apologetically, "I am not perfectly certain which one—"

"The prettiest housemaid," Anne said, fighting for patience, "the slender one with hair the color of guinea coins, and enormous blue eyes. Surely, you must—"

"Oh, yes, I know the one." Michael looked again at Bagshaw. "I must say, she seems quite competent. Perhaps in view of that, and Lady Michael's preference, some other course of action . . ." He paused suggestively.

"I could not recommend any other course, my lord. I assure you, her behavior does not warrant clemency."

"She returned last evening half an hour after the maids' curfew," Anne said flatly. "Surely, to discharge her for such a small offense—" She broke off when Michael's gaze shifted, and turning quickly, she saw Bagshaw shaking his head. Squaring her shoulders, she said with an uncharacteristic edge to her voice, "My lord, if there is more to tell—as he is so clearly indicating to you, if not to me—pray, ask him to explain the whole."

Michael said, "Indeed, Bagshaw, I confess I am curious to know the reason now, myself."

"Certainly, my lord, but since the tale is not one to relate in the presence of her ladyship, perhaps we might speak privately."

Having no doubt that Michael would send her away, Anne said grimly, "I hope you do not mean to ask me to leave the room, sir, because I care a great deal about what becomes of Jane. If she is to be sent away with no recourse other than to seek shelter where she can find it, without benefit of a proper reference, then I am determined to know the reason. I am neither a child nor an idiot, and though I do not want to oppose your authority, I do intend to get to the bottom of this one way or another. Surely it would be better to hear it from Bagshaw, who at least professes to be concerned for my sensibilities, than from one of the servants."

To her surprise, Michael said, "Her ladyship makes a perfectly valid case, Bagshaw. Perhaps you had better tell us both."

The quiet command disconcerted the butler, who said in obvious wonder, "But, my lord, truly, the subject is not one for delicate ears. Perhaps when I tell you the girl admitted visiting Mrs. Flowers in the village, you will understand my extreme reluctance to explain the whole in her ladyship's presence."

"Mrs. Flowers, eh?"

"Indeed, my lord. An entire evening, and one during which the wench apparently lost all track of time."

"I see."

"Well, I do not," Anne said. "Who is Mrs. Flowers? I do not think I have met her."

Lord Michael's mouth twisted wryly, and he exchanged another look with the butler before saying, "She is, as Hermione might say, no better than she should be. Her past, my dear, is a rather lurid one, and I am thankful to know that you do not number her amongst your acquaintances in the village."

"I see," Anne said thoughtfully.

With undisguised relief, Michael said, "Then you will agree that Bagshaw knows his business best."

Instead of yielding, as he so clearly expected, Anne said firmly, "You may leave us now, Bagshaw, but see that you do nothing more about Jane Hinkle until further notice."

"My lord," Bagshaw protested, "surely you will not allow this . . . this—"

"This what?" Lord Michael prompted, his tone gentle but carrying a sudden, unmistakable note of danger.

Bagshaw recovered his composure at once. "I beg your pardon, your lordship. There was no intended criticism, I assure you." He bowed to Anne, adding, "Your ladyship, I must beg your pardon, too, if I have overstepped my place out of concern for your ladyship's sensibilities. I hope you will forgive me."

Anne was watching her husband. She had made her stand, and he seemed willing for the moment at least to support her authority to do so, but she was not feeling gracious enough to forgive the butler. Moreover, she did not dare say another word—not yet. The next move was Lord Michael's.

His gaze was fixed steadily on her now, but he said quietly, "I will ring when I want you again, Bagshaw."

"Yes, my lord."

Scarcely daring to breathe, Anne stared at a point beyond Lord Michael's head until she heard the library door close behind the butler. Even then she hesitated to look at her husband, and a tense silence fell between them, broken only by the sound of a log shifting in the low-burning fire on the hearth. She counted to ten, trying to recover her temper, knowing she had to proceed cautiously if she were not still to bring all to ruin. She would gain nothing for Jane, or herself, by arousing Michael's anger.

When she finally looked at him, she saw to her amazement that he was regarding her with wry amusement. Moving to the front of the library table, and leaning against it, he said, "You are very assertive today, my dear. Where have you hidden the dependable Lady Serenity with whom we have all become so pleasantly familiar?"

Without a thought, she leaned forward in her chair and said bluntly, "Am I mistress in this house, sir, or not?"

Eyeing her more warily now, he said, "In as much as I am master here for the present, you are certainly mistress."

"Then Jane stays," Anne said flatly.

He shook his head. "No, Jane does not stay. I am afraid you do not perfectly understand the whole, but Bagshaw is quite right, and one should never keep an immoral servant."

"Immoral? Jane Hinkle? Nonsense." Anne stood up, unable to bear sitting a moment longer. "I would wager my own reputation on the fact that Jane is a good girl, sir, with excellent morals."

"Anne, really, you are beyond your depth here, for there are things you simply don't understand. Believe me, you would do much better to let Bagshaw and Mrs. Burdekin deal with the servants."

"Not one minute ago you agreed that I am mistress of this household," she reminded him.

"Yes, but—"

"I have been well trained to manage a large household, my lord, *and* its servants. One's first duty in domestic management is not only to keep a close eye on things in order to be certain the servants carry out their duties, but also to promote their welfare. To turn Jane off without a character is patently unfair, particularly when the poor creature has nowhere else to go and no one else to turn to. Merely for having been a little late and having had the poor judgment to visit a woman with a sullied reputation, she is to be tossed away like useless trash, condemned to a fate much worse than that of Mrs. Flowers."

"Look here, my girl, Mrs. Flowers's reputation is more than a trifle sullied. If you *must* know details, the woman is no more than a common trollop. That Jane apparently knows her and chooses to visit speaks a great deal about Jane's own morals, I'm afraid."

"Good gracious," Anne said, shocked, "that cannot be true. What on earth would such a woman be doing in our village?"

"She has a house there, actually, and poses as a widow," Michael said as one goaded. "Folks accept the pose only because she claims the favor of . . . of a prominent man in the district."

"She was your mistress, in fact," Anne snapped incautiously, unable to ignore the horror rising inside her.

"No, not mine," he retorted, straightening to his full height.

"I heard you hesitate over the identity of her patron, sir, and since the only other prominent man hereabouts whom I can call to mind just now is Sir Jacob Thornton, an elected Member of Parliament, who is also married and has numerous children—"

"Thank you very much," Michael said grimly. "I would remind you that I, too, am married and, though they are admittedly not my own, I am responsible for two children—for all the difference either factor makes to the particular topic at hand."

"But I meant . . . that is, I thought you must have known her before we were married," Anne said, adding hastily when she saw that her explanation only made him angrier, "It must be Sir Jacob, of course. I can readily believe it, and I do see what you mean about it's not mattering—marriage, that is, or . . . or children. How foolish you must think me not to have understood at once, particularly since he— But that is not the point," she added quickly before he could agree that she had been foolish or demand to know what she had nearly said about Sir Jacob. "Even if Jane was so misguided as to visit the woman, that is no proof that their morals are similar. Jane may have had quite a good reason, you know. No one has even asked her, I'll wager. And in any case, I shall explain to her that she must not go there again."

"And she will simply obey you." His tone was sardonic, his disbelief unmistakable. "Even if that were true, a female with loose morals—or even one with poor judgment, for that matter—is quite likely to do other unacceptable things."

"When servants know their employer has a compassionate and generous regard for their comfort and well-being, sir, I believe they try to show their gratitude in every way they can. I also believe that protecting and encouraging virtue is the best preventive against vice. Bagshaw would do more to improve morality in this house by rebuking the footmen when they press the maids for favors or pinch their bottoms than he will by turning Jane off for having made an unfortunate mistake."

"I am afraid it is the nature of men, especially footmen, to do such things," Michael said with a sigh. "It is only when the maids let things go too far that unpleasant consequences result, which is precisely why Bagshaw is right to want to get rid of a young woman with questionable morals."

"Do you pinch their bottoms?" Anne asked curiously.

A mixture of emotions crossed his face, and she was glad to note a trace of amusement among them. Ruefully, he said, "I was known to do such things in the past, but I have a distinct feeling that I would be wise just now to promise never to do them again."

"Yes, sir, you would."

He held out a hand to her, and said coaxingly, "Come, Anne, calm yourself, sit down again, and let us discuss this in a more friendly fashion. I miss your serenity, my dear. It is a quality generally rare in this household, and I value it highly."

She nearly put her hand in his, but caught herself before she did, saying quietly, "First I must know where I stand. Assuring me that I am mistress here is perfectly absurd if you mean constantly to support the servants against me."

"I won't do that."

"But you do; you have. At meals, they do not even look to me for orders. When I attempted to reduce the number of fires lighted each night, you refused to support me. When I suggested that Frannie look after Sylvia, the notion was rejected out of hand without a murmur from you. Indeed, whenever I try to effect the smallest change, if Bagshaw or Mrs. Burdekin object, you say they know best how things should be done and I should let them do their jobs. Not once have you supported my position against theirs. Not until just now with Bagshaw, at all events," she added with a sigh.

"I am sorry you view my behavior that way," he said. "I did not intend to make you unhappy, but since you are a new-comer and Bagshaw has been helping to manage things here for years, I suppose I just thought . . ." He spread his hands in a clear invitation for her to see the matter as reasonably as he did.

Relieved that he had not dismissed her or her argument out of hand, she said quietly, "I am tempted to point out that if this household were well managed, it would be a happier one, but I don't want to befog the issue, for I must make plain to you how difficult your attitude makes things for me. Every servant in the house believes you will not support my authority. Thus, I have none."

He frowned. "Has anyone dared to be rude to you? You need only speak his name, and I will dismiss him at once."

"Even Bagshaw?"

"Good God, don't tell me he was ever even disrespectful. I'd find that nearly impossible to believe. I've only seen him shaken from his dignity once, today, when his concern for the proprieties made it so hard for him to speak to me in your presence."

"No, Bagshaw has never been rude," Anne admitted with a sigh. "Rudeness would almost be easier for me to bear than the casual way he dismisses any suggestion of mine as not being the way things are done here."

"But he does know how things should be done." Michael moved toward her, adding with a smile, "I know it must be difficult to come into a new house and find things managed so differently from the ways to which you are accustomed, my dear, but no doubt, in time, you will see that our ways have merit, too."

Anne began to stiffen the moment she realized he intended to dismiss her, that he had not accepted her argument. Still, had he not put a hand on her shoulder, she might have held her temper in check. But when he touched her, all the irritations, annoyances, and resentments that had clouded her days at Upminster came together with a nearly audible snap.

Stepping back, she said angrily, "Do not treat me like a child again! My first night here you sent me to bed as if I had been ten years old. When I went into the garden without Elbert, you took me to task before the family and the servants. And although when you married me, you said you wanted a mother for the children and a mistress for this house, whenever I attempt to speak to you about either subject, you act as if my words were of no consequence. I cannot perform either of those duties well if you won't support my authority, my lord, and just because things have been done a certain way since the dawn of time does not mean they are being done correctly. Surely, if you must spend as much time as you do on your brother's affairs, they cannot have been in good order, and if his business affairs were not in order, I cannot imagine why you should assume that his household was."

"Anne, lower your voice," he said, glancing toward the door. "Such conduct is unseemly and most unlike you."

"How do you know what I am like? You have made no effort whatsoever to find out."

"That's not true," Michael said, struggling to control his own temper. "If I haven't given you the attention you expected, it is only because I have had so many other things on my mind."

"Then let others help you," she said, giving her frustration free rein. "Lord Ashby is willing to do so, and I could help you much more if I knew what was vexing you, and did not have to exert such elaborate tact with everyone. But you tell me nothing, and I must constantly cajole and persuade in circumstances where I should simply be able to say 'you will.' "

When he did not reply at once, she said more calmly,

"When you were in the army, sir, did you not frequently delegate authority to subordinate officers?"

"Yes, of course, but I cannot see what my junior officers have to do with the matter at hand."

"If one of them gave an order to his men that they did not like, did you assume the officer was wrong and tell him to listen to his men and let them decide what to do?"

"No, of course not. I would never undermine an officer's authority in such a fashion. But, Anne, really—"

"Even if the soldiers who objected had been in the army longer than your junior officer?"

An arrested look leapt to his eyes. He said slowly, "It actually is, by and large, much the same thing, isn't it?"

"Yes, it is," she said, hardly daring to believe he really understood at last what she had been trying to tell him.

He was silent for a long moment, thinking. Then with a rueful look, he said, "You ought to have spoken up sooner."

"What could I say? Everyone has been kind and polite—indeed, Bagshaw has been practically paternal—so whenever I try to press a point, it sounds like petty complaining. But this business with poor Jane is too important to let be, sir. I know what will become of her if she is discharged without a character. I cannot allow that to happen, not to someone who has served us well."

"Well, as to that little matter, I'm afraid I still think Bagshaw is right."

"I disagree, however, and in this instance, I believe you must support me if I am ever to be mistress here. You cannot just pick and choose those occasions when you will do so, you know."

"But, damn it, Anne, Jane Hinkle deserves to be dismissed."

"No, she does not. If she must be punished for lacking judgment, then let her forfeit her next day out."

"A full month of days out."

"Done," Anne said, knowing that she had won. "Thank you, sir." When he reached for her, she grasped his hand, gave it a warm squeeze, and said, "If you will excuse me, I want to tell Jane the good news myself."

He caught her hand tightly, saying, "No, Anne, that you cannot do. Only recollect your own advice to me," he added swiftly when she opened her mouth to protest. "In this instance, you are the superior officer and Bagshaw the subordinate. He must be the one to tell Jane. I'll ring for him now, and we will inform him together of what we desire him to do. And, Anne, if I truly treated you like a child, I do apologize most sincerely. You are not a child, my dear, not by a long chalk."

Dear James,

I lost my temper today in what Grandmama would condemn as a most unladylike way, but although I do agree that a lady ought never to give way to her emotions before others, I cannot say I am sorry I did. In point of fact, considering the excellent result, if shouting at people can help me define and secure my position as mistress of Upminster, I may quite soon become known throughout all Derbyshire as Lady Virago.

Perhaps a slight setback, he thought as he settled himself for the evening's entertainment, but scarcely a rout, and really, quite unavoidable under the circumstances. Nonetheless a wife with a temperament would soon prove intolerable, and thus strategies that had, until now, played but a minor role would have to be accorded greater significance. Perhaps a bit more misdirection might be in order, if only to provide him time to teach her better manners.

As to other matters, the wager appeared to be creating more trouble than he had anticipated. Ridiculous not to come right out and tell the world how great a fool Edmund had been, but honor and an overnice sense of courtesy must ever lie as obstacles in the path of a man with a dilemma. Beggaring Upminster was no part of his plan, certainly, but silence at this juncture was no doubt the will of Providence.

The room was hot, but the pretty young woman approaching him much too slowly on her hands and knees no doubt appreciated its warmth, for she wore not a stitch of clothing. She did not know him, for as usual here, he was masked. He crooked a finger, urging her to greater speed, and opened his robe, baring himself, wishing all women were as submissive—and as eager to please—as this one promised to be.

Nine

The following afternoon, Lady Hermione, obeying a foot-man's gesture and stepping through the open doorway into Anne's dressing room, paused dramatically with a hand to her bosom, to exclaim, "My goodness me, what's all this upset? This room looks as if you were moving out, my dear—furniture, baggage, and all!"

"Good afternoon, ma'am," Anne said, adding hastily, "Don't run away, John. I want you to help Frannie take down those wall hangings, and the bed curtains in the other room as well. If you think you will need more help, send for Elbert or someone else to assist you. How kind you are, ma'am, not to mind being dragged all the way up here to find me," she went on, turning back with a smile to her guest. "As you see, there is far too much to-do for me to leave, even to enjoy the pleasure of a comfortable coze with you in a nice, tidy parlor elsewhere."

"So I should think," Lady Hermione said, gazing about. "This room looks like someone turned it upside down and shook it."

"I suppose it does," Anne agreed, "but it is tidy compared to my bedchamber, I promise you."

"But what on earth are you doing, my dear?"

"Precisely what it looks like I'm doing," Anne replied placidly. "I am refurbishing these rooms a bit."

"A bit?"

"Well, perhaps more than that," she admitted. "Yes, Frannie, take those cushions out, and ask Jane Hinkle where she thinks they can be put. I should think she can distribute them amongst several rooms without disturbing the general appearance. I mean to embroider new pillow covers for these rooms," she told Lady Hermione, "but until I do, I'll keep only that small pile there in the corner."

Lady Hermione chuckled. "I never did understand how Agnes could endure this oppressive grandeur. Only saw these rooms a couple of times before, mind you, for she very nearly always entertained me downstairs in the drawing room when I called."

"You look very grand today," Anne said. "I collect you did not ride over, for once, but actually let yourself be driven."

Lady Hermione's eyes twinkled. "To be sure," she said, "and you ought to feel much honored by such an exertion on my part. In point of fact, however, I recalled your saying when I was here the other day that you meant to begin making calls in the neighborhood. Thought I'd offer to bear you company."

"How kind of you," Anne said, blushing when she added, "Everyone has been so warm and welcoming, and I have paid practically no calls in return. You will think it odd, I daresay, but I've found it a bit daunting to pay calls where I am so very little acquainted with anyone. Of course, the longer I put it off, the more difficult it will become."

"No one expects a bride to begin paying calls before the first month of her marriage is out, my dear. It was only to be expected that you would spend at least that much time getting to know your new husband and family. But I did think that having formed the intention to begin, you might like some company."

"I shall like it above all things, thank you. Hello, Sylvia," she added, seeing the little girl peek through the doorway from the bedchamber, as if she were deciding whether to enter or flee. "Is this not an amazing mess we've created?"

The child stood silently, gazing at the upheaval, and then, to Anne's dismay, tears began trickling down her pale cheeks.

"Oh, my dearest one," Anne exclaimed, moving swiftly to kneel before her, a gentle hand on each thin shoulder, "please, don't cry. I promise you, we are not turning your mama out. We are merely making these rooms more comfortable for me to live in. Look here, at what I've set aside just for you."

She got up and went to a painting leaning with its face against the wall and turned it toward the child. "I have already spoken to Andrew," Anne said, "to ask him if he had any objection to your keeping this lovely portrait of your mama in your own bedchamber. I think it is much nicer than the formal one hanging in the picture gallery, and both Andrew and I thought you might wish to keep it near you. Would you like that?"

For a moment there was no response while Sylvia stared at the painting of her mother. Then, slowly, she faced Anne, tears still sparkling on her cheeks and eyelashes, but her eyes were shining now. She nodded.

With a tremendous sense of relief, Anne said, "John will take it to your room straightaway. You must go with him to show him just where to hang it, and then you may come back to help supervise what we are doing here. Will you do that at once, please, John, and then collect some men to go with you to the salon near the first-floor landing, where you can hang those curtains in place of the blue ones we took down earlier? The wall hangings are to go in the north gallery, opposite the windows. They will get no direct sunlight there to damage them, but there will be light enough for visitors to see them clearly. Oh, and you had better ask Mrs. Burdekin to look at them when you hang them, to see if any need to be sent out for cleaning. I know my mother has ours done by the Axminster people about once every five years, so I suspect that someone should at least be sent for to look at them, but Mrs. Burdekin will know."

"Will she indeed?" Lady Hermione said *sotto voce* when the footman had left the room with Sylvia. "You are very decisive today, my dear. I confess, I almost expect Bagshaw to appear at my shoulder, suggesting that all this ought to be left for another day, or done differently, or not done at all."

Anne grimaced, glancing hastily about to see who might have overheard her outspoken friend. No one else was in the room just then, however, except for Maisie, who was stripping the cushions from the window seat, much to Juliette's apparent outrage. When the little cat humped its back and spat at her, Anne chuckled. Then, turning back to Lady Hermione, she said quietly, "I do not think Bagshaw will express disapproval of my actions today. At least, I hope he will not, for I feel quite militant and capable of routing all challengers."

Lady Hermione raised her eyebrows. "Dear me, did I miss something? You are indeed different today, my dear."

"Am I? I suppose I am, at that." Seeing her friend's bewilderment, she laughed and said, "I cannot tell you the whole, for there are bits that are not mine to repeat, but I can tell you that Bagshaw wanted to sack one of the housemaids and I prevented it. Perhaps that does not sound like much to you, but it felt like a very great victory to me."

"I'm sure it did," Lady Hermione said. "He is very strict, and I know he has discharged other maids for small offenses, for Ashby has said as much to me. There was one last year, in fact, whom Ashby said was an excellent chambermaid. I assumed that meant she was pretty—considering the source, you know."

"Most of the maids here are very pretty," Anne said, "so it would not be odd if she was. In this case, I simply thought the infraction was too small to warrant the punishment. I would not have been able to influence the outcome, however, had Lord Michael not agreed with me."

"Ah, but I suspect there is more to the matter than that," Lady Hermione said, "for I no longer see the careful, submissive wife I have grown to know and sympathize with. I believe you have taken a step forward, my dear, and I congratulate you."

"Let us say only that I won a minor skirmish, ma'am, and

hope that larger battles do not lie in wait for me ahead. Do you not think blue curtains will look well in here?"

"I do, indeed." Apparently accepting the abrupt change of subject, she gestured toward the gaudy carpet. "Are you having this awful thing taken up, as well?"

Relieved that Lady Hermione seemed disinclined to demand further explanation, Anne said wistfully, "I would certainly like to banish it to some other room, but I don't know if I dare throw out everything. I'm concerned about Sylvia's feelings."

"She will survive," Lady Hermione said. "In my opinion, you should finish the whole business now that you have begun it. Only think how much more difficult it will be to take up the carpet after you have attended to everything else and find that you simply cannot bear to live with it."

Half convinced, Anne said, "I did think the blue and cream Aubusson in the salon off the upper hall would look well here, for I want softer colors throughout. But I've already robbed that room of its curtains, and if I put the red curtains and carpet in there, it will be nearly as garish as this room was."

"No, it won't, for the walls there are cream-colored and the molding is picked out in gilt. All those colorful tapestries will be elsewhere, and as I recall them, the furnishings in that salon are dark with cream-colored upholstery. I think you should do it. That floral Aubusson is the very thing for this room, and if I am not mistaken, there is a similar one in one of the guest bedchambers in the northeast wing, where I slept some years ago. In my opinion, that one would do very well for your bedchamber."

Anne needed no further urging, and when Jane Hinkle passed through to the bedchamber a few minutes later, carrying a silver-embroidered pale blue satin bedspread and matching pillow covers, Anne gave the necessary orders to have the carpets taken up and replaced. Jane smiled, her approval unmistakable, but instead of hurrying to execute Anne's orders, she said diffidently, "I wonder if I might speak a moment privately with your ladyship."

"Not just now, I'm afraid," Anne said. "As you see, Lady Hermione has come to call. I will speak with you later."

Within minutes, two under-footmen were rolling up the gaudy red and purple carpets in each room. Watching them, Anne said suddenly, "Good gracious, I quite forgot that I shall have to change my dress if I am to pay calls with you. What am I to do?"

"Use Michael's dressing room," Lady Hermione advised promptly. "You've only to have Maisie carry your dress in there and post one of the other maids as a look-out to keep Michael's valet out until you are decent again. Go ahead. I'll wait for you here and keep things going while you're dressing."

"I can't ask you to do that, ma'am."

"Nonsense, I shall enjoy myself hugely. I can see just what effect you are attempting to create, so I shan't do anything you won't like, and I shall enjoy feeling needed, you know. My brother don't let me give many orders, for he's a crusty old bachelor, set in his ways. I thought he'd welcome a female to run his household, particularly since he complained before I came that his housekeeper seemed more and more taken up with the needs of her ailing mother than with him, but since my arrival, she has been most dependable, so he just wants things to go on as they have these past twenty years and more. Though he never misses the races at York or Newmarket, and frequently takes a bolt into Chesterfield on affairs he does not see fit to confide to me, I'm afraid Wilfred has not the least sense of adventure."

Anne grinned at her. "What a pity, ma'am, when yours must be as great as ever Lord Ashby's is. Well, you may give any orders you like in here, and if anyone questions them, just send them to me. Maisie," she added, "pray, collect what clothing I will require to pay formal calls, and bring it to me in Lord Michael's room." Then, asking Frannie, who returned just then from her previous errand, to stand guard at the gallery door to that chamber and warn away anyone who might attempt to enter, Anne stepped from her dressing room into her husband's.

She enjoyed the sensation of being alone in his room, where the very scent was different from her own. The windows stood wide open, inviting the fresh spring breeze to enter. The hearth was clean, with a new fire laid ready to light later, and when she peeped into the adjoining bedchamber, she saw that its windows, too, stood open to the elements. The high bed was curtained with dark blue silk hangings, which, except for being embroidered with the ducal arms and bordered with strawberry leaves, matched those at the windows. She wondered if Lord Michael felt any sense of awe, sleeping in the ducal bed, and was a little surprised that Andrew had not insisted upon occupying the late duke's bedchamber.

A light citrus scent wafted on the breeze, reminding her of the Hungary water Michael frequently used, but the lingering scent of wood smoke reminded her only to speak yet again to Mrs. Burdekin about the extra fires in the public rooms, and even a modern fireguard for the kitchen. Perhaps now, she thought, her suggestions would be heeded. If they were not, she would insist, and hope Lord Michael would remember his promise to support her.

The sound of a door opening in his dressing room took her quickly back into that chamber, expecting to find Maisie with her clothing. Instead, she discovered her husband standing in the doorway from the gallery, glaring at her, with Frannie peeping around him from behind, looking disconcerted and apprehensive.

"What the devil is going on?" Michael demanded. "I no sooner step into the house than I am greeted by the astonishing news that all the family rooms are being turned inside out, and that new furnishings are to be ordered for them all."

"Then you were misinformed," Anne said calmly.

He did not seem to hear her. "Look here," he said angrily,

"I know I said you were mistress of the house, but I expect you to discuss any extreme changes with me before you order them put into effect. You cannot possibly know how much such alterations will cost, but I can tell you, because Edmund wrote to tell me how many thousands he had spent refurbishing these same rooms. I can't and won't have that sort of thing, Anne, and I should have thought you would realize that. With things here in the tangle they are in— Not that I expect you to understand that exactly, for I don't, but you ought at least to have asked permission before you turned this entire floor into an almighty cataclysm."

While he continued to rant and rave, Anne saw the door from her dressing room open a crack and shut quickly again. Lord Michael had not seen it. "I know you will say I should have explained matters more thoroughly to you," he said at last, "but the fact is that I have had neither the time nor the inclination. Though I'm finally coming to have a better notion of how Edmund's affairs stand, that knowledge has not come easily, for he did not trust his affairs to one solicitor as most men do. He dealt with several, and when he died, I was not skilled enough in such matters even to know what questions to ask them. I still am not skilled enough to know which of them I can trust. Nor am I in the habit of explaining business affairs to females. Damn it, Anne, at least Bagshaw understands that nothing new can be acquired for the house just now."

"As do I, sir."

"And furthermore— What did you say?"

"I, too, understand that you do not want to spend money unnecessarily. I have spent none. Nor do I intend to spend any on these rooms at present."

"Well, good God, woman, why didn't you say so at the outset? You ought to have spoken up at once."

"Not only did you give me no chance to do so, sir, but I have discovered through experience with Papa and my brothers that it is as well to let a gentleman get all his blustering over and done before one tries to explain matters to him."

"Oh, it is, is it?"

"Yes, for then he is more likely to listen to what one wants to say. You did not listen to me at the outset, you know."

"Nonsense, you said nothing to me."

"But I did, sir. You said that you had been informed that all these rooms were being turned out and new furnishings ordered, and I said that you had been misinformed."

"I don't recall your saying that at all."

"No, sir, for you did not pay me any heed."

"Then you ought to speak up louder," he said with a reluctant twinkle in his eyes. "Did you really say that, Anne?"

"Yes, I did."

"Then I am a knave for not listening."

"I should not call you so," she said demurely.

"Should not, or would not?"

She smiled.

"Very well, we are agreed that I have behaved badly. Can we begin this conversation again, civilly?"

"Certainly," Anne said. "Let me see, the first thing you said was, 'What the devil is going on?' "

He bit his lower lip, then narrowed his eyes and said, "Do you remember every word I said?"

"Yes, of course."

"There is no 'of course' about it, and I do not think I want to hear more of my unmannerly phrases on my wife's soft lips."

"Do you not, sir?" A new, unfamiliar tension had entered the room. The way he looked at her now not only told her he was no longer angry, but sent tremors racing up her spine. He looked as if he were seeing someone he had never seen before. She said quickly, "Truly, sir, you need not be concerned about the cost, for there will be none. I have merely taken furnishings from other rooms of the house to replace those I do not like in my own rooms. Surely there can be no objection to that."

"None," he said, still looking at her in that odd fashion. He stepped toward her. "You may do as you please in your own rooms, certainly."

"May I?" Her throat seemed oddly constricted.

"You may," he said, his voice unnaturally low. He reached toward her, his hand touching her cheek, feeling rough against her sensitive skin. He looked right into her eyes, searching them, as if he had never seen them before. Clearing his throat, he added, "I told you, you are mistress here for as long as I am master." As he spoke the last word, his eyes seemed to darken. He moistened his lips, as if they had felt too dry.

Aware suddenly of her own parched lips, Anne wet them, still watching him, overwhelmed by his size and the blatant desire emanating from him. "I-I must change my dress," she murmured. "Lady Hermione is waiting for me in the next room."

"Perhaps I will send her away," he said, still looking at her in that odd fashion, his hand still gentle against her cheek.

"Y-you mustn't," she murmured. But when he moved his hand slightly, caressingly, she felt warmed from tip to toe, and she wanted him to go on touching her, not just on her cheek but other places as well. She imagined him touching her ear, then her neck, pulling her nearer so that he might kiss her, and although she wondered at herself for having such wanton thoughts, she made not the least attempt to suppress them.

As if he read her mind, Michael did move his hand along her jaw line to the back of her neck, caressing the skin between the coil of her hair and the top edge of her gown, then clasping her neck in the curve of his palm and holding her, gazing at her with that new, hungry look in his eyes, searching her face and eyes as if he would find the answer to some unspoken question there.

Anne looked steadily back at him, hoping her tension was not revealed by her expression, that the lustful yearning his touch had ignited within her did not burn in her eyes for him to see. She did not want to reveal herself so plainly to him, not yet, not until she had assessed these new and unwieldy sensations in her body and understood how he had stirred them so quickly to life. Once again, she remembered Lady Hermione.

"I really must go, sir," she said, astonished that the words came steadily from her tongue.

"The devil fly away with Hermione." His gaze was hot now, visibly filled with the same desire she felt in her body. He licked his lips again and muttered, "Where did you say she is?"

Hypnotized by the look in his eyes, distracted by her own swelling lust, she still managed to say, "In the next room, but pray, do not send her away."

"Damnation, why not?"

"She has offered to accompany me to pay calls in the neighborhood, and truly, sir, not only do I have no wish to offend her but I have put off that duty much too long."

"A good wife submits to her husband's wishes," he murmured provocatively.

"Yes, sir, she does." But she had collected her wits and knew she could not trust Hermione not to burst into the room and demand to know what was keeping her. Even knowing that Michael was with her, as she must by now, would not stop Hermione.

"I see by the look on your face that you have made up your mind," Michael said. "Something tells me my Lady Serenity is not going to be as submissive a wife as her father promised me."

She said daringly, "Perhaps not, sir. I find that I gain more when I am not so biddable."

"Do you, Anne?" His hand was still at the back of her neck. He moved it slightly, urging her toward him. "I hope you do not think always to rule the roost, my dear."

She swallowed hard. "No, sir."

"I think I would prefer your submission to my will—in some ways, at least."

"Do you, my lord?" She resisted the pressure against her neck, albeit not so much as to make him think her unwilling. "I think I would prefer a partnership."

He chuckled. "Partnerships are for tradesmen, little wife, not for marriage. I think you must be satisfied to have won your point yesterday and to have disarmed me today." He drew her slowly nearer.

She certainly did not want to debate partnerships with him, for she wanted to know what he meant to do next, and wondered if she ought to remind him yet again that Hermione still waited.

His lips were but inches from her own when the pressure against her neck relaxed. "Kiss me, Anne," he said, the expression in his eyes challenging her to refuse.

"A command, my lord?"

"If you want it so."

"And if I dislike commands?"

His gaze held hers for a long moment. Then he said, in exactly the same tone as before, "Kiss me, Anne."

Though she continued to wonder what he would do if she refused, she did not think she wanted to know just then. Their relationship was still too new and untried, and she had seen enough of the St. Ledgers temper to last her for a time. Then, too, this was a new side to him, one she had not been privileged to see before, and she rather thought she liked it.

He was waiting. His hand was light against the back of her neck. Submitting to a delicious new sensuality within herself, she leaned back against his hand, smiling at him, teasing him in a way she had never been stirred to tease a man before. Her eyelids drooped, and she licked her lips slowly, seductively. "Take your kiss if you want one, sir. I do not give them away so cheaply that I bestow them upon every knave who demands one."

He did not wait for a second invitation but caught her hard against him and took his kiss. The pressure of his lips was hard, demanding a response, and though he had never before kissed her in such a way, having exchanged only token kisses with her in the performance of his connubial duty, she responded as though she had done such things all her life. The thought crossed her mind that he might actually think her more experienced than she was, but she did not care, and when his tongue sought entrance to her mouth as it had their first night, she welcomed it, her curiosity sufficient to overcome any lingering aversion, had she chanced to think about it.

His other hand moved from her shoulder to her waist, holding her close, and she felt his body stir against hers. He set her back on her heels, looked down into her eyes again, and said, "I think we have more to learn about each other, Lady Michael."

"Yes, my lord," she said with mock submission.

He chuckled. "I could wish Hermione at the devil, but I own that I too have duties to attend this afternoon. Tonight, however, we shall begin to become much better acquainted."

"Shall we?"

"Don't flutter your lashes at me like that, or you'll pay no calls today, madam wife. Or get any dinner, for that matter."

She chuckled. "I think you had better leave if you truly mean to do so, sir, so that I can let Maisie in to help me change my dress. I have been thinking these past five minutes that Hermione is likely to burst in on us at any moment."

"What are you doing in my room anyway?" he demanded, as if the realization had just struck him that she was not in her own.

She explained, and he went to the door to her dressing room and pulled it open, calling, "Maisie, come help your mistress dress. Hello, Hermione. Yes, you may come in, too, and you needn't look daggers at me. I haven't eaten her. I'll see you later, Anne."

He turned to leave by the gallery door, but he no sooner opened it than he found John on the point of knocking. "What is it?" Michael demanded.

"My lord, Mr. Bagshaw thought you would wish to know

at once that His Grace has suffered a slight mishap with your lordship's racing curricle, and . . . and with the bays as well, sir."

"The devil he has! If he's harmed those horses—"

"Was he hurt?" Anne asked quickly.

John, still looking at Michael, said, "According to what your groom told Mr. Bagshaw, sir—for, knowing the bays to be your favorites, he did ask—they suffered no permanent damage."

"Just what did that young rascal do to them?"

"Was he hurt?" Anne demanded again.

Trying this time to answer them both, John said, "His Grace was apparently attempting to drive to an inch, sir, through a rather too-narrow gate, but fortunately, madam, he was not hurt."

"Fortunate, indeed," Michael said grimly, "but if he's so much as scraped the knees of those bays or the paint on that curricle, he will not boast long of that good fortune."

Ten

Anne turned quickly to follow Michael, but Lady Hermione caught her arm, saying firmly, "Now, my dear, there is no good you can accomplish by interfering in that business."

"But he's furious. He'll murder poor Andrew."

"Nonsense, he will do nothing of the sort. Moreover, he will summarily order you from the room—as, indeed, he should before he rakes Andrew down—and you will have nothing to do but obey him."

When Maisie seconded Lady Hermione's advice, Anne bowed to their counsel and scrambled into a gown suitable for paying calls. But when they reached the front hall to discover Lord Ashby on the point of going outside, she said urgently, "Have they come in yet?"

"No," he said, "I just got word of Andrew's mishap and thought perhaps I'd take a toddle down to the stable." Glancing warily at Lady Hermione, he muttered, "Hope I ain't too late, by Jove."

Lady Hermione demanded, "What's that you say?"

"Spoke plain enough. Not my fault you don't choose to hear."

"I suppose you mean to interfere, Ashby. If you will take the same advice I gave Anne, you will do nothing of the sort."

"Don't want your advice. Boy needs protecting if he's damaged Michael's rig or upset that first-rate team of his, for it's not right that Michael should be so hard on the Duke of Upminster, by Jove, not right at all. If the boy's a bit arrogant, it's because he knows his worth, which is exactly how it should be. And if he's ordered out Michael's horses and rig, it's because he believes he's entitled to use anything in his own stable." He glared at Lady Hermione, adding, "And who shall say he ain't entitled."

"I agree that Michael is too hard on the boy," she said, "but Andrew asks for it. He may be Duke of Upminster, but unless you want him to turn into another Edmund, you'll let Michael go to work with him." She paused indignantly. "You're not listening to me, Ashby. What on earth are you staring at?"

"That housemaid," he said frankly, indicating Jane, who was wielding a feather duster at the back of the hall. "By Jove, when she turns her head like that, she looks dashed familiar. Can't put my finger on it. Know she's new, and I don't think I know her from somewhere else. Still and all, there's something about her that stirs a memory. Don't suppose you'd know what it could be."

"No, I don't, but you take the palm," Lady Hermione said, exasperated. "Here we are, in the midst of a disagreement, and you pay more heed to a fool housemaid than to what I'm saying to you."

"Nothing odd about that," he retorted scornfully. "Ain't my fault you don't say anything I want to hear. You're dashed quick to criticize and to give advice, Hermie, but when it comes to action, I'm the fellow that's wanted." With that, he strode out the door without giving her a chance to reply.

"Well, if that doesn't beat all," she said. "Whatever has got into him, may I ask?"

But Anne was looking at Jane Hinkle. "She is very pretty, of course," she said in a musing tone. "Do you suppose that is the only reason she seems familiar to him?"

"My goodness me, child, I don't know. All the maids at the Priory are pretty. Always have been. One thing about dukes of Upminster is they've a fine eye for females. And not just the dukes but their younger brothers, as well. Not that I mean

Michael does— Well, he does, of course, or he would not have taken you for his bride, but I didn't mean—" She broke off, clearly feeling she had got into rocky territory, then added decisively, "We'll take my carriage. No use taking Agnes's landaulet, for all it's more the fashion. I don't like knowing the coachman can hear every word I say, and though Wilfred's coach may be ancient, we'll have proper privacy to talk as much as we like."

Discovering from the porter that her carriage had not yet been brought round, she added when he had stepped outside to keep watch for it, "We'll go first to Maria Thornton. The woman gives me a pain and puts me all out of patience, but you must return her call, and we might as well get it over with. She has some cause for her megrims, God knows, what with six children to look after and a husband with a roving eye. They say he keeps a doxy right down in the village, if you can believe it."

"I do," Anne said. "Michael told me. What is it, Jane? You have been hovering about for some minutes now. Is there something you wished to say to me?"

Jane Hinkle, looking self-conscious, said, "As to that, ma'am, I'd take it most kindly if you could spare just a moment to speak with me. I-I'd like very much to thank you properly . . . That is, there is something I'd like to . . ."

When she hesitated for the second time, Anne said quickly, "There is nothing you need say, truly. I did very little. All you need do now is show everyone that I was right to support you."

"But I did wish to explain, ma'am. That is . . ." She glanced doubtfully at Lady Hermione.

Anne said firmly, "We are going out to pay calls now, Jane. Perhaps later you and I can talk if you still wish to do so."

"Yes, please, ma'am," Jane said, effacing herself when the porter returned to tell them Lady Hermione's coach was at the door.

No sooner were they settled inside it than Lady Hermione

said, "What was that about?" When Anne hesitated, she added firmly, "There is no use trying to snub me, you know. I'm as nosy as a Peeping Tom and much more difficult to ignore. That is the second time today I've heard you put that girl off. I collect she must have something to do with the business you mentioned earlier."

"Yes," Anne said, seeing that there would now be no avoiding the issue. "Jane came in a half hour after the maidservants' curfew night before last and walked bang into Bagshaw. Nothing could have been more unfortunate, I'm afraid. He told her on the spot that she was to be turned off without a character."

"And you overruled him."

"Not so easily as that," Anne said with a rueful laugh. "He insisted we put the matter to Michael's judgment, and . . . and fortunately for Jane, Michael sided with her."

Lady Hermione's gaze was shrewd, but she did not press for details. Instead, she said curiously, "Then why have you avoided letting her express her thanks to you?"

Anne drew a breath, then said, "That she feels obliged to me makes me uneasy, you see, for I do not think I deserve that. In point of fact, ma'am, I have come to believe that I stood up to Bagshaw—and to Michael too, for that matter—for myself, not for Jane, and the thought is a rather lowering one."

"Good God, child, why?"

"Because I don't want to admit even to myself that I used Jane's predicament to further my own cause."

"Poppycock."

Anne smiled weakly. "I only wish it were poppycock."

"Well, it is, and I'll tell you why. You did need something to stir you to rebellion, my dear. You had been saying yes and amen to everything anyone said to you. No man wants a wife who is no more than a decorative cipher. He mayn't know it at the outset, but he wants someone to share his burdens, and strong though he may be, and capable, he is never so proficient that he requires no help. Even so, he will never ask for it. In my experience, the creatures are too stuffed up with pride to ask. My own husband, rest his soul, was as puffed up in conceit as any of them, but he soon saw that I was as strong in my way as he was in his."

"I don't doubt that, ma'am."

"Well, don't smile like that. It wasn't easy teaching him to heed me. Men always think they know everything, and even when they learn that they don't, they hate asking a female for help."

"Most people dislike asking for help," Anne said.

"True, but now, you listen to me, my dear. You let that young maid express her thanks to you properly. There is nothing to be lost in the exercise, and everything to be gained by it. The servants here, for the most part, are inbred and uncommunicative, except with one another. You won't easily break that linkage, but what you *can* do is develop your own lot amongst them, as and when you find opportunity, who will be loyal to you."

Knowing that advice to be sound, Anne found her thoughts returning to Lady Hermione's words throughout the afternoon that followed. Their calls were pleasant, even at Thornton House. Sir Jacob was not home, but his absence was not missed.

Anne had met Lady Thornton only once, when her ladyship had paid the obligatory bride call and sat with her the obligatory twenty minutes, but she found that on home ground Lady Thornton was perfectly amiable. She did not complain about her health above once or twice, and took evident pleasure in making known to Lady Michael her two eldest daughters, both handsome young women who would soon emerge from the schoolroom.

After visiting other homes in the neighborhood, Anne and Lady Hermione ended their day with the squire's wife, a close friend of Lady Hermione's, who, to Anne's delight, was addicted to gardening.

"I am so glad to hear you are putting the gardens at the Priory to rights at last," Mrs. Hazlitt said.

"I only wish the work could go faster," Anne said. "I can see just how everything ought to be, but although the kitchen gardens are in better trim now, we have not yet hired more men to begin in earnest on the lawns and borders."

"False economy," Mrs. Hazlitt said, not mincing words or pretending to misunderstand her. "It will cost a good deal more to replace lawns and shrubbery that die from lack of attention than it will to tend them properly now. Indeed, it oughtn't to cost much at all. Let me see," she added thoughtfully, "what you need is an excuse that will galvanize your own people to action. When does Lord Michael plan to open the house to the public again?"

"I don't know," Anne said. "He thought it wrong to do so while the family remained in deep mourning."

Lady Hermione chuckled. "He can hardly insist that is still the case, not when he's been married a full month and more."

Thoughtfully Anne said, "I don't know that I can convince him to open the house on a regular basis yet, but I wonder if he might not agree to a public day. I know, at home, we have them at least twice a year, at midsummer and Christmas. Perhaps . . ."

"The very thing," her two companions agreed in unison.

Anne and Lady Hermione took their departure a few minutes later, arriving back at the Priory shortly before the dinner hour. When Anne invited Lady Hermione to stay for the meal, she accepted with alacrity, but added, laughing, "I've no wish to wear out my welcome here, you know, and already Ashby looks at me in annoyance when I arrive and demands to know if I've taken to haunting houses in my spare time. Today he wanted to know if Wilfred had thrown me out in order to entertain houris in my absence. As if Wilfred would do any such thing!"

Anne smiled at the sally. "You will not wear out your welcome, ma'am, on any account, and I doubt that there can be many houris in Derbyshire, even if Viscount Cressbrook were the sort to indulge in such entertainment."

"Men will always find entertainment, particularly when left to their own devices, which Wilfred has been for far too long."

Anne took her upstairs so they might tidy themselves, and when they entered her dressing room, she saw that the servants had been hard at work. The room was as neat as a new pin, everything was in place, and the effect was everything she had hoped it would be.

In place of the gaudy red, purple, and blue carpet lay the lovely Aubusson with a muted floral design in shades of pale pink and blue, with pale yellow accents. Pale blue curtains to match framed the windows. In her bedchamber the bed had been spread with blue satin and rehung with cheerful curtains embroidered with flowers, birds, and butterflies in a modern Chinese pattern.

"Much better than the red velvet," Lady Hermione said, giving her cloak to Maisie, who had been waiting to assist them. "Don't you agree, Maisie?"

"Oh, yes, ma'am, and not a quibble from anyone, Miss Anne, not even Mr. Bagshaw. I do think it's pretty now, and a much more becoming style for you. Them heavy dark colors made you look washed out and pale, and no lady ought to look anything but her best in her own bedchamber and dressing room."

"Indeed," Anne said, gazing about in pleasure. Hearing a familiar mewing sound, she turned and greeted the little cat, which had apparently followed them from the dressing room. "Hello, Juliette, I hope you approve of all these changes, too."

"She don't, Miss Anne. She spent most of the afternoon with Lady Sylvia and Nurse Moffat, reading fairy tales."

Anne picked up the kitten and began stroking her before a prickling sensation between her shoulder blades caused her to turn and say, "Sylvia, darling, I do wish you would not move quite so silently. If I were given to spasms, I am persuaded that you would have given me several by now, the way you pop up where no one was before. Pray, make your curtsy to Lady Hermione."

Sylvia obeyed at once, and then Anne handed her the kitten
while she let Maisie tidy her hair. Since Lady Hermione was
unable to change her dress, Anne decided not to change hers
either, and so was soon ready to go downstairs. She stood up
to let Lady Hermione take her place at the dressing table.

Maisie said, "Miss Anne, if you would like to speak to Jane
Hinkle before you go down, you have sufficient time, I think."

Encountering a speaking look from Lady Hermione in the
glass, and aware that Maisie was determined to act as Jane's
champion, Anne said quietly, "Where is she now?"

"I told her to wait in the sitting room at the end of the
gallery," Maisie said. "There must be a good twenty minutes
before they will ring the bell, Miss Anne."

Still hesitating, Anne said to Lady Hermione, "I ought not
to run off and leave you, ma'am."

"Poppycock. Sylvia and Maisie are all the company I need
until I am presentable, and then, if you still have not returned,
I shall simply go downstairs and annoy Ashby until you come
down."

"Sir Jacob Thornton is most likely with him, ma'am, from
what I hear," Maisie said, "and Lord Michael, too, of course."

"And His Grace, as well, don't forget," Anne said.

"No, ma'am." Maisie shook her head, casting a warning
glance toward Sylvia, who had moved away to the window
seat with Juliette.

"Oh, dear, then he is in the briars again," Anne said, keeping
her voice low. "How bad was it, Maisie? Do you know?"

"Bad enough," the maid said grimly, "not that your father
or brothers would not have done the same, Miss Anne, and
well you know it, if any one of you had taken out a half-broke
team of horses and a racing curricle and scraped paint off the
sides, trying to drive to an inch, which His Grace can't do, as
he's proved today."

"Oh, no," Anne said, remembering certain unpleasant epi-
sodes at home when her brothers had attempted similar feats
with similar results. "What did his lordship do?"

"Tore a right good strip off His Grace, by what Jane heard," Maisie said, "and not just with his tongue neither. That lad will be dining off his mantel tonight, and maybe tomorrow as well. At all events he won't be at dinner, because his lordship told him he didn't want to see his face till tomorrow, if then. And there's more, Miss Anne. There's been a new tutor hired for His Grace."

"Good gracious, Maisie, how do you know that? I'm sure no one said anything to me about a new man."

"No, they wouldn't, for Mr. Foster said the letter just came today by the afternoon post. There was two for you, as well, one from Lady Harlow and one from Miss Catherine—Lady Crane, I should say. But as to the tutor, my lady, by what Mr. Foster was able to make out from what Lord Michael said to him, though no one suitable responded to his lordship's advertisements, a fellow name of Pratt were recommended to him by Lady Harlow, and the man has agreed to come at once. He'll arrive in just a day or two, Mr. Foster says."

"I see," Anne said. "Well, no doubt, that will make matters easier for everyone."

"Certainly it will," Lady Hermione said. "What that lad needs is proper direction and a bit of good old-fashioned discipline."

Seeing a look of doubt on Sylvia's face, Anne said with a smile, "If Mr. Pratt is young and good at his job, darling, and Andrew takes a liking to him, it may prove a very good thing."

She could not see that her words convinced the little girl, but since it was extremely difficult to coax someone who did not respond verbally, she left Sylvia to Hermione and Maisie to look after, and went to find Jane Hinkle.

Jane was in the sitting room, just as Maisie had said, engaged in dusting pictures and porcelain that were already gleaming from earlier efforts. Turning with a start when Anne entered, she said, "Oh, my lady, I do hope you won't be cross with me for waiting here, but Maisie—that is, Miss Bray—said

I might, and I did so want to thank you properly for what you did for me."

"You are welcome, Jane," Anne said calmly, gesturing toward one of the chairs near the fireplace. "Draw that chair up and sit down, for I do have something to say to you that I ought to have said before, and that is with regard to Mrs. Flowers. She is not, I'm afraid, a suitable person for you to know. If you are going to remain in this house, you will have to forgo her acquaintance."

"Yes, ma'am," Jane said, sitting stiffly on the edge of her chair. A glimmer of amusement lit her eyes, and she added, "In the event, it would be difficult for me to continue the acquaintance when for a full month I am forbidden even to leave the house."

"Yes, I know," Anne said, "but you must realize that you are fortunate indeed to be allowed to remain here."

"Yes, my lady, and that is why I felt obliged to explain certain matters to you which I have kept to myself till now."

"Indeed?" Anne raised her brows. Once again, her impression of the young woman altered slightly. She had recognized Jane as a superior servant, and had wondered more than once how it was that she, who had not been raised at Upminster, had come to work at the Priory. "Where do you come from, Jane?" she asked abruptly.

"Gloucestershire, my lady."

"Good gracious, what brought you so far into Derbyshire?"

"That is what I mean to tell you, ma'am, but—and I know I have not the least right to ask this of you—it is my hope that you will agree— Oh, dear, I did not realize how difficult this would be. I haven't the least right to ask, nor you the least cause to agree to keep mum, but the fact is . . . the fact is I was not quite honest when I applied for work here, ma'am."

"I cannot promise to keep your secrets," Anne said gently, "but I will hear what you have to say, and I'll help you if I can."

"I have done nothing wrong, ma'am, except I was not entirely forthcoming when Mr. Bagshaw and Mrs. Burdekin interviewed me."

"Both of them?"

Jane smiled. "Mrs. Burdekin first, and then when she had decided I might do, Mr. Bagshaw spoke with me. I believed then and still do, ma'am, that the final decision was his."

"And what did you not tell them?" Anne asked, conscious of the passing minutes.

After a brief silence, Jane said, "I had a sister, my lady, who married poorly—a Derbyshire man, he was—and when her husband abandoned her, she sought work here in this house."

"I collect that she is no longer here," Anne said, watching her closely and seeing pain in her eyes. "Where is she now?"

"I did hope Mrs. Flowers might be able to tell me that," Jane said quietly. "That was why I visited her yesterday, but perhaps I had better begin at the beginning."

"Perhaps you had," Anne agreed. "How did you come to know Mrs. Flowers? I am told that she . . ." She let her words trail to silence, unable to put the thought into words.

Jane smile wanly. "I had a letter from Molly, saying her husband had abandoned her but not to worry because she'd been taken on as a chambermaid here. She'd done similar work in Gloucester, ma'am, at the same house where I worked before I came here, and I knew she was a good worker, so you can imagine my shock when she wrote again some months later to tell me she'd been turned off without a character. Still, she said not to fly into fidgets, that she'd landed on her feet, so to speak. She wrote that bit as if it were a joke, and I didn't understand then, but I'm afraid I do now, for Mrs. Flowers said it was not on her feet that Molly worked."

Jane was staring at the cold fireplace now, and Anne hesitated to urge her to continue, for it was obvious she was with her sister again in her mind, if nowhere else. At last, Jane looked up and said, "It was hard at first to learn anything. The servants here are as close as oysters, and the villagers not much better, but I began to hear about Mrs. Flowers and how she knew what became of such young maids, and so I went to see her. I had to wait for her. She only came in a few minutes before I had to leave. I truly did mean to be back here by seven, ma'am, and would have been but for taking the wrong fork in the path from the village. I thought I were taking the one along the river, but it doubled back and crossed to the other side at a little arched bridge. I ran then as if a dozen bandits was chasing me, but I missed my time, though not, I swear, by as much as Mr. Bagshaw said. His watch must not be in good order, ma'am, though I did not dare say that to him."

"But what did you learn from Mrs. Flowers?" Anne asked.

Jane hesitated. "I don't like saying this about my own sister, but what with what she'd wrote in her letter, and what Mrs. Flowers said . . . She said maids hereabouts who get turned off by their employers end up at a place called the *Folly,* ma'am. Used to run such a place herself in Chesterfield, she said, and knew how such things were done. I didn't know what she meant at first, but she laughed when I asked her—said it were plain I didn't hail from London, that another such house once floated on the river Thames. She said they call the *Folly* a . . . a pleasure boat." Jane looked directly at Anne then, with a quizzical expression on her face.

"That boat tied up north of the village," Anne said slowly. "No one mentions such things to me, of course, but I saw it when I went aloft with Lord Ashby, and again once or twice when we've gone into the village. I'm afraid I paid it little heed. You fear your sister might have sought employment there?" When Jane nodded, she said, "But surely, if she were so near, you would know by now. Would not someone have informed her of your presence?"

"No, ma'am, because not knowing what to expect when I came here, I said nothing to a soul about Molly. Folks here knew her as Molly Carver, you see, so no one would suspect

Jane Hinkle of being her sister, and no one except Maisie has even been friendly to me."

"I see."

Jane bit her lip. "Molly was used to write me weekly, ma'am. Her letters stopped coming, sudden like, as if she'd dropped down dead. That's my greatest fear, of course, and why I had to come. My only hope now is that she felt so besmirched when she saw what she'd got into that she couldn't bear to keep writing to me. She was—is—younger than I am, you see, and was not always as w-wise as she ought to be, though our father, God knows, exerted himself to teach us both. But she was a good girl before this, ma'am."

"Does Maisie know all this?"

"No, ma'am, only that I had personal reasons for coming here. I did not want her to feel she need keep secrets from you, my lady, but if you do not object, I do mean to tell her the whole."

"I have no objection," Anne said, "but if you were hoping for sage words of advice from me, I must disappoint you. Unless you are willing to put the matter before Lord Michael—"

"Oh, no, ma'am, I dare not! I can go back to Gloucester if I am turned away, but I don't want to go without knowing what became of Molly, and I won't have the means to keep looking for her if Lord Michael turns me off. And he would, you know. For all that you may understand my feelings, it is unlikely he would do so. He'd most likely think me unsuited to work in his house, and be incensed to find I've repeated such a sordid tale to your ladyship. And, after all—" She broke off, flushing deeply.

"What is it?" Anne asked.

Jane was clearly reluctant to continue, but finally she said, "I know that gentlemen view some things differently than ladies do, ma'am. They take their pleasure where they will, whilst insisting that their womenfolk stay pure and innocent. And I know, from my own old mistress, that some ladies are more distressed by that than others are. You mightn't think it to look at me, but I served in the same household for ten years in Gloucester, and I saw my lady turn a blind eye to my lord's activities, even to the mistress he kept for years in London and for whom he bought expensive trinkets that my lady ought to have had instead. Time and time, my lady would cry her eyes out by night and behave by day as if naught were amiss. I'll not like seeing you suffer the same way, ma'am."

An icy chill shot up Anne's spine, but her voice was dead calm when she said, "Just what are you trying to say to me, Jane?"

"When I took that wrong turning, ma'am." She looked straight at Anne, pausing, as if wondering whether to go on, but when Anne nodded, she said in a burst of words, "I saw his lordship there, ma'am, near the boat, talking with t-two females. And . . . and before I'd so much as turned away, he was walking onto the boat, up a sort of ramp from the dock, arm in arm with the pair of them."

"I see," Anne said, striving to retain her composure. In that moment she realized she ought to have paid more heed to her father, Lord Ashby, and Sir Jacob Thornton when each of them had talked so glibly about Michael's rakish past. That he consorted with women of the sort that inhabited the *Folly* was particularly shocking, for she knew well that such women were often diseased and that the diseases they carried could be passed on to others, even wives.

That was, in fact, precisely what had happened to her grandmother's sister. Great-Aunt Martha had died of syphilis passed to her by her libertine husband, a man who—according to Anne's plainspoken grandmother—had particularly delighted in frolicking with trollops. The thought that Lord Michael might have doomed his own wife to such a fate was too dreadful even to contemplate.

Eleven

"Miss Anne," Maisie said quietly from the doorway, "you had better be getting downstairs to your guests. Lady Hermione went on ahead a few minutes ago."

Grateful to be rescued from the necessity of continuing the uncomfortable conversation with Jane, Anne went at once, and was given yet more time to compose herself by the fact that, before her arrival in the drawing room, Sir Jacob and Lady Hermione seemed to have entered into a spirited debate.

"I asked him what he thinks he's doing in Derbyshire when to the best of my knowledge, Parliament is still in session in London," Lady Hermione explained in her usual frank manner.

"And I," Sir Jacob told Anne in a laughing voice, "said that having spent the months of February and March listening to a lot of fool arguments about marriage and divorce laws, all of which seemed fated to continue for much longer than my interest in them would hold, I pleaded ill health and brought myself home. And you will recall that I did go to Derby," he added virtuously, "which was for the sole purpose of helping one of my fellow Whigs compose an amendment to the bill, which he will present to the House."

"Ill health, indeed," Lady Hermione said acidly. "You sound like your wife, Jacob. But what he will have us believe, my dear, is that Parliament, being once more thrown into disorder by the difference in Scottish and English laws, is attempting yet again to alter the Marriage Act which was passed after the Scottish Union."

"With disappointing progress," Sir Jacob said, eyeing Anne as usual as if he were mentally undressing her. "Marriage law is the sticking point, of course, as it always is. Our members are more sensible about divorce, which in England is the privilege of the rich—as it should be. In Scotland, divorce is the right of all except the utterly destitute, which is just plain foolishness, but at least Scottish divorces are not recognized in England."

Lady Hermione said sharply, "Divorce in England, sir, is the privilege only of rich *men*. Parliament will accept a husband's suit on the ground of his wife's adultery, but they certainly will not accept a wife's suit on that same ground."

Casting her a look of dislike, Sir Jacob said, "Certainly not. How ridiculous! A husband, my dear Hermione, cannot present his wife with an illegitimate brat to raise as her own, at *her* expense. Consider that before you prate such nonsense to anyone else."

"He's got a point the better of you there, Hermie," Lord Ashby said, "but ain't it dashed hard for anyone to be divorced, Jake?"

"It should be," Sir Jacob said. "If it were not, every man who desired to get rid of his wife would take a mistress and desert the wife, thereby driving her to apply for divorce. And if it were so simple, wives would soon become uneasy about their position, which would create suspicions, endless quarrels, and a separation of interests between husbands and wives, all of which would be detrimental to the peace of the family and security of women."

"Good God," Lady Hermione said disdainfully, "how noble you make it all sound! The Scots are clearly wiser about such things."

"Nonsense, it is a very good thing that their divorces are not recognized here and a great pity that we cannot say the same for their marriages. Are you aware, dear ma'am, that a couple may travel to Scotland and contract a clandestine marriage, which must then be held valid by English courts despite the fact that the same clandestine marriage performed in England would not be valid? The Scottish law of marriage, I promise you, is such as no rational lawgiver could ever approve, for it demands only a declaration by both parties that they wish to be viewed as husband and wife. One must, after all, have a concern for property as well as for morals in such things. And even you must agree that the danger to property is enormous when an English heiress can elope to Scotland for the sole purpose of contracting a clandestine marriage, and thus avoid the provisions of that very Marriage Act you mentioned, which strongly forbids such marriages."

Bagshaw entered to announce that dinner was served, and Anne, aware that Michael had been silently watching her while the others argued, encountered her husband's gaze when she stood up. He was dressed more formally than usual, in a maroon velvet coat and cream-colored knee breeches, and he looked even more handsome than usual. She saw in an instant that he was remembering their earlier encounter, and no sooner did her eyes meet his than the sensations he had awakened in her body began to tease her again.

He offered his arm, and while her mind strove to overrule her body's yearnings, she obediently laid her hand upon it. When he placed his hand atop hers, its warmth stirred more imaginings. As she took her seat at the table, however, her imagination suddenly presented her with a picture of him lying with a diseased harlot, and unbidden, a second vision leapt from deep in her memory of Great-Aunt Martha, her face ravaged by the symptoms of syphilis.

That Michael might prove to be another such man as her great-uncle was appalling, and the thought of sharing her bed with him again, that very night, before she knew the truth of Jane Hinkle's observations, was unbearable. But how she could avoid him if he commanded her— She could not. She was his wife, bound by her sacred duty to obey him.

"You are very quiet this evening, Lady Michael," Sir Jacob said suddenly.

Her head jerked up, seemingly of its own accord, and she stared blankly at his florid countenance for several seconds before she said, "I . . I was thinking."

"Private thoughts, or do you mean to share them?"

"Share them?" She glanced around the table at the other interested faces turned toward her. The notion was ludicrous.

"Can't think why you're dining here again, Hermie," Lord Ashby said abruptly. "Must be the third time in a fortnight."

"Do you disapprove, Ashby?" the redoubtable dame demanded.

"How you do take a fellow up! I ain't so uncivil—not but what I shall know where to lay the blame if Michael begins carrying on about the price of beef or eggs, or some such thing."

Michael had been watching Anne, but he said to his uncle, "I won't let you abuse Lady Hermione, sir. The price of food is as nothing when compared to sulphur and iron. I saw today that you have begun to fill that damn-fool balloon again. I thought I told you after you took Andrew up that I'd frank no more purchases of inflammable air."

"So you did, lad, so you did. But the fact of the matter is that unless we English stay on our toes, those misbegotten Frenchies will get the better of us in the air. That wouldn't do at all, and so you must agree."

"I don't. I can see no good to be had from balloons, or aerostats, or whatever you choose to call them. They look like children's toys, and they act like children's toys, and until you can make them behave properly, that's all they will ever be."

"But isn't that just what I've been telling you?" Lord Ashby demanded. "I've a notion that a new sort of oar will be just the ticket, don't you know, but until I can try it out, we'll never know. As to my aerostats costing more than this house to run, for all you know, my discoveries may lead to great riches one day."

"Well, until they do, you'd better find another way to finance your experiments," Michael said, "for the estate will no longer stand banker for them."

Sir Jacob laughed, made a mocking comment to Lord Ashby about the difficulties of high finance, and the conversation drifted into new channels for a time. Anne remained silent, letting the others' talk flow around her, until Michael said suddenly, "Are you still thinking deep thoughts, my dear? You've scarcely eaten a bite."

She hesitated, but knowing she must speak up before one or another of the more forthright persons at the table demanded again to know what she was thinking, she said quietly, "Well, I did have just a small notion about his lordship's balloon, sir."

Michael said firmly, "I've no wish to discuss that fool thing any more tonight, if you please."

"Very well," she said, "but you did ask me."

"You did, lad, so you did," his uncle said with a grin.

"He did, indeed," Lady Hermione agreed.

Lord Ashby helped himself from a platter of sliced beef and said, "Anne girl, if you've come up with a notion for financing the venture, don't keep it under your tongue. I must tell you, I've been thinking, myself, and I recall now that Montgolfier— He was the damned Frenchie who began the business of aeronautics, begging your pardon, ladies. Nearly had the French government convinced to try aerostats as freight haulers. Once we solve the trifling problem of steering, I should think we could finance our ascensions merely by carrying freight for a fee."

The sound Michael made could only be called a snort, but Anne said hastily, "An excellent notion, sir! From what little I have seen of your talent for invention, I should think you will soon figure out precisely how to steer them."

Lord Ashby looked gratified, but Michael said blightingly, "The whole business is nothing but damned foolishness."

Sir Jacob was watching Anne again, and she wished he would not, but she was grateful for his support when he said,

"Now, now, Michael, who shall say what is foolishness and what is not?"

"That's right," Lady Hermione said. "Why, even I can turn a balloon on its axis by employing the speaking trumpet to good effect, so it is not outside the realm of possibility that Ashby might design an oar that will work exactly the way oars work in the sea to direct boats."

"Exactly so," Lord Ashby said, beaming at her.

"You are all mad," Michael said with a sigh. "You can't steer an aerostat, because by its very nature it drifts at the mercy of the wind. So long as the wind does not shift, you can perhaps predict with some accuracy where you will come to earth, but if it does shift, you cannot row against it and expect to make progress, design you how many oars. The sky is *not* the sea."

"Never said it was," Lord Ashby said, "but you're no expert, my lad, and I am. I tell you, one day we *will* steer the things, and when we do, you'll be talking out the other side of your face."

"That is just as possible, I suppose," Michael said with a slight smile, "as that you will ever successfully steer a balloon."

Lady Hermione said, "But your problem, Ashby, lies in finding the money you require to continue the experiments, does it not?"

"It does," Lord Ashby said, returning his attention to Anne. "So what is this famous notion of yours?"

"And *your* problem," Anne said, looking at Michael, "is to bring order to the various ventures upon which the Upminster finances depend, is it not?"

"Is that your problem, Michael?" Sir Jacob asked lazily.

Throwing him an enigmatic look in which annoyance seemed uppermost, Michael said, "That is a simplified description, certainly, but it lies close enough to the mark. Do we take it then that you have devised solutions to both problems, my dear? I must say you are very decisive today." He smiled at her but she was quick to detect an edge to his voice even before he added, "Having set the whole house at sixes and sevens, do you now propose to do the same to my business affairs?"

"You make it sound as if I were encroaching, sir," she said, half irritated by his comments but relieved, too, that he sounded only a little annoyed and had not flown right into the boughs.

"Do I?" His voice changed to a gentler note, relaxed and lower in his throat. "I did not mean to do that."

"I only want to help." Avoiding his gaze again, she found herself thinking that if the king of beasts ever purred, he must do so with a voice like Michael's. The sound warmed her to her toes and made her wish she had not talked with Jane Hinkle. But even as the thought crossed her mind, the vision of Great-Aunt Martha's diseased countenance intruded again, and shuddering, she knew she was glad Jane had spoken up, and hoped Michael had not already contracted some dreadful disease and passed it on to his wife.

Lord Ashby had been looking from Michael to Anne, and he said with some amusement, "Do tell us about your plan, my dear."

Shifting her gaze with relief to his cheerful face, she said, "Why, sir, there are two problems but, as I believe, a single solution. First, of course, there is the matter of your balloon."

"Yes, indeed."

"You ought to charge subscription fees to those who want to watch your ascensions. That is how it was done in London when I viewed an ascension from Hyde Park. The aeronauts cultivated patrons beforehand, who subscribed in the name of science, and then others who came to the park to watch subscribed toward the next ascension by purchasing spectator tickets."

Lord Ashby looked thoughtful, but Michael's expression was disapproving, so before he could utter the words she saw leaping to his tongue, she said, "And as for the other problem, I think we ought to open the house to the public again, not just a couple of days a month, as I believe you said was done in the past, but on a more regular schedule. We could charge an entrance fee and put up notices in nearby towns and villages, even in Chesterfield."

Seeing Michael glance at Bagshaw, who had begun to direct the clearing of the table, she added, "Is there some difficulty about opening the house, sir? I know other great houses are opened to the public for a fee."

"Certainly they are," Sir Jacob said. "Think of Chatsworth."

Lady Hermione and Lord Ashby remained silent, watching Michael, who said quietly, "What do you think, Bagshaw? Could we do such a thing to advantage here?"

"We are rather short-staffed for such an enterprise just now, my lord, but that difficulty could certainly be rectified in a trice. And though some might think it rather too soon after His late Grace's demise to be opening the house to the public, that is for you to decide. As to whether it would answer the purpose, as her ladyship supposes, I can say only that in the past, the cost of arranging such events far outweighed the income. His late Grace, I should perhaps point out, opened the house from a sense of duty to do so, and our entrance fee was naught but a mere token."

"Then we should charge more," Anne said.

Michael was still looking at the butler. "I believe you are frowning, Bagshaw. Speak up, man, for goodness' sake."

"Well, sir, it does occur to me that to open the house in such a fashion seems a bit beneath the dignity of the Duke of Upminster. An occasional, even a somewhat regular event, when the cost is negligible, is merely a sharing of our treasures with the local public. To do the thing as a commercial venture would be . . ."

"Vulgar?" Michael finished when the butler fell silent.

"Yes, sir. In my humble opinion, sir."

"I quite agree." He looked at Anne. "Would you want to charge a fee to let people look round Rendlesham House?"

"Well, no, but it is not quite the same. We have never opened the house up, even on public days. We give dinners in the servants' hall for tenants and their families at Christmas, of course, but that is the only time outsiders are actually invited in. It was only because you said the dukes of Upminster have quite commonly opened the Priory to the public that I thought . . ."

"I understand," Michael said, "but I think not."

When Anne fell silent again, he turned the subject, and while the servants cleared for the dessert course, the conversation remained desultory until Lady Hermione, casting a sympathetic glance at Anne, said, "What about a public day, Michael?"

"Could we, sir?" Anne asked, remembering Mrs. Hazlitt's advice with regard to furbishing up the gardens. "You said public days were used to be held frequently, sir, and since the family is no longer in deep mourning, I should think folks will begin to think you are shutting them out if we do not hold one soon."

"I've no objection." His eyelids drooped, and she could see that his thoughts were shifting even as he watched her, and that he was no longer thinking about public but about very private matters.

She turned to Lord Ashby. "You know, sir, if we do organize a public day, it would be the perfect occasion for a balloon ascension, and if you were to post notices as I suggested earlier, even as far away as Chesterfield, I daresay you will gather quite a large audience, and a large subscription fund, too."

His expression changed rapidly from dawning interest to delight to frowning hesitation before he turned to his nephew and said, "What do you think, lad?"

Lord Michael, still watching Anne with that sleepy look, said, "No objection, Uncle, if you don't turn the affair into a circus with all the ragtag and bobtail in the county descending on us."

"I won't," Lord Ashby promised. Turning with a grin to Sir Jacob, he added, "Here, Jake, you can be the first to contribute to my subscription fund. Support the march of progress, man."

Sir Jacob chuckled. "I suppose I could help you out, Ashby.

There's a certain irony in it, but mind now, I want my name carved in one of those oars of yours, and a banner hung round the gallery, telling folks to vote for me when next I stand for election."

"Done." Ashby turned to Lady Hermione. "Daresay I'll hit Wilfred up, too, Hermie. Might interest him, by Jove, and if it does, he'll be bound to cough up a respectable sum."

Michael said to Anne, "A public day creates a vast amount of fuss in my experience. Are you sure you want to undertake it?"

"Oh, yes," she said. "I shall enjoy it." Recalling another part of her conversation with Jane, she wondered if a public day might not provide a perfect opportunity for that young woman to learn more about her sister's fate. Everyone in the neighborhood counted as the public, even Mrs. Flowers, and if she should attend, and if Anne could somehow contrive to meet her, and find courage enough to broach the subject, perhaps Mrs. Flowers might even cast some light on Michael's activities.

Deferentially, Bagshaw said, "Begging your pardon, my lord, but even a public day requires preparation, and neither the house nor the gardens are in good form at the moment. Mrs. Burdekin has been turning out rooms right and left all month for her spring cleaning—as Lady Michael requested—and the gardens still require a vast amount of work before they will be presentable."

But this time, Michael turned to Anne with a smile. "What do you think, my dear? When do you want to hold this grand event?"

"I think we ought to plan it for a fortnight from now," she said at once. "The gardens still will not be at their best, but that cannot be helped, and they can at least be properly groomed, though we might have to hire more men to help Quigley. We'll offer entertainment and a picnic supper; and, as to the house, Mrs. Burdekin has nearly finished her spring cleaning, so we can open the public rooms and the state apartments. I'll make a few lists so we can have some notion of what is required. In fact, sir, since they are now putting your decanters on the table, if Lady Hermione is ready, we will bid you gentlemen good evening and run away to make those lists at once." She began to push back her chair, aided by Elbert who stepped forward to assist her.

Anne felt an overwhelming relief just to get out of the room, and when Lady Hermione did not linger, but bade her farewell and called at once for her carriage, Anne was not sorry to see her go. The older woman was far too shrewd not to notice that something was amiss and would surely demand to know what it was. Indeed, she had already asked once that evening if Anne was suffering a headache.

Well aware that she had not escaped the necessity to deal with Michael, Anne knew also that with Sir Jacob in the house the men would not leave the table very soon. She would have at least an hour to think of a way to avoid her husband's attentions.

In the yellow drawing room, she tried to make her lists but hoped no one would have cause to read them, for she was certain they would make little sense. Her thoughts would not remain fixed upon planning a public day, no matter how hard she tried. She could think only of what lay ahead. At last, she decided there was nothing to be done but to get on with it, to take her cue from Michael and decide what to say when she was face to face with him.

Gathering her lists, she went to her dressing room. Since it was still early, Maisie was not there, and as she set her papers on the little escritoire, she saw her journal portfolio where she had left it. Taking out the last page she had written, she began to note her feelings and to jot suggestions to herself about what she might say to Michael. Hearing a noise from the bed-chamber a few minutes later, and thinking Maisie must have entered that chamber directly from the gallery, she put away her pages, blew out the candle on top of the desk, and went to speak to her.

When the room appeared to be empty, she looked about, wondering if one of the servants had come in to add wood to the basket or stir up the fire, but she could detect no sign of recent attention. Then she heard a mewling cry from the curtained bed, and it was not one she had ever heard from Juliette.

The new curtains blocked her view of the interior, so she stepped closer, wondering if the cat was sick. The gallery door opened behind her just as she saw Sylvia, curled in a tight ball in the center of the high bed with one hand on the kitten, whimpering in her sleep. Anne turned to see who had come in and, finding herself confronting her husband, put a finger to her lips.

"What is it?" he murmured. "I came to—" Breaking off when she gestured toward the bed, he moved past her to look, and when he turned back he was frowning. "Her nurse will be wondering where on earth she's got to, you know. I'll send someone to fetch her."

"No, don't do that," Anne said quietly. "If she wants to sleep here tonight, I don't mind in the least."

"She takes advantage of your good nature," Michael muttered. "She must not be allowed to call the tune here, Anne, any more than Andrew should. You spoil her. Moreover, I don't want to share your bed with a third person." The smile accompanying his words told her he intended the words as a joke, but she shook her head.

"I think she needs spoiling, sir. There is a reason she does not speak, you know, and since it does not appear to arise from any physical ailment, it may derive from distress of some sort. In any case, I fear I must disappoint you tonight." When he frowned, she added hastily, "I-I have the most dreadful headache, and I think I'd prefer to fall straight into bed and sleep until I waken."

He looked more closely at her then, and she was grateful for the dim light in the room, hoping he could not see her discomfort. She was not a good liar, for she had never practiced the art, and she was nearly as certain as she could be that he would see her deceit in her eyes. He said, "Do you get such headaches often?"

"W-when I am particularly tired or . . . or distressed," she said. "I daresay this one is the result of all the adjustments I've made these past weeks, and perhaps a little from the intensity of some of the conversation tonight. I hope you will forgive me."

"Good Lord, of course I will. In point of fact, I wondered at dinner if you were feeling quite the thing. But you don't want that child here if you want to sleep well. I'll take her to her own bedchamber."

"You'll waken her!"

"Nonsense, if she hasn't wakened hearing us, she won't stir if I carry her to her own bed. I'll just set her down and cover her, and if you insist, I'll even tell Moffat not to disturb her."

"Really, sir," Anne said quietly, "I'd like her to stay. I think she is coming to trust me, which is a great thing for a little girl who has lost her mama—and her papa too, for that matter. I'd take it kindly if you would indulge her this once, and tell Nurse Moffat that the notion has your approval."

He gave her another of the penetrating looks that could so easily disconcert her, and though she managed to meet it squarely, she was relieved when Maisie came from the dressing room just then.

"Oh, I beg your pardon, my lady," she said. "I heard voices, and since the door was open, I just barged right in, but I'll— Mercy, what's that child doing in your bed?"

"Just what I wanted to know, Maisie," Lord Michael said wryly, "but it appears that *she* is welcome." Giving Anne an enigmatic look, he bowed, adding, "I will leave you to your rest, my dear. And I will deliver your message to Nurse Moffat. Your mistress has one of her headaches, Maisie. Look after her."

"To be sure I will, sir. Why did you not say so at once, Miss Anne? I'll mix you up a cordial at once."

"Just some hartshorn in water, please," Anne said, struggling to conceal her relief. Not even to Maisie would she reveal that she had no headache. What she had told Michael was true. She was sometimes subject to them, particularly when her siblings had been quarreling, or just before her monthly. But her head felt fine now, and when Maisie had mixed her some hartshorn in water and tucked her up for the night, she fell at once into a deep sleep.

When she opened her eyes the next morning to find Sylvia awake and staring solemnly at her from the other pillow, with Juliette energetically making herself tidy between them, she smiled at the child and said, "Good morning, darling. Did you sleep well?"

Sylvia nodded shyly, then bit her lip and looked anxious.

Anne said, "I won't scold you, but you ought not to leave your bedchamber without telling Nurse Moffat where you mean to go."

Sylvia cocked her head in puzzlement.

"You could leave her a note," Anne said, wondering why no one had thought of asking the child to communicate that way.

But Sylvia looked more anxious than ever, and shook her head.

"Can you not write?"

The child chewed her lip again but made no other reply.

"I suppose you have nothing you truly wish to say, and no one can really blame you for that," Anne said, forcing a note of cheer into her voice. "Never mind, but do try not to worry Nurse Moffat. She loves you, you know, so it is unkind to distress her. We will have our chocolate together, and then you must run back to her."

Sylvia settled back against her pillows with a look of contentment, and when Maisie entered the room a few moments later and flung wide the curtains to reveal an azure sky, she found the two of them waiting expectantly for their chocolate.

"A fine thing," she said in an affectionately scolding tone. "They say Nurse Moffat didn't sleep a wink last night."

Sylvia grinned at her, and Anne realized it was the first time she had seen such a happy expression on the child's face.

Anne got up when she finished her chocolate, and began at once to busy herself with preparations for the public day. For the next fortnight, she kept her attention fixed on her plans, sending out invitations to nearby gentry and causing notices to be posted for the general public wherever they might do some good. She did not neglect Sylvia, however, and whenever she found the child trailing like a shadow at her heels, discussed her plans with her, speaking just as if she were receiving normal replies in return.

They saw little of Andrew during that time, for his new tutor, William Pratt, soon arrived and, following orders from Lord Michael, kept the young duke's nose to the grindstone. Anne was a little concerned that if his supervision proved too rigid, His Grace would soon rebel, but she could think of no way to intervene without diverting her husband's attention to herself. As it was, Lord Michael was beginning to behave in an uncomfortably prickly fashion, for which she knew she was solely to blame.

She managed to keep him from her bed by various and devious ploys. Her headaches were good for two days, and then she had a legitimate reason for five days more. A message from a tenant on another of the ducal estates took Michael away for three days, but even so, by the end of the second week, she was certain he must be thinking her a most invalidish female.

To keep him at arm's length, she kept busier than ever, organizing a fortune-teller for their public day picnic supper and other last-minute entertainments, including a well dressing—for she had discovered that floral offerings made to ensure the wells would not run dry were a tradition of the county on such occasions. What with these and her usual activities, by each day's end, she was truly exhausted, and Michael did not press her when she pleaded fatigue. He did mention more than once,

however, that he would be delighted when they had put the
public day behind them.

Each time she encountered him, Anne experienced a fluttering sensation in her midsection, and wished she were certain
of the truth; however, he was frequently gone during the day,
and even some evenings, and on the latter occasions, she found
it rather too easy to imagine him disporting with the women
at the *Folly.* In her earlier imaginings, though she had known
of his rakish past, she had assumed that in whatever romantic
liaisons he had enjoyed, his companions had been ladies of
his own class—all comfortably unknown to her. Thanks to her
sisters and Lady Harlow, she was aware that many women of
the *beau monde* sought passion elsewhere than in their marriage beds—though not, it was hoped, before they had presented their lords with an heir. Until Jane's revelation, however,
Anne had never imagined that Lord Michael might have consorted with common prostitutes.

She enjoyed frequent visits from Lady Hermione, of course,
but the nearer they approached to the grand day, the less they
saw of Lord Ashby, for he was immersed in plans for his balloon ascension. On the day before that auspicious occasion,
he announced with pride that he had made enough money
through his subscriptions to pay for his inflammable air with
a good bit left over, which he meant to use toward the purchase
of a new balloon.

That evening Lady Hermione dined with them again, accompanied by her brother, Viscount Cressbrook. Cressbrook
was a solid block of a man some five years her junior, whose
still-dark hair was brushed severely back from his high forehead, placing his large nose into unshielded prominence. While
Bagshaw and his minions served tea and other refreshments,
the viscount complained that his housekeeper had gone off to
tend her ailing mother again. No one encouraged him to ex-
pand upon this topic, and the moment he fell silent, Andrew,
who took a deep interest in Lord Ashby's endeavors, demanded
to know how high his new balloon would go.

Lord Ashby replied, "Ain't the altitude but the distance that counts these days, my lad. What with the Frenchies trying to cross the Channel, and our lads trying to get to Ireland, we must be able to stay aloft a good long time, I can tell you."

"Well then, how far can you go?"

Looking modest, Lord Ashby said, "I daresay a good wind from the south would carry us right on up to Scotland, my boy."

Anne paid them little heed, for she was conscious of Lord Michael's keen gaze upon her and wondered what excuses she could offer to keep him at a distance after their public day was done. That night, confiding her problem to her journal, she was unaware that as she wrote, she soon stopped thinking about James.

Dearest James,

I do not know which way to turn next if I cannot bring myself to confide in Mrs. Flowers—and from what I am told of that lady, I daresay it will be most difficult for me to do such a thing. Indeed, I do not know that she can help me even if I can bring myself to speak of the unspeakable, for I have no good cause to believe she even knows you, let alone that she will know your habits.

The fact is that I have begun to care for my husband, and I do not want him to be guilty of anything so reprehensible as what I am led to believe. But Jane Hinkle is not one to make up stories about anyone, let alone about her master. I must know the truth. If I cannot learn it from Mrs. Flowers, I do not know what I shall do, for I cannot ask you, nor would I have good cause to believe what you said if I did ask. Life is such a puzzlement! To think that I was used to believe that if one were honest and dutiful, all would be well. How foolish and innocent I was then.

* * *

Clearly, he thought, watching the little maid put more wood on the fire, preparing the room for his night's entertainment, although Edmund's holdings were still in a tangle that would take months to unravel, certain things must soon come to light if, in fact, they had not done so already.

Edmund's private debts, particularly the wager, as it stood, put a colossal strain on the ducal assets, but at the moment, they served his interests well. He might be forced to reveal the truth before the deadline, but even that eventuality could be turned to good account. Indeed, with the least care, he would easily retain his own powerful position. He had seen as much during the past fortnight, except perhaps where Anne was concerned.

She maintained an unusual distance now, an aloofness, and as yet seemed to have developed no proper wifely fear of her husband, but once he had the other matters in hand, that small defect could be dealt with in its turn. In the meantime, kindness, courtesy, a light hand—those were the right tactics for the present.

He spoke to the maid. She looked wary but not unwilling, and when he spoke again, she put down the wood basket and moved obediently toward him.

Twelve

The morning of the Upminster public day dawned with clear blue skies and unseasonably warm temperatures. Wanting to be certain that all was in readiness in the gardens, Anne slipped from the house alone to have one last look around before people began to arrive. As she emerged from the cool, shadowy house onto the terrace and into the comparative warmth of the garden and a flock of white pigeons fluttered from the lawn to the roof, she drew in a long breath of satisfaction. Heat already quivered like gauze above the pebbled carriage drive where sunlight dried the morning dew, and the borders were bright with new blooms. The well-scythed turf was a brilliant green, and she could hear the buzzing of bees in the limes. The front garden was neat and tidy, if not yet at its best. In another month, she knew, it would blaze with summer color.

Beyond the gardens lay wilderness or woodland, composed mostly of beech and chestnut trees, and threaded by mossy paths that were presently thick with bluebells and daffodils. Anne had arranged for a children's scavenger hunt in the woods, and other activities throughout the gardens, to keep the youngsters amused while their parents chatted and visited.

The south garden, enclosed by a massive wall of the same golden stone that comprised the house, and dating to the time when bishops inhabited the Priory, offered a curious sense of seclusion and quiet now. Inside its walls, herbaceous borders lined long green walks connecting little square orchards of ancient apple trees, under which she had planted irises, pansies, and other humble flowers, which had sprouted but not yet begun to bloom.

Passing through one archway after another, she made a circuit of the house, then entered the woodland, now alive with chirping birds and chattering squirrels. Emerging near the outlet from the lake, she crossed the arched bridge and walked toward the river. Before she had gone far, however, she realized that she was no longer inspecting but merely enjoying herself, and decided that she ought to get back to the house. She wanted time to break her fast and inspect preparations inside before the first visitors began to pass through the gates. Turning to hurry back, she kept her eyes on the path to avoid tripping over a stray branch or stone until, halfway to the main entrance, warned by his looming shadow, she looked up to find her husband blocking her way.

The expression on his face was not encouraging, and Anne remembered, belatedly, his command to take her footman whenever she stirred outdoors. She had not recently been so careful to obey him, frequently forgetting to send for Elbert when she wanted a word with Quigley or one of the other outside servants. Often one of the maids had been with her, but only because Anne had been giving orders of some sort or other, and had simply walked outside with the maid hurrying to keep step with her. Even more frequently of late, she had had Sylvia at her heels. But the thought that her safety might ever be at risk when she stepped outside occurred to her only now, as she gazed into Lord Michael's stern countenance.

For a moment he said nothing at all. He merely looked at her in that searching way she had begun to notice more and more, as if he would read her thoughts in her expression. She could not have explained to anyone just then how she knew he was displeased. She was not even altogether certain that it was not her own guilty imagination that put anger where there was none. She knew only that she felt just as she had been used to feel when caught out in mischief by her father or, worse, her grandmother.

Anne's mother had never noticed particularly what she did, and although Rendlesham blustered and bellowed, and was known to employ more painful measures, her grandmother had been the one who always stirred the most fear, for old Lady Rendlesham was what the servants called "a proper Tartar." The little shiver that raced up Anne's spine now brought back most unpleasant memories of those few occasions when she had inadvertently annoyed the old lady.

"Good morning, sir," she said, outwardly calm, though her pulse was racing. Perhaps if she said nothing to remind him that he had commanded her . . .

"Where is Elbert?" he said, putting that fancy to flight.

She forced herself to meet his steady gaze. "I don't know. I came outside to see that all is in readiness, for I shall not have time later, you see, and the first guests will begin to arrive by ten o'clock. Before then, I must also have a look round inside, although I am perfectly certain that Bagshaw and Mrs. Burdekin will have all in train. It is just that . . ." She saw that he was not paying heed to her words but was merely waiting, patiently, for her to finish speaking. "I expect I ought to beg pardon for forgetting to send for Elbert," she said before he could say whatever he intended to say, "but I'd be telling an untruth if I said I forgot. I find it irksome, you see, always to have to seek him out. And, pray, do not say he ought to be following at my heels all day, for if he did, it would drive me to distraction." She paused, studying his face, then added with a sigh, "I suppose that does not weigh with you in the least. You might just as well say what you wish to say to me and have done with it."

He controlled his expression, though she was certain it went against the grain for him to do so. No doubt, she thought, he was keeping a rein on his temper so as not to create a scene where it might be overlooked by the servants. Finally, he said,

"Would you be more likely to obey me next time if I thunder at you now?"

She gave the question the consideration it deserved, then said with equal calm, "I don't suppose I would. I'm afraid I just don't understand why it's necessary to have a footman always at my elbow when I am inside our own grounds with our servants all about me."

"Are they all about you now, Anne?"

She bit her lip. "Well, no, not exactly, sir, but I am not so far from the house that, if I were to encounter some sort of ogre, someone would not hear me shout and come to my rescue."

"And have you stayed entirely within the grounds?" he asked in that same tone. "It seems to me," he added, when she opened her mouth to assure him that she had not left them, "that you were coming up the path from the river when I encountered you."

"Well, yes, I was," she admitted, "but truly, I did not go more than a hundred feet. Still, you are right to remind me that I was unwise to venture down that path alone. I won't do so again."

A silence fell. Then he said, in that same even tone, "Am I now to retire, convinced that you will submit to my commands, madam? Do you believe that by such tactics you will escape the scold you deserve?"

"If you truly mean to rake me over the coals, sir, I wish you will do so at once, for I still have things to do and we shall both be too busy once people begin to arrive to have a moment to think, let alone to quarrel."

"Do you ever quarrel, Anne?"

"No, sir, not usually. I am thought to have a rather placid disposition, for the most part. I am generally accounted to be the peacemaker in my family, you see."

He grimaced. "You give me little peace, madam."

"I am sorry if that is the case, sir." She waited, certain he would say more and wishing he would get it over with. That she had displeased him distressed her, but she thought his command a nonsensical one and had too many other things on her mind just then to take the time necessary to soothe his anger.

He was watching her again, and she was conscious of an urge to stamp her foot and tell him to get on with it. Fortunately, before she could give in to such a foolish whim, he said, "I hope you were not meaning to attend the picnic supper you ordered for our guests this evening, my dear, for I've given orders to serve us privately inside. I have several things I want to discuss with you."

"But we must put in an appearance, sir. It will be expected."

"Nonsense, my uncle and Andrew can represent the family. Both of them will enjoy the exercise immensely." He paused, then added gently, "Don't force me to command you."

"I will do as you wish, of course, sir."

"Excellent. May I escort you to the breakfast parlor? I am told you have not yet broken your fast, but surely, you don't intend to go through this ordeal without doing so."

"No, sir." Taking his arm, she went with him into the house, racking her brain to think of an acceptable way to get out of the little supper he had planned for them.

From the moment the first guest arrived, however, she had little time to think about the coming evening, for crowds soon gathered and the day marched swiftly. She had asked Jane Hinkle to keep a lookout for Mrs. Flowers and to inform her the moment she saw the woman, if indeed she did come; but not until everyone had gathered to watch in awe as Lord Ashby prepared to go aloft in his balloon did Jane manage to slip up to Anne's side and say, "She's here, ma'am, yonder by that marble statue of the second duke. The lady in the straw bonnet and green dress."

Anne looked in the direction Jane indicated and saw a pretty, plump woman, carrying a parasol in one hand and a frivolous little reticule in the other. Her feet were shod neatly in kid boots, and her rosy complexion seemed to owe little to artifice. She smiled and chatted with a fat farm woman, looking as much at her ease as if she were one member of the *beau monde* chatting with another.

Slowly making her way in their direction, Anne tried not to look purposeful and kept a sharp lookout for Michael, or Bagshaw, or anyone else who might recognize her target and try to intervene. She turned away upon seeing Sir Jacob and Lady Thornton approach, but Viscount Cressbrook engaged them in conversation, and she was able to inch on toward her target. At last, timing her movements carefully, waiting until Mrs. Flowers had turned away from a woman to whom she had been speaking, Anne stepped up and said, "I do not believe we have met, ma'am. I am Lady Michael, you know."

"Yes, of course, your ladyship," the woman said, sweeping a curtsy. Her voice was not cultivated, but it was melodious, and soothing to one whose nerves were beginning to frazzle. "I'm right pleased to meet you, ma'am. I'm Fiona Flowers, from the village."

"Welcome to Upminster," Anne said, her courage ebbing swiftly. There was no way she could ask this woman about Michael, no way she could betray that she held any suspicion whatsoever of her own husband. Why, she wondered, had it not occurred to her before what a betrayal of her marriage vows such questions would be? Instead, smiling cordially, she said, "I believe one of our housemaids has spoken of you, ma'am, and most kindly."

"Did she? I believe I must know the one you mean, my lady, but I have met her only the one time, and then most briefly."

"I am afraid she stayed out that evening beyond her appointed hour, and has had to forego her days out since then."

"Knowing what I do about the strict rules at Upminster, I own I'm surprised she weren't turned off, if she were late."

"She very nearly was," Anne said, repressing a strong urge to look around and see if their conversation was being remarked by anyone. To give it even a hint of the clandestine would be fatal, she knew, and thus she held herself erect and said calmly, "Most fortunately, her fault was judged a minor one. However, I know she still has questions to ask you, for she thinks you may be of more assistance in her search for her sister. I hoped to enlist your help on her behalf. She has been forbidden to visit you again, I'm afraid, but perhaps if you do know Molly, you might ask her to communicate with Jane."

"If you know my reputation, ma'am, which I can tell you do, I am surprised you allow yourself to be seen speaking to me."

"At a public day, Mrs. Flowers, I am expected to speak at least a few words to as many of our guests as possible. No one will remark on our conversation unless it is judged to be of unseemly length. I merely wanted to tell you that Jane has my support in her attempt to discover what became of her sister. If you can contrive to speak to her today, please do so. She will be passing amongst the guests most of the day with refreshments."

"She won't want to hear anything I could say to her," Mrs. Flowers said. "Best she just stop asking questions about Molly."

"Then you do know what became of her?"

Mrs. Flowers's expression changed so swiftly that Anne knew they were about to be interrupted, and was not so startled as she might otherwise have been to feel a small hand creep into her own.

She smiled at Sylvia. "Hello, dear, are you having a good time?" The hand tightened around her fingers, and Sylvia leaned closer. Wanting to have at least a few more minutes with Mrs. Flowers, Anne looked around, and spying Andrew walking alone for the moment, she said to the child, "There is His Grace, looking for you, no doubt. You must go and watch the ascension with him, so that Mr. Pratt does not snatch him back to his books."

Sylvia grinned as if to say she knew perfectly well Mr. Pratt would do no such thing in the midst of a public day, but she ran away obediently, and Anne turned back to Mrs. Flowers, only to find that someone else had moved up to speak to the woman. A cheer announced the ascension of Lord Ashby's balloon, and Anne soon found herself in the midst of the excited crowd. Balked for the moment of any further chance to speak with Fiona Flowers, she continued to mingle with her other guests, and was soon drawn to take part in the well dressing, handing out wreaths and flower garlands to those who desired to observe the ancient custom. By the time she had a chance to look for Mrs. Flowers again, the woman was nowhere to be seen, but Anne soon learned that she had not been the only member of the family to exchange words with her.

Encountering Lady Hermione a short time later, she gratefully accepted a suggestion that they retire long enough to enjoy a glass of punch in the peace and quiet of one of the rooms that had not been opened to the public. Once safely inside the yellow drawing room, with the doors shut firmly, Lady Hermione sank back in her chair and put her feet up on an embroidered footstool.

"Ah, that feels better," she said. "My shoes pinch, and I am so sick of doing the affable with all these people, I'm afraid that without a respite I'll soon snap off someone's nose. To think there are actually people—otherwise perfectly sensible people, too—who really enjoy this sort of occasion. I'd rather be riding with the Cottesmore. It is not nearly so wearing."

Anne laughed. "I do enjoy this sort of thing, but I'll confess I'm weary to the bone and my feet probably hurt as much as yours do. The ascension went well, I think."

"Oh, yes, Ashby will be pleased. Even Wilfred was impressed, although how Ashby actually had the nerve to ask him to frank part of the next ascension, I shall never know. He complains that it's not his fault no one appreciates his genius, but this is the first time I've known him to do something about it. He is in a glow, too. One can practically feel it without even standing near him. But Michael, now, that's another story. What's amiss with him, my dear? Surely the two of you have not quarreled."

"No, we haven't quarreled," Anne said, mentally adding, *yet.*

"Then what is it, if you'll forgive an old woman for asking?"

"Nothing to speak of, ma'am," Anne said. "He is still concerned about matters having to do with the late duke's affairs. Evidently, he did not leave things in very good order."

"I should own myself amazed if he had," Lady Hermione said, "for Edmund had not the least head for business. His interests were gaming, horses, and women, not necessarily in that order, and since he was likely to bet on which of two birds would take flight first, he lost more wagers than he won. As to his women, I half expected to see one or two of his peculiars here today, but the only woman who looked to be alone was the one in the green dress with the pretty chip straw bonnet. Ashby told me she is a widow who has taken up residence in the village, and next I saw Jake Thornton speak with her—without Maria—so I thought I knew exactly who she was. But I saw you chatting with her later, and then young Andrew and Sylvia shortly afterward, so I expect I must have been mistaken about her. Who is she, my dear?"

Startled to learn that Andrew and Sylvia had made the acquaintance of Mrs. Flowers, Anne hesitated before she said, "Precisely who you thought her to be, ma'am. I spoke to her because we had not encountered each other before, and because, as you noted, she was alone and I thought it my duty. As to Andrew and Sylvia speaking to her, the last time I laid eyes on Sylvia, I was speaking to Mrs. Flowers—that is her name, you know. I sent the child to find Andrew, so perhaps the two of them were looking for me, and merely asked her where I had gone." Setting down her empty punch glass, Anne stood up, adding, "I had better look for them. I've stayed away far too long as it is, and really ought to make sure all is in readiness for the picnic supper."

She knew she was prattling, and Lady Hermione's expression had sharpened as a result, but the older woman made no objection to her departure, merely saying she would see her later. Anne had no wish really to speak to either Sylvia or Andrew, but she did think she ought to look into the kitchen to be sure everything was running smoothly there.

The odors of roasting meat and baking bread greeted her as soon as she passed through the dining room into the service passage, and she met servants hurrying along, who barely took time to bob a curtsy or a bow, but although the scene that greeted her when she walked into the kitchen looked chaotic, she saw at a glance that everything was in good trim.

"Mercy me, your ladyship," exclaimed Mrs. Burdekin, bustling up to her, "surely you ought to be outside with all the visitors! Is something amiss, madam?"

"No, nothing at all. I merely wanted to assure myself that everything was running smoothly, and to take a moment to look over the menu for our private supper tonight. Since Lord Michael decided rather on the spur of the—" Breaking off at the sound of a panicked scream, she whirled to see that one of the younger kitchen maids working near the great open fireplace was dancing about, shrieking for someone to "Put it out, put it out!" Flames licking at her hem suddenly flared higher, and she screamed again, twisting and turning in her futile attempts to extinguish them.

Without a thought, Anne dashed to the girl's side, catching her by the arms and forcing her to the floor, then flinging herself atop the burning skirt. Beneath her, the girl sobbed in terror.

When Anne was certain the flames must be out, she shifted her weight and sat up, saying calmly, "You are quite safe now. Don't cry. Mrs. Burdekin, make sure every spark has been extinguished, and then apply vinegar and water to any burns she received, until the pain is removed, when you can apply some soothing ointment." Getting to her feet, she realized for the first time that everyone in the kitchen was silent, staring at her.

The housekeeper's face was ashen. She began to speak twice before she managed to say, "That were the bravest thing I've ever seen anyone do, my lady. Come, Clara love, you are quite safe, as her ladyship said, so dry your tears. She's my niece, ma'am, come in to help just today, on account of the upheaval and all. I am beholden to you for saving her life, which I'll be bound you did."

Anne said gently, "There was nothing brave about it, Mrs. Burdekin. My grandmother taught me long ago what to do in such cases, and when I saw that no one else knew what to do to help Clara, I simply took action myself."

"But to fling yourself on a burning person! Why, you might have been burnt to a cinder yourself, ma'am!"

"The mischief that arises from this sort of accident," Anne explained, "is owing to the party standing erect, because flames ascend, you see, and feed and accumulate in intensity as they do. When the person is laid on the floor, the flames will do little or no harm and can be easily smothered."

"I declare, ma'am, that may be so for all I know, but I never heard the like before."

"My grandmother was acquainted with Sir Richard Phillips, the man who originated this treatment," Anne explained, "and he proved its worth to her with two strips of muslin. When he set the first afire and held it perpendicularly, it burned with an intense flame in less than half a minute. The second, laid horizontally, took twenty minutes, she said, before it was consumed, and the flame remained relatively harmless the entire time."

"Quite astonishing that is," Mrs. Burdekin said. "When one thinks of the number of persons, particularly female servants, who are grievously injured or killed in such accidents each year, particularly through carelessness . . ." She clicked her tongue and looked at her niece, adding, "What were you about, child, to have let your skirts drift so near the flames?"

"I-I were wishful to see her ladyship," the girl said, avoiding the housekeeper's eye. "I turned quick when I heard you speak her name, and . . . and—" Her voice broke on a muffled sob.

"Land sakes, if that don't beat all! But it weren't all your fault, love," the housekeeper added, shooting Anne a rueful glance. "Had I heeded her ladyship when she said we should ought to have a proper modern fireguard by that fire . . . We'll soon have one now, I can tell you. Moreover, after this, I mean to see that anyone working in my kitchen learns what we all learned today."

"An excellent notion, Mrs. Burdekin," Anne said sincerely. "Teach everyone, but particularly the female servants, that if their clothes take fire, they must instantly throw themselves on the floor. Thus will they generally avoid serious injury. Indeed, were that precaution generally known, such accidents would result in far fewer tragedies, I think. In the meantime, we will certainly order a better fireguard. I quite forgot, what with everything else, that I had meant to do so long since. Now, about the menu for Lord Michael's little supper tonight—"

Mrs. Burdekin soon produced the menu, which Anne quickly approved, adding only a fricassee of mushrooms, before leaving to rejoin her guests. Encountering Bagshaw in the dining room, she smiled and said, "Everything is going excellently well, Bagshaw. Please extend my compliments to the staff for all their help."

"Thank you, madam," he said with a polite nod. "I shall relay your approval in the appropriate quarters. Oh, and, madam," he added just as she turned away.

She turned back. "Yes?"

"His lordship asked me to tell your ladyship that he has set your little supper back a half hour, so that we can be certain all is going smoothly with the picnic in the garden beforehand."

She caught a niggling impression that the butler believed that to expect the servants to serve both a picnic supper to their many guests and an intimate supper indoors at the same time was rather too much, and that it was all her fault, but Anne merely nodded calmly and said, "Thank you, Bagshaw," before walking away.

Aware that, since she did not want to think about that private supper at all, she had very likely attributed thoughts to the butler that he was not guilty of thinking, she made up her mind to be extra civil the next time they met. After all, the smoothness with which the day had progressed was due in a very large degree to his impressive efficiency.

At Rendlesham, nearly every public day resulted in at least one unpleasant incident, either because men a little the worse for drink engaged in fisticuffs, or because some careless, unsuspecting female servant allowed herself to be trapped behind a barn or in the shrubbery by a not-so-well-meaning servant or guest (most often one of the gentry, unfortunately). But today, one did not have to worry that a Priory manservant would so far forget himself as to be uncivil to any visitor, or even to the maids. Not only was it safe to assume that no man under Bagshaw's eye would dare taste the ale or wine that he was serving to the guests, but females at Upminster appeared to have better sense (except for their mistress, as Lord Michael would no doubt very soon point out to her again) than to wander about in the shrubbery, or behind the barns, without proper protection. They either went about in pairs or with one or another of the footmen nearby in attendance.

The afternoon passed swiftly into early evening. Anne continued to make her rounds of hospitality, greeting newcomers and speaking with as many persons as she could, but she did not see Mrs. Flowers again, and when she encountered Jane Hinkle during a slight lull in the proceedings, she learned that Jane had not had any success in extending her acquaintance with the woman.

All too soon, the tables were set for the picnic supper, and the servants began to lay out the food. Anne was discussing with Lady Hermione the expected return of the balloonists, when she saw Michael descending upon them with a purposeful step. When he reached them she hastily repeated the gist of their conversation.

He said, "They will be back in the next half hour or so, I daresay. My uncle meant to set down as soon as he reasonably could today, because he wants to get his precious balloon back to the meadow with as little loss of inflammable air as possible."

"Goodness," Lady Hermione said, "I should think he must release a great deal just in order to transport the thing."

"He says not. He says, in fact, that it will prove easier for the horses to draw the wagon if the weight of the balloon is lessened to such a degree that they are carrying next to no weight at all. No, really," he added with a grin at Lady Hermione's skeptical expression, "he tells me the French frequently transport theirs in such a fashion, and that the balloon will actually retain its air for upwards of thirty days. He thought I would commend such economic methods, and I do, ma'am, I certainly do."

She sighed. "I daresay he will be leading a parade when he does return if he means to pass along the highroad with such an outrageous equipage for all the rustics to see. No doubt we should tell Bagshaw to lay out food for another hundred or so persons."

Michael chuckled. "Bagshaw has everything in hand, ma'am, and can even handle an extra hundred, if there are indeed that many left in the county who have not already presented themselves here today." He smiled at Anne. "Shall we go in now, my dear? You will excuse us, I know, ma'am. I have arranged to enjoy an hour alone with my wife, so if anyone should chance to miss us, I rely upon you to extend our excuses."

"Certainly, dear boy," she said, smiling fondly at them both.

Anne avoided her gaze, lest the shrewd woman discern her increasing discomfort. Walking with Michael into the house,

she decided that she now comprehended some small portion
of what French aristocrats must have felt upon being led to
Madame la Guillotine.

Thirteen

Except for their personal servants, Anne and Michael dined alone. Bagshaw drew the curtains when they entered the dining room, shutting out the pale evening light and leaving the room lit only by candles in tall branches on the table and sideboard, in the numerous mirrored wall sconces, and in the great chandelier over the table. The effect was pretty, Anne thought, moving to take her seat at the end of the table. It was a pity there were just the two of them to enjoy it.

"One moment, Elbert," Michael said when the footman pulled out Anne's chair at the end of the table opposite him. "Her ladyship will be more comfortable seated nearer this end. Rearrange the covers, please."

Anne saw that Michael was smiling doubtfully, as if he were uncertain of her reaction to his command. She said, "That arrangement will certainly make it easier for us to converse, sir, if that is your pleasure."

"It is," he said, his expression relaxing.

Elbert seated her at Michael's right hand, and silence reigned while Bagshaw poured their wine at the recessed sideboard and two under-footmen presented numerous dishes for approval before placing them on the table.

Having endorsed the menu earlier, Anne watched Michael's reaction to each dish and made her own selections quickly, without hesitation. When she refused the white mushroom fricassee, Michael said, "Don't you like mushrooms?"

"Not much," she admitted.

"Then why do you order them so frequently?"

"Because I know you are partial to them, of course. It is not necessary for me to order only my favorite dishes. We always have a wide variety from which to choose."

"You take good care of us, my dear," he said, nodding for John to carve the roast.

Feeling heat rush to her cheeks at the compliment, Anne said to her own footman, "That is all I require, Elbert, thank you."

At a sign from Bagshaw, Elbert left with the underlings. When John finished serving the sliced beef and stepped away from the table to his place at the wall, the butler nodded at him to remain, then followed the others.

When the door had shut behind Bagshaw, Michael said quietly, "I've not seen much of you during the past fortnight, my dear."

"I've had a lot to do to see the house and gardens prepared for our visitors today," she said, keeping her eyes on her plate.

"I told you there would be a lot of fuss," he said, but his tone was light and without censure.

She said, "I enjoy fuss, as you call it, and I've done this sort of thing many times before, you know. Papa enjoys public days, but Mama thinks them a heavy responsibility, which is how I came to learn about organizing them. I do confess, we never entertained so many curiosity seekers at Rendlesham as I saw here today, but in fact, Bagshaw and everyone did an excellent job of seeing that the day ran smoothly."

"We received more than our share of gawkers, to be sure," Michael said, signing to John to refill his wineglass, "and I daresay that if my esteemed uncle succeeds in bringing his balloon home still filled with air, there will be a good many more. Your lovely gardens will be utterly overrun, I'm afraid."

It was the first time he had spoken well of the gardens, and the thought that he admired them brought another rush of pleasure. She said, "Several beds have been trampled, I know, but we will soon have everything back in order."

He nodded, then applied his attention to his plate, and she could think of nothing to say that would not smack of excessive pride in her gardens. She did not want to bore him by speaking too enthusiastically about them, for she knew he did not share her passion. Nor did she want to say anything that would remind him of their encounter that morning, lest he might still have more to say about that. And if she were to comment on the food he might think she was fishing for more compliments.

Twice they began to speak at the same time, apologized, and urged each other to go first. Anne considered speaking to him about Andrew, for she believed, from rumors she had heard, that the new tutor was keeping him too well occupied with his studies and might do better to teach the boy to swim; but she hesitated for fear that the mere mention of Andrew's name might stir Michael's temper. She certainly could not tell him that Andrew and Sylvia had encountered the dubious Mrs. Flowers. Not only would she never mention such a thing in front of the footman but she felt certain that Michael would not be amused by the encounter and would say she ought to have prevented it. Since she believed the same thing, she had nothing to say in her own defense. Silence was clearly her wisest alternative.

Abruptly, awkwardly—almost as if he had been wrestling with his thoughts in the same way she had been wrestling with hers—he said, "I suppose you have been too busy with the house and garden to pay much heed to Andrew or to Sylvia the past few days."

Wondering yet again if he had peeked into her mind and read her thoughts, she said with care and an oblique glance at John, "I have been occupied, certainly, but I hope you do not think I have neglected the children, sir."

"No, no, certainly not," he said hastily, and the glance he flashed at Bagshaw, entering just then with Elbert to serve their dessert, assured her that he too was aware of the servants. "I merely wondered if you think Sylvia is happy to be home again. What with her odd behavior in turning up in unexpected places and disappearing apparently into air, I confess, I know no more about her emotional state now than I did when she first returned."

"I think she is accustomed to being at home again," Anne said, feeling no more inclined to discuss Sylvia's difficulties before the servants than she did Andrew's conduct.

Their conversation while they ate their pudding went no more smoothly than that which had preceded it, and when Bagshaw set a decanter and a fresh glass at Michael's right hand, and Elbert moved up behind Anne's chair again, she said with relief, "I will leave you to your port now, sir."

She had begun to rise from her chair when he said flatly, "I don't want to be left to my port. I want to talk to you." When she sat down again, he added, "Pour her ladyship another glass of wine, Bagshaw. Then you and the others may leave us alone."

"Yes, my lord."

A moment later, the door shut with a muffled thump behind the servants and the only other sound was the muted murmur of their movements on the other side, signaling their departure to the kitchen with trays of dishes, cutlery, and platters of leftover food that would be dispensed—along with the leftovers from the picnic—to the lower servants for their supper.

Anne said, "Did you wish to speak more specifically about Sylvia, sir, or have I done something more to displease you?"

"More?"

"Well, you did say you had several things you wanted to discuss, and when you mentioned the children . . . Perhaps I have not kept as close an eye on them as I ought, but their own servants and Mr. Pratt are very much to be relied upon."

"Yes, of course, they are."

"Then it must be that you have more you want to say about this morning," she said with a sigh. "I wish you will not. I have already agreed that I was at fault, and though I disagree with the necessity, I will try not to forget Elbert again."

He did not answer at once but regarded her in a measuring way before saying quietly, "I have nothing more to say about that, for I believe you were quite right, and are quite capable of determining whether you need a footman at your side or not. Actually, the boot is on the other foot. I've been wondering what I have done to displease you."

"Me?" But she knew now exactly what he meant, and she could not bring herself to meet his steady, inquiring gaze.

"What is it, Anne? If I visit your bedchamber, you are either absent or already fast asleep. If I touch you, you suddenly think of some important task you must attend to elsewhere. What have I done to make you avoid my presence?"

She opened her mouth to deny that he had done any such thing, but shut it again, unable to lie to him. Reluctantly, she forced her gaze to meet his and said, "I am not certain that I can explain my behavior to your satisfaction, sir. The topic is not an easy one for me to discuss."

"Then I *have* done something."

She tilted her head. "You sound relieved."

"I *am* relieved. I had begun to think you simply could not tolerate my company. For God's sake, tell me what I have done."

Still she hesitated. Even thinking the words seemed brazen, and she believed her imagination must be shamelessly pictorial, for his supposed actions leapt vividly to mind despite the fact that she herself had never seen him do anything wrong. The last fact steadied her. She said, "In truth, I do not know exactly what you have done, and that is one reason I have found it quite impossible to approach you with the information I received."

"Someone has been carrying tales to you?" His displeasure now was palpable. "Who has dared to do such a thing?"

She shook her head. "I shall not tell you that, because the person who spoke did so with the greatest reluctance, and only because I insisted that . . . that the person do so," she added in a rush, unwilling even to reveal the sex of her informant lest he guess it had been Jane.

His countenance hardened before a glint of reluctant amusement softened it again and he said, "Really, my dear, I believe you must tell me the whole tale now."

"Yes," she agreed, "I suppose I must, but please understand my difficulty, sir. The topic is not, as a rule, mentioned by ladies even to other ladies, let alone to gentlemen."

"Are you truly so nice in your notions that you cannot speak of it, or are you just afraid to talk about it with me?"

"In point of fact," she said, grimacing, "I am afraid you will tell me it's none of my affair. Many men believe their wives have no business to know what they do outside their own homes—or inside them, for that matter—but I doubt I shall ever be able to turn a blind eye to activities that I know can prove harmful to my health as well as to yours."

"Good God," he said, "what do you imagine I've done?" When she still hesitated, he leaned toward her and said sternly, "Anne, I command you, as your husband, to whom you have promised obedience, to tell me the whole tale at once. I will promise before you speak that to the best of my knowledge I've done nothing—nothing, I tell you—that could harm you in any way."

His words rang with sincerity. His gaze held hers, and she could not look away. Her mouth was so dry that she could not swallow, but her mind worked swiftly. Shutting her eyes, she said before a second thought could stop her, "I was told that you consort with prostitutes, sir, and while I know that many women—most, in fact—are singularly ill-informed about the dangers of such unions, I know of at least one lady who became desperately ill and died as a result of a disease she contracted from her own husband, who was in the habit of indulging his . . . his passions with common harlots. The thought that I could be contaminated in the same way utterly terrifies me."

There, it was said. She kept her eyes shut, but she could

not ignore the tension surging through her body. In the long silence that followed, her stomach twisted into knots, making it hard to breathe. She wanted to look at him, to see his reaction, but she did not want to encounter disgust or anger when she did.

"Anne, look at me."

She shook her head.

He sighed. "Truly, you are a most disobedient wife. If I were half the husband you deserve for believing such a thing, I would no doubt beat you soundly."

Her eyes flew open, and she saw to her astonishment that he was smiling ruefully. "I thought you would be furious," she said. "I do know a wife should never interfere in her husband's activities, but truly, I could not be comfortable, knowing—"

"Knowing what, Anne? Just what proof did your informant offer you?"

"That you are known to visit that dreadful boat on the river, that you have been seen talking to the women who . . . who work there." She bit her lower lip. Telling him was easier now, but she still could not believe he would not become incensed with a wife who talked about such things.

He certainly frowned. "I would definitely like to know who has been so busy as to spy on me and bear such tales to you."

He paused, as if to give her another chance to explain, but she could not do so without putting Jane Hinkle's position at risk or, at the very least, without divulging to him Jane's reason for working at Upminster. In either case, she did not feel that she ought to speak for Jane without warning her first.

When she kept silent, he said, "You put me in a difficult position, because I can only hope you will believe me when I deny any wrongdoing. I cannot prove my innocence, I'm afraid, for I did indeed talk to several of those women. I had my own purpose for doing so, a purpose that does not pertain to this discussion and that I would prefer—for my own reasons—not to reveal to anyone just yet. All I can say in my own defense is that I have never sought sexual congress with a prostitute."

She opened her mouth and shut it again.

He said patiently, "Say what you want to say. I cannot defend myself against unspoken accusations."

Reluctantly she said, "You were not exactly inexperienced when . . . when—" She simply could not put those thoughts into plain words, no matter what he demanded or how angry he got. With fire burning in her cheeks, she looked at him helplessly.

He touched her shoulder, and she felt the warmth of his hand through the thin fabric of her gown. Looking into her eyes, he said, "Anne, my sweet, I never pretended I was a saint before we met. I didn't even deny the character ascribed to me by Jake Thornton. But what I was and what I did before we married need be of no concern to you now—not even if I still had time for such things, which I certainly do not. I give you my solemn word that I did not consort with harlots before we married and have not done so since, nor will I do so in the future. Such behavior is simply not in my nature. In short, I am not Jake Thornton."

"No, you are not," she agreed, feeling herself relax and her doubts dissolve as if they had never existed. "I see now, I was most unfair to think you were cut from the same bolt of cloth."

"Do you believe me then, Anne?"

"Yes, Michael, I do."

He stood up then and held out a hand to her, and she placed her own in his, letting him draw her to her feet. When he took the decanter from the table, she looked at him in surprise.

"Pick up our glasses, will you?" he said. "We are going to finish this conversation upstairs, and I do not want to be interrupted by a servant merely because I become thirsty."

When she picked up only his empty glass, he waited patiently, pointedly, until she picked up hers. Then he opened the door. When she stepped past him, he put his free arm around her, kicked the door shut, and urged her toward the stairs, murmuring close to her ear, "It occurs to me, little wife, that I have resisted the temptation to display my considerable expertise before now, fearing to dismay you, or even to frighten you."

Nearly dropping their glasses, she looked quickly up to see amusement in his eyes. "H-have you indeed, sir?"

"I have. And since you deserve at least some small punishment for so sadly misjudging your husband, perhaps the time has come to show you just what sorts of things I *am* capable of."

His voice was low, reminding her now not so much of the king of beasts but of Juliette's purr when the little cat was particularly contented. Anne's body responded to the sound in a way that shook her, as if every nerve had leapt to attention.

Upstairs, when she would have passed his rooms to enter her own, Michael stopped her, saying, "No, sweetheart, I don't intend to let you out of my sight tonight for a minute, and I don't mean to have my plans countered simply because you find young Sylvia curled up in your bed again."

"Sylvia is no doubt still outside with all the others, sir, but Maisie will be waiting to attend me."

"Then she will wait in vain," he murmured, opening the door to his dressing room.

Foster leapt to his feet when they entered. The wardrobe door stood open, and the valet held one of Michael's coats in one hand and a clothes brush in the other. "My lord," he exclaimed, "I did not expect you for several hours yet."

"It is not your business to expect me at all," Michael said. But then he chuckled at the crushed look on the valet's face and added affectionately, "Oh, don't be a fool. You know you serve me very well, but take that coat away with you now. You should be outside enjoying yourself. I shan't need you again tonight."

"But, sir, Miss Bray is waiting to attend her ladyship, and surely, you will not want to undress yourself."

"I have done so many times before," Michael said, "so you

need not pretend that I shall be lost without your services. In point of fact, tonight her ladyship will be pleased to serve me, so do be a good fellow and go away before her embarrassment reduces her to an unseemly fit of the vapors."

"Yes, my lord. Certainly, my lord." Foster appeared to be even more distressed by the thought of Anne's embarrassment than by that of his master undressing himself. Hastily shutting the wardrobe, he turned to leave, adding hesitantly, "Perhaps I ought just to stir up the fire first, my lord."

"I am not totally incompetent, Foster." Michael spoke calmly but with an edge that the valet evidently recognized as easily as Anne did.

"Certainly not, my lord. The wood basket is newly filled," he added, resuming his customary air of dignity.

"Good," Michael said. "Go away, Foster, and take Miss Bray with you."

The valet bowed and left the room, and Anne, recovering her composure with some difficulty, muttered, "Really, my lord, he must know exactly what we mean to do!"

"He probably does."

"Well, I could wish you had been less revealing in expressing your wishes to him."

Michael chuckled. "I'm a revealing sort of fellow, as I shall presently show you, my dear."

She licked suddenly dry lips but did not resist when he urged her into his bedchamber. The fire crackled merrily on the hearth, and despite the valet's surprise at seeing them, the room was in perfect order. The bed had not yet been turned down, but candles lighted the side tables and the step table nearest the fireplace. Their glow and that from the firelight flickered on dark blue silk hangings and on the golden tassels and fringe, creating gilded, shimmering pathways on the wine-red Turkey carpet and setting shadows swaying on the Chinese wallpaper.

"First, my dear little valet, you may pour us each a glassful of wine while I tend the fire."

"I have never drunk port," she said, holding both glasses carefully in one hand while she took the decanter from him.

"Then it is time you tasted some. Or do you mean to defy my very first command of the night?"

"No, my lord," she said meekly, suppressing a shivery little thrill at the knowledge that he intended to issue a good many more commands before the night was done.

"Excellent. Already the evening shows promise." He knelt to stir the fire, although Anne could not see that it needed tending. When he put on another log, the flames leapt with the roaring sound of added heat rushing up the chimney.

While she opened the decanter and poured wine into his glass, and much less into her own, she watched him. Her body already anticipated his touch, for her pulse was tumultuous. Her breathing quickened, her skin tingled as if he had already caressed her, and the tips of her breasts hardened, becoming more sensitive to the fabric of her gown. Michael still knelt by the fire, and its leaping orange flames highlighted his face and set shadows and light dancing over his body.

The room was warm, and the golden glow touching the satin interior bed hangings and heating the outer curtains made the bed seem cozily inviting. The tingling in Anne's body increased.

Michael straightened, and her pulse quickened again at the look of lusty intent in his dark eyes. He said, "First, I think you must prepare the bed. There is a warming pan somewhere hereabouts, but I daresay we won't need it."

Hoping the light was insufficient to reveal her blushes, Anne handed him his wine and moved to do his bidding. When she had folded the spread and turned down the bedclothes, she turned to find that he had drawn a side table and a little settee away from the wall, nearer the fire. The wine decanter and both glasses now reposed on the table.

He was watching her. "I like the way you move," he said, "almost as if you were floating. Take down your hair."

Obediently, though she suddenly found it difficult to

breathe, she raised her hands to release her hair from the twists and coils that Maisie had created in honor of the grand day. "Perhaps I should fetch my hairbrush," she suggested, though the words nearly stuck in her throat.

"I have a brush, Anne. Come here."

Swallowing, she moved to stand before him, increasingly aware of his size, and of his intent. He touched her hair gently, and she heard his indrawn breath before he said softly, "So smooth, like satin." Both his hands moved beneath her long tresses, and he lifted them, letting the strands slip through his fingers. Then one hand paused at the back of her head, still wrapped in her hair, and he drew her closer, lowering his mouth to capture hers.

The kiss was different from any he had given her before, longer, more gentle, both tantalizing and provocative. He tasted her lips, savored them, giving little licks with his tongue as if he had found something sweet and wanted to identify the flavor. The sensations he ignited inside her were disturbing, seductive, irresistible.

Anne responded, kissing him back and slipping her hands beneath his coat. When she encountered the soft material of his waistcoat and the feel of his hard body beneath it, it was as if her fingers had suddenly developed added sensory perceptions, almost as if they could see.

Her light touch was all the encouragement he needed. His arms enfolded her, catching her hands between their bodies, and his kisses became more urgent. His tongue pressed against her teeth until she parted them, but then it was as if he wanted to tease her, to explore the vulnerable interior of her mouth, to arouse and seduce her. She had thought, despite his boasts, that he would simply claim her again as he had done before, but this was altogether different from anything she had ever known.

Her body was alive, quivering with anticipation of what he might do next, and her lips moved against his with an urgency that matched his own. She even dared to play with his tongue, darting hers against it as if she would duel with him, and when, suddenly, he withdrew his, she hesitated only a moment before she sent hers plunging after it, delighting when he captured hers. His teasing encouraged her to explore his mouth in exactly the same way as he had explored hers.

That she might be, in any way, the aggressor in a match of seduction had never occurred to Anne, certainly not with Michael, who, before she had begun to evade his overtures, had always come to her bed as a matter of duty and out of the necessity to produce an heir. Had the notion occurred to her, she would have dismissed it, certain her husband would disapprove of such wanton behavior. He showed no sign of disapproval now, however, responding with delight to her every move. Only when he suddenly swept her off her feet into his arms, with his mouth still fastened hard to hers, did she realize that they still stood before the crackling fire. She did not care about that, or about her untouched wine, for a sudden mental vision of Michael as a conquering hero, bearing her off as the prize of war, made her chuckle against his increasingly ardent kisses.

When he looked at her in astonishment, she pressed her lips tightly together, attempting to stifle her merriment.

Michael sat on the settee with her on his lap, and said with mock sternness, "Do you dare to laugh at your husband, wench?"

The chuckle bubbled again. Suppressing it with difficulty, she said, "Not at you, sir, only at some foolish imagining."

"And what were you imagining, madam? Come, tell me. This sounds promising."

"Well, I daresay you would approve, at that, but I do not think it would be good for you to hear it. You are altogether too arrogant and sure of yourself as it is."

He regarded her speculatively for a moment, then said gently, "Are you ticklish, Anne?"

She gasped. "You wouldn't dare."

"Not if you tell me what you were thinking."

"A person's thoughts are private, sir."

"A woman should have no secrets from her husband."

"Should she not? I daresay I shall have any number of them, and I certainly do not mean to tell them all to you."

"Not all—certainly not tonight—but you will tell me what made you laugh just now." He shifted his hands to her ribs.

She stiffened warily. "I loathe being tickled."

"Then tell me what I want to know. I will only tickle you a tiny little bit, like this"—she shrieked—"and this . . ."

"Enough, Michael! I'll tell you anything you want to know."

Settling her more comfortably on his lap, he said, "You're too easily bested, sweetheart. An enemy would learn all your secrets in a trice. I daresay that is the reason women are not sent to war, you know. It has nothing to do with their imagined fragility or lack of a true fighting spirit. Heaven knows, Charlotte or my younger sister, Hetta, for that matter, would be a match physically for any puling Frenchman, so it cannot be general lack of strength. It must be because women are all so ticklish, and give in so easily."

Knowing he was only teasing her, Anne said with the same air of thoughtfulness that he had assumed earlier, "All three of my brothers are much more ticklish than I am, sir. Indeed, Harry has only to see a pair of hands with wiggling fingers to capitulate at once, and he is a grown man, not a boy."

A twitch of Michael's hands reminded her that he was still waiting for her to tell him why she had laughed, so she said, "Very well, I will tell you, though I still think you will make too much of it. When you picked me up just then, I had the oddest vision of a hero in one of those foolish romances Catherine is always reading—the conquering hero. Do you know the sort?"

"Well, I don't actually, since I have never read the sort of book you mean," he said, "and if only your sister Catherine reads them, I fail to see how you can know much about them either."

She chuckled again. "She is on the subscription list of every publisher in England, and receives her books as soon as they are printed. I confess, I have read several, but she reads every day and I don't have that much time on my hands. Moreover I like to read other things as well, when I do have the time."

He reached behind her, and for a moment, she thought he meant either to tickle or to kiss her again, but instead he picked up her wineglass and, handing it to her, said seriously, "You need not fear that I will mistake myself for a hero out of a book, Anne. I have far too many things to do to have time to rescue damsels from dragons. I'm afraid any afflicted damsel of my acquaintance would be well advised to rescue herself rather than wait for me to ride to her aid on a white charger."

She sipped her wine, watching him over the edge of the glass. The port was stronger than what she was accustomed to drink, but she liked the sensation of it on her tongue, and when she swallowed, she could feel it going down, warming her all the way. She took another sip, then said, "I am not so certain that you know yourself as well as you claim, sir. You have too strong a sense of duty to allow anyone for whom you feel the least responsibility to tilt alone at dragons. And since you seem to have a strong aversion to delegating your authority to anyone else, even in areas where you ought to do so, I think you would drop everything, snatch up your sword, leap on your white charger, and ride like the wind to the fair damsel's rescue."

This time he chuckled. He had taken up his wineglass, and he sipped from it, holding her easily. She saw increasing arousal in his expression and was not surprised to hear a new note in his voice when he said, "Finish your wine, Anne."

Setting down his glass, he laid his hand casually on her breast, watching her face as if to judge her reaction. His touch made it hard to pay heed to the wine and she swallowed hastily. The gown she wore opened down the front, and her chemise had a pale blue silk ribbon threaded through the edging of the bodice, gathering it *à l'enfant*. She barely dared to breathe when Michael opened the gown and untied the little bow, freeing her breasts. His fingers played lightly over their soft contours.

She still held her glass, but her thoughts were suspended. She could not think what to do with it. Awkwardly, she moved to set it down.

"Keep it," he said. "I want you to drink more wine."

"I don't want to get drunk," she said. Her voice sounded sultry, unlike herself, as if she talked through smoke.

"You won't get drunk," he said. His fingers tantalized her more, arousing sensations that radiated from her breasts to the rest of her body. "A little intoxication won't harm you. It will merely heighten your awareness, and I want you to feel everything that I do to you tonight." Without waiting for a response, he reached for the decanter and poured more wine into her glass. Smiling wickedly, he added, "Believe me, sweetheart, I don't want a drunken female in my bed, just one who will relax and enjoy herself."

"I feel like a wanton with my gown gaping open like that," she said, but she sipped obediently. She was relaxing, to be sure, but she did not know that the wine had much to do with it. Michael's expert touch and her own curiosity had much more to do with her feelings. When he eased her gown and chemise from her shoulders and bent to kiss her breasts, she sighed with pleasure, arching her back, welcoming his caresses. And when he had taken her clothing from her, one piece after another, and commanded her huskily to help him remove his, she obeyed gladly, even impatiently. And when he possessed her the first time right there on the hearth rug, she met his passion with her own, and wondered at the delightful new feelings he inspired in her.

By the time he swept her up into his arms again and carried her to the bed, she knew that she had been greatly mistaken to think the physical side of marriage held little excitement. She hoped her husband had much more to teach her, and that they would have many years together to explore new possibilities. In bed, she soon found there was more to learn that very night, and long before they slept the huge fire had burned to glowing embers.

Fourteen

The next day being Sunday, Anne attended the Communion service in the village with Michael, sitting in the private Upminster pew with him and the rest of the family. Mr. Pratt, Foster, and Maisie Bray accompanied them to the little steepled church facing the village square but sat nearer the rear with several of the other Priory servants. After the service, Anne stopped to exchange pleasantries with persons who approached her to comment on the success of the public day. She noticed that Michael, Lord Ashby, and Andrew were doing the same thing.

She had hoped to see Mrs. Flowers, but was not really surprised when the woman was nowhere to be seen. Lady Hermione and Cressbrook were there, as was Lady Thornton, with three of her daughters, but Sir Jacob was not. Andrew had been in higher spirits than usual when they set out for the village, and even now, although he had reverted to his customary attitude, he appeared to be enjoying himself. He kept a protective eye on Sylvia, however, and Anne realized that she had never seen him direct his arrogance toward his little sister.

When they met Cressbrook and Lady Hermione, Lord Ashby said cheerfully, "I say, Wilfred, just you wait till you cast your glims over our new aerostat, which, now that the dibs are in tune again, will be stitched and delivered before Anne's cat can lick a paw. We'll call her the *Great Britain,* by Jove, for great is what she'll be. Modern valves, new design—

dashed if I won't have ribbons woven into the wicker to match the overhead netting. What colors do you favor? By Jove, you ought to have a say-so, since you're laying out most of the blunt for the thing."

Cressbrook regarded Lord Ashby with a fascinated eye and said, "Damme, Ashby, I don't want to be troubled with the details of the thing. Just said I'd like to be part of the venture, don't you know, not master of it. Said you could use the money, didn't you, and since Hermie said—"

"Oh, Anne, what a charming gown that is," Lady Hermione exclaimed, stepping right between her brother and Lord Ashby to take Anne's arm. Looking back over her shoulder as she urged her away from the others, she said, "Wilfred, if I stroll for a few minutes with Anne to tell her how much we enjoyed ourselves yesterday, you won't forget you did not come alone, will you?"

Her brother, looking bewildered, said, "How could I forget, my dear, when for the entire distance you kept interrupting what I was trying to tell you about poor Mrs. Medbury to bore me with your opinion of how much nicer the spring season is in England than in Ireland? What was I just saying? Damme, but I forgot."

"But it is nicer here," Lady Hermione said. "Not nearly so much rain, you know, and one never knows when one goes to bed at night what delights the next morning will hold. Come along, my dear Anne; and, Wilfred, do stop gabbling about your housekeeper. I daresay she's simply fallen in love with that nice doctor who's been looking after her mama. You were about to tell Ashby he needn't look to you for an opinion of every little step he takes, since you know he is the expert on aerostats. Was that not it?"

"Stap me, but so it was. Dashed amazing female," the viscount added. "Always knows just what a fellow wants to say."

Moving away with Lady Hermione, Anne said with a chuckle, "I doubt if you diverted Lord Ashby's thoughts, ma'am, as easily as your brother's. And if he thinks, as I do,

that you had anything to do with Cressbrook's decision to sub-
scribe to his venture—"

"Poppycock," Lady Hermione said. "Even if Ashby thinks
such a thing, he won't mention it, because he don't want to
take a chance that Wilfred might change his mind about the
money if he teases him. I just didn't want Wilfred thoughtlessly
suggesting that I had persuaded him to make his decision."

"But you did, did you not?"

"Oh, a little, perhaps. I must say, my dear, the men in your
family are looking unnaturally cheerful this morning. I had
got quite accustomed to them all going about with Friday
faces, but to look at them today one would think they had
been granted royal, or even divine, favor. I understand Ashby's
delight, but what's got into the other two?"

Anne smiled. "As to Andrew, I haven't a notion, but as to
Michael—Lord Michael, I should say—you hit the mark yesterday when you suggested that he was troubled. It was not
that, exactly—more like being unhappy—and I cannot tell you
the whole, of course, only that a slight misunderstanding between us has been set right."

Lady Hermione nodded wisely. "That is just what I thought.
I must say, it's good to see him looking relaxed again. That
heavy look he's worn the past six months don't suit him at
all. Oh, look, there's Jake Thornton! How wicked of him to
have missed Mr. Dailey's excellent sermon. Looks a bit gray,
don't you think? Usually, his complexion is quite florid, but
no doubt he drank too much last night, out carousing as he
no doubt was. I've a notion to tell him what I think of his
behavior. Sure as check, Maria won't dare even to take him
to task. I've never known such a meek marshmallow as that
woman. If my husband had treated me the way Jake treats her,
I'd have bashed him over the head with an anvil, damme if I
wouldn't."

"Ma'am, really!" Anne stifled a gurgle of laughter.

"Oh, don't heed my unruly tongue, my dear. I'm just all
out of patience with the woman. It's all very well to moan

about her poor health and to wish her husband understood her need for constant comforting, but if I were she . . ."

"Yes, I know what you would do. You'd bash his head in."

Lady Hermione grimaced. "I daresay I wouldn't, you know, any more than she has. But I'd like to think I would. Now, what do you suppose that confrontation is in aid of?"

Anne looked in the direction of her ladyship's frowning gaze and saw Michael speaking earnestly to Sir Jacob. Sir Jacob shrugged, whereupon Michael's countenance hardened in a way that she recognized only too well. The look was gone in an instant, however, and just then other movements caught her eye. Mrs. Flowers appeared as if from thin air and approached the minister, while at the same time, Andrew turned abruptly from the man with whom he had been speaking, and moved toward Mrs. Flowers.

Making a hasty excuse to Lady Hermione, Anne started after him, only to find that she had not shaken off her companion.

"What is it?" Lady Hermione demanded, striding alongside.

"I must keep Andrew from speaking again to that woman," Anne said in an urgent undertone.

"What woman? Oh, that woman. Good gracious, my dear, why do any such thing? It isn't as if he's got Sylvia with him. At the moment . . . yes, there she is yonder, with your Maisie."

Still keeping her voice low so as not to be overheard by anyone else, Anne said, "That woman is Sir Jacob's mistress, ma'am, as I told you yesterday. Michael won't approve of Andrew's enlarging his acquaintance with her."

"Are you certain of that?"

Amusement underscored the words, and stopped Anne in her tracks. She stared at her friend in astonishment. "What can you mean, ma'am? That woman is no better than she should be, and Andrew ought not to associate with her."

"My dear, I know all about her now. After I talked to you yesterday, I quite unscrupulously assaulted Wilfred and made him empty the budget to me. You'd be surprised what Wilfred knows. A quiet fellow for the most part, and never stirred a step over the mark in any way that I know about—except, perhaps, for wagering more than he ought when he makes his annual treks to Newmarket and the York races—but he does keep his finger on the pulse of the county, for all that. He said Fiona Flowers hails from a Chesterfield bordello, that she was actually running the place when Sir Jacob found her there and bedded her. He was so smitten, he moved her to the village, bag and baggage, where he's kept her ever since—in fine style, too, by what Wilfred said."

"But that is all the more reason that Andrew should not talk to her," Anne protested.

"Poppycock. Where do you suppose the males in this country learn what they need to know to procreate. Just imagine what would happen if a woman had to depend on her instinct rather than her husband's prior knowledge when she first approached the marriage bed. My goodness me, Anne, think of your own ignorance and imagine that scene compounded by Michael's knowledge being as small as your own. My dear, it don't bear thinking of!"

Anne, remembering the experience not only of her wedding night but of the one she had just spent with him, barely stopped herself from agreeing heartily with the older woman's sentiments. Forcing her thoughts relentlessly back to the young duke, and noting with relief that the minister had intervened in time to prevent his speaking to the dubious widow, she said, "Are you saying that Andrew ought to acquire such experience from the likes of Mrs. Flowers, ma'am? Surely, he is much too young."

"Fourteen, ain't he?"

"Yes, you know he is."

"Quite old enough, in my opinion, to speak to her."

Anne was shocked. "You can't mean that! He's only a boy."

"Mrs. Flowers will no doubt treat him like a man, however, and therein will lie her attraction, particularly when Michael persists in treating him so strictly. I am not saying she will take him to her bed, you know, only that she will behave to him as if he were grown up, and without toad-eating him. Only look at the boy now, trying to keep his attention on what Mr. Dailey is saying to him, whilst his gaze keeps drifting to her."

"But what can she be doing here? I am certain she did not attend the Communion service."

"No, Wilfred says she never does, on account of sinning the way she does and not wanting to take Communion on account of it. She attends morning or evening prayer instead, he said. Wilfred did say she serves as a sacristan now and again," Lady Hermione added with a knowing smile. "Even the most starched up pillar of rectitude could not refuse such an offer, you know—not with Mary Magdalene right there in the Bible, and all—and Wilfred said Mrs. Flowers occasionally puts flowers on the altar, as well. No doubt it is one of those duties that has brought her here now."

Whatever had brought her, Anne noted that when Mr. Dailey directed Andrew's attention to someone else and Mrs. Flowers approached the parson, her conversation with him was as amiable as Michael's parting words with Sir Jacob had seemed to be. Sir Jacob and his wife had gone home, and it was not long before Michael said it was time for the Priory group to leave as well.

He was preoccupied, and if after the warm interlude the previous evening, Anne had hoped to increase her understanding of the man she had married, she soon discovered her error. He spent that afternoon and night, and the following two days with whatever business it was that kept him so frequently occupied, and she scarcely saw his face. Though he visited her bedchamber Monday night, his stay was brief, more like those preceding their fortnight apart than the one that ended it. He apologized for his lack of ardor, but even the apology was perfunctory, as if his thoughts were already on something of greater importance.

On Tuesday, at dinner, he announced his intention of spending the next few days in Castleton.

Lord Ashby said, "Trouble at one of the mines, is there?"

"That is what I mean to discover, if I can. I've had a letter from Alsop, our steward there, complaining that yet another shaft has flooded, and demanding money for a new sough."

"What's a sough?" Andrew asked curiously.

Lord Ashby said, "Just a drain, boy, as you ought to know, since you own as many lead mines as you do, not to mention the two tin ones you've got down in Cornwall. By Jove, you ought to go along with Michael now and again just to see what a mine looks like. Fascinating places they are. Castleton is the Snake Mine. Isn't that right, Michael?"

"Yes, sir, but don't encourage Andrew to ask to accompany me this trip. I'll have no time for his questions. What with a new crushing wheel and new bellows at Bradford last month, and a new haulage road at Castleton begun in March—not to mention breakage everywhere, the mines are costing more than they bring in. I do not need to explain why that state of affairs can't be allowed to continue—particularly when tenants here at home are demanding help with improvements on their farms, and our own farm requires money be put into it, if any good is to be got out of it."

"Well, the first thing I should do if I were running those mines," Lord Ashby said flatly, "would be to invent a means to get more of the lead out of the second wash than what they're getting now. You see, my dear," he said, turning to Anne, "the crude ore, after they first break it up, is washed on a sieve over a large vat. They skim off the lighter waste material and throw it on a hillock, and the lead ore is sent to the coe—that's the ore house—to await measuring. But the material passing through the sieve also contains lead particles. They wash it again in long troughs over a flowing stream of water—buddling, that's called—to try to regain more of the ore, but dashed inefficient is what that is. I'd soon find a better way."

"You sound as if you know a great deal about it," Anne said.

"Oh, aye, I suppose I do. Whimseys, gin-engines, kibbles, and skips provide no particular mystery to anyone with an interest in modern technology, you know."

"Well, they are mysteries to me," Michael said, "but I can't see that knowing more about them would help when I've got experts in Alsop and his ilk, and the immediate object is to discover why we are encountering so many problems. Lead mining in general is highly profitable, so this series of mishaps at the St. Ledgers mines is a cursed nuisance. No sooner does one begin to run as it should than something occurs at another. It must be stopped. Their income must become more reliable, and quickly."

Anne wanted to ask why there was such urgency. She had heard him speak often of the need to practice economy, but living in the midst of such splendor made it difficult to understand his concern. However, when Lord Ashby turned the subject and did not question Michael, she did not like to do so herself, particularly with Andrew in the room. It occurred to her that perhaps Lord Ashby already knew the answer, but to ask him something she did not feel confident to ask Michael also seemed wrong.

When Michael left the next morning before she went down to breakfast, she was not as sorry to find him gone as she might have been, for overnight she had realized that his absence would make it easier for her to speak to Andrew about his acquaintance with Mrs. Flowers without Michael's learning anything about it.

He had ordered Mr. Pratt to keep the boy hard at his studies and out of mischief, but in the short time since their public day, Andrew had formed a habit of disappearing, much like his sister's. When he showed himself, sometimes hours later, he would offer but a vague explanation of where he had been, lifting his chin and looking defiantly at anyone who demanded details of his absence, then suffering in stoic hauteur whatever punishment was meted out to him.

Anne suspected that he was slipping into the village to meet friends, for, thanks to a letter received from her youngest brother, Stephen, she knew that the half-term break at Eton had begun. Moreover, she had encountered Andrew on the river path after one such disappearance and when she asked where he had been, he had simply said, "Oh, out and about," much the way Stephen might have done. But if Andrew was going into the village, she knew she must speak to him, lest he encounter Mrs. Flowers there and attempt to extend their acquaintance.

The very day Michael left, Lady Hermione confirmed both fears, telling her when they drove out that afternoon to pay calls that she had seen Andrew in the village.

"Coming away from that large house at the end of the main road yesterday, just as bold as brass. I oughtn't to be telling tales out of school, of course, but I'd as lief you knew of it before Michael finds out, just in the event that you are right in your prediction of how he will react to that connection."

"The large house? You say that so meaningfully, ma'am, but I do not know whose— Oh, good gracious," she exclaimed when the truth struck her, "you don't mean Mrs. Flowers's house, do you?"

"Well, it was used to be Sir Morton Foxgrow's house when I was young, but he died before I'd been in Ireland five years, and I recall Wilfred saying Sir Jacob had purchased it. He never lived in it, of course. Hired it out to folks who wanted it, for it backs onto the river, you see, and provides quite a pleasant view, or would if it weren't for that boat tied up at the curve just beyond it. But when Wilfred said Jake had set his bit of trifle up in style, I just assumed that was the house. And it was that one I saw Andrew strolling away from, looking more puffed up in his own esteem than even what's usual for him."

Anne's heart sank. Lady Hermione might believe in an established masculine conspiracy to train youths in the art of seduction, but Anne was as sure as she could be—despite the fact that Michael remained in many ways as much a mystery to her as the St. Ledgers mines were to him—that her husband would react with fury to the news that Andrew was visiting Mrs. Flowers.

Before that happened she intended to explain to Andrew just why he must not encourage the connection. However, just as when she had discovered she could not speak candidly to Mrs. Flowers, she soon discovered a similar difficulty with Andrew.

Knowing Mr. Pratt would keep him occupied until dinner (if indeed Andrew had not disappeared again), she spent the hour after returning to the house and before she had to change her dress for dinner, in replying to numerous letters that had accumulated while she had busied herself with preparations for their public day. She replied first, with enthusiasm, to Lady Harlow's letter informing her that her ladyship had very likely found just the person to instruct Sylvia, if Anne did not mind waiting until the end of the term when the young woman would leave her present position.

There were letters from her family, as well. Besides the brief one in Stephen's schoolboy scrawl, informing her of the advent of his half-term and his wish that he had been free for her wedding, there was an even briefer note from her mother, asking if Anne recalled what had become of the plan they had drawn up for a new knot garden on the south lawn.

Her sister Beth in Sussex was expecting her fourth child, and Catherine's letter from London overflowed with social pleasures, for now that the Season was drawing to a close, it seemed that everyone wanted it to end in grand style. Lady Crane wrote with delight of a crowded Drawing Room at St. James's and described in detail her gown for the Duchess of Gordon's ball. She had also, uncharacteristically, filled nearly half a page with her opinion of some recently submitted designs for the new Houses of Parliament, but when she added that her husband was a member of the committee that would decide which plan was to be selected, Anne was better able to understand her enthusiasm.

Once she had replied to these letters, it was time to change her dress for dinner. Only Andrew and Lord Ashby joined her at the table, but since she did not want to include Lord Ashby in her discussion with the boy, she waited to waylay Andrew after the meal, inviting him to accompany her to the sitting room near her bedchamber. "I have something of a private nature to discuss with you," she said.

"Very well." His expression did not encourage her to believe he welcomed the interview. Nor did he deign to speak to her again until they had made their way to the family wing and the room at the end of the gallery. "Well, what is it?" he asked curtly, looking down his nose at her after she had shut the door.

"Won't you sit down?"

"No, no, I cannot stay long. Pratt's set me any number of bothersome tasks to do this evening."

Repressing the urge to point out that Mr. Pratt's orders had not kept him tied to the schoolroom before when he had not wished to stay there, she said calmly, "I hope you do not mean to go into the village again while your uncle is away, Andrew."

"I do not know how my intended activities can concern you, madam," he said, his tone carefully controlled.

"Well, I don't suppose they do," she admitted. "I am not your guardian, after all, but I am concerned about your well-being, just as anyone who cares about you must be."

"There is nothing about which you need be concerned."

Noting the increasing edge of annoyance in his tone, Anne realized that in approaching the matter in the way she would have used with her younger brother, she had made a mistake. Andrew was not Stephen, not by a long chalk. Stephen would have appreciated any intervention that spared him an unpleasant interview with his papa. Andrew did not appreciate intervention from anyone for any reason whatsoever.

She tried again, keeping her tone calm and reasonable. "Andrew, I do not wish to interfere in your rightful business, I assure you, but I think perhaps you do not understand the gravity of your present activities, or their likely consequences."

"And what activities are those, madam?"

"Your visits to Mrs. Flowers," she said flatly.

He lifted an eyebrow, and his gaze became more supercilious than ever. "If you do not wish to interfere in my business, madam, then you should not do so. If—and I do say *if*—I should choose to visit anyone in the village, that is certainly my business and none of yours."

"But you don't understand, Andrew."

"Then explain it to me, Anne."

She realized that despite the fact that she had long since given him permission to call her by her first name, it was the first time he had done so, and she had an instant and adverse reaction to it. Not only was his tone boyishly insolent but she had a sudden vision of the man he would become if he were allowed to continue along the route he had been traveling. Nonetheless, she held her tongue, knowing that to issue the rebuke dancing so impatiently there, would be a greater mistake than any she had yet made with him. In any case, she did not know what to tell him to call her if she refused him permission to call her Anne.

Worst of all was the fact that she realized on the instant that she could not explain her concern to him without first knowing what, if anything, he had been told about relations between male and female persons. Not having the least wish or desire to explain such things to him herself, even if he allowed her to do so, all she could say in the end was, "Mrs. Flowers is not a suitable person for you to know, I'm afraid."

"I will be the judge of that, thank you." And with that, he turned abruptly and left the room.

Anne fought down the urge to run after him and box his ears; however, his continuing attitude of arrogant disdain over the next few days made it impossible for her even to sympathize with him when Michael returned from Castleton and responded to Mr. Pratt's complaints of his pupil's frequent unexplained absences and otherwise dilatory behavior by sternly commanding Andrew to accompany him into the library after dinner.

Lord Ashby, always the boy's champion, protested vehemently. "Dash it all, Michael, you can't always be condemning the lad merely for knowing his own worth. Pratt drives him devilish hard, and so do you, by Jove, so it don't take a genius to see why he chooses to play least in sight instead of keeping his nose glued to his books all day."

"He will learn to do as he is bid," Lord Michael said grimly, watching Andrew stride across the hall and into the library. "I have no intention of allowing him to grow up to be the care-for-naught his father was."

"Here now, don't forget you are speaking of the dead," Lord Ashby said, shocked. *"De mortuis nihil nisi bonum,* my boy."

"In Edmund's case," Michael interrupted sharply, "it's more a matter of *de nihilo nihil,* sir—nothing comes from nothing. You were not left his snarls to untangle, if I might remind you of the fact. Nor have you been of much assistance in untangling them. I'll also point out that had I possessed the same general lack of scruples as my brother, I'd have taken the easiest way around all the difficulty. Indeed, I might still have to—"

"By Jove, you wouldn't sell off the unentailed land!"

"I haven't sold anything, sir. Not yet. But only by agreeing to outrageous demands have I been able to avoid that course. I do not know how much longer it will be possible if some of the other holdings do not begin to produce their maximum income." He cut off Lord Ashby's next question abruptly, pointing out that Andrew was waiting for him in the library.

Anne, listening in dismay to their exchange, concluded that matters were even more serious than she had believed. Once again, she was tempted to approach Lord Ashby for answers, but noting that he had transferred his attention to the decanter at his elbow, and collecting her wits, she decided that she had first better attempt to learn what she could from her husband, and perhaps convince him to share some small part of his burden with others who were willing and able to assist him.

Knowing that Andrew would prefer not to encounter her again that night, she waited in the little salon off the upstairs hall until she heard him emerge from the library and pass by on his way to his own room. Then, gathering her courage, she went back downstairs, and finding that the boy had left the library door ajar, she silently pushed it open.

Michael stood staring down into the fire. One booted foot rested on the fender, one hand gripped the mantel. Some small noise she made must have warned him that he was no longer alone, for he straightened and turned. The annoyance on his face softened when he saw her. "Come in, sweetheart. I hope you have not come to continue my uncle's protests against my treatment of that young scoundrel, for I warn you, my patience will not stand it."

Anne shut the door quietly and, moving toward him, said, "I must own, sir, that Andrew's behavior during your absence may well have justified anything you chose to do to him to-night."

The weariness in his expression vanished, replaced by a frown. He said sharply, "Was he discourteous to you?"

She smiled ruefully. "I think my notion of courtesy does not march precisely with that accepted in dukes of Upminster, sir. Certainly, what passes for his customary attitude would not suit my father; and my grandmother would have sharp words to say to anyone, duke or commoner, who dared speak to her in the tone Andrew employs in merely responding to a casual greeting."

Michael grimaced. "My brother chose to be amused by his cocksure posturing when Andrew was scarcely out of leading strings, and my sister-in-law denied him nothing. Thus, his servants came to think the arrogance was expected of him.

And, indeed, Edmund himself behaved in much the same way, so Andrew's demeanor is not to be wondered at, I'm sure."

"Your sister Charlotte said that dukes of Upminster think themselves grander than God," Anne said, smiling. "I did think before that you were too hard on him, and I'm not certain I agree even now that to keep him so restricted is the wisest course, but I do agree that he must be made to see the error of his ways if he is ever to be a credit to his position. Would it be so very dreadful to send him to school, sir, where boys his own age and older might be counted on to have an improving effect on him?"

She saw his countenance tighten and braced herself for rebuff, but even as the thought crossed her mind that he was still not ready to share his problems with her, his expression relaxed. He said, "You underestimate the thickness of the lad's skin and his belief in his own superiority. It's a belief he comes by naturally, of course, for Charlotte was right about the dukes of Upminster. My grandfather was at least a force in politics and held several positions of high order, but my father, though just as arrogant, was less benevolent, and Edmund . . . Edmund had other interests. Not many hereabouts were surprised by his end, I'm afraid. He thought himself a devil of a fellow, but in my opinion, he was no more than a reprobate who went his own way without regard for himself or his family."

"Was that why the duchess killed herself?"

"I don't know," he replied. "No one knows why she did it."

Encouraged by his apparent willingness to talk, she said, "Will you tell me why you are so concerned about money, sir? My father said you had reason to retain control of my portion, and though he did not explain, I have seen for myself that you are in a constant worry about the state of Andrew's fortune."

"Your dowry is not being used in Andrew's behalf," he said quickly, almost gruffly. "Moreover, it will be repaid."

"I don't question its use or repayment," she said. "I merely asked because I believe there are economies that can be practiced in the house, and in the garden as well now, but without knowing what is required, I cannot judge whether they would be worth the effort to arrange them."

He smiled. "Do you still find yourself at loggerheads with the servants whenever you wish to instigate change, sweetheart? I had thought that problem resolved."

"There is always resistance to change, sir," she said, not thinking this quite the moment to tell him that her decision to order a new fireguard for the kitchen fire had been accepted by the housekeeper with such enthusiasm that Anne did not think even Bagshaw would quibble over the expense. Moreover, since Mrs. Burdekin had warmed to her considerably since the kitchen maid's accident, Anne did not anticipate further difficulty from that quarter. Choosing her words carefully now, she said, "What I mean to say, sir, is that I'd like to know if saving five or ten shillings a month will help solve the problem you face."

"In short, no, it won't. The problem is much greater than that. Twenty thousand pounds, to be precise—a debt my dear brother incurred in a wager at the October meeting at Newmarket. Aye, you've every reason to gasp. I did myself. The full amount ought to have been paid at once, of course, but the bet was with Jake Thornton, and with Edmund's death coming so soon afterward, Jake gave me until midsummer quarter day to repay it. That's less than three weeks from now. In view of the enormous sum, I did ask him for more time, but he refused, so unless I can think of another way, I will have to sell off at least a portion of Andrew's property. The unentailed parts—which are the only ones that *can* be sold— are unfortunately also the ones upon which his income most largely depends. So now you know the worst, and you must agree there is nothing you can do to help."

"But I don't understand. How could anyone bet such a vast sum on a horse race? And if Edmund made the wager at the

October meeting, which is generally the first week of the month, why had he not already arranged to pay it before his death, which did not occur till at least a fortnight later? My brothers have frequently said that debts of honor must be paid at once."

"Your brothers are perfectly right, too, but Jake explained it to me when he informed me of the wager, by saying they had engaged in a second bet after the first. Had Edmund won the second one, he would have wiped out the whole debt."

"But even if they bet on a second race—"

"They did not bet on the horses," he said with a sigh.

"But you said the wager was made at Newmarket."

"I did, and it was, but according to the vowel—which was properly witnessed, by the way, by none other than Wilfred, Viscount Cressbrook—Edmund's bet was that Jake would not induce a certain lady of title to . . . to yield to his charms."

"What lady?" Anne demanded before she could stop herself.

"She is mercifully unnamed. You will begin to understand now," he added dryly, "why I have been reluctant to discuss this matter. Evidently, Jake succeeded in his quest. The second bet was whether Edmund would enjoy success in a similar venture, I believe. It was scrawled right after the first wager in what must have been Jake's handwriting, for I remember it was different from that in which the first was recorded."

"How distasteful, but surely, if you explain to Sir Jacob that payment of such an enormous sum will mean decimating Andrew's birthright . . ."

"Jake Thornton has fewer scruples than my brother had, my dear. He cares naught for Andrew or his birthright. I put all that to him last Sunday, but he believes he has been forbearing enough merely to agree to wait till Midsummer Day for his money. He even had the brass to remind me that my own honor is at stake. To hear Jake Thornton preach honor," Michael added grimly, "was nearly more than I could stomach. I wanted to throttle him."

Anne could well understand that. The whole tale shocked her very much, but not nearly so much as did the news two days later that Sir Jacob Thornton had died.

Fifteen

Anne's first thought when she heard the news of Sir Jacob's death was that Michael would no longer have to worry about the enormous (and, in her mind, outrageous) debt that the sixth duke had contracted with him. Upon that thought had followed another, much less pleasant one, however, that made her extremely glad that everyone accepted without question that Sir Jacob had died in his sleep of a heart attack.

"Although," Lord Ashby said thoughtfully that night in the yellow drawing room when he first relayed the news to the family, and to Lady Hermione and Cressbrook, who had come to dine with them, "I should not have been at all surprised to learn that Maria Thornton had poisoned him, by Jove. Treated her like the very devil, Jake did, and what with all his goings-on about how wrong it would be ever to allow a woman to divorce her husband, he might even have been the one to put the notion into her head."

"I am sure he treated her badly," Anne said thoughtfully, "for not only have I heard others say so, but he had no very great opinion of the female sex in general, I think. He had a way of looking at women that was most unnerving."

"As if," Lady Hermione said grimly, "he were stripping one's clothes off with his eyes. I never liked him. Indeed, if anyone were to be suspected of murdering him," she added with an oblique smile at Anne, "it would no doubt be my humble self, for I once told Anne that, had I been so unfortunate as to have been the one married to him, I'd have bashed his head in with an anvil."

"Now, damme, Hermie," her brother said, "you know dashed well you'd have done no such thing. And whatever you thought of him, Jake was an excellent Member of Parliament for the district until he began to fail in health. I don't doubt there will be scores of fine things said of him at his funeral, which, by the bye, is to be held on Wednesday. His widow don't want to wait, and with this unseasonable heat, one don't rightly blame her."

"Well, I shan't have to hear what they say," Lady Hermione said flatly, "and it is just as well, for I never did hold with his nonsensical notions, certainly not about marriage and divorce. No doubt, there are inequities in the laws applying to the Scots and the English, but to insist that the most restrictive laws are the best ones and ought to be applied to all was utter lunacy. I had no patience with such idiotic thinking."

Andrew, silent until now, said abruptly, "Is it true, what Sir Jacob said about Scottish marriages being legal in England, even if the same one would not be if it were performed here?"

"True enough, I expect," Lord Ashby said.

Anne, recalling that Andrew had not been present the night Sir Jacob had expounded on the law, said, "Where did you hear such a thing?"

"Oh, I'm sure he talked of it often enough," the boy said glibly. Turning to Lady Hermione, he said, "I don't know why you didn't like him. He seemed all right to me."

"No doubt he did, for you are a man, or as near as made no difference to him. As we've just been saying, it was his behavior toward women that was execrable, and if he weren't dead, by heaven, I'd still like to give him a piece of my mind."

Lord Ashby said tartly, "We know that. You tell us all the time, old girl, but you never exerted yourself to *do* it whilst the fellow was alive, did you? You might at least give Jake credit for fighting for his beliefs and doing what he could to see them through. Not that he succeeded this time, mind you," he added with a thoughtful air. "Read in the *Times* this morning that his amendment to the Marriage Bill failed in its second reading and won't be brought up for a third. The House has gone on to discuss raising the duty on whale blubber, of all things."

"Well," Lady Hermione said tartly, "I can tell you that if this nation were not so misguided as to deny women the right to serve in Parliament, we'd soon see that matters which affect the so-called weaker sex—which certainly includes marriage and divorce laws—would never take second place to whale blubber. And if that was meant to be an illustration of Sir Jacob's efficiency in the Commons, all I can say is *poppycock.*"

"I suppose you approve of clandestine marriages," Lord Ashby said, shooting her a provocative look.

"Now, don't you go putting words in my mouth, Ashby, for I won't tolerate it," she snapped. "I don't believe in doing anything clandestinely. If you are going to do a thing, I say, do it right smack in the public eye."

"Anything?" He raised his eyebrows, smiling wickedly.

"Don't be idiotic!" But when the others chuckled, she blushed, adding, "You know what I mean. I don't hold with runaway marriages, and I don't hold with the Scots calling them legal, all for a man's having jumped an anvil, or whatever it is they do, and declared himself married to a woman—or child, as they certainly are in some instances. But no more than that do I hold with the notion that a woman has got to put up with her husband's philandering whilst he can divorce her for cause when she imitates his habit. That behavior, at least, poor Maria will no longer have to tolerate." She said to Anne, "You won't be attending the funeral on Wednesday, either, of course."

"No," Anne said. "Only the gentlemen will go, although perhaps Andrew . . ." She paused, glancing at the boy, who had for once been listening avidly and in becoming silence. It occurred to her only now that perhaps several of the comments that had been made were not exactly suitable for him to hear.

He returned her look steadily, but said, "I think I should go, don't you, Uncle Michael? After all, I am head of the family, for all that you did not let me attend your wedding."

Lord Ashby said, "He is certainly old enough, Michael, and there are those who would consider it a slight if he did not go."

"Yes, you are right," Michael said, "and you and I must go, sir, but there is no cause for any of the women to attend."

Lady Hermione said with a decisive nod, "Just what I thought, but I daresay we shall have to pay a sympathy call on Maria, Anne. It would be best to go the morning after the funeral, don't you agree? Shall I call for you?"

Before Anne could reply, however, Lord Michael said, "I don't want to put a rub in the way of your visit, ma'am, but I mean to accompany Anne when she pays her call at Thornton House. I have a certain matter to discuss with Lady Thornton that I prefer not to discuss with her man of business unless she asks me to do so, and I cannot, with propriety, call upon her alone at such a time as this."

"Look here, Michael," Lord Ashby said hastily, "you ain't thinking . . . That is," he went on hesitantly after a glance at their guests, "that business ought not to be discussed with a female, by Jove. It's not right, not right at all."

"It certainly ought not to be discussed at present," Michael said firmly. "I will do as I think best, Uncle."

"Of course, lad, of course. Ah, Bagshaw, there you are at last. Don't mind telling you, I'm famished. By the bye, Wilfred," he added, turning to the viscount, "you will be pleased to know that I had word they mean to deliver the new aerostat tomorrow. We can begin filling her just as soon as we've got all the materials on hand, in a day or two, and I mean to put it about that we'll take her up for a maiden voyage on Sunday afternoon. Do you mean to accompany me?"

"No, no," the viscount said hastily. "Damme, Ashby, I've told you before, I'm financing a scientific experiment, not taking part in one. If man had been meant to fly, he'd have been born with feathers, man, not flesh!"

"Exactly what I've told him any number of times myself," Lord Michael said cordially as he got to his feet and offered his arm to Lady Hermione. "Shall we go in?"

The talk at dinner proceeded desultorily. No further mention was made of Lord Michael's intended discussion with Lady Thornton, although Anne did not know what passed between the gentlemen after she and Lady Hermione left them to their port. She assumed Michael wanted to talk with Sir Jacob's wife about the wager, but she was afraid of receiving a setdown if she asked him outright to tell her what he meant to do, so she contained her soul in patience until the day following Sir Jacob's funeral.

Preceding him into Thornton House that afternoon, she found herself hoping he would not order her from the room in order to direct his conversation with Lady Thornton in privacy. From the speculative glance he shot her as they were shown into the drawing room, she deduced that he did want to exclude her, but trusted that his notions of propriety were too strong to allow him to ask the widow to grant him a private exchange.

Their hostess, enveloped in black crape and a languishing air, invited them in a faltering voice to sit down.

"We are sorry for your loss, ma'am," Anne said, arranging her skirt as she took her seat on a Chinese Chippendale chair, and being careful to avoid the chair's mock bamboo back, which she knew from experience was likely to poke her shoulder blades painfully. "His death was so very sudden."

"Indeed," gasped Lady Thornton, "such a shock. I don't know what I'll do. Six children, you know, to be provided for, and all so young yet."

"I imagine he left you all well provided for, ma'am," Michael said matter-of-factly. "Have you not had his will read to you yet?"

"Oh, no, for his man of business was in London, you see,

and it was not thought wise to delay the funeral until his coming. He will be here tomorrow," she added faintly. "So kind of you to come. Everyone has been so kind, but indeed, I do not have the least notion of how Sir Jacob left his affairs. I do not even know whom he will have named as guardian to his poor children, for he did not think me wise enough, of course."

"But surely, you ought to be their guardian," Anne said impulsively.

"Oh, no," Lady Thornton said, looking shocked. "I am only a woman, after all. What could I know of such things?"

Anne was tempted to tell her she ought to make it her business to learn about *such things,* as she called them, but Michael said with an air of one steeling himself to an unpleasant task, "There is a matter that I must in honor bring to your attention, Lady Thornton, though perhaps your husband had already mentioned it to you."

"And what is that, sir?"

"A wager that my brother, Edmund, made with him shortly before his own death. Naturally, I am still bound to pay it."

"Indeed, sir? My husband said nothing of this to me, but I have left all his papers for his solicitor to deal with, for Sir Jacob never discussed any of his affairs—of any sort—with me," she added on a more bitter note.

"The wager was a large one," Michael said.

"Was it? How large?"

"Twenty thousand pounds."

She sat up straight. "So much, my lord?"

He grimaced. "I'll not equivocate with you, ma'am. Even if my brother's affairs had been in good order, such a sum would have been difficult to collect. Unfortunately, they were not left in good order, and in point of fact, I'm still having the deuce of a time sorting out what he owned and what he didn't. He dealt with several solicitors, you see, rather than putting all his affairs with one, and he even seems to have managed a few things on his own. In at least one instance, I have discovered that he must have operated with a partner, and did not put the details in the hands of any of his men of affairs."

"Are you suggesting, sir, that my husband was that partner?"

"I do not know if he was or not, ma'am. I'll discuss that with Sir Jacob's man of affairs; however, since the wager appears to have been a private matter between them—and since there are distasteful elements in it that I am persuaded you would not want to know about or to have brought to light—I should like to keep it that way for the present. I own, I do have certain business matters in train that would not be assisted by public knowledge of such a large debt against the estate. I hope you understand."

"Not really," she said, "but I have no objection. Indeed, if the wager was as distasteful as you say it was, I daresay I should not care to benefit by it; but Mr. Styles—Sir Jacob's man, you know—will be bound to know all about it and most likely, the record of the wager will be amongst Jacob's papers."

"There was certainly a vowel, ma'am, for Jake showed it to me when he informed me of the debt. He was kind enough, in view of my difficulties, to agree to postpone payment till midsummer."

"That sounds very unlike him. I should think he would have insisted upon being paid at once."

Michael stiffened. "There was nothing written down between the two of us, if that is what you mean. It was an agreement between gentlemen. There was no need for a second document."

"My husband's sense of honor was not so fine as yours, my lord," she said gently, "though it pains me to say so. I think, you know, that unless he did not leave enough to the children to keep them comfortably—for I do not hesitate to confide to you, sir, my belief that he left the bulk of his wealth outside this family—I will not take your money. Wagers are nonsensical, and I should be most reluctant to profit by such a distasteful one."

"We'll see about that. I could not reconcile it with my conscience to take advantage of innocent feminine scruples in such an important issue. I see I shall have to confess at least the wager's existence to your man of affairs when he arrives."

"As you wish, my lord, though I warn you, I mean to tell him that to accept such money would distress me prodigiously."

They stayed only a few minutes after that, for other visitors arrived to pay their respects, and when they were in the carriage, away from interested ears, Anne said, "If it is not improper for me to ask, sir, why would she fear Sir Jacob's leaving his money away from his family? Would that not be a most peculiar thing for him to do?"

"Peculiar, perhaps, but not unheard of where an estate is not entailed to the eldest son—though I don't think her son's inheritance concerns her as much as her widow's portion."

"But, good gracious, sir, to whom would he leave that if not to her?" When he remained silent, his lips pressed together, she said quietly, "What sort of man would leave money to his mistress that ought by every right to go to his wife?"

"I did not say he would do any such thing," Michael replied. "In fact, I don't believe he did. What I do believe is that Lady Thornton thinks he did, and I have no doubt there are others who would not be surprised if she were to prove right."

After considering his words for some moments in silence, she said, "Must you still pay off that dreadful wager? Even if she does not want to take the money?"

"Indeed I must, sweetheart, and by Midsummer Day. Since she is entitled to the money, she must have it without a quibble, if I have to sell my own estate to accommodate her."

Shocked that he would consider selling his inheritance to protect Andrew's, Anne said impulsively, "You said you did not mean to use my dowry, sir, but surely—"

"Your dowry went to pay my own debts so that I could be

free to deal with Edmund's," he said bluntly. "Don't look so amazed. You know I was no saint. I won't spin you excuses or insist that I've learned my lesson, though I certainly have. I tell you now only because you are determined to understand the whole."

"Did you spend every penny of it?"

"No, of course not, but I did spend a portion of what your father provided in the settlements, and the last quarter's income from what you had from your godfather. Your father is no fool, sweetheart. I control only your income, not your capital, which is held in trust for you and your children."

"But if there is more, could you not borrow it? The estate could pay it back, once you have it running properly again."

"I can't do that. Really, Anne, you must leave this to me." He sighed, adding, "You just don't understand, sweetheart. I'll know more about where I stand once I talk to Jake's Mr. Styles."

So much for partnership, she thought. She was quickly learning that although he was willing to support her position in the household—although now that she enjoyed Mrs. Burdekin's support, she needed little from him—Michael was more willing to help her than to accept her help. Not, she was the first to admit, that she had the slightest idea how she might be of assistance to him in his present troubles. She had begun to wonder if perhaps some evil force was at work against him, for it did seem as if he no sooner solved one problem than another jumped up in his face.

Even burdened as he was, however, he seemed to regret his neglect of her. The very next evening, instead of retiring alone as usual to deal with estate matters, he left the table when she did and invited her to join him in the library. She saw at once that he was determined to be affable, but when he made a point of remarking on the improvements she had wrought in the gardens, she nearly laughed at such an obvious stratagem.

"They were never in such good trim before," he said.

They had made themselves comfortable. She was curled in

a chair, and he sat near her in its mate. The curtains were drawn, and candle and firelight glowed warmly against the heavy, dark curtains and reflected from the gilding on the covers of the books shelved along two walls of the room.

Anne had been surprised by his invitation. She had even wondered briefly if she had somehow managed to displease him, but his casual demeanor eased her fear, and his comments about the garden banished it completely. Then wryly he added, "I find it hard to believe the whole business hasn't cost a small fortune."

"But it hasn't," she protested. "You pay the gardeners anyway, you know, and it is much better that they earn their keep. We have merely transplanted plants from one location to another, and I ordered all the ponds cleared and the shrubbery clipped, and the weeds removed, and the lawns scythed—"

"Enough," he said, chuckling. "I believe you. You need not explain the whole business to me. It sounds, in fact, as if everything was let go to a ruinous degree before you came here."

"It was," Anne said, smiling back at him, "but all that was needed was organization. Quigley did not have the courage to proceed without orders from you, and before that, your brother had taken no interest in the gardens. If anything was done, it was the duchess who ordered it, which is no doubt why, of all the servants here, Quigley was the least opposed to taking orders from me when I first arrived."

"Well, I think you deserve a reward," Michael said, smiling warmly at her.

"What did you have in mind?"

"The garden room at Rendlesham," he said, watching her.

Puzzled, she said, "But what can you mean? The garden room at Rendlesham is at Rendlesham. Unless, of course, you mean I might pay a visit there. It is rather soon for that, I think."

"Indeed, it is, sweetheart. I shouldn't know how to get on here without you. I meant only that I remember that room quite well from our wedding breakfast. A very charming room,

I thought it. I particularly like the way it opens right into the garden, and since you are so partial to our gardens, I thought you might like to reproduce it here. Could that be done, do you think?"

"Oh, yes, certainly. The yellow drawing room would be perfect, for it faces directly out onto the southwest gardens. The increasing elevation there would make it fairly easy to open it to the outside, just as Papa did at home. But it would be an enormous expense, sir. I do not know who designed ours, but he was some fashionable architect or other, and I know Papa complained forever about the cost of the whole project."

Michael grimaced. "Well, we cannot do the thing at once, but I thought you might like the notion. If I can get everything straightened out, we'll talk about it some more, and if we cannot do it here, perhaps we can do it at Egremont."

Encouraged by the warmth of his manner, and the fact that he did not, for the moment, seem to be thinking of selling his estate, she said, "You know, sir, I have been thinking about all that, and it occurs to me that perhaps Papa might be persuaded—"

"No, Anne."

"But, really, sir—"

"I said no. I have revealed as much as I intend to reveal to your father about the difficulties arising from my brother's death. I won't go to him with my hat in my hand. Moreover, things have got a bit more complicated, I'm afraid. I managed to have a talk with Jake's man of affairs today, and not only was he unable to help me with that partnership matter I mentioned to Lady Thornton yesterday, but he cannot find the vowel Jake showed me when he informed me of the wager's existence."

"Then you need not pay it! If there is no record—"

Regarding her soberly, he said, "A debt of honor does not require a record, Anne. It must be repaid."

She would have pursued the subject, for she could not imagine that anyone should be held responsible for a debt of which there was no record, but they were interrupted before she could do so.

Lord Ashby, who had missed dinner in order to see to the bestowal of his precious new aerostat, which had arrived on a carter's wagon that very afternoon, entered the library clearly big with news, with Andrew at his heels. Without ceremony, Lord Ashby demanded, "Did you know Jake Thornton's man, Styles, arrived at Thornton Hall this morning, Michael?"

"I did. I've spoken to him."

"Dashed foolishness, if you ask me, to have brought that matter up with him or with Maria. Now the whole untidy business will be chatted about in every household in Derbyshire."

"Good Lord, Uncle, would you have me cheat her?"

"No, no. But look here," he added with a glance at the interested and rather stormy-faced Andrew, "that ain't what I came to tell you; although, by Jove, it's amazing to me that nothing's been said about it long before now. You'd think the rumor mills would have got hold of it straight off. They usually do, in my experience, no matter what one does to prevent them."

"If that is not your news, sir, what is it?"

"Thought you might already have heard it, but I can see it ain't come here yet, for you're both looking at me as if I were speaking in tongues, which it stands to reason you wouldn't be if you'd already heard. Can't say too much in present company, by Jove," he added with a glance at Andrew. "In any case, I needn't explain it to you in great detail, for you'll understand well enough when I say that one of my lads heard Jake left every dashed penny he had to Maria and the children. Word is, it was such a shock to the poor woman that she dropped down in a swoon and couldn't be revived for all of twenty minutes."

"I hadn't heard," Michael said. "I didn't ask Styles how things were left, of course. None of my affair. And I readily confess I don't get the local news as easily as you seem to do."

"It's not fair," Andrew muttered so low that Anne was not sure anyone but herself had heard him.

Uneasily certain that she understood his meaning, she shot him a warning look, but he was glaring at the world in general and did not heed her.

Michael said, "I'm glad to hear that Jake did as he ought. It would have been a pity if he had done anything else."

"The house, perhaps," Lord Ashby said delicately with another glance at Andrew. "That, at least, wouldn't have shocked anyone, particularly if he had arranged the matter quietly."

"There's already been scandal enough without that," Michael said. "But you are quite right, sir, in that we ought not to be talking of it now. Where have you been keeping yourself since dinner, Andrew? I trust you've done nothing to outrage Mr. Pratt, for I've found it most pleasant these past several days to receive no complaints of your behavior."

"I went for a walk along the river with Sylvia," Andrew said, looking up from his shoes at last. "She likes to walk there sometimes, you know."

"No, I didn't. I hope you also brought her back."

"Of course, I did. I'm not a fool, though you certainly take me for one often enough."

"Steady on," Michael said sternly. "You won't help matters by taking that tone with me. I acquit you of wishing to drown your sister. I collect that she went upstairs."

"Yes," Andrew said with a sigh. "We met Uncle Ashby coming from the meadow, and walked with him. Sylvie stepped in a puddle and got her feet wet, so I sent her up to change her shoes, although, once Moffat gets her hands on her, she will probably find herself straightaway tucked into bed. I came in here because Uncle Ashby did, but you needn't all continue talking in riddles. I have already heard all about Sir Jacob's will."

"Nevertheless, it is not a matter for you to discuss."

"I don't see why not. I have as much right to an opinion as anyone does, I should think. This is still a free country."

"It is," Michael said evenly, "but that does not mean that we want to hear the comments of a stripling on matters that do not concern him."

"It does concern me, for I care prodigiously about what happens— That is, I think . . . I think the whole business is an outrage, and most unfair, and for them even to be taking Fiona's house away is the outside of enough!"

A horrified silence filled the room, and Anne, seeing the dawning expression of outrage on Lord Michael's face, felt a pulse begin to thud in her temple and her knees begin to quake.

Sixteen

Andrew did not appear to be nearly as affected by Michael's growing wrath as Anne was, but Lord Ashby said as if he felt a need to defuse the situation, "By Jove, we're a fine set of gossips, are we not? And I, at least, have little time for such chatter, for I've any number of things to do before the lads and I can begin filling the new aerostat tomorrow. I think you ought to take a stroll down to the meadow first thing, Michael, my boy, to have a good view when we begin to fill it. Not taking it up till Sunday, of course, but must check the new bag for leaks, you know, before the grand ascension. Wouldn't do to have the thing sit flat before all its subscribers, now, would it?"

Michael was not even looking at him. His gaze was still fixed on Andrew, and it was plain to the meanest observer that he was keeping a tight rein on his temper. He said, "Would you care to explain that last remark of yours to me?"

"I cannot see that any remark of mine requires explaining," Andrew said stubbornly. "Sir Jacob's will was unfair, that's all, and I think someone ought to help her."

"Help whom?" Michael's tone was dangerously gentle.

"Fiona, of course."

Lord Ashby said hastily, "I'll just take myself off now, if you all will excuse me. Much to do, much to do." He turned sharply toward the door.

"Hold on one moment, sir, if you will," Michael said, standing up. "Do you know aught of this business?"

"Only what I can deduce for myself, which I can't say I like one little bit," he declared with a harassed look at Andrew. "I didn't introduce them, if that's what you think, though if you do, you've a dashed poor notion of my character and good sense, and that's all I'll say about that, by Jove. I'm off now."

Silence reigned until the door had shut behind him. Anne sat rooted to her chair, scarcely daring to breathe lest Michael turn his attention to her and demand to know what she knew of the matter. The thought weighed heavily on her conscience that, had she not spoken with Mrs. Flowers herself at their public day, Andrew would have been unlikely ever to have encountered her, and augmenting her guilt unbearably was the knowledge that duty alone had demanded her intervention the moment she learned he had formed the habit of visiting such a woman. The thought of how greatly she was to blame for the present scene turned the beating pulse in her right temple to a throbbing pain.

"Where do you think you are going?" Michael demanded when Andrew turned on his heel as if to follow Lord Ashby.

He stopped but did not turn. "I have things to do, too."

"Not yet, you don't. Step forward, sir."

With a sigh, Andrew turned around and did as he was told.

"Stand up straight."

Resentfully, the boy glanced at Anne, but he made no comment, merely obeying stiffly as he had before.

"By heaven," Michael said angrily, "you will show proper courtesy and respect and a little less of your ducal pretension, or you will wish you had. Put your hands behind your back, sir, and look at me when I speak to you."

Seeing the boy stiffen indignantly and glance her way again, Anne collected herself at last, standing up and saying, "I will leave you now, my lords."

"Don't go," Michael said curtly. "This will not take long."

"I am sure you would prefer to be private with His Grace," she said firmly, repressing an urge to rub her aching temple and taking care to accord Andrew an extra measure of dignity, in hopes that it might mitigate his humiliation at being reprimanded in her presence. She was anxious to leave, not on his account alone, but also for her own sake. She was certain that Michael would soon learn all there was to know about the boy's visits to Mrs. Flowers, and she did not trust Andrew not to reveal that she had known about them for some time.

"I would rather be private with you," Michael said, giving her a steady look, "and as soon as I have dealt with him, I shall be. Moreover, there is no real need for privacy. I mean to say nothing to him that you should not hear."

"Nonetheless, sir, I ought not to stay, for it is—"

"You may say all that you want to say to me in just a few minutes," he said gently. When she had sat down again, he said on a much firmer note, "Am I given to understand from your comment a moment ago, Andrew, that you have, by some means or other, developed an acquaintance in the village with the woman called Fiona Flowers?"

"Yes, of course I know her."

"You will have to forgive me," Michael said, moving a little away from him to sit on a corner of the library table he used as a desk, "but there is no *of course* about such an acquaintance. Did she have the effrontery to approach you?"

"No, and it would not have been effrontery if she had. *She* treats me with respect, which is more than I am accorded around here, I can tell you."

"You may certainly tell me anything you like," Michael said evenly if—in his wife's opinion, at least—quite inaccurately, "but you would do better to moderate your tone if we are not to fall out again. If Mrs. Flowers did not accost you, then how, may I ask, did you chance to meet her?"

Anne held her breath. She had relaxed a little when Michael moved away from the boy, but the small throbbing pain that had begun in her temple had already enlarged itself to encompass most of the area around her right ear.

Andrew stared straight ahead, not meeting Michael's gaze. He said, "I spoke with her at our public day. I tried to speak with as many of our guests as I could, just as you said I should. There is nothing in that to call for reproach, I hope."

"I know she was there," Michael said, "but if you merely accorded her a few polite words of welcome, I cannot imagine you would exclaim as you did a few moments ago. Would you have me believe that is the only time you ever spoke with her?"

"No, of course not. But she was kind to me then, and I said I should like to pursue the acquaintance. And you needn't think she jumped at the chance, for she did not. She said it would not be thought suitable, and I said, if you *must* know, that I didn't care a rap for what others thought. And then she said that if I wished to visit her in the village, I would always be welcome. She said the same to Sylvia, too," he added with an air of throwing down the gauntlet.

Michael's expression hardened. He said with deceptive gentleness, "And did you take Sylvia with you, sir?"

To Anne's relief, Andrew quickly saw that he had erred, and moderated his tone when he said, "No, for whatever you may think of me, I do know that such an acquaintance would not do for her. But I am nearly a man, for all you treat me as though I were still in leading strings, and when I am old enough to mount a mistress of my own—"

"Good Lord," Michael snapped, "what sort of relationship have you had with this woman?"

"She has been kind to me," Andrew said grimly. "I like talking to her, for she talks to me just as she would to any other man—although with proper deference to my rank, of course—and she has always made me feel welcome. She doesn't treat me like a child, either, but talks to me about important things, like . . . like what's going on in Parliament and what she thinks about matters one does not expect females to care about."

"I can understand that you feel flattered, but—"

"It is *not* flattery or . . . or toad-eating, or any other such despicable thing. She is kindhearted and considerate, and I feel more respected and valued in her house than in my own! And it *is* her house, whatever anyone else says to the contrary, for she has lived there nearly five years now and was told she would be well looked after and would live out her days there."

"There is nothing that can be done about that, I'm afraid, and say what you will, it has nothing to do with you. You cannot know what the exact arrangement was—"

"But I *do* know! *She* does not keep secrets from me but talks openly about herself, and I know just what sort of arrangement she had with Jake Thornton. I think he treated her damnably in not providing for her when he had paid all her debts these past six years and more, not to mention giving her the house to live in and leading her to think it was hers forever. Damnable is what I call it now, and what I shall always call it," he repeated, his voice trembling with rage now. "If I had control of my fortune, by God, I would mend matters, that I can tell you, and that is precisely what I mean to tell her when—"

"You are not to visit her again, Andrew."

"Don't say that! You can't stop me. She is the first real friend I have ever had, and I don't mean to abandon her just because everyone else does. You think that just because you came here and took over my estates you can order everything I do or say, but you can't! My father would never have objected to my knowing her. He had his own bits of fancy, after all, and—"

"That will do," Michael snapped, straightening to his full height. "By God, you young whelp, it is more than time that you learned both civility and obedience to your elders, and I mean to teach you those lessons before we are, either of us, much older."

Anne leapt to her feet again, hardly knowing whether she meant to try to intervene between them or to flee.

Andrew, tears streaming down his face, shouted back, "Do as you like then, but I'll be damned before I benefit from any teaching of yours!"

Seeing Michael stride purposefully toward him, Anne fled, but the echo of their angry voices still rang in her ears long after she had slammed the library door behind her and run up the stairs. By the time she reached her dressing room, her head was pounding, and all she could think about was finding the hartshorn Maisie kept on her dressing table. Acting as peacemaker between the various members of her own family was, she decided, mere child's play compared to attempting the same thing between the arrogant young duke and his autocratic uncle. At the moment, she felt that the latter role lay far beyond her capability.

Pouring a cup of water from the ewer on the washstand and stirring into it a dose of the excellent restorative, she drew a steadying breath, released it, and lifted the cup to her lips.

"Don't drink that, Aunt Anne. You will go to sleep and never wake up again."

Startled out of her wits by the clear, unfamiliar, childlike voice right behind her, Anne dropped the cup, whirled, and stared in stupefaction at Sylvia, who stood not a yard away in her long white nightgown and bare feet, gazing wide-eyed at her.

"Sylvia!" Anne fought to control emotions that threatened to overwhelm her, and said in a calmer tone, "Sylvia, darling, how you startled me! Oh, and look at the mess I made when I dropped my cup. How Maisie will scold!"

"I'm g-glad you dropped it," the child said. "I d-don't want you to die, too."

"Darling, I am not going to die for many, many years yet, I assure you."

"You will if you drink that," Sylvia said.

"What a pretty voice you have. Why have you kept silent for so long, darling?"

"I-I d-don't know," the child said, looking bewildered. "I can t-talk now, but when I tried before, nothing came out, so I stopped trying, because t-trying only made my head ache."

Anne had found a cloth and was doing her best to mop up

the spilled water. Her own head still ached, and she longed for the dose of hartshorn, but she feared to upset the little girl if she mixed another, or for that matter, if she allowed the tears of joy in her eyes to spill down her cheeks. Choosing her words with care, and continuing matter-of-factly with her mopping, she said, "What made you think I might die, Sylvia?"

"Because M-Mama did," the child replied. "She put something in her cup, and then she drank it, and then she sank to the floor and c-closed her eyes, as if she were asleep. But when I tried to wake her up, I c-couldn't."

"You saw your mama fall?" Anne could not keep the horror from her voice.

Sylvia nodded. Tears welled in her eyes, but she continued to regard Anne solemnly. "And . . . and when I t-tried to scream for someone to c-come help her, I could not make any sound."

"But your papa," Anne said. "I was told he was the one who found her. Didn't you tell him what you saw?"

"No, for when Papa came in, he banged the door back and shouted her name like he d-did sometimes when he was very angry, and I . . . I hid before he saw me there. And later, when he began shouting at everyone, saying he wanted them to tell him how she could do such a thing to him, I still couldn't speak to tell him I saw how she did it. I thought then that my voice must have died when Mama did, so I could never speak out of turn either."

"Speak out of turn?"

"Like Mama did."

Putting the wet cloth aside, Anne said, "I don't understand, Sylvia. How did your mama speak out of turn?"

The little girl looked at the floor, and for a moment, Anne feared that she would not speak again, but when Sylvia looked up with tears streaming down her face, she hugged herself, gave a great sob, and cried, "I . . . I d-don't know!"

Swiftly Anne gathered the child into her arms. "There,

there, darling," she said. "Everything will be all right. I am so glad you can talk again, I just want to hug you and make you feel safe. I know you must miss your mama quite dreadfully, and I cannot take her place, but I hope you know you can trust me to look after you. If you don't know how your mama spoke out of turn, can you at least tell me why you think she did so?"

"Sh-she said she did," Sylvia replied on another sob.

"She talked to you before she . . . before she drank from the cup?"

Sylvia shook her head.

"Don't stop talking again, I pray you," Anne said urgently. "If she did not speak to you— My dear, you are bewildering me beyond all bearing. Can you not explain the matter plainly?"

"She . . . she wrote a letter."

Anne gasped. "A letter! Good gracious, I was told she had left no message. What can you know of a letter?"

"I found it." The words this time were barely a whisper.

Struggling with her emotions, knowing that to exclaim again, particularly if she were to make Sylvia feel that she had done something wrong, might well cause the little girl to lapse back into her long silence, Anne said quietly, "Can you show me?"

Sylvia went very still, and the next moment passed so slowly that Anne had plenty of time to fear that she would not speak, but at last she said, "It is in my bedroom."

"Shall I go with you to fetch it?"

Another silence fell, but the little girl's expression was thoughtful this time, not frightened, and after a moment, she said, "If I go alone, Moffat will make me go back to bed."

"I won't even let her scold you," Anne said firmly.

Sylvia looked at her, her watery gaze searching Anne's face. When she put her hand in Anne's and squeezed her fingers, Anne sighed with heartfelt relief.

They encountered a worried Nurse Moffat bustling toward them in the corridor near the nursery.

"Oh, my lady, there she is! You naughty girl, Sylvia. Why, here I've thought you were all tucked up and safe asleep, and I go in to put out your night light and find your empty bed. I don't know what I'm going to do with you, and that's a fact."

Sylvia's hand tightened in Anne's. She did not speak.

Anne said calmly, "I will attend to her ladyship, Moffat. You may safely leave her in my hands for tonight."

"Well, as to that, ma'am, I hardly like to do so when she has been so naughty, but then I don't seem to have the knack of getting her to change her ways, do I?" Giving Anne no chance to reply, she went right on, "Like as not she ought to be punished for slipping out again, as she has, but one scarcely likes to be harsh with the little mite. I make no doubt there are some who think this new governess of hers, coming to take her in hand—which I'm told will be any day now—will be much more stern than what her old nurse has been, but I don't mind telling you, ma'am, I hope she ain't too harsh, for the child's that sensitive, you know, like one of them flowers that closes right up when a body touches it. I'd not like to see her made unhappy."

"I think we can prevent that, Moffat," Anne said, giving Sylvia's hand a reassuring squeeze. "I am well aware that no one else has served her as faithfully as you have, and if you are afraid that the new governess will replace you, you need not be. She will attend to Sylvia's lessons, but you will still have much influence, I promise you. As for tonight, you can safely leave her in my care."

"Well do I know that, your ladyship," the nurse said with a look of gratification at Anne's words. "My little fairy waif's perked up no end since she returned to us, and I don't think for a moment it was her time with Lady Harlow—kind though I know she was to her—that made for the change. I never saw her follow anyone else like a shadow the way she does you, not even her own mama, though the late duchess fair doted on her."

The little hand in her own trembled, and Anne said firmly, "We should not be talking like this just now, Moffat. I will take Lady Sylvia to her bedchamber. You may have the rest of the night to yourself, if you like."

With a sound of annoyance, Moffat said, "How right you are to reprove me, ma'am. 'Tis amazing how one begins to think that because she cannot speak, she does not hear. Not that I gave away any secrets, of course, but I do know I oughtn't to have spoke so in the child's presence." She looked lovingly at Sylvia, adding, "Now do go along with Lady Michael, my love, and let her tuck you up snug into your bed, and old Moffat will see you again first thing in the morning. She's already said her prayers, your ladyship, but— Good gracious, child, where are your slippers?"

Anne dealt with this minor setback speedily and soon sent the nurse on her way. When she looked at Sylvia again, and saw a fleeting smile at the child's lips, she said thoughtfully, "You know, darling, you had better mend your ways once everyone else realizes you can speak again. I've a fair notion you've been able to get away with quite a lot of misbehavior these past months, and they will not all be so gentle with you in future."

She almost wished she had not spoken, for the haunted, sad look reappeared on the child's face, and when Anne urged her toward the night nursery, she went obediently but with gathering reluctance. Inside the cozy room, Anne saw that the fire had burned down to glowing embers behind the stout nursery guard, but the coals cast a glow over the room, revealing the tumbled little cot and the washstand near the window with its ewer and basin. A low side table held a glass-enclosed candlestick, serving as a night lamp, with extra candles in a narrow dish beside it. The candle in the lamp had burned low, so Anne removed it and, opening the fireguard, lit a new one from an ember. Fitting it into the lamp and replacing the glass, she looked over her shoulder to see Sylvia, hands behind her, watching her solemnly.

"Where is the letter, darling?"

The child brought one hand from behind her back and held out a folded piece of notepaper. "I fetched it while you f-fixed the candle," she said, biting her lip. "It was in my secret place."

Anne took the paper, and as she unfolded it with shaking hands, she said, "You need not tell me where that is, of course. Everyone is entitled to a few secrets."

Sylvia looked relieved, but as Anne smoothed the single sheet on the side table near the candle, said abruptly, "I don't mind. There's a space behind the baseboard where it just fit."

"Why on earth did you keep it, darling? You ought to have given it to your papa or to your great-uncle Ashby."

"I was afraid to tell them I was there," Sylvia said simply.

Without further ado, Anne read the letter:

Your Grace,

I daresay you will not forgive me for what I am about to do, since it will undoubtedly bring scandal to the St. Ledgers name, and so I do not ask that of you. I will pray to God instead, though I do not expect Him to forgive my wickedness either. Perhaps he will understand, however, that I simply cannot submit to your barbaric decree, and know of no other way to avoid the dreadful fate you have ordained for me.

No doubt there are those who will declare that I ought to have spoken up—to Lord Ashby, perhaps—but you yourself said that even my own family would not believe me, and I am sure you are right. Who would ever accept that the Duke of Upminster is so villainous that he would send his duchess to a brothel to train her to be a better wife? To threaten to hand me over to your so much admired Lord M to punish me for speaking out of turn, as you call it, was an iniquitous thing to do, Edmund, but I

cannot doubt, knowing what I now know of you—and
have just learned about him from Molly—that you will
do it. Rather than submit to such treatment, I have taken
the decision to end my life.

My greatest concern on this evil day is for my innocent
children. I pray that the Almighty will do all in His power
to protect them from your villainy, now and forevermore.

Goodbye; from your wretched
Agnes

Seventeen

"What is a brothel?"

Stunned by what she had just read, and still trying to comprehend its full meaning, Anne did not at once realize what Sylvia had said. But when the echo of her question pierced the numbness in Anne's brain, she gave herself a mental shake and said, "A brothel, darling? Why, it's . . ." Not wanting to snub the child at such a time, she searched her mind for something at least marginally acceptable to say. "It is a house for abandoned females, I'm afraid, and not any place of which you need have more knowledge, or one that you should discuss with anyone else. I know you must have read this letter and been very much shocked by it, just as I am; but, indeed, I cannot think that your papa would ever have sent your mama to such a place, for she could in no way have ever been mistaken for an abandoned female."

"N-no," Sylvia said doubtfully. After a moment, her face cleared, and she said, "Abandoned means having no one to take care of her, d-doesn't it? Like when a mama b-bird abandons her fledglings to look after themselves?"

"Why, yes, that is just what it means," Anne said, hoping that the same Almighty who looked after innocent children would forgive her for the slight deception.

"Then Mama was wrong to think she would have to go to such a place," Sylvia said. "She could never have b-been thought to have b-been abandoned while she had Papa and Andrew and me."

Recognizing that she would be wrong to encourage this line of thought, Anne racked her brain once again for a response that would be acceptable to the child without being even more at odds with her own principles of truth. Before she could think of one, however, Sylvia said thoughtfully, "D-did Mama know that what she stirred into the cup would make her d-die? People said that she k-killed herself. Did she, Aunt Anne?"

"People ought not to have said such things where you could hear them," Anne said, vexed but not very much surprised.

"I think it was like Moffat said, and they forgot I c-could hear because they knew I couldn't speak. But did she really kill herself? I wish she had not, and since she was not abandoned, she needn't have. Was it not a wicked thing to do?"

Tears stinging her eyes again, Anne said gently, "I can't explain it all to you, darling, but there must always be a better way to solve one's difficulties. We don't know exactly what happened. Only your mama knew that, and she cannot tell us more than what she wrote in this letter, which was not very much."

"No, it wasn't," Sylvia agreed. After a pause, she looked uneasily at Anne and said, "Are you v-vexed with me for keeping it? Must I show it to Uncle Michael?"

Giving her a hug, Anne said, "No, I am not vexed. You did what you thought you had to do at the time, and that is all that matters. As for showing it to Uncle Michael, we must certainly tell him that you have found your voice again, but I think that for the moment, if you like, we can continue to keep the letter's contents private between us." Her conscience pricked her, but she needed time to think about the contents of that letter—particularly the mysterious reference to *Lord M*—before sharing them with anyone, least of all Lord Michael.

Sylvia was plainly relieved. "I'm g-glad," she said. "Can I sleep in your bed again tonight?"

"May I?" Anne corrected automatically. Then, smiling at how quickly she had gone from being delighted at hearing the child's speech to correcting it, she said, "You have had an upsetting time of it tonight, so if you will feel better sleeping in my bed, you certainly may do so."

She put out the light then, and with Sylvia's hand tucked in hers, went with the child back to her own chambers, where, to her dismay, she found Michael waiting for her in her dressing room.

He had been standing, gazing abstractedly into the fireplace as he frequently seemed to do when he wanted to think quietly, but he turned at once and looked with disfavor at Sylvia, saying flatly, "That child should be in bed."

"She is going to bed," Anne replied, "in my room."

"I see."

"Where is Maisie?"

"I told her you would not require her services tonight."

"Oh." She glanced from the child to Michael and back again, and decided that the first order of business was to banish the look of anxiety that had leapt to Sylvia's face the moment she saw him. "I promised Sylvia that she could sleep in my bed tonight, sir. I am sorry if that vexes you, but I do believe in keeping my word, especially to children."

"It does not vex me to know that you try to keep your word, sweetheart. That must be accounted a virtue in anyone. But unless you also promised Sylvia that you would sleep in that bed with her, and that at once, I will request some few moments of your time in my dressing room. I have something to say to you."

His even tone of voice gave her no indication of the state of his temperament, but she was certain, after the scene she had witnessed between him and Andrew in the library, that she would be wise not to test it. To Sylvia, she said, "I do not precisely recall what I promised you, darling, but a wife, you know, must generally do her husband's bidding. Moreover, I also have news for Uncle Michael, do I not? I will tuck you in before I go, of course, and you will be quite safe here until I return."

A small frown creased the child's forehead when Anne mentioned having news for Michael, but she turned obediently toward the high bed, jumped in without assistance, and let Anne draw the covers to her chin. Aware that Michael was close behind her, Anne bent to kiss one soft cheek, murmuring, "Good night, darling. Sleep well."

"Good night, Sylvia," Lord Michael said over Anne's shoulder. "We'll be just in the next room, you know, if you should chance to become frightened."

"I won't. G-good night, Uncle Michael."

Hearing his gasp, Anne said swiftly, "That is what I wanted to tell you, sir. Sylvia has recovered her voice. No, no, do not tax her about it now, if you please," she added, seeing questions leaping to his lips. "She has been talking for the past half hour, and will no doubt have a sore throat tomorrow from the exertion, which is precisely why I want to let her sleep in here. If Nurse Moffat were to learn the good news at once, she would question her till midnight. But let us go now, so that she can sleep, and I will soon tell you the whole."

Relieved when he did not oppose her, Anne waited only until he moved toward the door before bending down to murmur near the child's ear, "Don't fly into a fidget, love, I won't tell him anything but exactly how you came to speak to me."

"But he will make—"

Anne silenced her with a finger to her lips. "Hush now," she said. "Trust me, and go to sleep. Yes, I'm coming," she added when he turned in the doorway to see what was keeping her.

No sooner was the door shut than Michael said abruptly, "How long have you known of this turn of events?"

She looked calmly back at him and said, "You must know that I just learned of it myself."

"For all I know, you have been chatting with her for weeks. I scarcely ever see her, after all."

Anne said nothing. Neither of them had taken a seat, and she stood now, facing him, wondering if he meant to conduct the entire conversation from just inside the door and wondering, too, just how long she would be able to avoid telling him all she had learned from Sylvia.

He said with a sigh, "Those last remarks were both petulant and unfair, and I beg your pardon. You have never given me cause to believe you would keep any secret from me, let alone one of such magnitude as that. Why are you looking at me like that?"

Feeling her conscience stir again, because she did mean to keep at least one secret from him—at least until she had determined for herself that it was safe to tell him—she cocked her head, and said, "I had begun to wonder if you really wanted an explanation or if your whole intent in seeking me out was to force a quarrel on me, but now you have quite taken the wind out of my sails by apologizing."

He looked rueful. "I certainly don't want to quarrel with you. In point of fact, I came in search of you because I wanted to apologize for something else. You were quite right before to try to check me when I began taking Andrew to task. I am sorry now that I did not heed you, and I wanted to tell you so."

If his first apology had surprised her, the second caught her off guard completely. She had accused him of wanting to quarrel with her more out of a wish to give herself time to think, and to divert his thoughts from Sylvia, than from any desire to take him to task. Having learned in her dealings with her siblings that if she forced one combatant in a dispute to defend himself against a minor, unrelated charge, she could sometimes get him or her to think more sensibly about the major one, she had attempted the same tactic with Michael.

"You surprise me, sir."

"Do I? You must think me nearly as arrogant as Andrew if I can surprise you merely by offering an apology when one is due."

"Oh, no," she said, "just stubborn, and a little inflexible at times, perhaps."

"I will not say you are wrong about that, Anne. Tonight showed me just how foolish I can be not to heed your advice where the children are concerned."

"I suppose you thrashed him," she said. "He deserved it, perhaps, but I wish you had not."

"Then your wish has been granted. Your abrupt departure from the room stopped me in my tracks and made me take a good look at myself, and I confess, I did not like what I saw when I did. Andrew had already thrown me one leveler by calling that woman the first real friend he has had, and saying he feels more valued in her house than in his own, but when he became insolent, he made me as mad as fire. For some reason, he has a knack for stirring my temper even more quickly than his father could."

"You simply don't tolerate insolence, and I am sure no one can wonder at that. From all I have heard about the late duke, surely he did not tolerate it either."

"No," Michael said. "At least, in my own experience of him, I can say he did not. And though I rarely saw the two of them together—for I was away most of the time, you know—I doubt if Edmund accepted insolence from Andrew, but I doubt, too, that any was offered. As near as I can make out, Edmund never denied him anything. You have seen how the servants bow and scrape to him, as if he were a prince of the blood royal—although, come to think of it, I'm persuaded that Bagshaw, at least, would consider the present royal family to be much lower in consequence than the Duke of Upminster. That's better," he added when she smiled. "I was beginning to think you would not smile at me tonight."

The look in his eyes was a warm one, and she knew from her reaction to it that she would have to take care if she was not to reveal to him everything she had learned about the duchess's death. Drawing a steadying breath, she said matter-of-factly, "Since the servants have taken their cue from their late master, and from Bagshaw, of course, and since Lord Ashby, too, is always reminding Andrew of his vast consequence, surely you understand that his dignity is very large, sir, and fragile, as well. I am very glad you did not thrash him. That scene was humiliating for him, and quite painful enough to bear without that."

"It became more painful," he said grimly, "for I did not spare him the tongue-lashing he deserved, and the punishment I gave him will last a good deal longer than a thrashing."

"What did you do?"

"Aside from making it plain that his association with the unsuitable Mrs. Flowers is absolutely over, I have forbidden him to ride or to fish for a week, and ordered him to double his study hours with Pratt for that same length of time. Despite the fact that he threatened to show me that I am not his master, he will think twice before he shouts at me again, I believe."

Anne was not so sure, but although she hoped Michael would eventually learn to resist such authoritarian tactics with the boy, she was too much relieved to learn that Andrew had escaped more painful punishment, to take issue over what she still believed were overstrict penalties for the offense. Andrew had stepped beyond the line of polite behavior, certainly, but it was no wonder to her that he had responded so quickly and emotionally to Mrs. Flowers's treatment or her offer of friendship, and she thought his hot words should have been, if not forgiven, at least dealt with in a more tactful and understanding manner.

Michael's present attitude made it clear that she was beginning to gain some influence over him, and she could hope to gain more as the days progressed. Therefore, she said, "I think you will not be sorry you were lenient, sir. Andrew, in his own way, is nearly as sensitive as Sylvia, I think."

"I cannot agree with you there, but I won't argue either," Michael said, drawing a sofa up before the fire and gesturing for her to sit down. "Tell me about Sylvia now. You could have knocked me over with a feather when she said good-night to me."

"I believe you, for I had an even stronger reaction when she spoke to me," Anne said, remembering the drink she had spilled. When he sat down beside her, she went on, "To say that she startled me would be an understatement, for I did not even realize she had followed me into my room, or that she stood right behind me. I thought I was alone, and when she saw me stir a dose of hartshorn into a cup and raise it to my lips, she said, 'Don't drink that, Aunt Anne, or you will fall asleep and never wake up.' I dropped the cup and nearly jumped out of my skin."

"I am glad to know she has such deep concern for you. She mistook your hartshorn for laudanum, I daresay, and has heard someone warned against taking too large a dose. Why were you taking the stuff?"

"That has nothing to do with Sylvia."

"It has much to do with you, however," he said, settling himself more comfortably beside her. "I want to hear all about Sylvia, but first I want to know why you felt obliged to dose yourself with hartshorn."

"Well, if you must know, I had a headache."

"Poor Anne." He stroked her hair, gently. "Have you still got it? Shall I rub your head for you?"

She realized that her headache was gone, and much though the thought of him rubbing her temples appealed to her, she said firmly, "I am quite well, sir. Once away from the cause . . ." She paused meaningfully.

He sighed. "Very well, you have convinced me that I do not want to hear more about this headache. Tell me about Sylvia."

"There is little more to tell. Once she had spoken, she seemed to have no difficulty, other than a slight stammer from time to time, in continuing to speak. One would think her vocal cords would have become weak from lack of use."

"Apparently, they did not. But why on earth has she remained silent for so long? I should have thought such a feat far beyond the power of any child."

"She did not do so of her own desire, sir. She—" Anne broke off, perceiving that an explanation would not be as simple as she had hoped. She was tempted to unburden herself to him completely, for sitting there beside him, she could no more imagine him a villain than she could imagine any one of her siblings in the same role. But she was wise enough to realize that a villain might well be as charming as Michael was, if only to gain his own nefarious ends, and she knew she would be wiser to keep her peace until she had at least attempted to learn more about the duchess's accusations against the late duke.

Michael's arm was around her now, and she felt the warmth of it upon her shoulders. Involuntarily, she snuggled into the curve of his body and leaned her head into the hollow where his shoulder met his broad chest. She could feel his heart beat.

For a wonder, he had not demanded that she continue, and she realized now that his silence was uncharacteristic. Tilting her head a little, she looked up into his face, searching it for some sign of his mood. The gleam in his eyes made it clear to her that he had been waiting for her to do that very thing. She felt warmth in her cheeks, and licked dry lips, trying to recall precisely what she had said to him thus far.

He said, "Are you trying to tell me that Sylvia was afraid to speak? I can imagine you would hesitate to say so, thinking I'd declare you quite mad, but although I can't for the life of me think what might have frightened her so, I have learned my lesson, sweetheart. Your understanding of my brother's children is greater than mine, so if you are convinced she held her tongue out of fear, I hope you mean to explain your reasons to me."

Anne's thoughts were racing. She had learned that it would not be easy to deceive him. Not only was deception generally foreign to her nature, but she had long since discovered that she was more likely to speak her thoughts and opinions plainly to him than to wrap them in tact or diplomacy. She would have to tell him more of the truth than she wanted yet to disclose, which meant she would have to be careful if she were not to reveal the existence of the duchess's last letter.

Accordingly, she moved a little away from him, turning as if she meant only to look at him directly, and said quietly, "The reason is rather dreadful, I'm afraid. You see, she was in the room when the duchess killed herself. I do not know if you are aware of how she accomplished the dreadful deed . . ."

"She took poison, I believe." When Anne did not immediately continue, his own thoughts caught up with him, and he exclaimed, "Good God, are you telling me that little Sylvia actually saw her take it, that it was mixed into some potion that Agnes drank, and that is why she spoke when she saw you about to drink something?"

"Exactly so," Anne said quietly.

"I don't know just what she took," he said, frowning. "As I recall the matter, Edmund wrote only that she had taken poison and caused the devil of a scandal up here."

"I should think it would have caused a scandal the length and breadth of England," Anne said thoughtfully, "on account of her rank, if for no other cause. I cannot think why I never heard a word about it."

"Edmund moved heaven and earth to hush it up, as you might suppose," he said grimly. "Parson Dailey helped by agreeing to accept her death as an accident, so she might be buried properly, and our servants here are an unusually closed-mouth set. Still, Edmund told some folks hereabouts—Jake Thornton, for one—and the little that did get about did not redound to his credit, for though I doubt that anyone blamed him directly, it was natural for them all to wonder why she was so unhappy in her life with him that she put a period to her existence."

"Yes," Anne said, but she knew the moment she said it that she had allowed her opinion to color even that simple word,

and was not surprised when he shifted his attention sharply
from his own thoughts back to her. She held her tongue.

Michael said quietly, "I know you have heard much about
Edmund's character since you came to the Priory, and I have
not tried to conceal my own opinion of him, so you have been
given little cause to think him anything but a philanderer, but
surely you cannot think that his . . . his open ways with other
women drove Agnes to kill herself. Why, if that were the case,
half the women in England—if not more—would follow her
example."

"No one can ever know precisely what thoughts exist in
another person's head," Anne replied carefully, "and what I
have heard of the late duchess leads me to believe that her
character was by no means a strong one. Lady Hermione said
she was entirely dominated by her husband, and I have certainly learned nothing since then to make me doubt that assessment."

"It's probably true enough," he said, "though in point of
fact, I knew as little about them as I did about their children.
When Edmund married Agnes, I was still at Eton, and even
when I came home for my holidays, I generally enjoyed a
schoolboy's lack of awareness of the adult relationships around
me. When Andrew was born, I was a month short of my thir-
teenth birthday. My father was still alive then, of course, and
he doted on the new heir just as much as Agnes and Edmund
did, so it is no wonder, I suppose, that I thought everyone here
was perfectly happy."

"Children rarely pay heed to the adults in their families,"
Anne said thoughtfully. "They are much too taken up with
their own concerns to do so—other than to keep out of their
papa's way if they have been naughty, of course."

"I did that, certainly, and kept out of Edmund's way, too,
at such times, for being ten years my senior, he was as apt as
my father was to rake me down." He chuckled. "I can see by
your expression that you would like to point out that, having

had to put up with Edmund, I ought to have more sympathy for Andrew's attitude toward me. Don't spare me, sweetheart."

"I am never surprised when people fail to learn from their own experience," Anne said with a sigh. "I think it is human nature to resist doing so. You were not still at Eton when Sylvia was born, I collect."

"No, I was at Oxford by then, and in the army when my father was killed in a fall from a horse six years ago. I was posted to London at the time, so I came home for his funeral, but I left immediately afterward, seeing no good cause to linger. Since then, I'd spent no more than a few days or a week at a time here until Edmund's death. He did not write to inform me that Agnes had died until after she was buried, so I did not come home then, and I certainly never expected to have the entire business of the estates thrust into my lap less than two weeks later. And what a mess that has become."

"I still do not think it right that you should carry the entire burden yourself when there are others who would be glad to help you. Lord Ashby knows about the mines and, I daresay, a host of other things, and I—"

"In time, perhaps," he said, drawing her gently back into the curve of his arm. "I've felt obliged to keep most matters to myself so far, and although Jake's man was not as helpful as I'd hoped he would be, I got a message today from Alsop, the manager at the Snake Mine near Castleton, telling me he has learned something that might supply answers to a number of our questions. He did not trust the information itself to the post, of course, so I mean to go there tomorrow to talk to him personally. But we have spoken enough about me and my family for one night, sweetheart. Have you quite recovered from your headache?"

When she admitted that she had, he soon turned her attention to other activities, and although she was able to congratulate herself upon having successfully diverted his thoughts from the ticklish matter of the duchess's suicide, she had done nothing whatsoever to answer the questions in her own mind.

Both her instinct and her increasing desire for Michael told her that he was a good man, not a wicked one, but she could not ignore the reference to Lord M in the duchess's letter, and until she was able to put her fears to rest, she did not feel justified in revealing more to him than she already had. To make the letter public would give rise to dreadful scandal, and yet to keep it private while revealing its contents to the wrong person might well serve to thrust herself and even Sylvia into danger.

Unable to sleep, she got up at last, taking care not to waken Michael, and tiptoed into her own bedchamber to check on Sylvia. The child was sleeping soundly, curled up in the exact center of the bed with the kitten beside her. Anne straightened the coverlet, then lighted a candle from a glowing ember on the hearth and took out her journal. Though she began, as usual, by addressing the entry to her dearest James, she found herself almost from the outset writing as if to her husband instead.

. . . and so I come to the difficulty at hand, which is to say, how one knows when to trust another with one's innermost secrets. Though our relationship is founded upon certain basic needs of yours and your convenience, my heart tells me you are deserving of trust and that I am the wicked one for keeping secrets from you. One moment I want to run to you and speak every thought in my head, the next I know I must not—not yet.

I love you. There, I have put the words down on paper, so I know they are real. I know, too, that the sentiment is real, although indeed, I do not yet know if it will prove to be a blessing or a curse. I wish you could know how much I love you and how very much I fear discovery of the truth about you. One moment I think it will be for the best, and the next I believe that, if I were sensible, I would fear for my life.

To catalog details here where others might read them

would be dangerous, I think, but to write in this fashion
to you helps me clear my head and order my thoughts,
though I know you will not respond. Indeed, I see now
that my trust in you is of the greatest import. You do not
speak of loving me, of course, and in my opinion, you
have not always acted wisely, but you have never given
me cause to believe you would act without integrity. With
that in my mind, I see now that I have little reason not
to go to you at once and put my whole confidence in you
to set everything right.

Lying in his bed, alone for the moment, he turned his
thoughts to the news that had reached him from Castleton that
day. No doubt there had been a misstep, but he would not
know where he stood until he had learned the whole. In any
case, he was safe where the *Folly* was concerned, for there
was no longer much danger of the trail leading to him. As to
the wager, he had not yet decided what to do. No one had
known the truth but Jake, Edmund, and one other; and, since
Jake's widow seemed bent upon refusing any Upminster
money, that one would most likely never hear the wager had
not been paid. Providence had been with him thus far, certainly. With any luck, all would yet be well.

She was coming back now. He could hear her. A pretty little
thing, and proving to be more sensible than most, really. A
pity she was beginning to bore him.

After thinking first that perhaps she ought just to get into
her own bed and sleep with Sylvia, Anne gave in to her yearning and went quietly back to Michael's bed. He did not stir
when she crawled in beside him, but when she curled up next
to him, he turned a little, and she felt his arm slip around her.
Thinking he might have wakened, she wondered if she ought
to tell him the whole tale immediately, but when his deep,

regular breathing informed her that he still slept, she decided not to waken him.

She would tell him everything first thing in the morning. Moreover, she would show him the duchess's letter. And thus, with her mind relieved at last of this care, she slept so soundly that she slept past her usual time. When she wakened at last, and found herself alone in the great bed, she rang at once for Maisie, only to learn that his lordship had left the house very early that morning, bound for the mines at Castleton.

Eighteen

Discovering that Sylvia was up and had been for some time, Anne dressed quickly and went downstairs to the breakfast parlor, intending to waste no more of the day than she had already. Entering the room through one door just as Mrs. Burdekin entered through the other, the pair of them startled the two other persons already there.

Elbert instantly let go of Jane's arm and stepped away from her. Blushing furiously and shifting her gaze to avoid Anne's, Jane bobbed a curtsy and murmured an apology.

Vexed, Anne said, "Elbert, how many times must you be warned to leave the maids alone? If you have an acceptable explanation for this behavior, I should very much like to hear it."

Mrs. Burdekin, clicking her tongue, glared in displeasure at the two miscreants. "By your leave, your ladyship, I'll deal with this, and quickly, too." To Anne's surprise, she said nothing to Elbert or Jane but strode back to the door through which she had come and said in minatory tones, "Mr. Bagshaw—here I say, Mr. Bagshaw—be so good as to step in here this minute and explain to me just what one of your lads thinks he is about, to be manhandling one of my housemaids!"

Bagshaw, stately as ever, entered the room, bowed to Anne, and said, "Good morning, your ladyship. Is something amiss?"

Anne glanced at the two servants. Elbert stood as straight as a stick, his chin high, not looking at anyone else in the room. Jane, white-faced now, her hands pressed into her white cambric apron, stared at the floor. Anne said, "Mrs. Burdekin will explain, Bagshaw, but first, if you please, Mrs. Burdekin, I would like some tea and toast, and perhaps a boiled egg."

"Certainly, madam, at once," the housekeeper said. "As to you, Jane Hinkle, you've no call to be in this room at this hour, so you just step along upstairs to the small salon and see to the dusting there. That room looks as if it ain't seen a duster in a week of Sundays."

"Yes, Mrs. Burdekin," Jane said, bobbing another curtsy but casting a gloomy sidelong glance at Anne as she did.

Seeing at the same time that Bagshaw was eyeing the house-maid askance, Anne said firmly as Jane left the room, "I ought perhaps to mention at the outset that I do not want anyone to lose his or her position over this incident."

"Certainly, madam," the butler said, "it shall be as you wish. I might point out, with respect," he added dulcetly, "that I did offer a warning some time ago as to what would be the outcome of keeping immoral persons on the staff."

Mrs. Burdekin said sharply, "In that instance, sir, it is your menservants who ought to look to their behavior. The idea, always blaming my maids—" She broke off at a sharp glance from the butler, and Anne judged it time to intervene again.

"I see that the pair of you will know just how to deal with this problem so as to cause the least disturbance," she said quietly. "Now, if you please, I should like my breakfast."

Her meal was produced within minutes, and although Elbert waited on her, he did so silently. She made no attempt to discuss his latest breach of behavior further, preferring to leave that task to the butler; however, when she dismissed Elbert as soon as she had finished eating, she said, "I will ring if I require your services later. In the meantime, I suggest you give some serious thought to improving your deportment if you want to continue as my personal footman."

"Yes, your ladyship. Begging your pardon, ma'am," he added as she turned away, "but me and Jane . . . that is, well, perhaps I were speaking a bit sharp to her, but I think she's . . . well, the fact is I'm right taken with her, your ladyship, and once I can persuade her of my exact sentiments, I'll wager she won't behave like she does now. Why, in the old days, before His Grace died . . . But I shouldn't be talking out of turn, I expect."

The phrase bit hard at Anne's memory, and she fought a strong urge to demand to know exactly what he meant by it, but she managed to say calmly instead, "I am glad to hear that you have some consideration for Jane, Elbert, but you ought not to carry on your personal affairs when you are on duty, you know."

"No, ma'am, that I do know, but Jane were wishful to know where she might find your ladyship, and I were just telling her that your ladyship had not come downstairs as yet."

This bland description did not in any way fit the scene Anne and Mrs. Burdekin had interrupted, but Anne did not question him further, because Bagshaw returned just then and said in a stern tone, "When her ladyship does not require your services, Elbert, I shall want a few words with you in my pantry."

The footman's expressive grimace was nearly enough to make Anne change her mind and say she had other duties for him to perform, but she restrained herself, deciding it would do the young man no harm to hear what the butler had to say to him, and might well do him a great deal of good. Thus, she said, "Go with Bagshaw now, Elbert. If I want you, I will ring for you."

"Yes, your ladyship," Elbert said unhappily.

Leaving them, she went at once in search of Jane Hinkle and found her in the salon at the top of the stairs, energetically wielding her feather duster. She turned when Anne entered the room and, flushing, said, "Oh, your ladyship, I do beg your pardon. Is Mrs. Burdekin very cross with me, do you think?"

"I think, for once, the blame is being laid upon the right

shoulders," Anne said. "I left Elbert with Bagshaw, who did not look in the least as if he were going to commend him for his stupid behavior." When the maid still looked doubtful, she added with a reassuring smile, "I do think you are safe for now, Jane, truly. Elbert said you were looking for me."

"I was. He wanted me to tell him why I was in such a twitch, but I didn't think I ought to do so, and you know what men are, madam. He wouldn't take no for an answer. H-he fancies me, I'm afraid, and the footmen here seem to think that's all that's required to make a girl leap into bed with them. Indeed, they take it as a right, and I know for a fact that a number of the maids go in fear of them, but I've locked my little room at night since I came, and I'll continue to do so."

"An excellent idea," Anne said, "but you should speak to Mrs. Burdekin, you know, if you have any more difficulty with Elbert. Was that all you wished to say to me?"

"No, ma'am." Jane hesitated, then blurted, "I-I had my first afternoon out yesterday and . . . and I'm afraid I went to see her again—Mrs. Flowers, that is—and oh, my lady, she were in flat despair herself, on account of she says she is to be turned out of her house, and she said straight out that I were wasting my time searching for Molly." Tears welled into her eyes, and she looked hopelessly at Anne. "Molly's long since dead and buried, she said."

"I'm so sorry, Jane. Is she quite certain?"

"Yes, ma'am, and it weren't such a shock as you might think. I've feared from the beginning that Molly might be dead. Mrs. Flowers said she'd talked to one of the women on that boat down on the river, ma'am, who told her flat out Molly got killed. She said it were an accident, but I could tell Mrs. Flowers didn't believe that part of it. I'd say she knew, or guessed, more than what she was telling me, but she didn't tell me any more."

"Perhaps she wanted to spare your feelings."

"Perhaps, but I could see that she were too taken up with

her own problems to care much about mine. And I do think," Jane added on a harder note, "that what Sir Jacob did to her were a scandal, ma'am, though I know well I oughtn't to say such things. Lady Thornton's man already told Mrs. Flowers she's to be out of the house by Monday, and that's not fair, my lady, indeed it's not, for she's no place to go but back where she come from—if she's even got money enough left to get to Chesterfield—or else she'll have to work on that dreadful boat. It's a crime, ma'am, or ought to be. She's at her wits' end, I can tell you."

Sorry though she was to hear of Mrs. Flowers's predicament, Anne could think of no way to help her. "What will you do now, Jane?" she asked. "I hope you do not mean to leave us."

"As to that, my lady, I can't say. On the one hand, I still want to know exactly what happened to Molly, and on the other, knowing she's dead, I expect I ought to be thinking of myself."

"I'd like you to stay on here if you can bear to do so," Anne said. "You are the best housemaid we have, and I have no doubt that once we have a complete staff again, you will soon move up to a higher position."

Jane's smile was brief, but there was genuine amusement in it. "A fortnight ago, I'd have said you was all about in your head to suggest such a thing to me, ma'am—begging your pardon for the liberty—because, not having been born and bred here at Upminster, I knew I was lucky to have got my position at all, and would never stir a step upward from it. But since the day you snatched young Clara from the flames, Mrs. Burdekin's not stopped singing your praises, and she's been more than pleasant to me, as well. Still and all, I was that surprised to see her go for Mr. Bagshaw this morning, for I'm sure she never before did such a thing in her life. It was all yes and amen with her before, whenever he crooked a finger, but not anymore, I expect."

When Anne encountered the butler a few minutes after she

left Jane, she could not see that he had lost a jot of his customary dignity in the brief skirmish with the housekeeper. According Anne his usual nod of greeting, he said, "I have come to inform you that Lady Sylvia's governess has arrived, madam. A Miss Johnson, whom I have left sitting in the hall, not knowing precisely where your ladyship would choose to receive her."

"Good gracious," Anne exclaimed, "I did not know she was coming today."

"No, your ladyship, so I apprehend. According to what the young woman related to me, it was Lady Harlow who commanded her to come. A very well-mannered young woman she appears to be, I might add," the butler added deprecatingly.

"I will see her at once, Bagshaw. Show her into the yellow drawing room, please." Giving him time to do so before she followed him, Anne hoped the young woman would prove acceptable. Remembering Lady Harlow's forthright manner, she had little doubt that she would take offense if the governess of her choice were turned away from Upminster. When she entered the drawing room to find a sensibly dressed young woman with soft brown hair and pink cheeks, she was reassured, and the twinkle in Miss Johnson's hazel eyes bolstered an instant, instinctive conviction that Lady Harlow had chosen well. "How do you do," Anne said, smiling. "I am Lady Michael. I hope your journey was a pleasant one."

"Very pleasant, thank you, your ladyship," she replied in a well-modulated voice. "I collect, from your butler's reaction, that my arrival was not anticipated. My headmistress warned me that Lady Harlow might be acting precipitately in commanding me to come here straightaway when school let out for the half-term holiday, so I will tell you at once that I have relations in Derbyshire to whom I may go. Furthermore, should you decide that you will not require my services after all, I am assured that I may return to the school at Michaelmas term." She withdrew a packet of papers from the sensible reticule she carried and held it out. "You will find my references in order, my lady."

"I'm sure I will," Anne said. "I admit that, not having a very good notion from her ladyship's letter of when you would be free to leave your position, I did not expect your arrival. I'm afraid I was a little delayed in my response to her letter, too, but nonetheless, as I informed her, I have every confidence in her choice. You want to meet Sylvia at once, of course."

"Yes, please. I might add, ma'am, that Lady Harlow was kind enough to explain the child's affliction to me."

"That, thank heaven, need no longer concern us, for I am happy to tell you she has begun speaking again. Come, I will take you to her now."

They went upstairs to the nursery, where they found Sylvia chatting contentedly with Moffat. The nurse said, "Oh, your ladyship, ain't it grand to be hearing her voice again?"

Anne saw that Sylvia, although she had risen at once to her feet when they entered, now seemed to be avoiding her gaze in much the same way that Jane Hinkle had done earlier. She said to the nurse, "This is Miss Johnson, Moffat. She is to be Lady Sylvia's new governess. Mrs. Moffat is Sylvia's nurse, Miss Johnson, and will no doubt be of much help to you. Shall I ring for a servant to show you to your own rooms now?"

"If it please your ladyship," Miss Johnson said in her pleasant voice, "I would prefer to stay here for a time and get to know Mrs. Moffat and Lady Sylvia. Then perhaps, Sylvia would be so kind as to show me where I am to sleep."

"Very well," Anne said. "Sylvia, Miss Johnson's rooms are at the end of this corridor. You know the ones, do you not?"

"I'll show her," Sylvia said quietly. She glanced at Anne, then looked guiltily away again, making Anne wonder what mischief she had been up to. Deciding that now was not the time to pursue that matter, however, she left them to get better acquainted and went to attend to her usual household duties.

She had scarcely had a chance before then to think about the decision she had made the previous night, but now she found it hard to concentrate on anything else. The spring cleaning was all but done, and despite Mrs. Burdekin's acid comment to Jane about the salon, the great house sparkled from its attics to its cellars. Every cupboard and chest had been turned out and its contents inventoried, and every nook and cranny had been scrubbed and polished until it smelled as clean as it looked.

Blanket chests had been rubbed with lavender oil, new muslin bags of dried lavender scented the linen presses, and the potpourri jars in the main rooms had been scrubbed and refilled. Each room now boasted its own delicate fragrance, from damask roses in the state drawing room to the mixture of bay leaves and tonka beans in the library.

Though Anne might have attended to any of a dozen minor duties, she knew she would not concentrate. Thus, having approved the dinner menu and discussed with Mrs. Burdekin two projects for the month ahead, she fled the house for the gardens, where she had always been able to think more clearly. One of the dogs followed her outside, but it soon wandered off to explore the home wood, leaving Anne alone with her reflections.

Had Michael been at home, she was certain she would have taken Duchess Agnes's letter to him straightaway; however, with time to think, her doubts soon returned. The only Lord M in the entire neighborhood, to her knowledge, was Lord Michael. But according to what he had said himself, he had not even been in Derbyshire at the time of the duchess's death or at any time in the several years before it except for brief visits. Moreover, knowing him as she did now, she could not imagine him conspiring with his brother in such a distasteful way as the note described.

But while the emotional half of her mind insisted that the very idea was absurd, common sense told her it was entirely possible that Michael had lied to her all along. Certainly he had kept secrets from her, and was still doing so.

Kicking at the gravel path in a most unladylike way, she realized that her thoughts were not helping, and wished she had the nerve to visit Mrs. Flowers, who seemed to know a good deal about matters quite foreign to one who had been raised in a more sheltered fashion. For a fluttering moment, she even dared wish she might visit that dreadful boat on the river. There, she knew, she might learn about many things.

Smiling at herself in the knowledge that to visit either one would surely bring Michael's wrath down upon her, she realized that she was about to take the path toward the river. Once again, she had come out unattended, and recalling Michael's views on that subject—being fairly certain in spite of his kind words the last time the subject had come up that those views had not really changed much—she was about to turn back toward the house when she saw Mr. Pratt strolling toward her. She waited for him to come up to her, surprised in view of Michael's having ordered Andrew's study hours doubled, to see the tutor walking alone, and wondering if it might be a good time to ask if he might be able to teach the boy to swim.

"Good day to you, your ladyship," he said.

"Good day, Mr. Pratt. Have you left Andrew alone with his books to contemplate his latest sins?"

He looked surprised. "Why, ma'am, surely you know he went with Lord Michael today. I believe they rode to Castleton so that his lordship might introduce His Grace to the mine there."

All thought of swimming lessons vanished, and stifling her first inclination, which was to deny that Lord Michael had done any such thing, Anne murmured a vague reply, excused herself, and hurried back into the house. No longer were her thoughts possessed by what she would or would not tell Lord Michael. She wondered instead where on earth Andrew had got to.

Having no doubt that the tutor, still being unacquainted with his charge's ability to seize the initiative when he wanted to do something forbidden to him, would have believed whatever the boy had said to him, she looked first in Andrew's bedchamber, half expecting to discover him there. Finding it empty and showing no sign that he had been there since leaving it that morning, she was tempted to ring for his manservant, but she decided against it. Until she could discover precisely what Andrew was up to, the fewer people to know he was missing the better—for Andrew, at any rate.

Paying a visit next to the stable to see if his horse was gone, she found it in its loose box, munching hay. When she walked outside again, wondering if it would be worthwhile to walk to the meadow where Lord Ashby was overseeing the filling of his precious new balloon, she met his lordship coming back, strolling alongside Lady Hermione, leading her horse for her.

"Hello, my dear," he exclaimed. "Coming along to see the grand sight, are you?"

"Well, sir," she said, forcing a smile and trying to decide if she should tell him Andrew was missing, "I did think I'd have a look. I suppose there must be quite a crowd of folks there."

"No, there ain't," he said. "Just my two lads, standing guard. We don't encourage gawkers, you see, on account of wanting to admit only those who purchase subscription tickets. Makes them much more valuable, don't you think? Pity you didn't come along a half hour ago, though. Took Hermie up, I did."

"Goodness," Anne said, adding when she remembered the unexpected length of her own voyage, "but how could you have done such a thing and be here now, sir? Where did you come down?"

"Kept the *Great Britain* on a tether," he said smugly. "Didn't even rise above the hilltop. Just wanted to give Hermie a taste of what it will be like tomorrow, and then too, we wanted to fill the bag enough to be certain it suffered no leaks in being transported. Seemed an excellent chance to show Hermie how the new valve works, and to get some practice with the mechanism myself, since it's a bit different from the old one."

"No one else went with you?"

"Not a soul," he said, grinning. "You afraid for Hermie's virtue, my dear? Assure you, no need to be."

"No need at all, you knave," Lady Hermione said. "Since I can manage the thing as well as you do yourself, and wouldn't need you to get down again even if we hadn't been tethered, one finger out of place and I'd have pitched you over the side."

He grimaced, saying, "Dash it, Hermie, don't make ridiculous threats. You're always doing it, and you know dashed well you'd never do any such thing. You preach resolution, but the fact of the matter is you are as meek and proper as the next female."

"I am not," she snapped.

"Well, don't look as if I've insulted you," he retorted. "That was by way of being a compliment. I may tease the life out of you about being too timid ever to attempt a real adventure, but if you ever did even the half of the things you threaten to do, you'd put yourself beyond the pale, woman. Think of that!"

"Poppycock." Turning pointedly to Anne, she said, "Do you mean to go look at the thing? It is a pretty bag, I can tell you—green and gold stripes—and larger than the *Royal George.*"

"No, if you mean to go up to the house, I'll go with you, of course. I look forward to a comfortable coze with you."

"Tried to talk her into a nuncheon, myself," Lord Ashby said, "but she will have it that she can't stay. She was on her way to the village to post a letter to the Chesterfield registry office, of all things."

"The village?" Anne realized that she ought to have thought of the village before.

Lady Hermione grimaced expressively. "Yes, and I mustn't linger, I'm afraid. I've already spent too much time with Ashby and his aerostat, for I promised Wilfred I'd take a letter into the village for him, you see, so the postboy can take it with him when he leaves at two for Chesterfield. Wilfred forgot to hand it to him when the morning post was delivered, and so now, if you please, it's got to go at once, today."

"It must be important then," Anne said. Still trying to think what she ought to do, she was not really listening.

"Oh, important is as important does, of course, but Wilfred is in a state, to be sure, for he received notice from his housekeeper. Just as I foretold, the thoughtless woman intends to marry her mama's doctor, and to think I once fretted over having too little to do at the Hall! Now Wilfred turns to me for everything, expecting me to manage his household for him, so that he can save a few pounds a month. But I won't do it, and so another housekeeper must be hired as soon as one can be found."

Making up her mind, Anne said casually, "I hope you will stop by on your return, ma'am, and perhaps stay to dine with us—that is, if your brother will not object."

"Much good it would do him if he did," Lord Ashby said with a chuckle.

"Oh, go along with you, Ashby," Lady Hermione said, adding when he just grinned at her, "No, no, I mean it now. I want a private word with Anne."

"Very well, but mind you don't let that gray nag of yours run away with you," he advised, turning away to ascend the steps, swinging his stick in a jaunty manner.

"Odious man," she said, watching him. "Now, my dear, what is troubling you? No, don't poker up, I can see that something is amiss. Tell me."

"I own, I am a little troubled," Anne confessed. "Andrew threatened to show Michael that he is his own master, and now he seems to have disappeared again. I'm afraid he might have gone into the village, but I don't know for certain, or I would go after him myself. I have not even made a proper search here. Indeed, till Lord Ashby mentioned the village, I never thought—"

"Say no more. Ashby told me what happened last night, and I understand your fears. Andrew seems determined to flout Michael's every order, does he not? I shall keep my eyes open in the village, I promise you, and if I see him, I'll send him straight home with a flea in his ear. You may rely on me."

Watching her ride off, Anne hoped she was not making a mistake by not organizing a collective effort to find Andrew. Reluctant to stir up a fuss, she decided to search for a time on her own, and await Lady Hermione's return. An hour passed before she remembered Sylvia's guilty behavior and wondered if she had knowledge of her brother's whereabouts.

Hurrying to the nursery, she found the child alone with her nurse and looking not a little disconcerted to see her.

"What have you done with your new governess?" Anne asked in her usual calm manner, but watching Sylvia narrowly when she did.

Moffat answered, "Our nice Miss Johnson has gone away to change her dress, my lady, so we can show her over the gardens after we have our bit of nuncheon, which they will be serving in the schoolroom in just a few minutes now."

Still watching Sylvia, Anne said, "Moffat, have you forgotten that Lady Sylvia can speak for herself now?"

The nurse chuckled. "Not likely, ma'am, though I did just answer your question out of plain habit to speak for her, I suspect. But it ain't likely I'll forget she can talk again, for she's been just chattering away all morning long, making up for lost time, I suppose we ought to say."

"Well, I wish to speak with her privately for a moment," Anne said, noting that Sylvia seemed reluctant even to look at her, let alone to enjoy a private chat. "Perhaps you can go to fetch Miss Johnson, Moffat, so that she knows where to go. I have not taken time yet to explain her duties to her, or even to think about where she will generally take her meals. In time,

I expect, she will accompany Sylvia to the family table when we do not dine in company, but for now, you may tell her that she and Sylvia will take their meals here with you."

"Yes, your ladyship."

Anne said nothing more until the nurse had gone, leaving her alone with Sylvia, who was looking more uncomfortable than ever. She looked at her feet and fidgeted until the door had shut behind Moffat. Then, when Anne still did not speak, the child finally looked at her.

"I think you have something to tell me," Anne said gently.

Sylvia shook her head.

"Come now, darling, this is no time to forget how to speak. I wondered when I brought Miss Johnson up to you why you looked so oddly at me. Have you done something naughty?"

Sylvia shook her head again.

"This will not do, Sylvia," Anne said, her tone stern now. "When you could not speak, such a reply was acceptable. It no longer is, however. Respond to my question properly, if you please. Have you done something naughty?"

"No, Aunt Anne. At least . . ." Her brow wrinkled as she considered the matter.

"Well?"

Sylvia looked directly at her at last. "If a person obeys one person, but in obeying him is maybe vexing another person, is that being naughty?"

Anne gave a sigh of relief. "Then you do know where that wretched boy is. Tell me at once."

"But I don't know," Sylvia said. "At least, if you mean Andrew, he did not say where he was going."

Realizing that she had taken a misstep, Anne said at once, "Perhaps you had better explain the matter from the beginning."

"Will you be cross with me?"

"I don't know," Anne said honestly. "It would be foolish of me to promise not to be if what you are going to tell me is something that will make me cross with you. If all you did was obey a command that Andrew gave you, I probably will be cross with him, not you. I can tell you, however, that if you do not explain matters quickly now, you will vex me very much. When did you see Andrew last?"

"When I got up this morning, I went to tell him I could talk again. He was still having his breakfast, and Mr. Pratt had not come in yet, so we were able to talk alone for a few moments. He was very pleased, and he said it quite decided him to do what he must to show Uncle Michael that he was a force to be reckoned with, and not a mere child to be ordered about. I asked him what he meant, but he would not explain. He said only that he had to make haste if he was to succeed, and he scribbled a letter."

"To whom?"

"To Uncle Michael, and he made me promise not to give it to anyone else who might come looking for him, and not even to Uncle Michael until tomorrow morning when, Andrew said, it will be quite too late for him to stop him doing what he means to do. He said I should just tell everyone that I don't know anything. But I don't think," the little girl said with a shudder, "that I could have told lies to Uncle Michael, even for Andrew."

"I should hope not," Anne said. "Where is the letter?"

After a pause, Sylvia said, "You know. My secret place."

"Run and fetch it, please, at once."

Sylvia obeyed, and once Anne held the sealed letter in her hand, and saw that it was indeed addressed in Andrew's bold but scrawling hand to Lord Michael, she hesitated only a moment at the thought that she should not read a note addressed to someone else before she cast her scruples to the wind and ripped it open.

Sir:

I take leave to inform you that, having had a surfeit of your discipline, I have decided to take matters into my own hands. Henceforward, I shall answer to no one but myself. As a first step toward that end, I have decided to marry Fiona Flowers, since to do so will resolve both her problem and mine.

She has always been most kind to me. Moreover, she once told me she would be glad to be my wife, and would marry me in an instant, were the opportunity truly hers. Once I have informed her of my sentiments and have explained matters properly to her, I have no doubt that she will agree to elope to Scotland with me.

Upminster

Nineteen

"What did Andrew write?" Sylvia asked in a small voice.

Scarcely heeding her, Anne looked helplessly at the note, trying to convince herself that she did not believe it. Glancing at last at the anxious child, she said, "He wants to do something foolish, my dear, but I mean to stop him, so you must not fret. Say nothing to anyone about this letter, unless by some mischance your uncle should return from Castleton before I have found your brother. Then, if he should ask you about Andrew, tell him only that you gave me a letter he had written and that I am attending to the matter. You need not say what was in the letter."

"I don't know what is in it," Sylvia pointed out. "But what will you do, Aunt Anne?"

"I don't know," Anne admitted, "but you can help me by going along now to eat your nuncheon with Moffat and Miss Johnson, and by keeping silent about this. Can you do that?"

"Yes, ma'am."

"Good." Catching up her skirt, Anne went in search of Bagshaw, encountering him on the stairs to the front hall.

"Bagshaw, do you know when Lord Michael means to return?"

"I am sure I could not say, madam."

"Does that mean you do not know, or that you will not tell me?" she demanded impatiently.

He seemed to stiffen at her tone, but collected himself at once and said in his usual polite way, "Lord Michael has

driven in his post-chaise to Castleton, madam, to look into
some matter or other to do with the mine. With a pair of horses
and one postillion, such as he had this morning, to get there
and back takes at least three hours, perhaps more, and one
cannot doubt that his purpose in going there must occupy
rather more time than that. May I be of service to you, perhaps?"

"No, thank you," Anne said distractedly. She turned away
only to turn back, saying, "Have you seen His Grace today?"

"Not since breakfast, madam. I believe he left the house
soon afterward."

"I see." She thought quickly. Andrew had several hours'
head start, but although she did not doubt that he believed
the extraordinary notion he had taken into his head, she could
not imagine that Mrs. Flowers would agree to it. Even if it
was a bit late to hope Lady Hermione might find the boy
still kicking his heels in the village—for even Andrew would
not have been so unmannerly as to present himself before
he was certain Mrs. Flowers was up and decently clad to
receive him—surely, the woman would send him straight
home again. In any case, Michael's discovery of this latest
start must somehow be prevented. The thought of the painful
scene that would undoubtedly follow such discovery stirred
Anne to gather her wits.

Forcing her attention back to the patient butler, she said,
"Is Lord Ashby still in the house, or has he gone out again?"

"I believe his lordship is in his sitting room, madam, ex-
amining the final preparations for tomorrow's ascension."

With a sigh of relief that yet another obstacle had not been
flung into her path, Anne hurried to find Lord Ashby.

He looked up when she entered his pleasant little sitting
room, and said cheerfully, "Hello again, my dear. You will be
most pleased to hear that we have collected more than enough
subscriptions to cover the entire cost of tomorrow's expedi-
tion."

"Never mind all that now, sir. We have something much more important to discuss, I'm afraid."

"Nonsense, what could be more important than the ascension? What with that penny-pinching nephew of mine carrying on over every few hundred pounds' worth of inflammable air, I thought—since the subscriptions were your own notion, you know—that you would be delighted to learn how well they have succeeded."

"I am very pleased, sir, certainly, but the present matter is extremely urgent. I'm afraid Andrew means to try to persuade Mrs. Flowers to elope with him to Scotland." She paused, watching him, half expecting him to laugh.

Instead, Lord Ashby said crossly, "Drat the boy! What can he be thinking of, to offer himself to such an unworthy piece?"

"I am persuaded that he is acting only out of his resentment toward Michael's attempts to control him," Anne said, "but Andrew cannot be thinking properly, for the notion of such a marriage is perfectly absurd. He is only fourteen years old, after all, and Mrs. Flowers must be all of thirty-five. I do not doubt that she has tried to persuade him to come home, but I fear she must have her hands full, for he was extremely upset last night. I mean to go after him myself, but Michael would be extremely vexed if I were to visit her on my own, and I might well miss Lady Hermione on her return, so I am hoping you will ride along with me, sir."

He had not tried to speak, nor had he seemed really to be listening, but he frowned now, saying, "Doubt he'll have any trouble persuading her, by Jove. She'd become a duchess, after all, with all the rights and privileges of the rank. Woman in her position would be mad to turn him down, particularly when Jake's will has as good as thrown her out of her own house."

"But they cannot really marry, can they?" Anne said, aghast. "Andrew is a minor. Surely, he cannot marry without permission."

"Not here in England, he can't, but you said they're bound for Scotland, did you not?"

"That is what he wrote here," she said, handing him the note, "but he is still only a boy, sir, and though he is tall for his age, no one could mistake his lack of years or believe it to be an acceptable match."

Lord Ashby grimaced. "He may be only a boy, and a minor under English law, but he has reached the age of consent, and in Scotland he will not have to contend with any recalcitrant parson or marriage license as he would here. Don't you recall what Jake Thornton told us that night about the ease with which a Scottish marriage may be arranged?"

"Marriage by declaration," she said, sitting down abruptly in the nearest chair when her knees threatened to betray her. "But surely Sir Jacob was talking about grown men abducting heiresses to Gretna Green, and other such clandestine alliances, not about boys running away with thirty-five year old—" She broke off, unable to think what to call Fiona Flowers that would not offend her own already overstrained sense of propriety.

"Aye, but the law applies to all, my dear, whoever they be and whomever they might carry off to Gretna or any other damned place in Scotland. And what it means in Scotland is not the worst of it by a long chalk, I'm afraid."

"No," she said. "I remember now. Sir Jacob said that any marriage declared legal under Scottish law is also recognized as legal in England, so if their union is truly a lawful one in Scotland, it will be here, too. But surely you misjudge Mrs. Flowers, sir. I have met her, and I simply cannot believe she would be party to so dastardly an arrangement."

"Bound to leap at it like a trout to a mayfly," Lord Ashby said cynically. "What with her protector dead, not so much as a sovereign left to her, and knowing she's to be evicted from her house at once, the way I see it, it's the only recourse left to her, other than to return to some broth— That is," he added with a guilty look, "she's naught to lose and much to gain, which, if you ask me, is rather too much motivation for her to accept that misbegotten brat's proposal of marriage."

"Then we must go after them at once."

"Someone should. They won't be bound for Gretna from here, you know. Much more likely that they'll make for Wakefield and meet the Great North Road just south of York. Where the devil's Michael? He'd catch them quick enough with those bays of his."

"He's gone to Castleton," she said, "and by the time he gets back, it will be too late. If they are really bound for Scotland, sir, we must go after them ourselves."

Lord Ashby did not look pleased, but he nodded and said with a sigh, "I'll send a message round to the stables." Then, more cheerfully, he added, "Now I come to think about it, I daresay we'll find them still in the village if we're quick enough, or—what's even more likely, in my opinion—we'll meet Hermie on her way back, dragging the brat along with her by an ear."

"Andrew's been gone several hours," Anne said.

"No matter. Flowers woman was bound to want to pack up her things, at least, and in my experience, packing consumes a vast amount of time—far more than one ever expects it will. But you needn't come along, my dear. I'll go myself. Might miss Hermie, as you say, and Michael is quite right to want you to keep your distance from that Flowers woman."

Reluctantly, she agreed but urged him to make haste, and turned to ring for a servant herself, to send the order to the stables. Just as she put her hand on the cord, however, the sitting-room door opened and a man she recognized as one of those who helped Lord Ashby with his balloons entered, saying, "They are nearly ready now, my lord. Her ladyship said to fetch you down to the meadow at once."

"Fetch me to the meadow," exclaimed Lord Ashby. "What the deuce are you blathering about, Douglas?"

"The ascension, sir. She said you mean to practice again today with a bit more weight in the basket, so as to be perfectly certain there will be no difficulty tomorrow. The bag is nearly filled to capacity now. They are just waiting for you."

"They?" Speaking at once, Anne and Lord Ashby exchanged startled looks. He demanded, "Who, exactly, is waiting for me?"

"Why, everyone, sir. His Grace, Lady Hermione, and a third lady that her ladyship said you had invited to accompany you."

"What direction is the wind?" Lord Ashby snapped, getting to his feet so quickly that his chair tipped and nearly went over, and snatching his stick from its place against the wall.

"From the south, sir, and steady, about twenty miles per hour. If it keeps up, you could ride it straight to Scotland," he added with a chuckle.

Heading for the door, with Anne and Douglas right behind him, Lord Ashby said, "I've got a devilish premonition that things are a sight worse than we thought, by Jove."

When they emerged from the house, the first thing they saw was the bright green and gold striped balloon rising gently into the sky. Three figures occupied the wicker basket beneath it, and to Anne's astonishment, all three had the audacity to wave.

Lord Ashby's second man could be seen now, running toward them across the stable yard. He began speaking before he reached them. "My lord, my lord, I swear 'twere none o' my doing! She cut the tie-ropes first with that knife what you keeps in the basket, and then damned if she didn't cut the tether as well!"

"By Jove, I'll murder the lot of them," Lord Ashby roared. "Tell them to bring my curricle round at once, Douglas, with a full team hitched to it, damn your eyes! I'll take Lord Michael's bays, if he didn't take them himself!"

Douglas was staring at the rapidly rising balloon, his eyes round with shock, his mouth agape. Only when Lord Ashby prodded him with his stick did he leap to action.

"I'm going with you," Anne announced, "and it is no use

to try to stop me, sir, for I mean to be there when you catch them if we have to drive all the way to Scotland."

"I'll not waste time arguing with you," he said. "I need to fetch my driving coat, in any case. You fetch a cloak, too, for it's bound to be a dusty ride and there's every chance we won't catch them before nightfall. And leave word for Michael," he called after her as she ran ahead of him back into the house.

She obeyed him as far as fetching her cloak was concerned but as she scrabbled through her wardrobe to find a hat with a veil to keep the dust off her face, she decided not to leave a note for Michael. To write a full explanation would take too long, she reasoned; therefore, the less anyone said to him, the better it would be for all of them. When she hurried into the stable yard ten minutes later, still pinning her hat into place, she found Lord Ashby already on the point of climbing into his curricle, aided by both of his men, who were clearly chagrined at having allowed his precious aerostat to escape their custody.

Striving to look and sound much calmer than she felt, she said to them, "We can scarcely pretend to you two that the balloon broke free, but I will ask you to extend that explanation to anyone else who might ask about it. At least"—she looked anxiously from one to the other—"I hope you have not already told anyone else what you told us."

"No, your ladyship," they said in unison, and the second man, scraping his boot through the dust and avoiding her eye, added in a small voice, "Didn't want no one else to know we was outsmarted by her ladyship, ma'am."

"Excellent," Anne said approvingly. "I am very pleased that you showed such good sense." When they both began to look more cheerful, she added kindly, "There is little cause for concern, you know. His lordship has shown Lady Hermione how to manage the aerostat, and she will no doubt bring them down quite safely, so I hope you will continue to behave sensibly. I will be most displeased if I find everyone gossiping about this when I return. Say nothing at all. Do you understand me?"

"Aye, my lady," the men said, tugging their forelocks.

Lord Ashby said, "It's doubtless no more than a damn-fool prank of His Grace's, Douglas, but in any event, get the wagon moving as soon as you can. Just follow the balloon—but you know that much. They think they're headed for Scotland, but I daresay they won't get that far. Still, when it comes down, you'll have to ask for help as you go, for I'll not wait for you. And don't dawdle talking to folks. I know a good many will be thinking we've cheated them by sending the damned thing up today instead of waiting till tomorrow. We'll deal with that problem later."

He grimaced, then shot his unhappy henchmen a grim look, adding, "I'll have something to say to you both later, but for now, just do as you're told. Keep a still tongue in your heads, as Lady Michael commanded, or, by Jove, I'll cut them out— aye, and your livers too, while I'm at it. Stand away from them now!"

They rolled down the drive, picking up speed as they went, and it was plain to Anne from the way Lord Ashby feather-edged the first corner that he did not intend to spare Lord Michael's favorite team. Anne knew the anxious henchmen would follow as quickly as they could with the wagon, but they would be of no help in the chase. She just hoped she and Lord Ashby could keep the balloon in sight. Although pres-ently it appeared to be drifting along the same course as the main road, she knew from her own experience with the un-predictable craft that one could not depend upon it to do so for long.

She could hear Lord Ashby's voice above the loud clatter of hoofbeats and rattling wheels; however, since he was ap-parently not speaking to her but only muttering threats and epithets, she kept silent, making no attempt to listen or to speak to him until he took a bend in the road at such speed that she had to clutch the side of the curricle to keep from being flung out.

"Please, sir, slow down," she cried, grabbing her hat with her other hand when a gust of wind threatened to snatch it from her head. "We won't catch them at all if you overturn us or if one of those horses breaks a leg."

His muttering increased in volume, but since he was driving Lord Michael's bays, the last named possibility was terrifying enough to make him draw in a bit, and when the team slowed to a trot, he snapped, "Damned foolishness!"

"It is criminal, not foolhardy," Anne said tartly. "Why, this is no more than an illegal abduction, plain and simple."

"Idiotic female," Lord Ashby growled, using his whip deftly to deter the offside leader from kicking its wheeler.

"I do not think she is idiotic at all," Anne said. "She is just plain mercenary, that's all, and I wouldn't have thought it of her. There must be a law against what she is doing, and if there isn't one, they ought to draft one in Parliament."

"Laws never meant much to that totty-headed wench," Lord Ashby said more calmly, shooting her a look of wry amusement.

"Goodness, sir, I did not realize you knew her as well as all that."

"Known her most of my life," he said, looking surprised. "Never been much amazed by any maggot she's taken into her head before, but this takes the prize."

"Well, I should certainly hope so," Anne said. "Stealing a child must be about the worst thing anyone could do."

"By Jove, it ain't the brat she's stolen," Lord Ashby said indignantly. "It's my brand new balloon!"

"Well, in all fairness, I don't really think we can blame Mrs. Flowers for taking the balloon, sir. I daresay she—"

"Who the devil said anything about Mrs. Flowers? I'm talking about that damned scamp Hermione. She had no business encouraging that brat and his . . . his . . . whatever she is, to steal my balloon to take them to Scotland. Nor she hadn't any call to go along with them. Only look at those clouds gathering yonder over the moors. If they ain't thunderheads, you may call me a Dutchman. They'll be devilish lucky if they ain't blown out to sea or struck by lightning before this mad escapade is done."

Anne saw at once that he was right about the clouds gathering in the north, and repressed a shiver of fear at the sight. The puffy white thunderheads did not really look ominous yet, but she feared Lord Ashby would prove to be right. In any case, the balloon was drifting steadily toward the clouds.

"Can they really make it all the way to Scotland, sir?"

"Could, I expect," he said, still watching the balloon. He cast an eye northward again, and she saw him frown. "Doubt they will do so today, however. Unless I miss my guess, those clouds gathering like they are mean there will soon be a shift in this wind. Look up at the ones forming right over our heads now."

She did so, and saw that there were a few wispy clouds scattered above, all moving at the same speed as the balloon, which no longer seemed to be rising. She said, "Everything above us is going steadily north, and the balloon is moving well ahead of us. If they don't come down soon, I'm afraid we'll never catch them in time."

"Can't be helped," he said brusquely. "The wind must be moving between fifteen and twenty miles per hour. These horses might do twelve to fourteen on a good road, but not for long, and I don't want to change teams at Sheffield, since we didn't bring our own groom along to leave with them. Michael would have a fit if we left his precious bays with strangers. They'll get us well past Sheffield, however, and in any case I wouldn't want to leave them at the George in Calver, which would be the best place for them, for they are certainly known there, but Michael might well see them there when he returns from Castleton. Did you bring any money, by the bye?"

"Only what I had at hand," she said. "Don't you have any?"

He grimaced. "None to speak of. Didn't think to take any out of the subscription fund, and my own pockets are to let. Well, there's no hope for it. If we do have to change teams somewhere and they won't tote up the reckoning to the estate, we'll just have to pledge something."

"Then I hope you've got something to pledge," Anne said with asperity, "for I've nothing but what I stand up in, which is to say my dress, my cloak, my shoes, and my hat."

"You've got your ring," he pointed out.

"If you think for one minute that I would pledge my wedding ring, sir, even to fetch Andrew home, you'd better think again. I'd leave you behind for surety before I'd pledge this ring."

He chuckled, but fortunately they did not have to pledge anything, for long before the powerful team was spent, they had other things to worry about.

"That balloon is awfully far away now," Anne said a half hour after they had passed through Sheffield. She had to squint to see it, although the sun looked like a big orange ball perched in a nest of gray haze and gathering, darkening clouds.

"The distance between us ain't what I'm worried about at the moment," Lord Ashby said grimly.

"But if we lose sight of them," Anne said, "we'll never catch them in time to prevent that dreadful wedding, and what Michael will say to us then doesn't bear thinking about."

"Then, by Jove, don't think about it," Lord Ashby advised, urging the bays to greater speed, and having his hands full just keeping them together. "They won't make Scotland by air today, that's certain."

"But how do you know?"

"Anne, use your head. You're shading your eyes against the sun, ain't you?"

"Yes, of course." His meaning struck her even as she spoke. "They are drifting to the west!"

"Yes, and if I don't miss my guess, they'll soon be drifting south again unless that blasted wind blows them out to sea.

Those clouds to the north look like they're moving right toward us now, however. That will teach them, by Jove."

But Anne saw that he was looking more grim by the moment. She said, "What is it, sir? Isn't that a good thing?"

"Wind blowing before a storm can be strong and cold," he said. "She's managed that balloon as well as I could have done myself till now, but she's had no experience with heavy winds, and the landscape hereabouts is unknown to her, and has far too many hills and trees to suit me. Landing safely will be more difficult than she realizes."

Anne could see that the balloon had shifted direction again. Now it looked as if it were hovering, staying in the same place, but before long it began to look as if it were growing larger, so she knew it was coming straight toward them.

The sky was darker, and the wispy clouds overhead had grown more solid looking. She heard thunder and knew the low rumbling sound would have been louder but for the noise of horses and carriage. "The storm is building fast," she said anxiously.

He did not answer. He was watching the balloon.

"How far away are they?" Anne asked.

"Not certain. Distance is deceiving, particularly from this angle. I think they're between Huddersfield and Holmsfirth."

"But that must be twenty-five miles from here!"

"Aye, and rugged country—lots of hills and odd bits of forestland. She's got to bring it further south, to Stocksbridge, at least, before she dares to set it down."

When they passed through Hoyland Nether, he made no mention of pausing to change horses, though the bays were clearly tired. The balloon was lower in the sky and seemed much closer, but when Anne said so, Lord Ashby shook his head.

"Still too far, and look how that basket is moving. Watch the stripes. You can see the balloon is turning on its axis. That's a fine thing if one wants to do it, not so fine if it's making them dizzy and she can't keep it in position. The storm's still hours away, but the winds ahead of it are unpredictable, and she's bound to encounter crosswinds near the ground."

Anne said nothing. She wished the balloon would come down. Not only did it seem to her that the danger was greatest while it remained so far above the ground, but the longer it stayed up, the more likely it was that they would not get home before dark. Michael would be worried, and would no doubt grow angrier by the moment, just as he had the last time. Perhaps she ought to have left a message, after all, she thought, a soothing one. Surely someone would tell him about the balloon if not all the details about its passengers, and he would assume that she was following it. Not, she realized with a sigh, that the assumption would console him much. That thought not being one upon which she wished to dwell, she fixed her attention firmly on the balloon.

"They're coming down," Lord Ashby said tensely. "South of Stocksbridge over Broomfield Moor, I think. Wish I knew the countryside better. Know it for hunting, of course, but one thinks differently when it comes to good landing places, and I don't think she's going to have much choice in the matter. Oh, steady on, old girl. Hold it steady now. That's it, gently, gently. They're throwing out ballast, trying to slow their descent. Thank God, she still has some left."

That there would not be much ballast left aboard now Anne knew. The voyagers must have thrown out nearly all they had before the fickle wind had turned against them, keeping only what they would need to slow a normal descent. That this one would not be normal was growing more apparent by the moment.

"They must be cold," she murmured, pulling her cloak closer around her. The wind on the ground had risen. It was by no means a harsh wind, and under other circumstances, she doubted she would have noticed it. But knowing from her own experience how even a slight crosswind could unsettle a balloon, she bit back words of fear and simply kept her eyes on the balloon.

It was at treetop level now, close enough that she could see the basket swinging beneath the balloon but still some distance from the road, and a good distance ahead of the curricle.

"They're not drifting toward the road," Anne said a moment later. "They're still moving south, but not toward us."

"They'll come down north of Bamford, I think," Lord Ashby said. "There's a turning ahead. We'll take it."

The team was lathered now and would not be able to maintain the pace for long, but she soon saw that it did not matter, because the new road was not built for any speed above a walk. The balloon had disappeared behind a rise in the landscape, and when they topped the next hill, she saw a village nestled by a river, but the balloon was nowhere to be seen.

"Far too many trees," Lord Ashby muttered, urging the horses to a faster pace. "Thought it would be clearer."

Anne held on for dear life when the curricle bounced and jolted over ruts and holes in the road, praying that the wheels would not come off but saying nothing, knowing he would pay her no heed. The road smoothed a little when they drove into the village of Bamford, and he shouted at an urchin in the nearly empty street to ask if he'd seen a balloon.

"Whole village gorn ter see it," the lad shouted back. "Me pa said it looked ter come down in Farmer Kirby's field, he did."

"Come on, show us," Lord Ashby shouted. "Climb on the back, and hang on tight. How is it you ain't with the rest, boy?"

"Me pa said he'd lick me silly did I leave afore I fed the pigs," the lad replied, adding with a smirk, "but they'll all look nohow when I show up in this rig, won't they? Just on ahead, it be, past them gates."

Emerging from a cover of trees, they saw the balloon, deflating rapidly, in the center of a large field of new corn.

"Good girl," Lord Ashby said with a sigh of relief. "She opened the valve."

Anne, with the end in sight and knowing now that they had

stopped Andrew's flight to Scotland, shot her companion a mischievous look and said, "I believe you care more than you will admit about Lady Hermione, sir. You've been worried sick that she might be injured."

"Pooh, nonsense," he snapped. "I was worried that she might rip that bag to shreds through her damned carelessness. As it is, the damned wench has lost all my inflammable air."

"But, surely, even though the balloon will have to be refilled, you will be glad to find her safe and well, won't you?" Anne persisted.

"Aye, I will that," he agreed grimly, "because when I do, I mean to strangle her!"

Twenty

They saw the erstwhile aeronauts in the center of an excited cluster of about twenty villagers. Without checking the bays, Lord Ashby drove the curricle as near to the group as he could.

Lady Hermione saw them first and strode to meet them, as awestruck villagers stepped hastily aside to make way for her.

"A female," one man said in a voice that carried easily to the occupants of the curricle. "Did ye see that, lads? 'Twere a female a-guiding that balloon! I swear, I never saw the like."

Anne realized that Lady Hermione had made a sensation with her audience, but one look at Lord Ashby was enough to tell her that he was not at all amused. "Please, my lord," she said in an anxious undertone, "don't create a scene here."

"Me," he exclaimed in a tone of outrage. "I am not the one who has created a dashed scene, Anne. Just look at her. Scarce a hair out of place, though she must have been tumbled about on that landing, and as pleased as Punch, she is, by all the attention she's getting. By Jove, I'd like a few private minutes with her, that I would. Hermione! Here, I say, Hermione, you come here, woman, and hear what I have to say to you."

"Don't get your whiskers in a bristle, Ashby," she called, pausing to shake hands with a villager who had stepped into her path. "I'm coming straightaway."

Anne said, "If you'd like to get down to speak with her privately, sir, I can hold the team for you."

"Well, I don't know about that," he said, shooting her a speculative look. "They're prime bits of blood, you know. A

little tired, but I daresay if we don't push them, they will get
us home again. Michael won't be pleased if we leave them
here, that's certain. Hope Douglas and Haydon can find us. It
may be that I'll have to go look for them, you know, though
what with the wagon being so much slower and all, they might
well have seen where the bag was bound to come down before
ever they reached Sheffield. Damnation, now look at that
woman," he added testily. "Thinks she's a May queen, receiving her subjects. Here, I've got to deal with that." Thrusting
the reins into Anne's hands without further ado, he jumped to
the ground.

She had no trouble holding the team, for the horses were
tired, but she did begin to feel like an exhibit at a fair. The
villagers had observed the curricle's arrival and were gazing
as curiously at her as they had gazed at the balloon, if not
with the great amazement they had accorded to Lady Hermione.

Having detached herself from her admirers, Lady Hermione
was speaking with Lord Ashby, but their exchange did not take
long. His lordship soon turned on his heel and plunged into
the crowd, the speed and length of his stride indicating that
his temper was still ruffled. Lady Hermione walked at her
usual pace to the curricle and looked up at Anne with a rueful
smile.

"I suppose you are ready to murder me, too," she said.

"Where is Andrew, ma'am? Was anyone injured? We were
persuaded that you were coming down much too fast."

"The wind dropped just as we neared the ground, and I
thought we would make a perfect landing, but then the grappling hook caught on a tree and tripped us up. The Flowers
woman twisted her ankle rather badly when the basket tipped,
and lost her balance, and now, that young rascal insists he's
going to stay right with her to see that she's well cared for.
Myself, I'd like to box her ears—his, too, for that matter—for
a worse coil than this I can't imagine. Poor Ashby is beside

himself, and no wonder. He wouldn't even listen to me when I tried to explain why we took his precious balloon."

"Why did you?" Anne asked, adding quickly, "You had better come up here to talk to me, you know, for I'm quite sure those people would like nothing better than to hear what you will say."

Lady Hermione climbed obediently into the curricle, talking as she did. "They're no longer interested in me, now that Ashby has gone to tend to his expensive bits of silk and wicker. They are interested only in that. Lord, but I'm glad to be safe on the ground again! It was a near thing, I can tell you, and lucky we were to find this field when we did." She settled herself, but when Anne did not respond, Lady Hermione looked directly at her and said, "I expect you still want to know what I was about."

"Yes, I do."

"Well, it's simple enough. I talked them into taking Ashby's balloon, though I did not tell him that, of course. Not yet. He did all the talking. Didn't give me a chance to say a word, and I'll wager he will have a good many more things to get off his mind before I get a chance to explain my actions to him."

"Forgive me, ma'am, if I say you are making no sense whatsoever," Anne said bluntly. "Did you say that *you* were the one who actually decided to take the balloon?"

"Certainly, I was. And you see how well it answered the purpose. I tell you, I began to think I could not count on the wind at all, for we kept going straight on toward the Highlands, as if we were on a string being pulled by some brawny Scotsman. Just when one counted on the wind being capricious, too."

"You didn't mean to go to Scotland then."

"No, of course not. Do you take me for a ninnyhammer? I'd have thought that you, at least, would have had more sense. But I'll begin at the beginning, shall I? If I don't, I daresay you will never understand. I met them in the village, you see."

"I hoped you would, but I did not expect this, ma'am."

"Well, but you see, they were just coming out of the Flowers woman's house, and I could see by the way young Upminster was looking up and down the street that he was up to mischief, so I made it my business to go bang up to him and ask him what he was doing. Now, one might expect the lad to have prevaricated in such a case. Certainly, anyone else bent on such a mad course would have done so. But not his high-and-mightiness. Oh, no!"

"Goodness, never tell me that he blurted straight out that he meant to marry her!"

"He did," Lady Hermione said with a bemused shake of her head. "As cocksure as his father, that young snip, and needs taking down a peg, if you ask me. I hope Michael flays him for this. He's still insisting he's going to marry her, you know, even now, so I don't know what we'll do. In the midst of this lot, I can't see us dragging him back to the Priory, can you?"

"I think I can prevail upon him to go with us," Anne said, "but what about Mrs. Flowers? I must tell you, ma'am, I was as shocked as can be to see that she had actually gone with him."

"Well, you wouldn't be so surprised if you could but hear the poor woman. That rascal Jake Thornton evidently told her to her face that he had signed the house over to her, and that he had arranged for her to be comfortable for life. But she says he never gave her the deed to the house, which, as we know, is held by Maria's solicitor. As to the money Jake promised her, she's not telling the whole tale there, I think, but she does not put much faith in its existence, I can tell you that, and I certainly don't blame her. I don't suppose we can blame her for succumbing to Andrew's pleading either, though I think she's had second thoughts about that. She is no adventurer, you see, and though she got into the basket as meek as a nun's hen, she was downright terrified once the wind caught us, and couldn't get out fast enough once we were down, which is how she came to twist her ankle, of course."

"But you have not explained why you took the balloon in the first place," Anne said. "At least, I collect that you thought you could somehow keep them from going to Scotland, but surely you knew you would be at the wind's mercy."

"But that's just what I counted on," Lady Hermione said with a wicked grin. "Don't you see, my dear? I could never have talked them out of going, for they were both dead set on it, and I couldn't just let them drive off in Fiona Flowers's gig, which is what they had planned to do. Upminster, apparently feeling that it would be unwise to take his horse or any sort of vehicle on his elopement, had walked to the village, you see. Rather foolish of him, I thought, but then he hasn't had much practice at this sort of thing, has he?"

A bubble of laughter escaped Anne's lips, and she said, "He was in disgrace, ma'am, and didn't dare show his face in the stables. In the course of last night's confrontation, Michael told him he was not to fish or ride, and commanded him to double his study hours with Mr. Pratt. Having told Pratt early this morning that he was off with Michael to Castleton, Andrew had to disappear, but I'm persuaded he must have believed Michael had given orders that he was not to take out a horse, so he dared not show his face there. Instead he no doubt spent a couple of hours playing least in sight, until he could slip into the village and visit Mrs. Flowers at a civilized hour."

Lady Hermione shook her head. "Really, one hopes he will improve before he takes command at the Priory. His father did a lot of outrageous things, but Edmund would never have lowered himself to such an extent as to attempt to run off with the likes of Fiona Flowers, and I must admit, it quite shocks me to think that such a top-lofty young dog as Upminster would lower himself so much."

"He counts her as a friend, ma'am. Indeed, he said she is the first real friend he has ever had, which I think very sad, don't you? And as you said yourself, she seems to be the first person ever to treat him like a man instead of like a boy. That must count for a good deal with Andrew, I believe."

"No doubt, but if he did this out of any reason other than plain unmixed pique, I'll call myself a Dutchman."

"No," Anne said with a sigh, "that's just what it was, I'm afraid. He was humiliated last night, and livid with Michael, I'm sure, for he resents anyone who holds him in check. But in fairness, though I should not say so, I agree with Lord Ashby when he says Michael has been too strict."

"You'll get no disagreement from me on that point," Lady Hermione said. "Why, when I think what a rascal Michael was at the same age, and remember things said about his activities in London, I own I should have expected him to be more tolerant."

"I think it is because of his experience that he is strict," Anne said. "Papa was perfectly iron-handed with my eldest brother, and said it was because he knew from his own experience what mischief Harry could get up to if he were given the chance. He was strict with Bernard, too, but is much more lenient with Stephen, having seen that neither of the elder two was ever tempted to step far beyond the line of what Papa would tolerate."

Before Lady Hermione could reply, a lad ran up to the carriage and said, "Beg pardon, me ladies, but his lordship said ter tell ye to come help with the lady what hurt her foot, if ye please. I'm ter hold the horses fer ye. He gimme a shilling, he did," he added with a grin.

Getting down and making their way to the center of the group of people, the two found a harassed Lord Ashby, trying to give orders and talk with Andrew and Mrs. Flowers at the same time. He greeted their arrival with exasperated relief.

"Take these two away from here, will you?" he said sharply. "I've sent a pair of lads running to the village to keep a lookout for the wagon, and I've got a couple of others helping to gather up the bag, but I dare not leave it for an instant, lest some of these folks try to tear off bits of it for souvenirs. Here, you," he called to one of the men helping with the balloon, "don't snatch at the silk like that! If it gets caught on a branch, disentangle it gently. Wait, I'll show you. Andrew, if you don't mean to help, at least keep out of the way and stop striding back and forth like a maniac."

"But you don't seem to care that she's hurt," Andrew snapped. "All you care about is your damned balloon."

"Watch your tongue, lad. Ladies present."

Andrew glared at Anne and Lady Hermione, then turned on his heel and went back to Mrs. Flowers, who was seated on the ground, looking windblown and ill at ease. When Andrew realized that Anne and Lady Hermione were following him, he turned back and glared again, saying in a voice that trembled, "Take care what you say to me or to my intended wife, for I'll not have her offended. I have not changed my mind, you know, and though I daresay you think you can stop me, you cannot. I know my own mind, and I won't be ordered about like a commoner any longer."

His attitude and the fact that Anne was well aware of the number of ears cocked to hear their conversation made her understand perfectly Lady Hermione's desire to box his ears, but before he had finished his declaration, she had detected both fear and frustration in his voice, and the sparkle of unshed tears in his eyes. Remembering that he was still young and had been badly spoiled, she said with her customary composure, "Your Grace, I think Mrs. Flowers would be much more comfortable a little away from this crowd. I do not think she should attempt to climb into the curricle, but perhaps she would prefer to sit on a rock instead of flat on the ground, which is, I believe, a trifle damp. Do you think you can help her move toward the stream I see at the bottom of this hill? We can make cold compresses for her ankle there, you know."

At first, she thought he would refuse, but then he seemed to realize that Mrs. Flowers was anything but comfortable where she was. When he spoke to her, she nodded quickly, and with his help got awkwardly to her feet. Anne moved to her other side to help, and took comfort from the fact that the woman seemed unwilling to look at her. She had feared for a

moment that Mrs. Flowers might prove to be as huffy and
stubborn as Andrew.

Her ankle was clearly giving her a great deal of pain, but
she bore it stoically, and Anne was grateful when none of the
villagers tried to follow them, for she suspected that Andrew
wanted the whole business over as much as anyone else did,
but she knew he would not easily admit as much, and would
not be at all reasonable if he were taken to task before an
audience.

Glancing at Lady Hermione, she saw that the older woman
was looking thoughtful, and hoped she would not make the
mistake of scolding the boy. Evidently she had not given in
to her temptation to do so before, however, so Anne was hopeful that she would continue to keep her vexation to herself.

When they reached the tumbling stream, and Mrs. Flowers
had been assisted to a position some little distance from the
water, where two boulders formed a semblance of a chair, Anne
took her handkerchief from her reticule and said to Andrew,
"Go and soak this in the stream, if you please, sir, whilst we
help her to remove her shoe."

He made no objection to performing the service, and when
he walked away, Anne said quickly in an undertone, hoping
the noise of the stream would keep him from overhearing,
"Mrs. Flowers, I depend upon you to help me. You must know
that he cannot be allowed to marry you."

"Lord, my lady, I've known that from the outset, or as near
as makes no difference. To be sure, it did sound like the answer
to a prayer when His Grace stepped into my parlor this morning and said he wanted to make me a duchess. Well, I ask
you, ma'am, wouldn't anyone's head be turned? And for a
woman finding herself in the bleak position I've been thrust
into this past week— Well, the fact is my mind was affected
and I didn't think proper, and that's the truth of it. But what's
to be done now?"

"I don't know precisely," Anne said, "but I'm very relieved
that you will not aid and abet him more than you have."

"I'm as sorry for the lad as I can be, for I can see he's got it into his head that by marrying me he will solve all his problems, which of course, ain't the fact at all, but he's that set on it, and he's at that age where youngsters must be treated like men if they're to grow into men. His father treated him like a pet who amused him; his mama seems to have treated him like a lord, and now here's Lord Michael choosing the worst time of all to treat him like a child at last. What's more, he's got no friends to speak of. It's a pity, and I did think that I would be helping him, but I can see that I was all about in my head to think any such of a thing."

"You can serve no good purpose by berating yourself," Anne said. "We must think what to do to convince Andrew."

"What I say now," Mrs. Flowers said, unfastening her shoe and wincing as she did, "is that we must get him out of this coil, but without his dignity being overset, my lady; and how that can be managed, I don't know, I'm sure, for it's as fragile as can be, as you must know. But here he comes now, and this blessed shoe still ain't off. I thank you, Your Grace," she said when Andrew held out the wet handkerchief. "I've been dawdling, as you see, for the very thought of pulling off my shoe makes me queasy. Moreover, I'm as cold as I can be, what with being blown about like we were and then sitting on the ground like I did."

"You should have told me," Andrew said, frowning.

"Ah, but there was such a dust-up, what with all those folks descending on us, and Lady Hermione's making you help catch the balloon before it floated away, once we'd got out of it, that I didn't like to make a nuisance of myself by complaining."

"Well, I wish you had told me, that's all," he said, sounding this time more sulky than annoyed.

Anne said calmly, "There ought to be a lap rug under the seat of the curricle, sir. Perhaps you would extend your kindness by fetching it for her, or finding someone else to do so, although I'd as lief not be overwhelmed by helpful villagers now that we've managed to escape them for a few moments.

If there is no blanket in the curricle, perhaps one of the women who lives nearby would lend us one."

"I'll find something," he said, turning away at once. His relief at leaving them was unmistakable.

"There, you see," Mrs. Flowers said, watching him stride up the hill as she tried to pull off her shoe. "He wants to be safe out of this, but he don't want to admit it to a living soul."

"Then just tell him you've changed your mind," Lady Hermione said bluntly as she bent to help the woman.

"Well, but I don't know if that will answer," Mrs. Flowers said thoughtfully, sitting back to let Lady Hermione pull off her shoe. "I've said I would marry him, you see, and I don't know that he won't just think I've abandoned him to his uncle's brutality through deciding he's too young, or just through having given in to your entreaties or my own fear of Lord Michael—which I don't mind admitting is considerable at this point," she added with a grimace. "He's not a man one wants to cross."

Handing Lady Hermione the wet handkerchief, Anne said, "Do you know him, Mrs. Flowers?"

"Not to say *know,* exactly, but I've heard enough to make me right wary of bringing myself to his notice, my lady." She shifted her attention to her swollen ankle, fixing her gaze on the handkerchief that Lady Hermione was wrapping around it.

Recalling the duchess's note, and realizing she might never have a better opportunity than this one, Anne said quickly, "Lady Hermione, would you give me a moment alone with Mrs. Flowers?"

"Certainly," her ladyship said promptly. "I'll just go and ask Ashby how much longer he means to keep us here. If you hear an explosion, do not be alarmed. It will just be that he has decided to shoot me to put himself out of his misery."

Anne smiled but waited only until her ladyship was beyond earshot before saying, "You will think me ungracious to mention such a topic just now, Mrs. Flowers, but from what Jane Hinkle told me, and from other information I have received, I believe you may know something about that boat on the river beyond the village, something I want to know."

"The *Folly,* they call it, ma'am." She did not look up, and her voice was so low that Anne had to strain to hear the words.

She said, "Yes, that's right. Please, I must ask this. Is that boat owned by someone who might be known as Lord M?"

The woman hesitated, but then, drawing a long breath, as if she were making up her mind, she looked up, right at Anne, and said, "That's right, my lady. They call him Lord M, or just *his lordship,* as if he were the only lordship walking the earth."

Anne swallowed hard, wishing now that she could drop the whole conversation, but she had to ask one more question. "Is it Lord Michael, Mrs. Flowers, who owns the *Folly?* Answer me quickly, if you please, for His Grace will be coming back any minute now, and he must not be a party to this conversation."

Mrs. Flowers glanced up the hill as if she expected to see him then and there, then said, "I cannot give you a plain answer, ma'am, for I do not know. I can tell you there are any number of people hereabouts who believe that he is, but I've never actually seen Lord M, and from what I am given to understand, he wears a mask whenever he is on the boat. He visits the *Folly* only late at night, in general, and the girls don't rightfully know him. Not one amongst them would recognize him if she walked bang into him in the center of the village in broad daylight."

"But I'm told Lord Michael has visited the *Folly* in broad daylight, and spoken with at least two of the women there."

"That's as may be. I didn't say they don't know Lord Michael, for they do. I just said they don't know the identity of Lord M, and that's true enough, but I can tell you, they are terrified of him, and with good reason, I'm afraid."

"What can you mean?"

"I didn't like to tell poor Jane any more about her sister than what I did, but the plain fact is that Molly were beaten to death, my lady, and by what I hear, it were Lord M who killed her. No one dared speak to the authorities, and 'tis said she were buried somewheres far from here. She knew something she didn't ought to know, they say, and he meant only to teach her to keep a still tongue. Well, he did that, I expect, but if you was thinking of trying to expose him, ma'am—not that you would, I daresay, if he should chance to be your own husband. Still and all, I'll tell you to your head that you'd best not do it."

The horror Anne expected to feel did not materialize, and she wondered if she had become emotionally numb. Surely, she ought to feel horror at the thought that Michael might have murdered some poor innocent maidservant. But her imagination boggled and would not accept the thought. Looking up the hill, she saw Andrew coming toward them, and was spurred to ask one last question. "Please, ma'am, do you know nothing more specific to tell me about this mysterious Lord M? Is he tall, short, thin, heavy— You must know something to help me."

Mrs. Flowers, too, had seen Andrew. She began to shake her head, then stopped, saying, "He is tall with broad shoulders and a lordly bearing, ma'am, but that don't help you at all, I know, for it's the spit of Lord Michael that I'm describing. I have seen him from a distance, of course, though I've never spoken with him. And that's the one thing that might help, for they do say as Lord M's voice is one a woman never forgets. Like a cat's purr, they do say. Creepy, is what I'd call it, but if it *is* his lordship, my lady, pray have a care to yourself. Ah, there you are, Your Grace," she added in quite a different tone. "How very kind of you, sir, to bring me a blanket. I declare, I've begun to feel like a block of ice, for it's turned quite chilly."

The chill racing up and down Anne's spine had nothing to do with the approaching storm, however. How many times, she wondered, had she been reminded of a cat's purr when she heard Michael speak? She could not seem to think, however, nor did she have the liberty to do so, for Andrew's attitude was as prickly as before, and she had to gather her wits to deal with him.

Knowing, regardless of Mrs. Flowers's warning, that she would not rest until she had confronted Michael, she still had to exert patience to deal with Andrew, and she gave thanks for all the practice she had received in keeping her temper while dealing with her brothers and sisters over the years.

Andrew draped the blanket carefully around Mrs. Flowers, taking care not to add its weight to the injured limb. He said, "I got this from one of the village women, Fiona. She wanted to return with me to assist you to her cottage, where she said she would look after you more properly, but I told her you wanted privacy. Nonetheless, with the storm approaching, as I believe it is, we ought to think about finding you some shelter soon, and the woman does seem respectable."

Before Mrs. Flowers could reply, Anne said firmly, "I want to discuss with you just what is to be done about all this, sir. Mrs. Flowers will no doubt excuse you for a few moments if you will just step over here with me."

He looked rebellious, but Mrs. Flowers said gently, "Do go, Your Grace. I shall be glad to lean back and close my eyes for a few moments, and it would not do if I were to do so with you standing there, wanting to talk to me."

"Well, if you are quite sure . . ."

"Go along now."

He grimaced and turned with obvious reluctance to accompany Anne. She did not go far, for she did not want to leave Mrs. Flowers unattended, but once they were distant enough that she knew Andrew would not worry about being overheard, she said, "Now, Andrew, we must talk plainly about this business, and I am no doubt going to say things that you will not like to hear, but I want you to listen to me, and I hope you will not simply dismiss what I say."

"You can't tell me what to do," he said gruffly.

"Look at me, Andrew." She kept her voice gentle, resisting

the urge to touch him as she would have touched Stephen, just
to remind him that she cared for him. "If you cannot look me
straight in the eye, and talk to me, you cannot have very much
faith in the rightness of your position, my dear."

He looked at her then, his eyes glittering. "I suppose you
are going to tell me what a fool I am."

"I do not think you are a fool. I think you are frustrated
and angry, and I think you acted impulsively and unwisely,
but I also think you are sensible enough to know by now that
a marriage between you and Mrs. Flowers is quite out of the
question. She knows that if you do not."

"I suppose you threatened her with all manner of things,
and now she means to abandon me like . . ." He turned away,
and she knew he was fighting his tears.

"Andrew, I did not threaten her. She already knew she could
not marry you, but neither of you will be abandoned, I promise
you. What you offered seemed so much like a dream to her
that she was carried away a little, or I think she would never
have agreed to it. And if you are honest, my dear, I think you
know that you would never have suggested such a course if
you had not been so very angry with your uncle, and so determined to be free of his discipline. One day you will meet
a lady who will make you an excellent duchess. Of that I have
no doubt. But until then, you must do all you can to become
the best duke you can be, so that she will not be disappointed."

"But I am not allowed to be a duke. He treats me as if I
were younger than Sylvie."

"He is still learning, too," Anne reminded him. "He has
not been a guardian any longer than you have been a duke,
after all. But he is making an effort, Andrew, and you must
do the same. You must both learn to be more tolerant of each
other."

"He w-will m-murder me for this," Andrew said, his voice
catching on a sob.

Repressing a shiver at his untimely choice of words, Anne
said steadily, "I will not let him do any such uncivil thing.

Indeed, if you will help me, I think perhaps we can settle this without troubling him much about it at all."

"How? He will know the instant he returns to the Priory that everyone is gone, and he will soon enough learn why."

"Well, he may not return until late, you know, but if he should get back before we do, I'll try to think of something to tell him. It occurs to me that if we can all get home before it grows quite dark—which fortunately does not happen until nearly nine o'clock at this time of year—it will not be so bad as you think. Here come the others now. Gracious, a good many others," she added, seeing that Lady Hermione and Lord Ashby had apparently collected an entourage.

The reason was soon explained. When he reached them, Lord Ashby said heartily, "The wagon is coming along now, they tell me, which means we shall no doubt see it within the hour, but the storm is marching right along, too, and I cannot say I like the looks of those clouds moving toward us. Thought we'd best find shelter, don't you know, and several of these good folks have offered to house us till the worst is past."

"Good gracious," Anne exclaimed, dismayed, "surely you do not mean for us to remain here, sir!"

"Don't see why we shouldn't," he replied. "I must say, I expected Andrew to kick up a riot and rumpus, but not you, my dear. Surely you are not too nice in your notions to accept hospitality from these kind people, and I'm assured there is an excellent public house in the village, where the host puts up his own ale from an ancient and highly respected receipt. I mean to try that just as soon as the lads get here and can look after the *Great Britain*."

Aware of her audience, Anne said carefully, "Even if we do stay until the storm passes, sir, how do you intend to get us all back to the house afterward?"

"Why—" He broke off in consternation. "By Jove, if I didn't forget we've got my curricle. Can't take but two, maybe three at a pinch. Daresay we'll have to find a coach of some sort, and that might not be so easy here in Bamford." He looked around, as if he expected a coach to appear out of thin air.

One helpful man said he thought the public house owner might lend them the old coach he kept in his stable for when he and his family visited his wife's parents in Tilney.

"The very thing," Lord Ashby said, "and we'll want a driver, too, I expect. Won't want to fret about returning mine host's coach to Bamford." He started to turn away, evidently in the belief that everything had been decided.

Anne said, "I beg your pardon, sir, but I don't think it would be wise for us all to remain here longer than absolutely necessary. The sooner Andrew gets back to the house, the better, you must agree."

"Only if he gets back before Michael learns of this latest start of his," Lord Ashby snapped.

"In point of fact, my lord, I am in something of the same fix," she said calmly. "He will not be pleased to find me away from home either, and in view of his displeasure the last time I left the house with you and Lady Hermione, I think I had better get home now as quickly as I can, and take Andrew with me."

"But, look here, you left Michael a note, did you not?"

"Well, no," Anne confessed, "I didn't."

"The devil you say! Next, by Jove, you'll be telling me that you and that brat want to steal my curricle."

"Well, yes," Anne said, "we do."

Twenty-one

Lord Ashby became so choleric at the thought that first his balloon had been commandeered, and now his curricle was to be wrested from him, that his face took on an unhealthy color. He sputtered and tugged at his side whiskers. His angry gaze swept from Anne to Andrew to Lady Hermione, where it came to rest.

"You," he said accusingly, "are to blame for all of this."

"Am I, indeed?" she responded placidly.

"Yes, by Jove, and if it's the last thing I do, woman, I'll make you sorry you were ever born."

"Very well, if that is how you feel, I expect you ought to have your say, Ashby, but before you do, I suggest that we remove Mrs. Flowers to a cottage where she can be made more comfortable until we are able to transport her home. Moreover, I can think of no good reason for dear Anne or young Upminster to wait upon our convenience before departing. His Grace is quite capable of driving that team and looking after her, you know."

"Are you compounding all your other iniquities by suggesting that Andrew drive Michael's best team all the way back to the Priory?" Lord Ashby asked in a tone of outrage.

"Why not? It is not even ten miles from Bamford, I daresay, and I am persuaded that he can easily manage that team. Can you not, Andrew?"

"Certainly I can," he replied, straightening and raising his chin. Then, with a glance at Anne, he added in a less confident tone, "But I am not altogether sure it would be wise for me to do so under the present circumstances."

"Poppycock."

"Oh, yes, poppycock," echoed Lord Ashby in a sarcastic tone. "By Jove, I daresay Michael will be just delighted to see you drive that team again, lad. Go right ahead, with my blessing."

Andrew flushed, but Anne said instantly, "Thank you, sir, we shall take every care, I assure you, and we will leave at once, if you don't mind. Although the storm seems to have slowed its progress somewhat, I'd as lief get home without being drenched. Are you quite certain, ma'am," she added, turning to Lady Hermione, "that we are but ten miles from Upminster Priory?"

"No more than that, at all events," Lady Hermione said, watching Lord Ashby, who was still having difficulty containing his wrath. "You get along now, the pair of you. You'll be quite safe with the lad, Anne dear, and in the meantime," she added on a more provocative note, "I will do my possible to see that Ashby here don't explode or try to seduce poor Mrs. Flowers."

"Hermione! By Jove, woman, you and I are going to have a long talk, and I'll wager you won't enjoy a word of it. It's time and more that someone took you in hand, by God, and I'm just the man to do it."

"Are you, Ashby? To be sure, you are the one who is always telling me I ought to stop giving unwanted advice to people and exert myself to *do* something instead, but the moment I actually follow your advice, you see what comes of it. You have been shouting at me and carrying on like a wicked Russian ever since you arrived, and no m-matter what I s-say or d-do—"

"Here now, Hermie, you ain't crying! Dashed if I ever knew such a wench. Look at all these people gawking at you. Hermie, I say, Hermie, I didn't mean it . . ."

Obeying the emphatic gesture Lady Hermione made behind

her back, Anne grabbed Andrew by the arm, bade a hasty and low-voiced farewell to Mrs. Flowers, and made good her escape. When they reached the clearing where Lord Ashby had left his curricle, she took advantage of the comparative privacy to say, "Andrew, I hope you really can manage these horses, for even as tired as they must still be, I don't trust my skill with them at all."

"Lord, yes, of course I can manage them," the boy said in much his customary tone. "Uncle Michael taught me himself, for he said he didn't want me employing my father's slapdash methods with any of *his* cattle."

"I didn't realize he had taught you to drive," Anne said. "If that is the case, I know I can entrust myself to you."

"He most likely won't agree that I'm ready to drive this team," Andrew confessed. "You will recall that he flew into the boughs the last time I did so, but that was because I scraped the side of his racing curricle, trying to drive at speed through a gate. Moreover," he added with a sigh, "in view of how angry he's bound to be about all the rest, I suppose what he thinks about my driving is only a bagatelle."

"Don't anticipate trouble now," Anne advised. "In my experience, what one imagines will happen is frequently much worse than the actuality. We don't know yet that your uncle will even have to know about all this. Of course, since you entrusted your letter to Sylvia—"

"Is that how you found out? I told her not to give it to anyone before tomorrow, and then to give it to Uncle Michael."

"Well, I hope you do not mean to scold her for failing you, for she holds you in very high esteem, you know, and would be quite dashed down by your censure. I encountered Mr. Pratt in the gardens this morning, and was astonished to learn that he believed you had accompanied your uncle to Castleton. And when poor Sylvia looked at me with such obvious guilt in her eyes, I drew my own conclusions and confronted her. She is not to blame, Andrew. You ought never to have involved her in your plan."

The boy did not respond. His attention was fully engaged in guiding the team out of the field onto the uneven road, and he was clearly nervous of the responsibility he had accepted. Since the muttering thunder from the approaching storm was not likely to have a calming effect on him, or on the team, Anne made no further attempt to converse with him just then, hoping he would relax a little once they reached the main highroad.

It was more than ten minutes after they had done so before he looked at her and said soberly, "I have been thinking."

"Have you, dear?"

"I'll have to tell him about all this, won't I?"

She said matter-of-factly, "Well, you know, I do think it would be best if you made a clean breast of it. You will have all the advantage of making an honest confession, you know, which will be far better than if he were to learn of it from someone else. And that, I fear, we cannot be certain will not happen, for far too many persons have become involved in this tangle."

"He will still murder me."

"I wish you will stop saying that," Anne begged. "You cannot know how very much I dislike hearing it, particularly when I am certain that he will do nothing of the kind. Recollect, if you will, that he does at least try to exercise patience in dealing with your misbehavior, and that he did teach you to drive a team—and in fine style, too, I might add—when he must have been exceptionally busy with his new duties."

"He only taught me after I tried tooling random-tandem," Andrew said, shooting her a reluctant smile. "I'd heard from one of the chaps home at Christmas how it was all the rage in London and Oxford, and was determined to attempt it myself. And," he added on a harder note, "though Uncle Michael chose to dispute the point, the horses I had hitched to the phaeton were my own."

"And the phaeton?"

His lips twitched. "My great-uncle's. I'd have used my father's, but it sat a good deal higher off the ground, and I thought if I should come to grief it would be better in the lower one. It was not I who came to grief, however, but the phaeton."

"I see. A wheel?"

"An axle. Broke clear through. I took a turn too quickly, not realizing it was the most dangerous thing I could do with a pair strung out one behind the other. When a wheel hit the ditch and caught in the hedgerow, the axle ended up in two bits across a boulder that ought never to have been there. Uncle Michael threatened to lay his whip about my shoulders, but instead he taught me to drive both a pair and a team properly. He said driving tandem was only for worthless whippets and Jack Straws."

This artless conversation gave Anne food for thought. She said, "So he has not always treated you as harshly as he has seemed to do since I came to live at the Priory."

"He was pretty forbearing before, actually, though he bellowed a lot. I expect he just got fed up."

She said with a twinkle, "You haven't precisely given him cause to love you, have you?"

Instead of the responsive twinkle she expected, the boy frowned heavily and said, "I never give anyone cause for that."

Anne was shocked. "But, my dear, though I know you must miss your mama and papa sadly, surely they loved you very much."

He shrugged. "My mama doted on Sylvia, ma'am, as well she should have, but to me she showed only respect and duty. She never called me Andrew, as you do when you are not trying to make me feel my dignity"—he shot her a speaking look—"but always Tissington, which is how I was styled before my father died. As for him, although I daresay he was rather puffed up about having produced a son, he had no time for me. Indeed, his servants got more attention from him than I did, for he spent much more time conferring with Bagshaw than he ever did talking with me."

Anne was stirred by pity, but she knew it would be a mistake to let him see it, so she said in her usual calm way, "That must have been difficult for you. I am singularly fortunate, I know, to have parents who choose to spend most of their time at their principal residence. My mother is not a warm person, but at least she was nearly always nearby, and we girls had governesses, while the boys went to good schools. And my father, though not terribly interested in his children, still keeps watch over our activities. I hope that when you marry and have children of your own, you will remember these feelings of yours now, and be more conscious of your duty toward your children, as a result. I have frequently observed how very protective you are of Sylvia, and I suspect you will be so with your own offspring as well."

"Do you really think so?"

The mixture of anxiety and hope in his eyes was nearly too much for her, but she said warmly, "Oh, yes, I have often noted that persons who were ignored by their parents—or guarded too closely by them, for that matter—try to treat their own children more sensibly, and that people who were over-indulged as children tend to be more strict with their own. I was recently speaking of this phenomenon with Lady Hermione, albeit from an aspect that pertains rather more to your uncle than to you."

Seeing that she had his full attention now, she went on, "As I see it, since children who are overindulged by their parents or ignored by them altogether are, in effect, given complete freedom to do as they please, they frequently manage to get into all manner of scrapes and mischief. Then, later, as parents themselves, just knowing what can happen makes them more severe with their children than their parents were with them."

"But by your own logic, then, I shall be a strict parent," Andrew said, "for what makes Uncle Michael so determined to control my actions now, *he* says, is that I was thoroughly spoilt before by always having had complete freedom to do as I please."

"If you will forgive me for contradicting you, my dear, in my opinion, you have been given very little freedom at all, for you have been kept at the Priory almost like a prisoner. The cage is a golden one, to be sure, but your freedom, as you call it, has hitherto extended only to allowing you to behave in a manner that would not be tolerated anywhere else in a boy your age. I don't call that freedom. I call that plain foolishness."

He frowned, and for a moment she expected him to take offense, but then he shot her another of his slanting looks and said, "So, was Uncle Michael overindulged or overguarded?"

"Indulged, I think, but only in the sense that he was allowed to do as he pleased and given enough money to think he need not count the cost. In that sense, however, from what I've heard—though I ought not to repeat it to you—he must have been shockingly indulged, for he seems to have got into a number of scrapes and to have run up all manner of debts without counting the cost until he was forced to do so. But that very experience, I believe, produced the deep sense of duty he has now to protect you from all the evils he knows may be lying in wait for you."

"But I can take care of myself," Andrew protested.

"I hesitate to contradict you, dear sir, but where would you be at this moment had Lady Hermione not taken it into her head to interfere with your plan?"

He had the grace to look chagrined, but a moment later, she detected a lurking twinkle in his eyes when he glanced away from the team again to say, "And what about you, ma'am? Shall you be able to take care of yourself when Uncle Michael learns that you drove out with Great-Uncle Ashby to follow us?"

She speedily diverted his thoughts from this unpromising topic by warning him to keep his eyes on an approaching carriage that seemed inclined to remain in the exact center of the road, and by the time they had passed that vehicle, she had the happy notion of telling him about the arrival of Sylvia's new governess and then of asking him to tell her about the countryside through which they were passing. He was content to do so, and some time passed in this fashion, until a chance remark of his drew to her notice the fact that the road they traveled was the exact same one that Lord Michael would take from Castleton.

"Good gracious, will he?" Anne exclaimed. "I suppose, now that I look about me, some of this country does seem familiar, but I'm quite certain we did not pass through that last village—Hathersage, wasn't it—earlier today."

"No, you wouldn't have. If you went to Sheffield, you most likely turned off at Calver or Froggatt."

"Calver," she said with certainty, "and I remember now that Lord Ashby was concerned lest we encounter Michael there. I am all confusion, I admit. It was bad enough when Lady Hermione told me we were only ten miles from the house, after we had been chasing the balloon for what must have been hours, but to be back on the road where we began, and without passing through Sheffield again— We have traveled in a circle, I suppose."

"Very nearly."

He went on to describe what he thought must have been their route, but Anne paid little heed to his discourse. The storm was still behind them, but thunder muttered frequently, with an occasional rumble louder than the others that would sound enough like approaching carriage wheels to make her look anxiously over her shoulder. The thought that they might encounter Michael before they reached the Priory was more than a little disconcerting because she had not yet decided what she meant to say to him, and she feared if he caught them on the road—and driving his bays, at that—that she would be given little chance to explain anything for some considerable time.

That he would undoubtedly be harsh with Andrew if he were to discover in such an abrupt fashion all the facts of this latest escapade was another matter of concern, for he would be that much less likely to heed her if she suggested more patient methods. She had no doubt now that he had begun well with the boy, but suspected that Andrew's failure to respond quickly to tolerance and understanding with the behavior that Michael desired of him, coupled with Michael's increasing worry about other matters, had led to growing distance between them and greater inclination on Michael's part to be severe.

If she could discuss her feelings with him in an atmosphere of composure and tranquility, she believed she could make him see that he would do better to exert a greater degree of forbearance with his charge. But, if he were awaiting them now at Upminster, or if he should catch them on the road— Another mutter of thunder interrupted her thoughts, causing her to look back again, but the road behind them was reassuringly empty of traffic.

"Will he be angry with you, too?" Andrew asked abruptly.

Realizing that he had stopped talking about the countryside and must have deduced at least some of her thoughts from her distraction, she said, "I hope not. He can make life rather uncomfortable when he is displeased, can he not?"

Andrew agreed with enough fervor to make her smile, but the smile faded quickly. Though she made more effort after that to keep up her end of the conversation, she found her thoughts continually returning to Michael. Despite all she had learned about the mysterious Lord M, and despite the fact that to her knowledge Michael was the only Lord M in the district, she still could not seriously believe that he was the villain Mrs. Flowers had described. The most condemning evidence was the description of Lord M's voice, and surely many men had low, caressing voices that might, at least occasionally, inspire women to compare them to large purring cats.

He had a temper, to be sure, but he had never raised a hand to her, or even given her cause to think he might, though she had surely, at one time or another, given him what some men would consider to be sufficient provocation. And though he had without doubt been violent on more than one occasion in his treatment of Andrew, he had never done more to the boy than Lord Rendlesham had done to his sons, or to his daughters for that matter.

Mrs. Flowers had said that Lord M frequently used the women on the *Folly* for his own sexual gratification; yet, Michael had given his word that he had never indulged in sexual congress with prostitutes, and she had believed him. That she still believed him made her wonder if she was being naïve? Was it merely that she had grown to care for him, indeed to care passionately that he succeed in all his endeavors, whatever they might be? Was she just refusing to concede that she might have married a murderer. Was she mistaking hope for confidence?

Though she could not answer these questions, or other, similar ones her mind produced, she found she was quite capable of making a decision in spite of them. She would, she decided, confront Michael just as soon as they got home. If she achieved nothing else, his discovery that he was believed by many in the district to own the *Folly* ought to take his mind off Andrew's activities long enough for her to think of a way to approach that topic with enough tact to influence the outcome.

The decision made, she fixed her attention on her companion; and, finding him more willing than ever before to cast aside his arrogance and talk like a sensible person, she was able to direct his thoughts and conversation in such a way that the pair of them reached the Priory in perfect charity with each other. This signal success made her feel confident to tackle Michael at once, but when Andrew turned the bays over to one of his grooms, the man informed them that Lord Michael had not yet returned.

"That is to say, ma'am, he did return from Castleton nearly two hours ago, but then he rode off again in a hurry and didn't say whither he were bound," the man said. "Said not to fret if he were late. Said he didn't rightly know when he'd be home, but likely with yonder storm a-brewin' as it has been most of the afternoon, he'll get hisself back here a bit sooner nor what he thought. Like as not, m'lady," he added in a comforting tone, "he'll be home afore ye finished yer dinner, ma'am."

"Thank you," Anne said, exchanging a look with Andrew as they turned away and began to walk across the stable yard toward the house. Though she was glad that Michael was not waiting in high dudgeon for their return, having girded herself for battle, so to speak, she found it unnerving that her opponent had not yet stepped into the arena. She could only hope now that he would return before her courage failed her altogether.

"Do you think he rode after us?" Andrew asked.

"No, because surely we would have met him on the road if he had. He must have had other business to attend to."

Andrew was silent until they entered the house, but then he said casually, "I'll just go up to Sylvia, ma'am, to tell her we've got back safely, and I daresay I'll dine in the schoolroom with her, too, to keep her company."

"Oh, no you don't, you rascal. I know what is in your mind, but I tell you, it won't answer. You may go up to reassure her, certainly, and to make your greetings to her new governess, but then you come straight back here to bear me company."

He drew himself up and said stiffly, "I am not crying off, I promise you, for I mean to make a clean breast of it just as I said I would, and at the earliest opportunity. I just thought you would prefer to be private with him if he gets home in time to join you in the dining room."

"Well, I don't want to be private with him the minute he walks in, or to be left alone with my thoughts in the meantime, and so you may put that notion straight out of your head. In point of fact, if you are indeed going up to inform Sylvia of our return, I wish you will ask her and Miss Johnson to join us for dinner. I don't know if Sylvia fears thunderstorms or not, but if she does, the more company she has around her, the better, for although this one has been kind enough to hold off longer than I daresay anyone expected it to, it is bound to begin any time. I've heard thunder grumbling behind us all the way from Hathersage."

"I, too," Andrew said. "Once I even thought I was hearing the rattle of coach wheels, and glanced back to see if it was Uncle Michael bearing down on us from behind."

Anne chuckled and admitted that she had done the same thing, more than once. "But do go and ask Sylvia if she would like to join us for dinner."

"Well, I would," he said, "but you know, I believe she and her governess will already have eaten, for it is nearly seven o'clock, and Sylvia generally has her supper at five."

"Good gracious," Anne said, looking at the clock in the hall and seeing that it supported Andrew's statement, "I had no idea it was so late. I hope Bagshaw and Mrs. Burdekin did not assume we were dining elsewhere and put all the food away already."

"Oh, no, for before you married Uncle Michael, he was often out and about late on estate business, and Great-Uncle Ashby would get involved with his aeronautics or inventing some gadget or other, so they would both be late to dinner. More than once, I had finished eating before they ever entered the dining room, but that never disconcerted the servants in the least."

"You know, Andrew, the more I think about it, the more I believe you ought to be at school. You would never dine alone there, I believe."

"Well, I'd like to go, and that's a fact, but dukes of Upminster are always educated at home. It's traditional."

"Well, traditions can be broken. Do go up and speak to Sylvia, and I will tell Mrs. Burdekin we want to dine at once."

As Andrew turned toward the stair hall, Bagshaw appeared in the doorway, and for a split second, Anne's pulse leapt, for she thought he was Michael. But the instant was over in a flash. The butler, as stately as ever, looked down his nose at them in what Anne thought must be disapproval. Andrew said,

"I hope you told them to put dinner back, Bagshaw. There will just be the two of us, unless Uncle Michael joins us, because Great-Uncle Ashby's been detained and will likely not return until tomorrow. Have them serve enough for an army though, will you? My stomach is dashed well knocking against my backbone."

"Certainly, Your Grace. The kitchen was warned to expect a belated arrival. When would it suit you to dine, sir?"

Andrew looked at Anne, who said, "We'll not wait for Lord Michael, Bagshaw, but tell them to keep some food warm for him, if you please. His Grace and I will dine in twenty minutes."

"Very good, your ladyship."

Since there was no need for her to speak with Mrs. Burdekin now, Anne went upstairs with Andrew, who murmured mischievously, "I have just now realized why you desired Sylvia to dine with us, ma'am, and I must tell you, I think the notion a brilliant one. We must think how to contrive it, even if she has already eaten. My uncle will shout at neither one of us when she is present."

Anne grinned at him. "Don't be so cocksure of that, young man. I own, I had some such notion in mind, but by now your sister will be in bed or at least preparing to retire, and in any case, we'd only be postponing an inevitable confrontation. We both have some uncomfortable moments ahead of us, I believe."

"I know." But for once he did not seem concerned, and a moment later he turned again and said with boyish cheerfulness, "Do you know, I like it when you call me *young man* and *my dear* like you do. I don't believe anyone else ever has done so. Uncle Michael calls me *sir* when he is particularly vexed, you know. Quite puts a fellow off the word altogether."

Anne chuckled and impulsively reached out to give his arm an affectionate squeeze. "We'll brush through this, my dear, just you see if we don't."

When he had gone to find Sylvia, she found herself wishing

she really had as much courage as she had pretended to have. That Michael would disapprove of her careering about the country with Lord Ashby was as certain as that he would be determined to punish Andrew. And how she might deflect his anger with either of them long enough to say anything of consequence, she did not know. Somehow though, she had to confront him about the *Folly* and show him the duchess's letter. All in all, she thought as Maisie helped her tidy herself for dinner, the sooner the whole business was over, the better it would be for all of them.

In the dining room, she and Andrew talked of commonplace matters while Bagshaw and Elbert waited on them in near silence. Michael still had not returned by the time they finished their dinner and retired to the library together, and after the third time Andrew asked Anne when she thought he would be home, she sent him upstairs, deciding that she could deal better with her own apprehensions if he were not constantly reminding her of his.

"Will you promise to send for me when he gets here?" the boy demanded. "I want this over and done, ma'am."

"I know you do, my dear. So do I, but I will make you no promise that I cannot be sure to keep. Since I don't know when he will arrive or what mood he will be in, I cannot promise to send for you. You would probably do better now, in any event, to speak with him tomorrow, after you both have had some rest."

"Very well, but I do wish he would come."

It was still light outside, but the sky was darkening, and not long after she had settled herself in one of the big wing chairs with a book in hand, and two branches of candles on a side table to light its pages, Bagshaw entered in his usual dignified way, drew the curtains, and said quietly, "Would your ladyship care for a glass of wine or some other refreshment?"

"Not wine," she said, "but some lemonade would be pleasant, thank you. The roads were extremely dusty."

"At once, your ladyship."

His return was as silent as usual, and since she wanted to give at least the appearance of one engrossed in her book, she barely looked up to thank him. She thought it odd that he served her himself instead of sending Elbert or another servant, but the lemonade was welcome, albeit a little sweeter than she liked. She sipped it as she read, but refreshing as the drink was, she realized before long that the day had been extremely tiring.

Finding it hard to concentrate, even to keep her eyes open, she closed the book, snuffed the candles she had lit, and went wearily upstairs. The exercise, plus the necessity to converse with Maisie without revealing her tension, revived her a little. When she was ready for bed, and Maisie had gone, Anne took out her journal and began a fresh page. In her weariness and the hope of occupying her mind so as not to think too much of the interview to come, she did not even notice that she did not begin her writing in the manner she had employed for so many years.

Saturday, June 14

Dear Michael,

What a day this has been! I cannot begin to put it all into words, for to do so would take much too long, and I can scarcely think. There are so many things I want to write that I don't know where to begin, and at the moment, nothing makes much sense.

I suppose I am sorry for what I've done if it makes you angry, for I don't like you to be angry. I can sympathize with poor Andrew, even when you have cause to be incensed with him, because my knees are quaking right now when I think of what I want to say to you, and how you will react if I do. Indeed, sir, my good sense tells me to run far away as fast as ever I—

The pen slipped from her fingers, and, unable to keep her eyes open a moment longer, she slumped over the escritoire, lowered her head to her arms, and slept, undisturbed even by the loud crashes of thunder that accompanied the breaking storm.

They entered a short time later. "Keep watch for her woman," he said in an undertone to the man who stayed near the door. To the footman he said, "Take care; we don't want to waken her. Time enough for that when I'm ready to teach her who is master." Watching him lift Anne into his arms, he said grimly, "She is damnably interfering and sure of herself, but that state of affairs can soon be rectified, I believe. Do you recall what you are to say if you encounter anyone?"

"Aye, sir, that she's a maid what were overcome by illness, and we're taking her to her family to look after. And we're to say it in such a high-handed manner that none'll dare question us more, so if you'd just be so good as to fetch me a blanket from yonder bedchamber, *your lordship*— Won't do to let anyone see that fine flaxen hair of hers, will it? Recognize it in a flash, they would, and then your plan would surely come to grief."

"That won't happen, so you just watch your cheek, my lad." But his tone was idle, not threatening, for he was gazing down at what Anne had written. A long moment later, when he turned toward the bedchamber to get the requested blanket, he murmured in a satisfied, purring tone, "It is quite plain now to the meanest intelligence that I am meant to win this battle."

Twenty-two

At first Anne's dream delighted her. She rode with Michael through a shady woodland, one she did not remember ever riding through before, where sunlight filtered through the trees, and a stream babbled, tumbling over polished stones. The water was so clear they could count the stones beneath its surface everywhere except where swift currents churned up a lacy white froth. They chatted, laughed, planned, and then Michael vanished.

Raindrops touched her cheeks, her eyelids. A chilly breeze wrapped icy tentacles around her. Thunder crashed, and lightning outlined the trees with a flashing, fiery glare. Her body bumped along, awkwardly now, and except for the vivid flashes of lightning, inky blackness swallowed her. Her eyelids stuck shut. She could not open them no matter how hard she tried.

In the manner of dreams, the atmosphere changed abruptly. She heard voices, laughter, men and women, the tinkling music of a pianoforte, and the higher-pitched, plucked strings of a harp. Outbursts of laughter punctuated the gay and lively music. All these sounds floated to her ears from a distance at first, then grew nearer and became mixed with smells of food, heavy perfume, and more fundamental human odors. The sounds and smells diminished again, though they were still nearer than when she had first heard them. Sounds of the storm faded, too, and the chill. She felt substantially warmer.

Someone carried her. In her dream Michael had returned

and was carrying her upstairs to her bedchamber. He was not angry in the least, and the room felt cozy and warm. A fire crackled on the hearth. She could still hear distant strains of piano and harp, as if Michael had hidden musicians downstairs in the library, or outside in the garden. He laid her on the bed, but it felt oddly hard and the counterpane was scratchy against her cheek. Silence fell again, and darkness.

Someone shook her. She stirred, and the dream vanished. The music and laughter still echoed oddly, however, lingering even when she blinked. Her eyelids felt heavy, too heavy, and sticky as well. She blinked again. She was not in her bed. She was not even in her own bedchamber. She was lying on a hard, stiff-backed sofa.

Two branches of candles and a crackling fire lighted the room in which she found herself, revealing that whoever had decorated the room favored the color red above all others. Not only did a dark red Turkey carpet with gold, dark blue, and green in its elaborate pattern cover the floor but deep wine-red velvet curtains, tied back with golden tassels, adorned the one window she could see from where she lay. Even the sofa upon which she reclined, two nearby chairs, and the footstool in front of the nearer one were all upholstered in a red Turkish tapestry nearly as garish to behold as the carpet.

She still heard voices close by—in the next room, perhaps— and laughter, and the harp and piano from her dream. Oddly, the room seemed to rock and sway, and the gentle motion made her dizzy, for she was not accustomed to such a sensation. Thunder crashed, as it had in her dream, and the wind outside blew in gusts strong enough to puff wood smoke from the fire into the room. She could smell it. And, surprisingly nearby, she heard water slapping rhythmically as if against a shoreline.

Her head ached when she tried to think, worse when she tried to turn it, and she still found it hard to focus her eyes, but she knew suddenly that she was not alone.

A man, a stranger, stepped into view. Plump and well

dressed, with red cheeks, an unpleasantly moist mouth, and eyes that swept over her impersonally, he said, "Welcome, madam."

"Who are you?" She tried to sit, but the blanket covering her seemed amazingly heavy—especially since she recognized it as one from her own bed—and her arms and legs refused to cooperate, feeling sluggish, almost numb.

"Call me Maxwell," he said. "Do you want a glass of wine?"

"I would prefer water, thank you. Where am I?"

"You are with his lordship."

Feeling her heart leap with relief, Anne paid no heed when, instead of water, the man poured wine from a decanter on a small side table into a glass. "Michael is here?" she cried. "Where is he? Oh, do fetch him to me at once. I want to see him."

"You may see his lordship if you will but turn your head, madam. He has awaited your awakening with no little impatience."

She turned her head too quickly and winced, both at the pain and at a wave of dizziness that threatened to overwhelm her. She saw him at once. "Michael?"

He stood silently some distance beyond the chair with the footstool, beside a large, mahogany desk, one end of which lay beneath the sill of a second red-velvet curtained window. His face was darkly shadowed, although the branch of candles lighting the cluttered, paper-strewn desk top revealed his maroon velvet evening coat, tight cream-colored breeches, clocked stockings, and well-polished shoes. The close-fitting coat set off his slim waist and broad shoulders, and she recognized it as the one Michael had worn the night Sir Jacob had dined with them. The candle glow outlined his strong jaw and the lowest portion of his face, and she fancied that his lips curved in a sardonic smile, but still he remained silent.

Anne frowned. Her head was clearing rapidly, and she knew suddenly that her deep sleep had not overtaken her naturally.

"Someone must have put something in my wine at dinner to make me sleep," she said when the man called Maxwell handed her the wineglass. Its dark contents stirred with the motion of the room. "But why would they do such a thing?"

Maxwell said, "His lordship wished you brought here, madam, but quietly, so as not to cause any alarm or outcry."

Anne heard his words, but she ignored him and riveted her attention on the imposing, still silent figure by the desk. "I cannot see your face," she said uneasily. "Those candles light only the lower half, so I wish you would step out where I can see you. Indeed, I wish you'd send this man away and tell me plainly why you did such a thing. You had not the least need to render me unconscious. You must know I'd go with you anywhere."

"I am glad to hear you say so, my love." He spoke from deep in his throat, the cat's purr voice rather than the crisp tone Michael generally used. Perhaps he meant only to sound sensual, but his manner sent a shiver of ice up her spine when he added, "I believed that a certain sense of mystery would appeal to you."

"You were wrong," she replied. "Moreover, I must say such an attitude seems most unlike you." Struggling to collect her wits, she moved to sit upright, sliding her feet from under the blanket to the floor and reaching to steady herself on the nearby arm of the sofa. As she did, the wind blew another puff of smoke into the room and the gentle rocking sensation increased briefly. Realizing she still held the wineglass Maxwell had given her, and having not the least wish to drink any wine, she set it carefully on the carpet near her bare feet and, through a new wave of dizziness, realized something else. "I'm in my nightdress!"

"Would you prefer my men to have stripped you naked before leaving you here, my love?"

He had used the endearment once before, and despite the fact that of late she had longed to hear him speak words of love to her, she found she did not like to hear them spoken in that odd, purring tone. "I'd prefer that you had just come to my bed without subjecting me to any of this," she said, "but it occurs to me now that the reason this room sways, and water seems to be smacking against its very walls, is that I have been brought aboard the infamous *Folly.* I must suppose therefore that the truth is what so many suspect it to be, and you hold at least an interest in that sordid business."

"I own half."

She recoiled but said with forced calm, "I see. I thought better of you, sir. May I know who owns the other half?"

"The Duke of Upminster."

"Andrew? Nonsense, no boy could—"

"He inherited it when his father died."

For a long moment, she was speechless. Then, glaring at him, she said in a tone that ought to have withered him where he stood, "How could you?" Sitting bolt upright now, she pushed the blanket aside, but when the distant music and chatter suddenly increased in volume, she remembered they were not alone and looked swiftly over her shoulder to see that the door of the room was just closing behind Maxwell. With it closed, the sounds from the next room were muffled again.

Breathing a sigh of relief, Anne turned back and said sternly, "Do step into the light now, for goodness' sake. I do not like this air of mystery, as you call it. Nor do I like your games or your choice of a place in which to play them. No doubt you believe that stupid feline murmuring of yours to be a stimulant to passion, but presently it only irritates me, so do stop— Heavens," she exclaimed when he stepped out of the shadow at last, "why on earth do you wear a mask?"

"I told you," he said, moving slowly toward her, avoiding the low stool without so much as glancing at it, and still speaking in that throaty murmur, "I hoped you would enjoy the mystery of a little romantic pretense."

Niggling doubts that she realized had plagued her from the first moment of seeing him snapped now into certainty. "You are not Michael," she said flatly. "Until you moved, I could not be sure, but I know Michael's movements and gestures better than my own. I do not know who you are. I presume you hoped I would continue to believe you were he, but now that I know you are not, you might just as well reveal your true identity."

"I am the owner of the *Folly,*" he said without abandoning the cat's purr voice, "and in truth, I do not much care whether you know I am not Lord Michael, for it will make no difference in the end. I have long desired to meet the real woman beneath that serene facade you display, my dear, imperious little Anne." He paused as if to savor the taste of her given name on his tongue.

"What exactly do you want?" Her voice nearly stuck in her throat, but she got the words out somehow.

"I want you, my love, which is a supreme compliment, for I am accounted to be an expert in matters of feminine pulchritude. Indeed, I believe I am a connoisseur—not merely an aficionado, but a veritable gourmand, as it were. My tastes are varied but refined, and I have long wanted to sample your delicate charms."

"So you simply ordered me delivered to you, like a parcel?" She stared at him, outraged, anger quelling fear for the moment.

"More like a succulent dish, I think," he murmured. "I had you delivered to my table, as it were, an appetizing entree prepared for my private delectation."

"How dare you!"

"If you cooperate," he added softly, as if he had not heard her, "I will show you pleasures you have never even dreamed of before. We will soar to heights you could not reach even in that ridiculous balloon of my Lord Ashby's."

"You are demented."

"If you do not cooperate," he went on, his voice hardening, "you will not distress me much, though you will no doubt soon come to wish you had submitted. I shall merely indulge myself in other pleasures that I enjoy, to your much greater expense, and you will soon learn to behave as you should."

Certain now that his senses were disordered, Anne kept a tight rein on her fears and said in a voice that trembled only slightly, "I think you would be wise to summon a carriage to take me home straightaway, whoever you are. If you do so at once, I shall endeavor to intercede for you with the authorities, but if you do not, I fear there will be nothing I can do to help you."

"So you would intercede even for me," he said silkily, apparently not in the least disturbed by thought of her summoning the authorities. "You are indeed very much too busy, madam."

His last word struck a familiar chord, but she spared no time to wonder why, for she could no longer control her temper. "My husband will kill you for this, if I do not beat him to it," she said furiously. "If you dare to harm me—indeed, if you do not let me go at once—I will not answer for the consequences."

"There will be no consequences."

"Don't be absurd. When Michael comes for me—"

"He will not come."

"He will! He will search the earth to find me, and once he learns of your wickedness in bringing me to this dreadful place, even trying to make me think he owned part of it—"

"Lord Michael has departed for Scotland."

"Nonsense, why should he?" But his words triggered a dizzying sensation, as if she were spinning, being sucked into a vortex, her world turned upside down and inside out. From within the maelstrom, her captor's words sounded fiendishly cool.

"He has gone in search of a runaway wife, I'm afraid."

"But I did not run away." She fought for calm.

"He believes you did."

"How could he? You must be lying. He would never believe such a thing of me."

"But he does, my love. He came home today to discover you had fled the house without telling anyone where you were bound. He believes you ran off to be with your beloved James."

"James?"

"The same James, my pet, to whom you have written so many deliciously intimate letters. Truly you can't blame your husband for being so jealous that he leapt to false conclusions when you departed without leaving so much as a note of explanation."

Her mind reeled. Could Michael so badly misjudge her? She had indeed written her journal as if to a beloved man, and of late, she knew, she had frequently written more to Michael himself than to James. Moreover, she had grievously misjudged Michael by thinking even for a moment that he was financially involved in the *Folly*. But could any sensible man, knowing her and discovering her journal, truly believe she had secretly written and kept copies of so very many letters to another man?

"I don't believe you," she said, strengthened by her increasing confidence to stand and confront him directly, reassuring herself that her nightdress was no more revealing than a number of the gowns she had worn to balls and assemblies in London, and deciding the fact that she wore not so much as a stitch underneath it was of no concern to anyone else. "Michael would realize before he read more than three pages that they were not letters at all but merely pages of my journal."

"Ah, but you see, I'm afraid he did not see all the pages, only a carefully selected few, enough to make him believe you had a lover. Having written in one entry that you wanted to run to your James, you then wrote, and I recall the exact words, I believe, 'Do you even know yourself, I wonder, how much I love you and how much I fear discovery of the truth about you? One moment I think it will be for the best, and the next I believe, if I were sensible, I would fear for my very life.'

Can you doubt, madam, that having read that after hearing you had fled—"

"Good God, why did I not see who you are before now? Only one man could possibly know such details or have opportunity to arrange such a thing. I don't know how I could have mistaken you for Michael even for a second, Bagshaw, but you must know by now that your game is up. Why, when I tell him what you have done—"

"You will not tell him," he said as he reached to remove his mask, tossing it casually onto the cluttered desk.

"Don't be a fool," she snapped, incensed now. "I will tell the whole world what you have done to me tonight."

"Molly Carver also threatened to tell the world," he said, his voice no longer a lustful murmur but one of fuming menace. "Do you know what became of Molly, my impertinent little pet?"

"You murdered her," Anne said with a calm wholly at odds with the flame of terror his tone had ignited in her.

He stepped nearer, and though it required every ounce of courage she had in her not to move, she refused to give him the satisfaction of knowing how much he frightened her.

He said, "Do you know, I never really thought of it as a murder, but I suppose it was, at that. Of course, she was only a common whore, not anyone worth bothering about, so I doubt that a single soul will miss her."

"Of course people miss her. Her family misses her. They, none of them, have the least idea what became of her."

"And how would you know anything about her family?" he asked, his tone sultry now.

She opened her mouth to tell him about Jane, then snapped it shut, realizing that if by some mad stroke of misfortune she should fail to escape him, Jane would become his next victim. Needing to say something, she took a high tone again. "You have no business to question me, Bagshaw, as you know perfectly well."

He stood over her now, and when his face contorted with

fury at her rebuke, she stepped back involuntarily, remembering the wineglass only just in time to avoid kicking it over. The backs of her legs encountered the sofa. She could go no further.

When with a look of insolent mockery he reached out to touch her chin, she ruthlessly suppressed a scream and said in a shaking voice, "T-tell me how Molly died."

"She was foolish," he said. "You must be more sensible."

"What happened?" The two words nearly choked her.

"Like you, she discovered my identity and threatened to tell the world. I meant only to demonstrate the consequence of provoking my temper, but I fear I misjudged my own strength."

"In fact, you beat her to death to silence her," Anne said, amazed at how calm she sounded but certain he would discern the false note and know her fear of him paralyzed all other emotion.

"That was not my intention. I meant her to receive no more than the usual punishment allotted to misbehaving harlots."

"Merciful heaven, how can a harlot, who has already sunk as low as a woman can go, be said to misbehave?"

His laugh sounded perfectly demonic. "How much you have to learn," he said, "and how much I shall enjoy your lessons. Our little birds of paradise here on the *Folly* frequently misbehave and must be shown the error of their ways. Maxwell is quite adept with a whip and rarely does permanent damage, but I tend to let passion rule my arm, I'm afraid, which is precisely what happened with the Carver slut. She defied me. Not only did she refuse to promise to keep silent, even when most of the skin had been lashed from her back and her gown was in bloody shreds, but she was insolent. Had she begged for mercy and promised to obey me, she would still be alive today. Remember that, my pet."

Anne felt sick. The image his words painted in her mind was more than her stomach could tolerate. "How could you? Molly was only an innocent young girl."

He shrugged. "She was, like most maidservants, a trollop,

a whore—as you said yourself, the lowest of the low. What difference can one more or less of that sort matter? She chose her lot in life."

"You know she did not," Anne said, forcing the words out between tight lips and gritted teeth, wanting to strike him, or better yet to shoot him right between the eyes. "I see now how it is, the way you threaten maids like Frannie and Jane. I daresay you demand favors for yourself from any maidservant you believe to be unprotected, and most are afraid to withstand you. If one refuses to submit, you turn her off without a character, rendering her unemployable elsewhere and leaving her no choice but to seek work here at the *Folly,* where she soon finds herself at your mercy. The wonder to me is not why *some* of our maids have become prostitutes but how so many have avoided it. You are a complete villain, Bagshaw, and will certainly be hanged."

"Harsh words, my pet," he said, stroking her cheek.

Anne wrenched away from him. "Don't touch me!"

"Oh, I shall do more than just touch you, my love."

"And don't call me by those horrid words. I am not your love or your pet. I am not your anything!"

"So it is possible to shake your calm," he said, sounding smug. "I wondered, you know. Much of your great allure lay in wondering what it would take to shock you, to break through that serenity of yours and free the passion I was certain lay beneath. How gratifying to learn that instinct did not mislead me." With an evil smile, he added, "We must cultivate this more passionate nature for the pleasure of others. I will teach you myself."

"You will do no such thing," Anne said, horrified. "Good God, do you think you can keep me here forever? You *are* mad."

"Oh, not mad, my pet. I run no risk by keeping you aboard my boat. No one who cares about you has the least notion of your whereabouts. Lord Michael learned of your precipitate departure from the stable boys, of course, but they insisted they knew no more than that you had driven off in furious haste with Lord Ashby. They mentioned Scotland, however, which sent him haring after you at once. It all seemed quite providential, really."

Remembering that she and Lord Ashby had both commanded his men to tell no one else how the balloon had got loose, Anne could not at this juncture think highly of Providence. She said, "Only you would say such a thing, Bagshaw."

"Ah, but the whole business was clearly providential, you see, for I had been wondering how I might arrange to teach you manners—particularly after you worked your wiles on Burdekin—so I took advantage of your being out of the way today to search your rooms, and there were your papers sitting there, just begging to be used. When only a short time later his lordship mentioned your abrupt departure to me, the temptation was quite irresistible to encourage him to believe the worst. I've become rather adept of late at sending him off on little errands to keep him out of my way."

"All the accidents and mishaps at the mines and elsewhere!"

"Just so."

"But why?"

He narrowed his eyes. "The Priory is my domain, you see. Edmund was content to leave it so, but Lord Michael, not having the same exquisite tastes as his brother, was by far too likely to interfere. Thus, he was kept busy and out of my way. I controlled him like a puppet," he added with a reminiscent gleam.

"Poppycock," she said, using Lady Hermione's favorite word. "Next you will be telling me you were responsible for that dreadful wager that—"

"Don't look so conscious, my pet. You are not speaking out of turn now, for I know all about Edmund's little wager. He was in his cups, of course—he frequently was—but even he would be surprised at how much vexation it has caused Lord Michael."

"Well, how you can refer to a wager of twenty thousand pounds as *little,* I'm sure I don't know. Such a sum must cause vexation to anyone who had to deal with it."

"Indeed, it must," he agreed with visible amusement, "particularly when he cannot, with any propriety, speak openly of the details. Another clear indication of the hand of Providence at work, just as it must have been at work when Lord Michael said nothing to anyone else about your departure."

"You cannot be certain of that!"

"Oh, but I can, for when he saw your 'letters' he swore me to secrecy. He was hoping to whisk you home again before anyone knew you had gone, you see, and for all anyone else knows now, you are sound asleep in your own bed."

"People saw me! Elbert, His Grace, men in the stable yard, not to mention Maisie!"

"When he returns I will simply tell him that you came back, discovered what he had believed about you, and then ran away in earnest. What you wrote tonight will serve as your farewell letter very nicely, for you actually addressed it to him this time, you see. He will be distraught, of course, and I will be sadly remorseful, but you . . . you will disappear—forever, I'm afraid—since it clearly would not be at all sensible to let you return to the Priory. And he will be unable to marry again, of course, so this little problem will not arise again. I shall be left in peace to rule my little kingdom as I see fit."

"You never meant me to return," Anne said in a small voice, "not even if I had failed to recognize you."

"Well, no," he admitted. "Even in that event, I could not allow you to speak of where you had been, you know, and I doubt that I'd have trusted any promise you made to keep silent."

"I'd never have offered such a promise," she said flatly.

"Oh, I think you would promise almost anything in time," he said dulcetly. "Once I have taught you to behave, I shall remove you to a house in London in which I also hold an interest. In fact, perhaps it would be best to convey you to

London as quickly as the journey can be arranged. Our people there know exactly how to deal with recalcitrant young women."

Anne shivered. "Even you could not do such a thing."

"Certainly I can. I'll have no use for you here once I tire of you myself, for I cannot risk letting anyone see you who might reveal your whereabouts to his lordship."

She wanted to keep him talking, to prevent his touching her again. "Why do they call you Lord M?"

"For Mephistopheles, a little conceit of mine."

"But people believed you a member of the nobility! Surely you must have encouraged them to do so."

He sneered. "That misconception was not of my making. When Edmund brought me in to help run this place—not long after he purchased the boat and had it brought here—the first of our little tarts assumed when they met the pair of us that I, rather than he, was the nobleman. Not surprising, really, for the nobility have become sadly slipshod in manner of late, and in any case, my deportment was always more polished than his. You have seen the same phenomenon for yourself many times, I expect, for upper servants who behave with more elegance of manner than their master or mistress have become distressingly common. I believe that such informal behavior on the part of a master quite lowers the tone of a house. I would never behave so shabbily."

Anne stared at him. "You dare to criticize your betters when all the while you intend to ravish me? You are not only mad, you are ridiculous." She moved to turn away in disgust.

Catching her chin to force her to look at him, and gripping her arm so hard when she tried to pull away again that she knew he would leave bruises, he said harshly, "You will soon learn not to speak so disrespectfully to any man. You stepped beyond the limit of my tolerance when you incited that fool, Burdekin, to stand against me. She will be the next to be reminded that a properly behaved female must submit gracefully to her master."

Aware that more resistance would only infuriate him, she stood still, combatting her roiling emotions, trying to focus her thoughts, to devise a way to stop him, fearing that no acceptable way existed. "You cannot want to harm me," she said as steadily as she could. "A true gentleman would never behave so basely."

"Gentlemen do many things their womenfolk know nothing about," Bagshaw said. "Only consider who my customers are. Sir Jacob Thornton was not the only Member of Parliament to visit this place. Even your precious Michael has been known to visit, and there are others all up and down the river—gentlemen, noblemen, and even wealthy tradesmen. I am not so nice in my ways that I turn my nose up at good money, and nor was Edmund. But now, my pet, I think we will begin your first lesson. For all my association with the nobility, I have not yet tasted the charms of one of its feminine ornaments. You will be my first."

Desperate to keep him talking, she said hastily, "Did you know that your late master was so iniquitous that he intended to make you a gift of his own duchess?"

Bagshaw leered. "Generous of him, was it not? Such a pity that she took her own life before he could honor that pledge."

"She took her life because she knew exactly what he meant to do," Anne snapped, looking him right in the eye as she did.

He shook her. "I cannot think how you would know that, but I've warned you before about flaunting your disrespect, my girl. We don't tolerate impudence from our little birds, I'm afraid."

"I am neither your girl nor one of your birds," Anne said, still looking directly at him. "Though you can ravish me, even beat me, you cannot alter that state of affairs."

"Do you think not?"

She knew she had spoken nonsense. One touch of the whip that had flayed the skin from Molly's bones and she would submit to anything he demanded. Even now, the tense fury in his voice and the igniting fire in his eyes were such that she thought it a wonder her nightdress had not been seared from her body.

The hand that held her arm moved to grip the back of her neck, and the other, the one holding her chin, slid down to grasp her left breast. Anne froze. Her lips dried, her heart pounded, and her knees threatened to betray her. Awareness of the last sensation suggested what she should do, and when he bent his head to kiss her, she let herself go limp. Ignoring the sharp pain in her scalp when the fingers gripping her neck caught in her hair, she kept silent as her body slipped from his grasp.

Bagshaw tried to catch her, but the way he had been holding her, and the fact that she had startled him, impeded his efforts. She crumpled to an awkward position, half sitting on the sofa, slumped forward over her knees. Her hands nearly touched the floor. Quick as thought, even as he was bending to yank her upright again, Anne snatched up the wineglass near her right foot and dashed the contents into his face, catching him hard just under his nose with the edge of the glass.

The effect was much more than she had hoped for. With a cry of outraged pain, Bagshaw staggered backward, tripped over the tapestry footstool, and fell headlong, cracking his head against the edge of the desk and collapsing to the floor, unconscious.

Twenty-three

Terrified that someone in the next room might have heard Bagshaw's cry, or that he might regain his senses as quickly as he had lost them, Anne leapt to her feet and ran to the nearest window, shoving the curtains aside to find the latch, only to see that the rain-streaked window had long since been painted shut. She could not budge it. Without wasting a moment, she turned to examine the second window, the one blocked by the desk.

Snatching up her nightdress, she stepped to the chair seat and then to the desk top. Finding the latch free, she pushed open the window and scrambled to the wet sill, paying no heed to the havoc her movements wreaked on the cluttered desk. The blotter slipped beneath her feet, and she heard things crash to the floor, but thinking only of the noise and the likelihood that someone must hear it, or that Bagshaw might come to his senses in time to stop her, she did not hesitate on the sill long enough to glance back, but flung herself headfirst into the black night, realizing with horror only in the scant seconds before the chilly waters of the Derwent enveloped her that the window might as easily have looked onto the dock as over the river.

She sank quickly, making no effort at first to surface, letting the river current carry her, for she was aware that even in the darkness, it would take no more than a candle's glow to reveal her white nightdress against the dark water. Only when she could no longer hold her breath did she allow herself to rise, at which point she discovered a new problem. She could not swim in the voluminous garment.

Material that had first billowed around and above her, threatening to swim away on its own, now grasped at her legs, trapping them, tangling around them, threatening to drag her under again. She fought welling panic, struggling mentally as much as physically to force her limbs to relax. Then, turning onto her back with her head upstream, she let the current carry her away from the *Folly* feet-first, floating in a way she had not done since she was a child learning to swim. Though she swallowed a good deal of water in her attempt to reach the button at the back of the gown's close-fitting neckline, she managed at last to rip it open. And when the water caught the gown and swept it upward, she let the current strip it from her body, catching it at the last minute with both hands just before the sleeves slipped free of her arms.

Determined not to lose the gown altogether, she dragged the ends of both sleeves to her mouth as she turned back to her stomach, biting down hard. Then she began to swim at an angle toward the shore, visible ahead of her now in an odd glow of light. The current was more gentle away from the center of the river, and soon she could feel the muddy river bottom beneath her feet. She realized then that the rain had stopped. Slipping and sliding in the mud, bruising and scraping her feet on hidden rocks, she made her way to the bank. Only then did she look back, and stare in astonishment at what she saw. So intent had she been upon her peril that she had been completely unaware of activity behind her, but fiery orange flames blazed against the night sky. The *Folly* was burning.

Motionless now, with her head out of water, hearing feminine screams and shrieks of panic mixed with masculine shouts and the rattling of numerous carriage wheels, she realized that most of the customers were hastily departing, no doubt in order to avoid the embarrassment of meeting anyone who might come to help fight the fire. So fascinated was she by the sight of the burning boat that she had no sense of danger to herself until a hand shot out from the shrubbery and grabbed her arm, and the menacing, purring voice that she had come to hate and fear said, "You will pay dearly now for your insolence, my pet."

Startled and panic-stricken, Anne screamed and fought like a madwoman to free herself, ignoring the rocks, stones, and mud beneath her feet. In her terror, she imagined she heard someone call her name, and she screamed again, punching Bagshaw with her free hand and kicking him as hard as she could without thought of her sore feet. Amazingly, it was the river that saved her, for her bare skin was wet and slippery, and in his attempt to grasp her more tightly, he stepped in the mud and his feet slid out from under him. Falling heavily, he nearly took her with him but let go in his struggle to save himself. He lurched to his feet again only to step on a large rock that tilted crazily with his weight, then seemed to cast him headlong into deep water.

He came up once, sputtering, "Can't swim!" Then, as Anne watched in helpless horror, the swift current swept him away.

"Anne!"

Turning at the sound of the beloved voice, she scrambled up the bank and flung herself into Michael's arms. "Oh, Michael, Bagshaw fell into the river, and he can't swim!"

Michael held her tight against his warm chest. "My darling, I saw the whole while I was crashing through bushes, trying to reach you from the road, but I have no interest in searching for him, other than to murder him with my bare hands. Or was I mistaken in what I saw? Were you merely dancing naked on the riverbank with him when he fell?"

"I was doing no such thing!"

She heard his relieved chuckle. "Forgive me, sweetheart. It was a dreadful thing to say when I know you must have been terrified beyond belief, but in my relief at finding you safe, I seem to be a little light-headed and could not resist the urge to tease you. What, may I ask, have you done with your clothes?"

Looking down to see that the firelight from the *Folly* cast her whole body in a rosy glow, Anne gasped in shock. "I had my nightdress," she said, adding as she looked vaguely around, "somewhere. But it is quite soaked, I'm afraid."

"Take this," he said, releasing her long enough to slip off the heavy cloak he wore and to wrap it around her. Then he swept her up into his arms and carried her to his waiting horse.

Only when they were mounted and she could lean comfortably against his broad chest and hear his heart beat did Anne think again of Bagshaw. "Did he drown, do you think?"

"I have enough faith in both God and the Devil to believe the latter has claimed his own," Michael said grimly. "Did he hurt you, sweetheart?"

"No, I got away before he could do anything too dreadful. In fact, I think I hurt him when I hit him with a wineglass."

"I'll do more than that to the villain if I ever see him again," Michael promised, "but now I mean to get you home and tucked safely into a warm bed."

"But what about the people on the *Folly?* I'm nearly certain that I started that fire, because I heard things fall from the desk when I escaped through the window. I think a branch of candles must have begun it. Should we not help?"

"No," he said bluntly. "There are plenty of people dashing about, and there is nothing we can do that they cannot. If you like, we can assist some of the women later to find respectable ways to make a living, but tonight we will look after ourselves. We'll stay on this side of the river until we reach our bridge. I've no wish to ride through the village—nor do you, I daresay."

"No, sir," she said, leaning contentedly against him and letting her eyelids droop shut. They rode in silence for some moments before she said sleepily, "I'm glad you found me. How did you come to be there?"

"To begin at the beginning," he said, "Alsop had discovered that someone at Upminster was behind the troubles at the mine in Castleton. He actually had caught one of the rogues in the act of weakening some underpinnings and choked the information out of him. But since the fellow would say only that *his lordship* had ordered him to cause a bit of damage—"

"That is how they call Bagshaw at the *Folly,*" Anne said, "but I don't doubt poor Alsop thought the fellow referred to Lord Ashby, or even Cressbrook, if not yourself."

"Alsop never suspected me," Michael said, "but he had heard murmuring before, including references to a mysterious lord. And though I could not seriously suspect my uncle, I had just enough doubt to keep me from asking for his assistance."

"I thought you foolish," Anne said. "His knowledge of mechanical devices would certainly have been helpful to you, but I can see now why you kept things to yourself."

"I'd have done better to shout my concerns to the world, I suppose. What I don't know is why Bagshaw created such havoc, if in fact he really was behind it all."

"He was," Anne said. "He was kind enough to disclose his reasons to me. In point of fact, he enjoyed an exaggerated view of his power, and saw both you and me as threats to his dominion over the household." She repeated what Bagshaw had said, adding with a sigh, "He said it was easy to keep you out of his way."

Michael chuckled. "But not so easy to deal with you. I see how it was, sweetheart. I married a seemingly nice, submissive female, who for a time was willing to be told that she must not interfere with the household, but once you took the bit between your teeth, there was no stopping you."

"Yes, I even suborned Mrs. Burdekin, he said."

"I knew that Edmund had left control of the house to him, and he seemed so efficient and . . . and so—"

"—so lordly," Anne said. "I remember, that was my first impression of him, and even Lady Hermione said that when she asked him to do something, she felt as if she were ordering King George about." Anne nestled more comfortably against Michael, tucking her bare toes up under the warm cloak, and said, "But how did you find me? Bagshaw said you had gone to Scotland, believing that I had run away from you. I wouldn't, you know."

"You believed worse of me, did you not?"

"Nonsense, what could be worse than that?"

"You believed I owned part of that damned floating brothel."

Having forgotten that little detail, Anne squirmed at his tone, and said in a small voice, "I suppose you must have somehow encountered Lord Ashby and Lady Hermione—"

"And their very odd companion. It was she who told me what you had learned from her."

"Yes, well, I am sorry if you are vexed, Michael, but I also knew, you will recall, that you had been seen aboard the *Folly;* and if you believed I wrote letters to a secret lover and then ran away with Lord Ashby, I think we must be very nearly even."

"I don't know what I believed, thinking back on it. I was tired, and feeling frustrated, and when I returned to the stables, I heard tales of a missing balloon, and a hurried departure to Scotland, all mixed together. I do recall thinking at one point that you must have taken off in the balloon and my uncle was following you, or the other way around. I could get no sense out of the stable boys, and everyone else seemed to be missing, so I applied to Bagshaw for information."

"And he showed you my supposed letters."

"Exactly. Behaving in quite a distracted manner himself, he said one of the maids had found them, and like the exhausted fool I was by then, I reacted at once instead of thinking sensibly. Somehow he managed to imply that you were bound for Scotland, believing you could apply for a divorce there, in order to marry your lover. I recalled enough of what Jake Thornton had said to believe you might believe such a thing possible, so I shouted for a horse, thinking that if I rode cross-country, I might head you off before you reached the Great North Road."

"If you did not take the main road, that explains why we did not encounter you on our return," Anne said.

"Does it?" His voice had taken on an edge she did not quite like. "I might say at this point that I had not ridden more than halfway to Sheffield before I realized I was being foolish beyond permission. But although I did indeed encounter my uncle and his party and learn that you had been with them and had returned to the Priory believing I was guilty of—"

"Pray, sir, say no more about that. I was wrong to believe such a thing even for a moment. I collect that Lord Ashby and the others did not remain in Bamford overnight as they intended."

"No, I met them in Froggatt, where they were in the process of exchanging an antiquated coach for a more comfortable chaise to convey them here. According to what my uncle told me, Lady Hermione objected to spending the night in a tawdry public house, or for that matter in a posting house. She said it was unseemly enough for her to be jauntering about the countryside in his company, with only Mrs. Flowers as a chaperon, a view with which her brother will no doubt agree. He was at the Priory when I got back, demanding to know where we had misplaced her."

"Good gracious, do you think he is still there?"

"I shouldn't doubt it," Michael said, "because in view of the fact that Hermione seemed to know exactly what Mrs. Flowers had told you, I think she must have got the tale out of her soon after you left them, and then was driven by her own curiosity to get back. If that is the case, she will not leave the Priory without knowing the end of the tale."

"I wonder what they will do with poor Mrs. Flowers?"

"I believe Hermione intends to take her to Cressbrook Hall," Michael said. "She seems to think Wilfred will welcome the woman as a replacement for his housekeeper." When Anne stifled a choke of laughter, he said, "Just so. Perhaps, before we encounter them you would like to explain those letters of yours to me."

She willingly explained how she had begun to write her journal as a series of letters to her long-deceased brother, and when she had finished, he said thoughtfully, "That answer didn't occur to me, though I doubted the existence of a secret lover long before I met the others. I had learned some time ago, you see, that Edmund was involved in the *Folly,* for I discovered that he had actually purchased the boat; however, I also unearthed the fact that he was not the sole owner, and I'd been trying to discover who his partner was, because I could neither sell it nor do anything else with it until I did so. You will recall that the subject came up when we visited Maria Thornton."

"You thought Sir Jacob had been that mysterious partner."

"With good reason, I thought. It seemed the sort of venture that would interest a man of his stamp. But there was no more evidence of a partnership than there was of the damned wager."

"You know, Bagshaw knew about the wager, Michael. He thought it was some sort of evidence that Providence had taken a hand in his villainy. He called it Edmund's little wager and said he was sure it caused you no small vexation. He was amused when he said it, too."

"An odd thing to say," he agreed. "I did not recognize the full extent of his villainy at once, of course, but when I learned that you had been with the others, and realized that he had purposely sent me on a wild goose chase, I rode back to the Priory as though twenty devils were after me, only to discover not only that you really had disappeared but that he was gone as well. I remembered how close he had always been to Edmund, and how much in his confidence, and the pieces of the puzzle began to fall together into a picture I did not want to contemplate."

Anne said, "When he told me what he had said to you, I could not imagine you would believe it."

"In the ordinary event, I would at least have asked a good many more questions, but after the day I had already endured, I simply was not thinking properly. And that reminds me," he added gently, "that I have a question or two to ask about my bays, which, I am told, were taken by my uncle, blast his eyes, and then returned by you and Andrew. It occurs to me just now, in fact, that I have heard singularly little mention of Andrew in all the many explanations I have received today."

Anne stiffened but did not speak.

"I think, in future, sweetheart, when I want information from you, instead of tickling you, I will hold you just as I am now, for your body tells me more than mere words ever would. Now, tell me what mischief that brat conjured up today."

She hesitated, not wanting to explain, knowing he would be angry with Andrew and perhaps with the rest of them as well.

He said, "I remind you that there will soon be others for me to question if you do not open the budget. Cressbrook certainly intended to wait for my uncle and Hermione, and unless I misread his mood, he is under the impression that somehow or other Ashby has compromised her reputation. I have my doubts that he will accept the Flowers woman as any sort of chaperon, either. Thus, I am very nearly certain that both my uncle and Lady Hermione will be glad to discuss Andrew's activities at length."

She sighed. "You are persuasive, sir, but I hope you will not be enraged by the tale, for I do not think my sensibilities can tolerate much more Cheltenham drama tonight."

"I will restrain myself then," he said quietly, holding her closer. "The sky is clearing, at least, so we won't be drenched again. Are you warm enough?"

She nodded, snuggling more comfortably against him. Then, she gave an accurate but concise description of the day's events. He interrupted twice, once to demand if his ears had deceived him when she said Andrew had intended to marry Mrs. Flowers, and the second time to describe in brief but graphic terms just what he meant to do to the boy for stirring up so much riot and rumpus.

"I hope you will do no such thing," Anne said. "In fact, I think the best thing would be to send him to school. Surely you must know people who would help get him into Eton or Harrow."

"Sweetheart, any school in the land would welcome the Duke of Upminster with open arms, but I should be flying in the face of tradition to send him away to school. Dukes of Upminster—"

"—are educated at home," Anne finished for him in weary tones. "I have heard that, sir, and indeed, I have heard about tradition until I am sick to death of it. In my opinion, persons dredge up tradition as the best excuse when they wish to avoid doing things differently. In any event, tradition has proved unequal to the task of preparing Andrew for the great position he will someday hold. As his guardian, you owe it to him to find a more efficient method. I know I am being odiously impertinent—"

"No, sweetheart, you are just odiously right."

"I beg your pardon?"

"I told you once that you were wiser than I when it came to the children, but I have discounted your wisest advice. I hope I have learned my lesson. Had I listened to you from the outset, I might have seen much sooner what sort of villain Bagshaw was."

"Not necessarily," Anne said. "He was very careful, I think. I've a strong notion he enlisted the aid of at least some of the menservants, and terrorized the maidservants, so it was nearly impossible to understand what was going on until I began to be such a nuisance to him. Indeed, until I undermined his authority, particularly with Burdekin—"

"Undermined?"

"Oh, yes, he said as much, himself. I prevented her niece being badly burned, you see, and she grew much kinder after that and stopped citing tradition to me whenever I desired an alteration in the way things were done. Unfortunately, Bagshaw saw any action of mine as interference in his realm and decided I required punishment for my presumption. He has done the same before, so of course, I believed he meant every word."

"When has he done the same before?"

She told him about Molly Carver, and had begun to explain about the duchess's note, and the reason for her suicide, when she suddenly thought of something else. "The wager, Michael! Could the duchess have been the woman involved, the one Sir Jacob seduced? Could that be why mention of the wager amused Bagshaw so? If Edmund would have given her to his butler—"

"No, sweetheart, the woman involved in the wager is the same whose husband fought the duel with Edmund, and killed him. I can scarcely go around Derbyshire advertising such facts, however; and that, plus the fact that I'm having enough trouble untangling the mess Edmund made of the Upminster affairs without letting it be known that such a huge demand exists against the estate, is why I generally chose not to speak of the wager."

They rode silently for the short time remaining until the Priory bridge loomed ahead of them, when Michael said abruptly, "When I think that devil had you in his clutches for as much as an hour, sweetheart, it makes me wild. Thank God, I encountered the others in time to get back here and find you."

Anne chuckled. "You sound as if you think you rescued me. I would like to point out not only that you did nothing of the kind but that you warned me not long ago never to expect you to rescue me from harm."

"I did nothing of the sort," Michael snapped.

"But you did," she reminded him. "You said I should never look for such favors from you since you are the sort who requires damsels to rescue themselves from the dragons who assault them."

He drew in his mount so sharply—right in the center of the arched bridge—that the animal whinnied in protest. Taking Anne by the shoulders to make her look at him, he said, "Listen to me, and believe me when I say that I would have moved heaven and earth to find you if you *had* run away from me."

"Heaven and earth?"

"That's what I said, and before you quiz me further, I just remembered something I meant to ask you earlier. We got talking about Edmund's partner in the *Folly,* and it went out of my head. Explain why, if you were writing to your brother in that journal of yours, you expressed yourself in such loving sentiments."

"It is the oddest thing," she said softly, "but of late I keep forgetting that it is James to whom I write. Indeed, though I was so sleepy, I do not recall doing it, Bagshaw told me that the entry I began tonight was addressed to you. He intended to tell you that although he had been mistaken about my first flight, I had got upset when I learned that you had so distrusted me, and ran away then in earnest. He was going to use my last journal entry to prove it, and I have no doubt, Michael, that it, too, was couched in loving terms."

"Was it, sweetheart?" His voice was low in his throat, the purring voice, and she wondered how she could ever have mistaken that lovely warm sound for the fiendish rasp that Fiona Flowers had described.

"Michael, by Jove, that you, lad? We've been on tenterhooks ever since we returned and found you were still amongst the missing, and then we saw the flames. What the devil's burning?"

"The *Folly,*" Michael said, gathering his reins and urging his horse forward to meet Lord Ashby and the two men with him. "I'm sorry you were put into a fidget, sir, but I've got her safe now, and I daresay the sooner we get up to the house, the better she will like it. She's a bit damp around the edges, you see."

"Is she, by Jove? What happened, Anne? Where have you been? Do you know Michael thought you had run away from him? We soon put him right on that score, I can tell you, but I don't understand why you should have left the Priory, damme if I do. I thought you were actually looking forward to speaking with Michael. And what's more, I can tell you that Andrew thought the same thing, and he tells us that he dined with you, too, so what Bagshaw can have been thinking to have told Michael you'd gone away earlier, I can't think. Fellow must be queer in his attic!"

Feeling unable to respond to his pelting comments and questions, Anne leaned more heavily against her husband's broad chest, and gratefully heard him recommend that they return to the house before indulging in lengthy explanations. But if she hoped for time to recover her energy before she faced the inquisition, she soon learned her error, for no sooner did they walk into the front hall than the others burst forth from the library.

"There they are," Andrew exclaimed. "I told you Uncle Michael would find her all right and tight!"

"I knew he would," Sylvia said, running from behind her brother to fling herself at them.

"Well, of course, he did," Lady Hermione said, looking on in satisfaction.

"And about time, too," Cressbrook said in an irritated voice. "Perhaps now, Hermione, you will have the goodness to accompany me home where you belong. Look at that clock, will you? You ought to have been home hours ago! I never knew such goings-on in all my days. Damme, when I was younger, women behaved a deal more circumspectly, that I can tell you."

"Poppycock," she said. "Why, in our younger days, women were forever doing things that would be frowned upon now. Come now, Wilfred, you must own that I'm right, for our own mother—"

"That will do, Hermione," her brother said gruffly.

Only too well aware that her sole garment was the cloak she clutched around her, Anne looked appealingly at her husband, who smiled at her and said firmly to the others, "Go back into the library, all of you. I am going to take Anne upstairs, and then I promise I will come back down to explain it all to you."

When the others took vocal exception to Anne's leaving

without answering their questions, she gathered her dignity as well as she could under the circumstances, and said, "If you will all just give me a few moments to make myself presentable, I will come back, too. Oh, Mrs. Burdekin, how glad I am to see you!"

"And I, to see you, my lady. I do not know where Elbert or Bagshaw are, but what with all the kick-up there's been tonight, I thought I should hold myself in readiness in the event that you wished for some refreshment."

"Bagshaw will not be back, I'm afraid," Anne said.

"Well, that Elbert's gone, too, ma'am, but Jane will help me serve, and John."

"Excellent," Anne said, "and perhaps—"

"Enough," Michael said firmly. "Mrs. Burdekin knows what to do, my dear. You are going to bed."

"If you think you are going to pack me away in cotton wool while you and the others determine the truth of all this, you are very much mistaken, sir."

"Am I, indeed?" His eyes were twinkling. "You are becoming very imperious in your habits, sweetheart. Whatever happened to my Lady Serenity?"

"She learned the error of her ways," Anne said with a look challenging him to contradict her.

Michael nodded to the others, and said with laughter in his voice, "You heard my lady, everyone. Go back into the library and possess your souls in patience until we return. I promise we will not keep you kicking your heels long."

Anne sighed, and leaned back against him again, content in having added yet one more small victory to a most successful day.

Twenty-four

When Michael and Anne reached her bedchamber, she realized at once that he had formed the intention of keeping her there by one devious means or another. To thwart that objective, she rang at once for Maisie, who arrived with such speed that it was obvious she had been awaiting the summons.

"Oh, my dear Miss Anne," she exclaimed as she hurried into the room, "Such an uproar as there has been, and the whole house awake, I'm sure! Where on earth have you been? It is long after midnight, you know, and I prepared you for bed myself, hours and hours ago."

"Well, it is no use to fuss at me," Anne said, "for I am not going to bed yet, in any case, so please just find me a gown I can put on at once without a lot of bother."

"Not going to bed!" Maisie looked instantly at Lord Michael. "If it please you, sir, she cannot know what she is saying, for I can see just by looking at her that she's had a hard time of it, and how she can expect me to make her presentable with her hair all in a wet tangle like that, and needing to be dried proper before a good fire, is more than I can say. Surely, she ought to be popped into bed as soon as may be."

Anne said with an edge to her voice, "You heard me, Maisie. If you don't fetch a gown for me at once, I will find one myself. I am quite capable of determining what I ought to do."

Maisie folded her lips together with the air of one who has

encountered such recalcitrance before, and continued to look at Lord Michael. He smiled understandingly at her but said, "Pray, do not look to me to interfere with your mistress, Maisie. She has taken a firm stand, and we must all of us leap to her bidding. Must I leave the room and stay outside, kicking my heels, whilst you are made presentable, Lady Imperious?"

The meekness of his tone did not fool Anne for a moment, but as if she took him at his word, she looked right at him and said, "If you will not play the fool, sir, you may remain, for dressing will not take me above ten minutes. Maisie, you will have to make do for the moment with combing out the worst tangles and plaiting my hair. I have no wish to keep everyone waiting whilst we dry it." As she talked, she reached to unfasten the cloak she wore, and when she let it fall to the floor, Maisie gasped.

"By all that's holy, Miss Anne, you've not got a stitch on! What became of your nightdress, may I ask?"

"I . . . I lost it," Anne said, avoiding Michael's eye. Letting Maisie help her into a shift, she said, "The gray wool, Maisie. It's high to the throat and warm, and that is what I care most about at the moment."

"I'll be bound you do, for you're beginning to shiver," Maisie said, clicking her tongue, "but what happened to you?"

"I was abducted by Bagshaw, or some of his henchmen."

"Bagshaw? Mercy me!"

"Yes, Bagshaw. I don't know who the others were, but Mrs. Burdekin said Elbert is also amongst the missing, so I wouldn't be surprised to learn that he was one of them."

"Bagshaw? Elbert?" Maisie clasped a hand to her bosom and stared in shock. "Whatever next?"

Michael said grimly, "I had hoped her mention of Elbert had escaped you, for I did not want to increase your alarms by discussing the likelihood of his involvement until you were somewhat recovered from your ordeal."

"Well, sir, if you mean to continue with such past habits, I warn you, we shall fall out again, because I've had a surfeit of being protected and treated as if I had no brain whatsoever. If you had been more forthcoming about your problems earlier, as I requested, I might have been more on my guard, you know, and between us, we should have known twice as much as each one knew alone. And, too, you ought to have talked things over more with Lord Ashby, because I daresay he would have soon led you into asking questions at the mine that would much sooner have uncovered the mischief there. Moreover—"

"Enough," Michael said in quite his old way. "I understand you, I think, but this is neither the time nor the place for this discussion. The others are waiting for us."

Looking from Maisie's shocked face to Michael's stern one, Anne realized she had overstepped the mark by going on as she had in her tirewoman's presence. Leaving her to tidy up the room, with orders to go to bed as soon as she had finished, Anne walked silently with Michael until they were well away from their own rooms before she said ruefully, "I must apologize, sir. I ought not to have spoken to you as I did just then."

"Possibly not," he said, turning his head to smile at her with more warmth than she had expected to see just then, "but I have a strong notion that I deserved to hear every word."

"Not in front of Maisie, however."

He chuckled. "You are generous, sweetheart. I recall at least one or two occasions when I scolded you in the presence of the servants, and several others when I certainly did not treat you with the respect you deserve. I have merely been served some of my own in return, that's all. In any case, after the fright you gave me tonight, I am too grateful to have you safely returned to me to take exception to your scolds."

"Well, in that case . . ." Anne began.

"No, no," he said, laughing, "don't test me too far. As it is, I am astonished by my own forbearance. I daresay that just now I would be able to confront even Andrew with equanimity."

They found the others awaiting them, if not with patience, at least with resignation, and she soon found that he had judged his emotions more accurately than she. Seeing Sylvia still with them, Anne said, "Darling, whatever are you doing still up and about? You must go back to bed at once."

"I woke up and went to your room, and you weren't there," Sylvia said. "I remembered what you said about not frightening Moffat, so I went back, but I couldn't sleep. And then, from my room, I heard lots of noise when the wagon and carriages came into the courtyard, so I came down to see what was happening."

Lady Hermione said cheerfully, "Don't scold the child. No one paid the least heed to her when she first came down, you know, for we were all intent upon learning whether Michael had found you here and then were set to fidgeting when we learned that he had gone in search of you. At all events, we certainly would not have been so cruel as to send her to bed once she learned you were missing, which, thanks to Ashby's blurting it out the moment we walked into the house, she did. Man never could keep a still tongue in his head."

Lord Ashby said calmly, "Now, Hermie, I won't have you talking like that, particularly not when we've just convinced Wilfred here that there was never any intention of our running off together, or of my compromising your reputation."

"Yes, yes," Cressbrook said testily, "but just saying that you have discovered today that you care more about each other than you ever knew before and think you might like to get married don't tell me much, not the way you two have flown out at each other every time I've seen you in the same room together. Damme, it won't wash any more than it will to pretend that your virtue was protected by that . . . that female yonder!"

Words failed him, and Anne realized that Mrs. Flowers, whom she had quite forgotten, was sitting quietly in a corner at a discreet distance from the others.

Lady Hermione said bluntly, "My virtue was never in doubt, Wilfred, and for you to suggest that it was is much worse than anything Ashby might have done. My own brother! You ought to be ashamed, sir, and just when I've found you the exact housekeeper you're in crying need of, too!"

Hearing a chuckle from Michael, Anne clapped a hand over her own mouth, but Andrew said approvingly, "That's a first-rate notion, sir, for she is an excellent woman and is quite in the habit of running a house, for she told me she had run quite a large one in Chesterfield before ever she knew Sir Jacob—And what I can have said to send you all into whoops," he added indignantly, "I cannot imagine. You did tell me you had done such a thing, did you not, Fiona?"

"I did, Your Grace," Mrs. Flowers said, "and indeed, I was most efficient, for I am of a saving disposition, you know."

"Well that, at least, will be a change," Cressbrook said.

"Then it's settled," Lady Hermione said hastily, "and a good thing, too, for what you and Michael no doubt heard Wilfred say, Anne, and very likely don't believe any more than he does himself, is that I have agreed to marry Ashby. We realized only today that the main reason we are always pitching at each other is that we each care prodigiously. It is the greatest wonder," she added, looking at Lord Ashby tenderly, "that we never before recognized the truth, for you must know we have known each other since we were the merest children."

"I think you will be very happy," Anne said, "and I hope you will both be sensible enough always to share your problems and never keep secrets. When Michael tells you what he learned at the mine today, sir, you will agree with me that he ought to have heeded his best instincts and asked your advice long since—yes, *and* taken you with him when he visited the mine, for I'm quite sure that you would have guessed all that was happening in the twinkling of a bedpost."

When Michael had explained, Lord Ashby said, "As to ferreting all that out in a twinkling, I daresay I shouldn't have done any such thing, you know, but I'd have been onto them before now, by Jove. And I daresay I'd have realized before Alsop did that there was a mischief-maker involved somewhere. It is one thing when a man has to deal with the results of mischief on a daily basis, and quite another when someone learns about it who understands what is required to produce such results. Aye, you ought to have told me straightaway, Michael lad."

"Well, don't be too quick to take him to task," Lady Hermione said thoughtfully, "for I shouldn't wonder if he thought you were too much involved in your own projects to want to hear about his troubles, or even that you were involved yourself in the mischief, just wanting to keep him out of your hair. You didn't give him much reason to trust you, Ashby, that's certain."

"Well, if that ain't just like you, Hermie! Dashed if I don't think I might be making a great mistake—"

"Not in the least," she said cheerfully, "but you are not the man I believe you to be if you cannot be honest enough to recall that practically the only time you even talked to poor Michael—by what you told me, yourself—was when you were trying to cozen him into giving you money for your experiments. Now, isn't that true?"

"Aye," he said, cast down, "it is. And ordering materials in spite of him, as often as not." Turning to Michael, he said, "I wasn't the least help, was I? If it weren't for me always running up the tab with my precious silks and inflammable air, you'd have soon paid off that dashed Newmarket wager, by Jove."

Michael laughed. "Now, Uncle, you are taking entirely too much blame upon yourself. How on earth do you think your experiments can have been enough to prevent my paying twenty thousand pounds to Jake Thornton? I'll grant you, you could send me flying into the boughs quick enough, and I did begin to feel as if everyone was in a conspiracy to wring money out of me, and out of the estate. Moreover, I daresay I felt guilty at first that my own debts formed a considerable part of the whole, but—"

"Twenty thousand?" murmured Cressbrook. "Newmarket?"

Recalled to his audience, Michael looked hastily around the room and said sternly, "Andrew, take Sylvia up to her bedchamber and then go to bed yourself. Neither of you has any business to be down here at such an hour."

"I am still Duke of Upminster, I believe," Andrew said, straightening and glaring at him. "If you are discussing Upminster affairs, you are discussing my affairs, and I won't be sent to bed like a child. I daresay you do not yet know to what extremes your actions have forced me—"

"I believe I know enough to know that you and I are going to have a long talk tomorrow, my lad," Michael said, cutting in swiftly and sternly. "Unless you want that talk to go more painfully for you than I had planned, keep a civil tongue in your head and do as I bid you. Do I make myself clear?"

Grimacing, Andrew muttered, "Yes, you do."

Deeming it time to take matters into her own hands, Anne said calmly, "You should know, my dear Andrew, so that you may consider your own feelings about it beforehand, that what your uncle primarily wants to discuss tomorrow is whether you think you will benefit from attending a good public school."

Lord Ashby exclaimed, "Now, see here, Michael, surely you ain't thinking of sending the Duke of Upminster to school! Why, it just ain't done. Tradition, you know. By Jove, I can't—"

"Be silent, Ashby," Lady Hermione said firmly.

To everyone's astonishment, he obeyed, clamping his lips together tightly.

Andrew stared from one adult to another. Then, looking much more cheerful, he said suddenly, "Come along, Sylvia. I don't know why you did not go up when Aunt Anne bade you do so, but you must go to bed now or you will look like a hag tomorrow." And with his dignity apparently undiminished the young duke left the room with his little sister following obediently in his wake.

When they had gone, Lord Ashby said, "By Jove, Michael, I know I oughtn't to have gone against you with the boy still in the room if, in fact, I *am* going against you. Come to think of it, you were not the one who said you was sending him to school."

"No, but I am certainly thinking about it," Michael said, looking at Anne with amusement in his eyes.

When she smiled back, the look in his eyes warmed to one that was even more familiar to her and to which she felt an instant, visceral response. She wished the others would go away.

Cressbrook said distinctly, "Not twenty thousand."

Lord Ashby looked chagrined and said to Michael, "Sorry about that. Talking out of school again, and you've every right to be vexed, for I know you don't want that wager babbled about. Look here, Wilfred, that ain't for public knowledge, you know. Edmund kept it quiet, and so did Jake Thornton for a wonder, and it ain't for you to go chatting about it to all and sundry now."

"But I attended the October meeting at Newmarket with Edmund and Jake," Cressbrook said simply. "Always go—spring and October meetings. Never miss one. Memory's not what it was, of course, but that wager had to do with hunting birds of quality, or some such thing. Unless I'm thinking of another one."

"No," Michael said, subjecting the viscount to a searching look, "it was at Newmarket, right enough. I don't have the record, but I've seen it, and that's just how it was written. The type of bird they were hunting did not bear wings, however."

"Damme, that's the one I know then, for I wrote the vowel myself. Edmund tried, but he was too much in his cups to write and demanded that I do it for him. Jake kept it. But surely that wager was paid! Gentlemen's honor, don't you know."

"There was an additional wager," Michael said with a grimace. "When I saw the vowel, it had been scrawled at the bottom. Had Edmund succeeded in matching Jake's success, the wager was to be declared null and void. He failed, however, and although I do not presently know the whereabouts of the record—"

"I have it."

Startled, everyone turned to stare at Mrs. Flowers, and Anne realized from the looks on the others' faces that, like herself, they had all forgotten her presence again.

Michael recovered first, and said, *"You* have it?"

"Yes, your lordship, I do." She opened the reticule she carried, and removed a folded paper, handing it to him. "I've had this for months now, and though I do not generally carry i on my person, I did today, thinking that if worse came to worst I could demand payment. Sir Jacob gave it to me long ago saying all I need do was present it to claim the money. Bu when I saw that the wager had to do only with hunting a bird I thought it ridiculous. And when I learned that he had made no arrangement for me in his will, that he had not even left a letter with his solicitor as he had promised to do, to show that he gave that paper to me after Duke Edmund's death, I feared no one would believe me if I said he meant that money to be my legacy."

"Good Lord, what a coil," Michael exclaimed. "I have already told Lady Thornton of the wager's existence, and promised to pay it. She did say she would not take the money, bu nonetheless, I cannot but think she would change her mind if she discovered where it was supposed to go. Twenty thousand—"

"Two thousand."

This time all eyes turned to the viscount, and with his color deepening accordingly, he said, "Remember thinking two thousand was an outrageous sum to wager on shooting a pigeon or two, but damme, for twenty, I'd have refused to write the vowel. Daresay I'd have told them both they were shockingly inebriated, and that I'd dashed well not stand witness for such a wager."

Michael had been swiftly reading, and he said now in a puzzled voice, "But it is clearly twenty thousand here."

"Don't understand that," Cressbrook said. "Moreover, they both knew the right amount. Can't think why Jake would have told this woman she'd be set for life on a mere two thousand."

"Well, I can tell you," Mrs. Flowers said bitterly. "Jake Thornton wasn't no better than he should be. A female learns in my line of work—my past line, I should say—that men are rarely to be trusted, but Jake was a piece of work, a real beguiler. Every time he made a promise, I believed him, and I think from what he told me of his wife, he could twist her round his thumb as well. When he gave me that paper, he said not to say a word about it unless something happened to him, and then to take it straight to Lord Michael without mentioning its existence to another soul. I tell you now, the way he made me promise to do it just as he commanded was one reason I feared something was amiss with it. And when I saw the cut of that solicitor of Sir Jacob's, I was right terrified that he or Lord Michael would have me cast straight into prison if I showed that note."

Lord Ashby began to protest, but Anne said thoughtfully, "Michael, what would you have done had Mrs. Flowers brought the note directly to you?"

"I would have explained that the estate could not bear so great a sum at once, but that I'd do all in my power to see she got the money, particularly since Cressbrook signed as witness."

"You would not have demanded to see proof that Sir Jacob had indeed given her the paper?"

"No, her possession would be proof enough of that, and I should not think it particularly odd in him to choose to provide for his . . . for her in such a way as not to fling her existence at his wife at such a time."

"No, in the normal way of things, Lady Thornton would never have known of the wager."

Cressbrook said, "May I see that paper?"

Michael handed it to him, and he looked it over carefully. "This first bit is in my handwriting," he said, "but I think that fifth naught was added later. Only look at the shape of it. I am certain I left a space on either side of the number, so that it would stand out. That is generally my habit with numbers. But here, as you see, there is space only on the left."

"There is a comma, however," Michael pointed out.

"Yes, indeed, but if a naught was added, so might a comma have been. I begin to suspect that Jake Thornton was less of a gentleman than even his critics believed. I shall be happy to confirm the proper sum wherever you will, Michael, for you must not pay twenty thousand when the wager was for two."

"No, nor allow the estate to be robbed of such a sum, but I hardly dare think much good will be served by explaining all this to Lady Thornton, so we are yet at a standstill, are we not?"

Lady Hermione said, "You let me deal with Maria Thornton. I know precisely how to manage that for the best. I shall simply tell her that Mrs. Flowers holds the vowel and that if she wants the whole thing to disappear as if in a puff of smoke she will say nothing more about it. I can even promise to take Fiona away with me when Ashby and I are married, though I should be sorry to do so, for that would be to deprive poor Wilfred of a no doubt excellent housekeeper."

"Are you leaving Derbyshire?" Anne asked, surprised.

"We will both want to make long visits here, of course, but I think that, for a time at least, we will live somewhere on our own. I can have the dower house on my son's estates in Ireland, you know, and Ashby has a sort of hunting box in Leicestershire. We haven't discussed it, but some arrangement can be made. I do think that Mrs. Flowers ought to get the two thousand, if the estate will bear it. Do not you, Michael?"

"Yes, but I don't intend to settle all this tonight. My lady is fast fading, as you all can see, and ought to be tucked up in bed before another hour strikes on the hall clock. Will you take Mrs. Flowers with you to Cressbrook Hall, ma'am, or shall I rout someone out to drive her home?"

"She will go with us," Lady Hermione said firmly, ignoring her brother's doubtful grimace.

"Then, if you don't mind, we'll see you to the door at once. I'm afraid we no longer have a butler to perform that service," he added dryly.

"My goodness me, that's quite right," Lady Hermione exclaimed. "I will not stir a step without hearing all that happened to you, Anne. Where did Michael find you? What befell you? Did that odious Bagshaw—I must tell you, I never really liked that fellow— Did he do anything really dreadful to you?"

"Hermione, take a damper," Lord Ashby said, grabbing her by the arm and hustling her toward the door. "Michael wants to get poor Anne to bed, and you are not going to keep her up till all hours answering your fool questions, for I won't hear of it."

"Why, Ashby," Lady Hermione was heard to say dulcetly as she was swept from the room, "how very masterful you can be. I never should have guessed it, you know."

"Now, Hermione, by Jove—"

Cressbrook said politely to Mrs. Flowers, "How rude my sister is to run off without so much as a word to you, ma'am. If you will take my arm, I shall see you safely to the carriage."

"Why, thank you, my lord. So very kind," she murmured, fluttering her lashes at him.

Anne squeezed Michael's arm.

He looked down at her and said gently, "Tired, sweetheart?"

"I certainly ought to be, don't you think?"

"I do, and I'll warn you right now that if I find young Sylvia in your bed, I'm chucking her right back to her own room."

"Andrew will have seen her tucked in. I'll be all alone in my bed, I promise you."

"Well, as to that," he murmured, "we shall see."

"First, we must say good-bye to our guests." But she made no objection to a farewell that under ordinary circumstances must be thought to have been performed with unseemly haste.

Back in the hall, Michael bade his uncle a firm good-night, but Lord Ashby did not seem to attend to him. Looking a little bewildered, he said abruptly, "See here, did I really offer for Hermie? Because if I did, I don't recall it myself."

Anne chuckled and said, "You will be very happy, sir."

"Do you think so, my dear? I wonder what sort of wind currents exist in Leicestershire. Perhaps Ireland will be—"

"Good night, Uncle," Michael said again. "Say good-night to him, Anne, or come morning, we'll still be discussing hot air."

Upstairs, she was not much surprised to find herself whisked into her husband's bedchamber instead of her own, and when he began to help her remove the wool dress, she said provocatively, "Did you ever really believe I had a secret lover, my lord?"

"For no more than a few moments," he murmured, pushing the soft wool from her shoulder and bending to kiss her bare skin. "Your hair is still damp," he said a moment later. "I'll kick up the fire a bit, so you don't take a chill."

Letting the gown slip to the floor as she watched him move toward the fire she said, "I collect that I am not to sleep in my own bed tonight."

"No."

"How quickly did you know—about the lover, I mean?"

His excellent profile was outlined by the glow of the fire when he looked over his shoulder and said, "Even riding madly toward Sheffield, I could not make myself believe such a thing of you. You had frequently exasperated me, had frequently not told me the complete and unvarnished truth, but I still knew you for a woman of principle and integrity. I believed in you, Anne," he said, coming back to take her in his arms again. "I could wish I deserved the same faith from you."

"But you have it," she said to his chest, her voice barely rising above a whisper.

He went very still. "What did you say?"

"I believed in you, too. I did not even know why, for it

seemed as if the evidence kept pointing to you, and although, when I first saw Bagshaw standing there, in your clothes—"

"The devil! Which clothes?"

"The maroon velvet coat. He is, or was, as large as you, you know, and much the same shape—although since he was your butler, one generally did not think of him so."

"Not my butler but Edmund's. I knew they were close, but I had no notion they could be so close as to be mixed up together in the *Folly*." His fingers moved to the ribbon of her chemise, loosening it.

Deciding it was more than time that he begin to divest himself of his own clothing, she unfastened the buttons of his waistcoat, murmuring, "I do wish you had discussed some of these details with me before now."

"If you will forgive my saying so," Michael said, as his fingertips tickled her breast, "a man does not discuss distasteful wagers over women of quality—or floating brothels—with his wife." Taking her by the chin with his free hand, he tilted her face up and kissed her lightly before he added, "To think that I am the most fortunate of men and did not realize it until it was nearly too late."

"I must remind you again," she said primly, trying without much success to ignore the sensations stirred by his moving hand, "that you did not rescue me. I saved myself."

"I hesitate to contradict you, my love," he said, his breath softly caressing her neck in a way that made her dizzy, "but have you considered that Bagshaw might have lied about his inability to swim, that even if he did not, he might somehow have made it safely to shore? Had I not been there, is it not possible that he might have found you again and worked his evil will on you?"

She shivered at the image he had drawn so ruthlessly in her mind, but said firmly nonetheless, "I got away from him twice, Michael, and I choose to believe I would have done so again. But I do confess that, since I never saw my nightdress again, the knowledge that I'd have had to make my way back here without a stitch to my name makes me very glad you arrived when you did."

"Just so you remember to show proper appreciation for my efforts," he said, moving both hands gently over her breasts. "You will soon find that I can become a veritable champion of marital partnership if I am but approached in the proper manner."

"Can you, indeed?" She pushed impatiently at his coat, whereupon, with a chuckle, he took his hands from her body long enough to remove his clothing. "You know, sir," she added when he picked her up without further ado and carried her to the bed, "I used to look at life as a series of complications that one had to resolve through compromises that rarely satisfied anyone. But now that I've learned to fight for what I want, and to do what I believe is right, instead of merely seeking peaceful settlements, I am beginning to regard life as a series of adventures instead."

"Are you?" He grinned at her and said wickedly, "Then let us proceed to see, sweetheart, just how adventurous you can be."

Epilogue

When Anne entered the newly finished garden hall in search of her family, the French doors stood wide open, and sunlight splashed across the tessellated floor in an inviting golden path. Right in the center of it, sleek, black Juliette lay stretched out asleep beside one of the dogs. A fresh summer breeze wafted in, redolent of roses and lavender, and outside, above the constant hum of insects and a chirping chorus of birds, Anne heard her daughter shriek with laughter. Stepping quickly to the doorway, she saw Michael at the top of the white pebbled path, holding the baby high over his head, laughing up at her as she waved her tiny arms and kicked her feet. Soft golden curls framed her head, glistening like a halo in the sunlight, and Anne felt a surge of joy at the sight of her.

Smiling, drawn by their infectious laughter, she moved impulsively toward them. Michael saw her first and grinned, lowering the baby to cradle it against his broad chest. "Her eyes sparkle just like yours do when she's happy," he said. "If she's lucky, she'll grow up to be as beautiful as her mama."

His voice stirred familiar sensations within Anne's body, and she knew by the warm look in his eyes that he would soon give the baby into her nurse's keeping and turn his attention fully to his wife. The thought stirred a glow of happiness. She had never known such love as these past months had given her, such pleasures, passions, and such desire. How lucky her tiny daughter was to have been blessed with the kindest, most loving man in the world for her father.

"She is a lucky wench," he said now, as if he had been eavesdropping on her thoughts. He moved closer to Anne, but his eyes were searching the garden, no doubt for the nursemaid who had tactfully left him alone for a few moments of paternal ecstasy with his daughter. "Our little Eliza couldn't have chosen a more perfect mama if she'd drawn up a list of requirements and presented them to a registry office."

The baby snuggled contentedly against him, showing no inclination to go to her mama, or anywhere else.

"Anne! Anne!" Andrew's voice floated up to them from the bottom of the garden, and a moment later the boy himself came into view, striding toward them, his feet crunching on the path. He was grinning widely, mischievously.

"You ought never to have told Aunt Hermione that she could occupy herself during their visit to us by creating a knot garden," he said, laughing. "She told Uncle Ashby to go tend to his balloons an hour ago, and she's had half the south-lawn flower beds ripped out since then. The poor lawn looks as if a herd of wild boar have been rooting there."

Another time Anne might have been stirred at least to view the damage, but today she was too much a victim of contented pleasure to care what Hermione did to the garden. She smiled lazily at Andrew and said, "It is your lawn, my dear sir. You had better supervise her efforts, don't you think?"

"Well, actually," the boy said, casting a speculative look at Michael, "I rather thought I might take that new yearling of Uncle Michael's out and school him for an hour or so."

Michael chuckled. "Tell you what, my lad. You go find the child's nursemaid, and send her to collect her charge, and you can spend your entire school holiday with the colt."

"I'll do better than that," Andrew said, looking astutely from Michael to Anne and back again. "I'll take her straight off to Martha myself."

"She's asleep," Michael said, gazing down at the baby,

whose eyes were shut and whose thumb was tucked safely in her mouth.

"She won't mind," Andrew said confidently as he reached to take her. "She likes me to carry her."

Michael relinquished the baby at once, and she scarcely stirred, merely tucking her thumb more firmly in her mouth and sucking rapidly for a moment when the transfer was made.

Watching the young duke walk off with his precious burden, Anne said, "I'd never know him for the same boy I met when I first came here. How much Eton has changed him! Why, he is even more protective of his little cousin than he is of Sylvia. Our Eliza will be spoiled to death before she even learns to walk."

"If she is," Michael said, his voice low in his throat, his hand warm on her back as he urged her into the house, "her brothers and sisters will soon show her the error of her ways."

"And just how many brothers and sisters did you have in mind to provide for her?" Anne asked, smiling lovingly at him.

"Well now, I don't know," he said, returning her look with a teasing one of his own, "but I've a strong hunch that if we keep on as we've begun, there will be many more where she came from."

Dear Reader,

After reading many books where the servants are described as being more stately, more aristocratic, more noble, or "higher in the instep" than their employers, I could not resist making the butler the villain of this story. Such descriptions have become practically throw-away lines in Historicals and Regency romances for years, so I decided I could probably let a number of persons mention Bagshaw's noble demeanor without giving away the plot.

The rest of the tale suggested itself when I found that throughout the eighteenth and nineteenth centuries, due to differences between Scottish and English marriage laws, a couple contracting a clandestine marriage would find it held valid by the English courts even if that same marriage performed in England would not have been valid; and the plot thickened when I learned that the groom could be fourteen years old, and a duke.

In case you are curious to know where an author discovers such stuff, the following exchange is taken from testimony of Lord Moncrieff, Lord Advocate of Scotland, before the Select Committee of the House of Lords* attempting for the umpteenth time (this one in 1844) to amend the Marriage Act of 1753:

---

*Patricia Courtney Otto, *Daughters of the British Aristocracy*, Stanford University (Doctoral Dissertation), 1974, p. 79.

Lord Chancellor: Suppose a young nobleman of fourteen is trepanned [lured or entrapped] into marriage by a woman moment would that be a valid marriage, and carry a Dukedom and large estates to the issue?

Lord Advocate of Scotland: It would.

Lord Chancellor: Does it require any domicile in Scotland for one minute more than the time the marriage is performing to make it a valid marriage?

Lord Advocate: No.

Lord Chancellor: Are you aware that such marriages (between a fourteen-year-old Duke and an English prostitute) would be, by all the courts of England and by the House of Lords, dealing with the legitimacy of the heir to the Dukedom, held a perfectly indisputably valid marriage?

Lord Advocate: I presume the House of Lords would hold it so.

Irresistible stuff, as I am sure you will agree. I just hope the story did it justice, and that you were entertained. That was, as always, the author's primary intent.

Sincerely,

Amanda Scott

P.S. If you enjoyed *The Bawdy Bride,* please look for *Dangerous Games,* coming in June of 1996. The heroine is Melissa Seacourt, one of the children from *Dangerous Illusions,* which was published by Pinnacle in June of 1994.

Dangerous Games

by
Amanda Scott

The First Player Sets the Stakes

Monday, 3 May 1824, Newmarket, England

"Main of seven, gentlemen, five thrown," declared the groom-porter at the Hazard table in the crowded main gaming room of Newmarket's famous Little Hell. "Odds three to two against the caster. Chance of five to win; seven loses." Collecting the dice from the table, he looked up at the large, dark-haired man who had just cast them. "Will you increase your stake, my lord?"

Nicholas, Lord Vexford, nodded. Taking the dice from the porter, he dropped them into the dice box and set more of his markers on the table. "Adding twenty guineas," he said in a deep voice that carried easily to the other players.

"Thank you, my lord. Who covers, gentlemen?"

When most of the others—some twenty in all at the table—moved to cover Vexford's stake, the much shorter, rather plump gentleman beside him said plaintively over the rumble of their voices, "By Jupiter, your luck's clearly in with the bones, Nick, but love's another matter, ain't it? Come to think of it, might be a dashed great mistake to be making such a show to this lot that you've got bored with the Hawthorne. They're bound to say even you can't expect your luck to hold with both women and gaming at the same time, particularly since that chit uglifies any other one unfortunate enough to be seen in her company."

Smiling lazily down at him, Vexford murmured, "But what makes you think I'm bored with her, Tommy?"

"Plain as a pikestaff," Lord Thomas Minley said. "At the Heath, she clings to you like a limpet whilst you watch the damned horses, and where is she right now, I ask you? At some dashed assembly or other, wondering where the devil you are, that's where she is right now."

"Clara knows better than to expect me to do the fancy here," Vexford said. "As to watching the horses, everyone does. That *is* why one attends the Spring Meeting, after all."

Minley snorted. "Dash it, I know that, though it ain't the only reason, and that's a fact. Gambling's the main reason, and don't say it ain't, my lad, not when you've had a monkey off me in less than an hour right here in Little Hell and another this afternoon before the first heats were over and done."

"But I need the money," Vexford said dulcetly. "The lady's damned acquisitive. Are you covering my stake, Tommy?"

"I am, though only a fool would believe you need my blunt to pay for Clara's baubles. Dash it, I saw that ruby bracelet you gave her." His gaze narrowed shrewdly. "Is that what it is? She wants too many pretties? I can well believe it. Too demanding by half, I'd say—for my taste, anyway. But then, I'd never be able to afford the wench in the first place. Be done up, paying for one of her shoe buckles, and don't tell me she don't wear 'em. That chit flaunts glitter wherever she can manage to put it. Now I come to think of it, Nick, maybe you'd best get rid of her. Dash it, you've enough luck to spare, even for finding a new light-o'-love."

Vexford looked pointedly at the other gamesters who waited for Lord Thomas to cover the stake. When he had done so, Vexford gave the dice box a shake, then cast a three and a two.

"There, you see," Thomas said in disgust. "Odds clean against it, and you throw chance. I'd have been glad if you'd just lived up to your name and nicked the board."

While the groom-porter called the odds, Vexford added to

his stake, and Thomas, shaking his head, covered again when the others did. Vexford threw an ace and a four.

Thomas groaned. "That's done it. I'm damned if I'll cover again. Look, there's Yarborne crossing his fingers, as if that will alter his luck. When you're in vein, Nick old lad, there's none can touch you, and certainly not by crossing a few fingers. That fellow's given to more superstitious nonsense than my maiden aunt Sarah, though he don't seem the sort, and that's a fact."

"Yarborne's got more money than your maiden aunt Sarah, and he's not nearly so tight with a shilling either," Vexford said. "He gives as much to the poor and needy as any man in London, which all goes to show that he must do something right, because he's said to be even more of a gamester than I am."

"Dash it, that can't be true—I don't mean the bit about Aunt Sarah, for she's as tight as a tick, but the gambling part. You live and breathe cards and dice, and Yarborne's forever organizing musicales, ladies' supper parties, and concerts to raise money for the poor. Not everyone likes him, I daresay, but one no sooner hears him accused of some dashed scurvy thing like usury than one hears he lent money to some fool, interest free, just to keep the bailiffs from his door. Good Lord!" he exclaimed when his errant gaze fixed suddenly on the entrance to the crowded room. "Here comes Dory! Don't tempt him to play, Nick, I beg you. It ain't right to take advantage of a man of God, in any event, and certainly not when he's my brother."

The Reverend Lord Dorian Minley, ten years older than Lord Thomas, strolled up to the table and watched with interest when Vexford cast again. When most of those gathered around groaned in much the same way that Thomas had earlier, the vicar said with a chuckle, "I collect that you've thrown in, Nicholas."

Thomas said with a snort, "He has. Cast chance four times in a row, which is against all the odds. Hasn't nicked once, which means—in case you don't recall, Dory—not only that he has failed to throw a main (which would mean paying off each and every one of us, and would serve him dashed right), but he ain't thrown a single combination but fives—his own winner. If I didn't know him for an honest player, dashed if I wouldn't call for a hammer to break those dice. But when," he added in a less bitter tone, "did you arrive in Newmarket, old man?"

"Earlier this afternoon," the vicar replied with a singularly sweet smile. The two brothers looked a good deal alike despite the difference in their ages, for both had the same hazel eyes, curly brown hair, and sturdy, plump figures. The second and fifth of the Marquess of Prading's six offspring, both were of average height, but standing next to the tall, broad-shouldered, loose-limbed Vexford, they looked nearly diminutive.

Lord Thomas exclaimed, "Dash it, how could you have arrived this afternoon, Dory? I didn't see you at the Heath."

"Fact is, I took a walk along Devil's Dyke," the vicar said, "and the oddest thing happened to me there. I'll tell you about it later. Too noisy by half in here for a proper conversation."

Thomas said at once to Vexford, who had been keeping an ear on their conversation while he added to his growing stake, "Look here, Nick, I'm famished. If you want to have supper with Dory and me, you'll have to pass that box on soon, or else I'll just toddle off along with him now to the supper room."

In response, Vexford cast again, and again the result was greeted with a groan. But this time, when the porter asked if he would increase his stake, he shook his head. "My luck can't hold much longer," he said, "so I'll take Tommy's excellent advice and pass the box." Handing the dice box to the man on his left, he began to gather his winnings, saying over his shoulder, "I'll be delighted to honor you and Dorian with my company, Tommy."

"The devil you will," Lord Thomas said tartly, watching

him gather his winnings. "You'll bloody well *pay* for our supper."

Chuckling, Vexford followed the Minley brothers to the supper room, where they were fortunate enough to find a corner table unoccupied. As they took their seats, Lord Thomas said to the vicar, "I've just been advising Nick here to expend some of that luck of his to find himself a new mistress, Dory. The one he's got is too avaricious by half. But no doubt you'll remind him that the Church of England frowns on such liaisons."

The vicar smiled. "I could do that, of course, but I should hate to think myself responsible for any young woman's being cast adrift without support or shelter." He shot Vexford a quizzical look, adding, "However, I daresay that our Nicholas would not abandon any friend of his to such a fate."

Thomas grimaced. "Good Lord, no. Clara could live for a lifetime on just the proceeds of the bracelet he gave her last week, and heaven only knows what else she's managed to cozen out of him. It's more likely that she'll refuse to accept her congé. Woman's a dashed limpet, like I was telling him before."

A servant approached, and conversation lapsed while the gentlemen discussed the evening's menu with him. But once he had gone, Thomas said as if there had been no interruption, "Mind you, I don't say he ain't been fair to her; I'm just saying—"

"You're saying rather a lot, actually," Vexford interjected gently but in a tone that caused the experienced Lord Thomas to fall instantly silent. "I'd prefer," Vexford went on, "to hear what the vicar's has been up to of late. I don't think we've encountered each other since last year's Spring Meeting."

"Perfectly correct," the vicar said with an understanding smile at Thomas, who seemed to have no more desire at the moment to speak. "It is difficult for me to get to London these days, you know, let alone into Hampshire, although I did meet your estimable sire right here in Newmarket at the Calver

Stakes a fortnight ago. I collect that he has not returned for
the Spring Meeting, however. At least, I have not laid eyes on
him yet."

"No, he and my mother are at Owlcastle," Vexford said,
referring to the Earl of Ulcombe's primary residence, which
occupied vast parklands in the county of Hampshire. "They
intend to return to town by week's end, I believe."

"Ah, well, I have formed the intention to visit London this
year, myself," the vicar said. "It has been far too long since
I did so. Indeed, I mean to attend the Epsom Derby next month.
Haven't enjoyed that exciting event since my Oxford days."

The servant returned with their wine, filled their glasses,
and went away again, leaving the bottle on the table, before
Lord Thomas said abruptly, "Look here, Dory, didn't you say
something odd happened to you in the Devil's Dyke today?
Can't think why anyone would want to go for a walk in a ditch
rather than watch the heats, after coming to Newmarket for
the races."

"Call it an impulse," the vicar said, "but indeed, the strang-
est thing happened. I really cannot account for it. I thought I
was quite alone, you know, and didn't expect to meet another
soul, but as I rounded a curve, I heard a chap talking. Found
him rather shortly after that, sitting cross-legged right on the
ground, chattering away to himself. I bade him good-day, and
took the liberty of inquiring about what he was doing there."

" 'Indeed, sir,' says he, 'I am at play.' "

" 'At play? With whom?' I asked. 'I see no one.' "

" 'I own, sir, my antagonist is not visible,' says he. 'I am
playing with God.' "

Lord Thomas exclaimed, "The devil he did! And what did
you say to that, Dory?"

"I asked what game they were playing, of course."

Vexford chuckled. "Good for you, Vicar. And what game
did the fellow say they were playing?"

"Chess."

"And did you see a chessboard?"

"None. Indeed, I pointed that out to the chap, and then—just funning a bit, you understand—I asked if he and God had placed any wagers on the outcome."

"And had they?"

"According to my newfound acquaintance, they had. And—would you believe it?—when I mentioned that he did not stand the least chance to win such a wager, since his adversary must be the superior player, he said, 'He takes no advantage of me, sir, but plays as a mere mortal.' Being naturally rather stunned, I asked how they settled accounts. 'Very exactly and punctually,' says he. 'And pray, how stands your game now?' I asked, whereupon the chap admitted that he had just lost to his opponent."

"And how much did he admit losing?" Vexford asked.

"Twenty guineas," the vicar said with an enigmatic smile.

"By Jupiter, Dory," Thomas exclaimed, "the poor fellow must be all about in his head! Did you leave him there all alone?"

"Patience, Thomas, I've not yet come to the end of my tale. When I asked how he would manage to pay what he owed, he said the poor were his treasurers. He said his opponent always sends some worthy person to receive the money lost, 'And,' says he to me, 'you are at present His purse-bearer, sir.' "

Thomas stared. "You're hoaxing us, Dory, admit it! Dash it, it ain't the thing for a man of the cloth to be telling such Banbury tales."

In response, the vicar reached into the pocket of his coat and withdrew a handful of guineas. "See for yourself. I would offer to pay for our dinner, but I am honor-bound to contribute it to the poor box. I just wanted to share the tale with someone else before I did so. Passing strange, is it not?"

Thomas gaped at the golden coins in his brother's hand, then looked at Vexford.

Though Nick might have suspected another man of lying, not for a moment did he think the vicar had done so. And although he knew that innocents were frequently duped by sharps of one sort or another, who allowed them to win money at a gaming table in order to draw them back again to play for higher stakes at a later date, this was clearly not such a case. Such dupes were, in his experience, more greedy and less honorable than the worthy vicar. And no matter what devious thoughts might have been in the strange chess player's mind, the fellow could have nothing to gain by giving the vicar money for the poor box.

The servant soon placed their supper before them, and conversation became desultory until they had finished eating. Then, when a second bottle of wine had been placed on the table, the vicar asked casually, "How's young Oliver getting on at our alma mater, Nicholas?"

Nick shrugged and said with a hint of amusement, "Haven't heard of any earthquakes or fires in Oxford of late, Vicar, so my guess is that my brother's been locked up or dug six feet under and they just haven't got round yet to telling the family."

The vicar chuckled, but Lord Thomas said with a grimace, "That brother of yours is a damned menace, if you ask me. I still remember that awful fortnight I spent with you at Owlcastle during a long vacation, when that brat put honey in my shoes and then made me pay him to guard my door against some villain or other who supposedly enjoyed putting tacks on the door sill each morning. Dashed if I didn't catch that scalawag, Oliver, doing the thing himself the very next day!"

"That was years ago, Tommy," Nick said, grinning at him, "and you asked for it by treating him with all the disdain of your superior years and education."

"Well, you didn't treat him so well yourself, as I recall the matter," Lord Thomas retorted. "When he snipped the seams of your leather breeches to make them fall apart when you mounted your horse, you pinned his ears back good and proper, my lad."

"Yes, that was to teach him respect for his elders. You might have done the same with my goodwill."

"Well, I might if I'd been a Goliath like you are, but even

then young Oliver was near as tall as I am. Moreover, though I might have had your goodwill, I'd not have had Ulcombe's." Lord Thomas gave an exaggerated shiver. "Your father's not a man to cross, and he fair dotes on that scapegrace brother of yours."

"He might have doted on Oliver then, Tommy, but the lad is fast losing his charm, I'm afraid. You may not credit the news, but my father complained recently that Oliver's been wasting the ready at an unbelievable pace. I won't be surprised if the lad's crest isn't soon lowered a bit."

The vicar said tolerantly, "As I remember that boy, he was always full of juice and ginger."

"He's spoilt rotten," Lord Thomas said, not mincing matters. "Oh, he don't trouble you any, Nick, but you mind my words. When they let him out of Oxford, London's where he'll head, and then you'll have your hands full. Just you see if you don't."

"Oliver doesn't trouble me because I don't allow anyone to do so," Nick said amiably. "I go my own road, Tommy, and let others choose theirs. You said a while back that my father is not a man one chooses to annoy. Would you perhaps say that I am the more easily crossed, old friend?"

Lord Thomas choked on his wine, and the vicar pounded him helpfully on the back, saying sternly to Vexford as he did so, "I have never thought you a heedless man, Nicholas, so I shall not pretend to believe you spoke as you did just now without thinking. Nor do I hesitate to tell you to your head that it don't become you to speak like that to Thomas."

"I'll speak as I choose when he plays the fool."

"No one expects you to cherish fools, but neither would anyone who knows you believe you could harm a friend. Indeed, I believe I know you as well as anyone does, so I shall go farther and dare to say that no one who knows you would expect you to ignore a fellow human being who appealed to you for help."

"I'll take issue with that, Vicar, for it would depend upon the particular human being in question. In my experience, most petitioners want only to have their path smoothed for them without having to exert themselves in any way. In the idealistic days of my youth, I lent money to friends and put myself out in other ways to help those I thought deserving of aid. In most cases not only was the money not repaid, but my so-called friends never expressed any gratitude and made it clear that they expected to be able to put a hand in my pocket whenever the fancy struck them. I soon learned to be more wary, I can promise you, and in the end decided it was best to be and let be."

"But surely you would not refuse a friend in need," the vicar protested, looking at him with a worried frown.

"Perhaps not, if he were really a friend and really in need," Nick said with a sardonic smile. He stood up, adding, "It is well after seven, I believe, so my man will have returned to the inn from the racing stables by now. Since I've got two horses running tomorrow that are favored to win, I ought to have a word with him before he goes to bed."

Lord Thomas looked surprised. "Do you mean to say you don't intend to go back to the tables? But, Nick, your luck is well and truly in tonight!"

Vexford smiled. "One reason my luck stays with me, Tommy, is that I don't push it when it's been strained. Considering what I've won the past two nights, I'd doubtless be wise to take to my bed now and get some sleep. However, you needn't fret, for I don't intend to do that, only to meet with my trainer. I'll return after I've spoken with him."

The vicar rose and shook his hand. "I daresay you are staying at the Rutland Arms, Nicholas. Above my touch, that is, but although I daresay I'll have taken to my bed before your return, I look forward to seeing you tomorrow. I'll put my money on your horses to win," he added with a smile.

Melissa Seacourt's room at the Rutland Arms Inn was small but well-appointed and tidy; however, although she recognized the inn as a first-class hostelry, she was anything but comfortable. The past few days had been one long exercise in self-discipline, and she was exhausted from what seemed to be an unceasing need to gauge her father's unpredictable and often dangerous moods, and adjust her own demeanor accordingly.

Mag, the serving girl Sir Geoffrey had hired to attend her, provided some relief, but not as much as might have been expected. Not only did Mag not have the least notion of Melissa's true situation but her hearty cheerfulness and frequently expressed delight in things she saw along the road irritated Sir Geoffrey. At one point, he had demanded that she ride up front with the driver, leaving Melissa alone to try to assuage his bad humor, a task made doubly difficult by the fact that, until four days ago, when he'd abducted her from her stepfather's garden in Scotland, she had not seen him in nine years.

Though he had soon revealed his reason for abducting her, even now she found his outrageous plan nearly unbelievable; however, when she had dared to suggest he had no right to marry her off to a total stranger merely to repay his gaming debts, his reaction had reminded her instantly of how dangerous it was to cross him. After that, she had not even dared to ask for more information about Lord Yarborne. What little she already knew suggested that the man was at least as old as Sir Geoffrey, which was enough to make her rack her brain for some means of escape.

None had occurred to her. She had considered enlisting Mag's assistance but soon realized the girl was not clever or discreet enough to trust with such a confidence. Moreover, Mag was utterly in awe of Sir Geoffrey, and Melissa did not think she would entertain for a moment the notion of defying him.

Since Mag slept in the same bedchamber with her at each inn, and Sir Geoffrey had scarcely let the pair of them out of his sight at any other time, Melissa had not managed until now

to have more than a few moments of solitude. But just befor
seven, Sir Geoffrey had set out in search of Yarborne, orderin
her to remain in her room until his return. When Mag suggeste
ordering supper served to them there, Melissa feigned a hea
ache and begged her to sup below in the coffee room. No dou
as anxious for freedom as Melissa was, Mag made no objectio
and thus it was that Melissa found herself alone at last.

Shuddering at the thought of what Sir Geoffrey would c
if he caught her, she waited only until the sound of Mag
footsteps had faded into silence before she threw her hoode
cloak around her shoulders, pulled on her gloves, and hurrie
to the torchlit inn yard, taking great care to avoid the coffe
room.

Pausing on his way back through the gaming room to ex
change a few brief comments with friends, Nick stepped ou
side at last and shouted for his horse.

The moon was already high, so there was no need to re
quest a boy to light his way. The Rutland Arms, located mic
way between Newmarket and Newmarket Heath, was
popular inn for the racing set, and since he had stayed ther
from the time of his first visit to Newmarket, Nick thoug
that even on a darker night his horse would know the wa
The road appeared empty of traffic, the cool night air revive
him, and he enjoyed the solitude of the ride. By the time h
reached the two-story inn, he was feeling refreshed, an
thought he might even linger in the taproom a while aft
he had spoken with Drax, if he found any acquaintanc
there. First, however, he had to see his horse safely into i
stall.

Though the stable area appeared to be deserted, he kne
that he had only to shout for a stableboy and one would appe
without delay. But though he did not make a habit of lookin
after his own animals, he did not in the least mind doing s
He rode straight into the dimly lighted stable.

Conscious at once of movement near the back of the building, he heard unmistakable sounds of horses being disturbed. Dismounting, he peered into the dimly lit interior. "Who goes here?" he called, stepping in front of his horse.

Silence greeted him. As he moved farther into the stable, he saw that one of his own hacks had been saddled, but there appeared to be no one near it. Then suddenly, a hooded figure enveloped in a long cloak threw itself into the saddle, leaned forward, and kicked the horse, which immediately leapt forward toward the open doors.

Though Nick stood directly in its path, he made no attempt to jump out of the way. He did step a little to one side, however, and when the horse would have shot past him, he reached out, grabbed the bridle, and held on until the animal plunged to a halt beside him.

An infuriated shriek was the rider's sole response.

"One ought never to ride full tilt out of a stable," Nick said calmly. "Such a lack of regard for others might well result in an innocent person's being run down."

"Let go!" The voice came from low in the rider's throat. In the dim light Nick could not see a face, but the strong emotion in the thief's voice intrigued him.

"I think you had better get down now," he said, "and explain yourself to me."

Instead, the rider kicked the horse and wrenched at the reins, trying by brute force to yank the bridle from his hand.

Shaking his head, Nick reached for the figure and dragged it unceremoniously from the saddle. He was surprised first by the lightness of the body he held in his arms, and then by its soft, slender shape as it squirmed frantically to escape his grasp. The hood fell back, and even in the gloom he saw at once that his captive was female, and a very pretty female at that, with long flaxen hair.

"What the devil!" he exclaimed.

"Oh, please, sir, let me go! You must."

"Oh, no, I don't think so," Nick said, grinning at her. "I think I've just taken the biggest prize of the night, my girl, and I've never been one to throw away good winnings."

Also by Amanda Scott